Please feel free to send me an email. Just know that my publisher filters these emails. Good news is always welcome.

Ashley Michelle - ashley_michelle@awesomeauthors.org

Sign up for my blog for updates and freebies!
ashley-michelle.awesomeauthors.org/

D1554526

About the Publisher

BLVNP Incorporated, A Nevada Corporation, 340 S. Lemon #6200, Walnut CA 91789, info@blvnp.com / legal@blvnp.com

DISCLAIMER

His to Claim

By: Ashley Michelle

BLVNP

ISBN: 978-1-68030-816-7

Table of Contents

Dedication

To my mother, for inspiring me to aim high even if it meant falling down. To my family, for being my first real fans. To the ladies of the round table (you know who you are), and all the hours spent plotting the demise of fictional characters. To all my lovely readers on Wattpad, for all your kind words and hours of sleep and sanity lost reading my book. And to my weasel, for distracting me with your hipping and hopping (I love you).

FREE DOWNLOAD

Get these freebies and MORE when you sign up for the author's mailing list!

ashley-michelle.awesomeauthors.org/

01

Scarlett

"—Shift."

I was jolted out of my daydreaming by the sound of a loud voice ringing in my ear. I turned around with raised brows to find Darlene, the shift manager of the small family-owned diner, staring at me expectantly with a tray of dirty dishes in one hand. I had clearly missed the important parts of whatever she had been saying to me.

A sheepish grin worked its way up my face. "What was that?"

She rolled her eyes and blew a stray hair out of her face. "I *said*, do you mind covering the end of my shift for me? My babysitter called. Apparently, Graham is running a pretty high fever."

I nodded my head. "Sure, no problem." It wasn't like I had any plans for the evening anyway, other than obsessively checking the mail. There were only two weeks left before graduation, and I was yet to hear from any of the colleges I had applied to.

Darlene let out a small sigh. "Thanks, Scarlett. I owe you."

I waved my hand. "Don't worry about it. I know how hard it is on you being left to take care of Graham while Troy is away. I'm happy to help lighten the load." Her husband had to travel a lot for his job, and that left Darlene with extra parenting duties.

She gave me a grateful smile as she turned away with the tray of dishes. "You're truly an angel, Scarlett."

I snorted at her comment. "I already agreed to cover you. You don't need to kiss my butt anymore, Darlene."

She gave me a playful wink before turning away, disappearing through the kitchen door. I slowly turned back around with a sigh. This was going to be a long night of nothing but the virtual emptiness of the diner.

I was happy when a familiar face shuffled through the front door of the diner, setting off the little bell that hung above the door. He lifted his hand to his head, ruffling his dark hair which was starting to look shaggy around the edges. This boy would look like a mountain man if it weren't for my constant influence in his life. He met my gaze briefly as he reached out and grabbed one of the cheaply made menus from an empty table. He flipped through the pages quickly before setting it back down.

I pulled the pen and pad from the front pocket of my stained apron. "What can I get you, Wyatt?"

He shrugged as he moved closer toward me. "I think a cup of coffee will be fine. It's been a long day."

"It's going to be a bit longer. Darlene asked me to cover the end of her shift," I commented with an apologetic smile. Wyatt had promised to pick me up after my shift ended while I was running out the door this morning.

He let out a sigh, running his hand through his hair. "Of course, she did. Well, there *is* a meeting tonight. Guess it's going to be extra long for both of us, sweetheart," he replied with a sarcastic grin as I poured him a cup of coffee and placed it on the counter in front of me.

Darlene approached us carrying her purse, her jacket slung over her arm. "You know the coffee here is shit, Wyatt. I don't know why you keep ordering it when you only ever have a sip and leave the rest."

Wyatt ignored her comment. The two of them were always at each other's throats for reasons unknown to me. He pressed his hands to the counter, breathing in deeply. His nose scrunched up a bit, and he looked over at me. "You smell." I frowned at my cousins greeting as he sat himself down on a stool at the breakfast counter, grabbing the coffee.

"Gee, you really know how to compliment a girl," I grumbled, my voice dripping with sarcasm. My cousin and I had a very close relationship, considering that my parents had taken him in after his father ran off and his mother got sick. He returned the favor when my parents died, taking me into his home and raising me like I was his kid sister.

"God, Wyatt…" Darlene remarked as she threw her arms into the sleeves of her jacket, pulling up the collar. "Even if a woman does stink, you shouldn't comment on it. And you wonder why you're still single."

Her words brought a smile to my face, and I gave him a pointed look. I snickered as I turned away from my cousin who was pouting at the blunt reprimand he had received. I could see Winston, our cook, slaving away over the grill through the small hole, singing along to some garbage being gurgled out of the old boom box he kept in the kitchen. The diner was my home away from home, and its motley crew was my self-created wolf pack even if they were only humans.

"Wyatt," she said his name in a flat tone. Darlene had never cared much for my cousin. Maybe it's because he had a knack for putting his foot in his mouth... or maybe because they had gone "grown-up" together and he'd been quite the fool back in his younger years.

"See you tomorrow, Scarlett. Thanks again," she called.

I turned around to give her a quick wave. "See ya, Darlene. Tell Graham I said hello and hope he feels better," I called back as she exited the front door, the bell ringing again.

Wyatt lifted his gaze to mine, staring at me expectantly with wide eyes as if he was waiting for something. I stared back at him, shifting my hands to my hips. "Why are you looking at me like that? Do I have something on my face?" I reached up with a hand and wiped it across my cheek, checking to see if there was any food splatter. It was a hazard of the job.

"Can't you feel it, Scarlett?" he asked me in a soft voice so that no one else could hear. Hell, if it wasn't for my extra-sensitive senses I probably wouldn't have heard him either.

I narrowed my eyes in confusion at his question. "What are talking about? Are you feeling okay, Wyatt?" I reached out and placed my hand on his forehead. He pulled back with a furrowed brow and looked at me as if I had two heads.

"After all the complaining and whining I had to listen to from you... are you seriously telling me that you don't feel even the slightest bit different?" he asked a little louder in an exasperated tone, waving his hand in the air dramatically. I had no idea what he was going on about or why he seemed so upset.

I looked around the small room at the other patrons who seemed content to ignore his outburst. I leaned forward, stuffing my notepad back into the pocket of my apron. "I don't know why you think I should feel different, but I feel the same as I always do. Unless you want to count the fact that my feet feel like I've been walking barefoot on hot coals. These ten-hour shifts have been killing me," I whined at him.

He gave me a slow blink, shaking his head. "Seriously, Scarlett?"

"What?" I questioned with a tired tone.

"Your scent—"

I held up a hand, cutting off his thought mid-sentence.

"I know. I know. I smell, but in my defense, you would smell too if you worked with greasy food all day," I snapped at him, growing tired of the conversation he was having with me. If I wanted to be insulted, I'm sure I could easily find one of my peers to satisfy that need without a problem. Human or shifter, they were all eager to tear someone else down to elevate themselves.

He shook his head at me. "No, your scent has changed, Scarlett. Your wolf has matured. I can smell her on you now."

I stared at him blankly as I digested his words. Had my wolf finally reached maturity without me noticing? I searched my mind for a sign of my wolf's presence. I had been waiting for this moment since I hit puberty. Most of my peers had already matured, leaving me as an outsider when it came to the pack.

All shifters had to go through two stages of puberty: the natural human one and the beast underneath. It could happen at any time, but basically, it meant that the connection between human and wolf was fully formed. It wasn't until this happens that we were allowed to attend actual pack events. Most of my friends had already matured. I had been left in the group of late bloomers. Sometimes, it happened that a wolf never matured. These people were seen as Omegas. They were still a part of the pack, but they would never be considered true wolves.

I shifted back and forth on my feet, concentrating hard. "I don't feel any different."

Wyatt took a sip of his coffee. "You will, trust me." He pulled the mug away from himself, peering down into the cup with a small look of disgust before setting it down. "But you know what this means?"

"What?" I questioned with a raised brow.

He met my gaze with a knowing look. "You don't have to wait in the car like the other pups during the meeting tonight. You're a true wolf now," he teased as he gave me a wolfish grin. I rolled my eyes at his comment, but on the inside, I felt a bubble of excitement.

I had only ever seen the pack house from the outside, having never been allowed to enter it before. I found myself getting anxious as I followed Wyatt down the dirt driveway and around the side of the house. In the back, there was another building, about the size of a guest house.

I could hear the sound of happy voices carried on the gentle evening breeze. My palms felt sweaty in the pockets of my sweatshirt as my nerves got the better of me. Wyatt gave me a grin as he opened the door. "So it begins."

I rolled my eyes at him as I walked past him into the large open room. The smells of other pack members overwhelmed me for a moment. My eyes scanned the crowd warily, looking for familiar faces. I found my gaze gravitating towards the front of the room where the stream of bodies seemed to be moving.

That was the first time I saw *him.*

He stood near the front, greeting people with a friendly smile. My heart hammered in my chest as I watched him from where I stood at the back of the room. I had no idea who he was, but I knew he was perfect. His dark hair was shaved close to his head as if it had been shaved bare at some point and was finally being allowed to grow out. My eyes followed the length of his body, taking in every part of him. He had a lean body that spoke of endurance-honed muscles.

Wyatt elbowed my side. "Don't just stand there, Scarlett. People are starting to look at us." He urged me to move forward. I had to force my feet to move from where I had been anchored. My whole world seemed to be shifting on its axis, and I couldn't be sure I was standing on solid ground anymore.

My heart was in my throat as I approached my mate— at least that was what my wolf was telling me. This perfect male specimen was our mate, the one that the Goddess had ordained for us at birth. But what if he hated me? What if I wasn't what he was expecting? Insecurities that I had never felt before began to flood my brain.

I dug my heels into the floor. "I can't do this. Let's go home."

Wyatt grabbed onto my elbow and led me on. "You're being ridiculous. We all had to go through this, Scarlett. Consider it your official initiation into the pack." I gritted my teeth as every step brought me closer to the finality of my situation.

The Alpha and his mate were standing together, greeting the other pack members as they filed into the room, grabbing seats for the meeting. I remembered them from the times they had visited my home when I was much younger, way back when my mother was still alive and my father held a prominent position in the pack. They looked older and a little more worn down, but that had to be expected of people in their positions.

"Alpha Aaron," Wyatt spoke formally as he reached out a hand, a common human greeting. I danced on the balls of my feet, wishing that I hadn't accepted Wyatt's offer to join him. I was still in my work uniform, smelling like grease and probably looking unkempt from the busy workday... not the way I wanted to make my first impression on the pack.

"Wyatt," he replied, shaking the hand that had been offered to him with a firm grip, "it is good to see you again."

Wyatt beamed at the acknowledgment, turning his eyes toward the female beside the Alpha, bowing his head. "Luna Victoria."

She gave him a kind smile. "Wyatt."

Alpha Aaron's dark gaze shifted in my direction, a smile still on his lips. "And who is this beauty?" he questioned, lifting a brow as he examined me further. My cheeks rushed with heat, and I felt the sudden urge to hide behind my cousin like I did back in my younger years where I would cling to my mother's leg.

Wyatt wrapped his arm around my shoulder, pulling me in protectively to his side, and that only made me feel more embarrassed. "This is my cousin, Scarlett."

Luna Victoria gave me a knowing glance as she leaned into her mate's side. "Sweetheart, it's Conrad and Elizabeth's daughter."

"Of course, she is," he replied as if he had already known. My lips twitched with the urge to smile when she looked at me with a playful eye roll at his expense. Alpha Aaron crossed his arms over his wide chest, leaning forward toward me. "I can see it now that I've gotten a closer look. You've got Conrad's eyes."

"And Elizabeth's beautiful face," Luna Victoria remarked. "If I recall correctly, your mother was a late bloomer as well." I felt my head sink a little lower at her comment.

"David..." Luna Victoria called, turning toward my mate with a smile, "come over here real fast."

She glanced back at me. "Conrad helped train David when he was a young boy. I'm sure he will be very interested in meeting you." I felt my nerves spike as he turned in our direction, and I realized that he wasn't an average member of the pack. This was *their* son, the next heir: an Alpha born male.

I wanted to run, but my feet kept me firmly rooted in place. I was afraid to look up from the ground. What would I see staring back at me? I swallowed hard, trying to prepare myself for what was about to happen.

His shoes came into view, and I felt my wolf stirring under my skin. Wyatt elbowed me in the side. "Scarlett..." he hissed under his breath in a warning tone. I lifted my face to meet his gaze with a bated breath.

His dark eyes widened in surprise as we drank each other in. Something in my mind snapped. I could feel it all, everything everyone had tried to explain to me about having a wolf. Her emotions and thoughts surged through me as I watched the corners of his mouth lift upwards into a smile.. a heart-stopping smile that was meant for only me.

I felt my own lips begin to mimic his. There was nothing and no one else in the room for us at that moment. This is what it felt like to have a mate, and I knew he was feeling the same sensations by the look in his eyes.

The moment was broken when a tall dark-haired female placed a kiss on his cheek. "I'm sorry I'm late, David. My shift went into overtime. I had to help Doctor McCarthy deliver the Johnson's twins. Those pups are going to be a handful. I can tell you that now." She finished with a soft chuckle of amusement.

I hadn't even seen her approach us I had been so lost in a different world. My smile faded quickly as my brows furrowed in confusion as I glanced between the two of them. He looked rather stiff as she grabbed a hold of his hand with hers, turning her face in my direction. "Hello. I don't think I've seen you before." She tilted her head to the side.

"That's because she's only just matured, Eva," Luna Victoria commented toward her, both of them sharing a look of understanding like two people who've already been through it.

"This must be very exciting for you then," she remarked with a bright smile, completely unaware of what had happened between me and the male she was holding onto as if he were hers. My wolf was growling possessively in my mind, struggling to free herself so that she could eliminate the competition.

"David, this is Scarlett," Luna Victoria introduced me. "Conrad's daughter," she supplied as if it were my own special title.

I felt like the rug had been pulled out from under my feet and I was falling without anyone to catch me. My stomach was in my throat, but I forced myself to speak. "Hi…" I replied in a tense voice, finding it hard to hold his gaze.

David pulled his hand free from Eva's grasp and took a step towards me. He lifted his hand slightly like he wanted to reach out to me, but he thought better of it, deciding to stuff it into the pocket of his slacks instead.

"It's nice to meet you, Scarlett." Goosebumps rose on my flesh, and I watched his pupils dilate a bit as he took in more of me. "Your father was a great man. The pack lost a great warrior when he passed away. I lost a dear friend," he added, trying to keep things from getting strange in front of all the onlookers. None of them seemed to know what had transpired between the two of us.

I gave him a small smile that didn't reach my eyes. "Thank you." He looked like he wanted to say something more to me, his lips parted slightly. Alpha Aaron stepped forward, his dark eyes calculating as he glanced between myself and his son. I lowered my gaze to the ground, clenching my jaw tightly.

"Well, we should get this meeting going." He wrapped his arm around his mate and pulled her into his side. "It's wonderful to have another true wolf added to the pack."

Wyatt grabbed my elbow, and I tensed slightly at the touch. Now that I could connect to my wolf, the world seemed too overwhelming. Every sensation moved through me like an exploding bomb. I let him lead me away to some empty seats, but my mind was adrift as I looked around the room. I had matured and met my mate, only to find out that he already had someone at his side. How could I compete with her?

My gaze focused on the female in question, Eva. She was a fully matured female compared to myself, who was still growing into my body, which was mostly knees and elbows. She seemed kind, and she didn't waver under the gaze of all the people in the room. She looked like a queen. I certainly wasn't much compared to her. That was why she was the one standing on the stage, holding his hand.

I sunk down lower in my seat. I could hear Alpha Aaron's voice as he spoke to the group, but none of the words were able to pierce through my racing thoughts.

"We are happy to announce that the mating ceremony of Eva and David will be held at the end of next month," Alpha Aaron said with pride in his voice, clapping David on the back as he stood next to a smiling Eva, hand in hand. My heart dropped, and I sucked in a painful breath. This wasn't how things were supposed to go. I was his mate, not her.

I couldn't sit in that room for another moment and listen to any more words. I leaned over to Wyatt. "I need to go," I whispered. He looked over at me in confusion as I rose up out of my chair and hurried toward the exit. I didn't look back, but I felt David's eyes on me, my body heating up everywhere his gaze drifted to. It was getting hard to breathe as I pushed open the door and flung myself out into the night, letting the cool air wash over me.

I sucked in ragged breaths as I tried to overcome the ache in my chest. No one had warned me maturing would be so painful.

02

Scarlett

The next couple of days turned into a blurred routine of waking up, going to school, going to work at the diner, and coming home. I tried everything I could to keep myself distracted from thoughts of my mate, and at first, it seemed to work. Slowly, though, the thoughts became too numerous to block out, and I had the image of him holding Eva's hand constantly flashing in my mind.

Eva… I had found myself coming to hate that name. I couldn't help myself, no matter how much I knew she wasn't to blame for my current predicament. It was not as if she knew that I even existed. Yet, knowing what she was to David, what she was going to be to him, only fueled the hatred I felt.

I found myself wondering how they had met. What had been going through their minds when they got together? Had they both simply gotten tired of waiting for their mates and said "screw it"? Or had they loved each other so much that none of that even mattered? Perhaps, she had a mate out there somewhere that she had disregarded as well. Though recalling the kind smile she had given me, I didn't think her the type to do something like that.

I was content, at the moment, to remain on the sidelines, because I really didn't have any other plan on how to handle the situation. They had seemed so happy together that a part of me wanted to let him go his own way and pretend that we had never met. However, there was another part of me that wanted to approach him and ask him to give me a chance. I was his true mate, after all, and she could never be what I could be to him.

It didn't help that my wolf and I weren't on the same page. Her constant whimpering and urging for me to go to him were only making me more frustrated. It was different having something else constantly in my mind with its own wants and needs. Her instincts were telling her to go be with her mate, but she didn't understand all the other factors revolving around the matter and that it wasn't that simple. It was exhausting, to say the least.

If I had known that this was what was in store for me when I reached maturity, I might have spent my nights praying to remain as I had been. I would have happily remained completely oblivious to the fact that I even had a mate who was planning a mating ceremony with the impeccable Eva while I was walking around like a kicked puppy.

I let out another heavy sigh as I continued to wipe down the counter, finishing up my closing duties before I head home for the night. Darlene leaned against the counter next to me, crossing her arms over her chest. "Alright, Red..." she started to say, using the name she had called me the first few weeks I worked at the diner. Apparently, she had trouble remembering my name in the beginning, and Red was close enough in her mind. "What gives? You've been walking around here for the past week like someone stole your best friend."

"It's nothing." I found myself sighing again.

Darlene rolled her eyes. "Yes because you normally walk around sighing like a lovesick teenager. Is that it? Do I need to beat up some boy for breaking your heart? Cause I'll do it." I couldn't stop the small smile that lifted my gloomy expression. The thought of Darlene beating up my mate was a funny one.

"I appreciate that, Darlene, but you don't need to beat anyone up. I'm just stressed about the fact that I haven't heard back from any of the colleges I applied to." It wasn't necessarily a lie because it was true I was stressed about college. There was no reason to try to explain to her how I went from no love life to having an over-complicated one practically overnight.

She gave me a pat on the shoulder. "I don't know why you're stressed. You're the smartest one out of all of us here at the diner. Those colleges would be stupid not to accept you."

I took a step back. "Thank you, Darlene. I appreciate the confidence, but it's not like it takes much to be the smartest around here. There's no competition."

Her eyes narrowed into a playful glare as she reached out and snatched the towel from my hand. She wound it up and snapped it toward me, and I let out a laugh as I dodged her attack. "Why don't you go ahead and clock out, smartass? I'll finish up here. Just lock the front door on your way out."

I didn't need to be told twice. I had been working a lot of shifts at the diner over the past couple of weeks in hopes of saving up money I might need for college. That was, if I ever got a response. I gathered my things and blew Darlene a playful goodbye kiss as I headed out.

I pushed the key into the front door, twisted it, then grabbed the door and gave it a good couple of pulls to make sure the lock had settled right.

I turned back around after checking to make sure the door was locked. And as I did so, I found David waiting there. I gave a small scream of surprise, hand rushing to cover my heart that I thought might explode out of my chest. "What are you doing here?" I asked in a breathless voice as I tried to calm myself down.

He looked a little apologetic for having scared me as he took a step in my direction. I found myself taking a step back away from him, suspicious of his reasons for suddenly appearing before me. "I came to see you," he stated with uncertainty.

I shifted the strap of my purse. "How did you know I work here?" I looked around the parking lot, noticing that there was a black Mercedes parked next to my cousin's beat-up truck. I hoped that Darlene was busy in the kitchen and didn't see me out here with him, or else, she would be waiting to interrogate me on Monday.

He gave me a look as if it should be obvious to me. "I asked Wyatt." I internally facepalmed myself. Of course, he had, and my cousin had certainly obliged him without a moment's hesitation.

I frowned as I chanced another peek back towards the diner. "You shouldn't have come here." I really hoped that Darlene couldn't see us.

"I just wanted to talk, that's all." He lifted his hands up in surrender, palms out towards me to show he meant no harm. There was a sad smirk playing on his lips as if he found some kind of humor in our current situation.

I had to ignore the way my body seemed to be drawn to him like a moth to the flame. I had already been burned once, and I was not looking to get burned again. "Okay." I lifted my chin a bit as I assessed him. "Talk. I'm all ears."

I noticed the way his lips twitched at my response as he lowered his hands to his sides. "A little demanding, aren't we?"

Inside, I felt like I had the right to be. He could have come to me sooner, but he hadn't. Still, my cheeks flamed regardless of what I felt as I registered the fact that I had spoken to the future alpha in such a disrespectful manner.

"Sorry," I apologized, dropping my gaze to the ground and internally reprimanding myself for talking to him like I had. He could have me punished for something like that, mate or not.

I heard the sound of his sneakers against the pavement as he took another step towards me. "It's fine, Scarlett. I was just teasing you. I deserve that and more, I'm sure."

I peered up at him, his dark gaze holding me captive. "I should have come to you sooner, Scarlett. I know that. And I wanted to come to you. I was just confused about everything. I needed time to think about this thing between us. It was unexpected... *You* were unexpected."

I had to resist the urge to roll my eyes. He was almost as bad as Wyatt when it came to putting his foot in his mouth. "Sorry to have sprung myself on you so unexpectedly," I remarked dryly as I shoved the diner keys into my purse, searching for the keys to Wyatt's truck.

"That's not what I meant," he replied quickly. "You're my mate. Of course, meeting you was the happiest moment of my life. Though it was unexpected, I wouldn't have changed it."

I lifted a brow but kept my mouth closed up tight, allowing him more time to explain himself. He must have understood that because more words came spilling out of his lips.

"I need you to know that my reason for staying away had nothing to do with not wanting you. I do want you, Scarlett. How could I not want you? You are perfect." His words made my wolf happy, smoothing over any hurt feelings she had about the fact he had disregarded us for the past week after finding out we were mates.

I was happy he was here and that he was saying he wanted me, but there was still one factor that I could not forget, a factor that he had failed to mention in all of his talking. "What about Eva? How does she fit into all of this? Where does this leave her?" I questioned him. I needed to know the truth.

He let out a heavy breath, lifting a hand to his head. His hand rubbed anxiously at the short stubble that covered it.

"I don't know, Scarlett. I don't want to talk about her right now. I can't think of her when I'm standing in front of you."

I clenched my teeth together at his words. "So when should we talk about her then? Before or after the mating ceremony?" My anger had me snapping at him. I noticed the immediate regret of his in his gaze, and he took a step towards me, leaving not much distance left between our bodies. I pulled the truck keys from my purse, ready to take off at a moment's notice.

He must have sensed that, "Scarlett, it's complicated..."

"No, it really isn't, David. Either you want to be with her, or you want to be with me, your mate." I tacked on at the end, "Until you make up your mind about that, I think you should stay away from me. It isn't fair to Eva, and it's certainly not fair to me."

He looked a little shocked at the words coming from my mouth, but he didn't argue their validity. "I don't know if I can stay away from you. My wolf doesn't want to let you out of our sight. I feel more at ease with you near," he admitted in a tone of defeat.

The truth was that my wolf didn't want him to stay away from us, and neither did I, but I knew that was the influence of the bond. The longer we were in each other's presence, the harder it would be to remain clear-headed. I shook my head, trying to sort out my thoughts. "I need you to respect my wishes, David. I don't want to be the second choice when it comes to my mate. So until you can choose, this is the way things will be." I felt a lump building in my throat, but I held myself together in front of him.

His expression looked grave, but he nodded his head. "I understand."

We stood there staring at each other, both of us lost in the heavy silence. What more was there to say? He hadn't made a decision about anything. He said he wanted me, but he still had Eva waiting for him at home. He *had* said he needed time to think. Maybe with time, he would realize that no one else could compare to your mate no matter how wonderful they might be. Or at least, I had to believe there was still a chance.

"Can I at least walk you to your car?" he asked with a soft voice that could have almost been a whisper. My fingers tightened around the keys in my hand, and my stomach twisted up in painful knots as I gave him a small nod. I should have told him no, but I wanted to be in his presence a little longer.

I crossed the distance between us, coming to stand near him but making sure to keep space between our bodies. I itched to reach out and touch him. His gaze roamed over me from the top of my head to the tips of the dirty sneakers that stuck out from under my baggy jeans. I felt my cheeks burn, wishing I could have worn something a little nicer today.

"Shall we?" he questioned, motioning for me to make the first move. This was so awkward. Was this how all mates felt when they met each other or was our situation out of the ordinary? I forced my legs to move my body forward toward my truck.

We walked next to each other in heavy silence. I tried to search for something to say to him that would take away the edge that had been created, but my ability to form words was failing me. By the time I thought of anything mildly interesting to say, we were already standing at the driver-side door of my cousin's truck.

"Well, this is me," I remarked, internally facepalming.

His lips curved upward with amusement. "It was good to see you again, Scarlett." His body inclined forward toward mine. I remained rooted in place as his lips brushed against the skin of my cheek. I felt the surge of pleasurable tingles race across the spot he had touched. He lingered for a moment as if caught off guard by the sensation as well.

As he pulled back, his lips hovered centimeters above my own, dark eyes meeting mine. I had to force myself to step back even though everything in me was screaming at me to steal a kiss. "Goodnight, David," I said, slightly out of breath.

"Goodnight," he said, giving me a small smile that didn't quite reach his eyes before I turned away and unlocked my door, scrambling up into the cab of the truck to put some safe space between us.

When I had gotten home, I dragged myself up the stairs to my bedroom and happily sunk into a much-needed sleep. So when I was awoken by a harsh pounding on my bedroom door, I was more than a little keyed up. I turned my head into my pillow, catching sight of the red numbers on my alarm clock blinking nine in the morning.

It was Saturday. Saturdays were the only days that I didn't have school or work and the only day I got to sleep in. I didn't like to be disturbed on Saturdays, and Wyatt knew that better than anyone. Only when the knocking became more persistent did I peel myself up out of bed. I stomped my way to my door, wrenching it open. "What the hell, Wyatt? You better be bleeding to death!"

My wolf was just as grumbly about being disturbed. I snapped my mouth shut when I noticed that Wyatt was standing with two warriors flanking him on either side. The one on the right met my shocked gaze. "Alpha Aaron has requested your presence."

A part of me felt extremely anxious over the fact that he had sent warriors as personal escorts. What did he want, and what did he think I was going to do? I shifted back. "Just let me get changed," I said before closing the door on all of them. I scrambled around my room with shaky movements, trying to make myself as presentable as possible.

The ride to the pack house was beyond tense. Wyatt and I were sandwiched together in his truck while we drove in between two large SUV's. I didn't know what to say to him about what was happening, and he didn't try to ask me. He kept his eyes focused on the road in front of us, fingers clasped tightly around the steering wheel.

The two warriors escorted us into the house, keeping us pressed closely together between them. Alpha Aaron sat behind his desk with a serious expression, his gaze fixed on the two of us as we were let into the room. Behind him, Luna Victoria stood dutifully, her elegant fingers wrapped around the top of his leather office chair. I held her gaze for a moment before I felt the need to look away.

The air in his office was heavy and suffocating the deeper I moved into it. Wyatt was pressed in at my back. I could feel his anxiety as well. He had no idea what was going on, but in the back of my mind, I had a horrible inkling this had to do with David and me.

The door closed behind us, and I jolted. I didn't like being enclosed in a small space, and neither did my wolf. I tried to keep my breathing as even as I could, hoping it would help me to keep myself under control. Shifting right now would not be a good thing to do.

Wyatt cleared his throat. "Do you mind me asking what all of this is about?"

Alpha Aaron leaned forward in his chair, the leather creaking under the sudden movement. His elbows graced the top of the fine cherry wood desk, fingers laced together. "Of course not, son. This is about your cousin and my son," his deep voice rumbled, "and their connection to one another."

I felt the urge to sink to the ground as he turned his dark eyes in my direction. Wyatt glanced in my direction with raised brows, questioning me silently about what I had been keeping from him. I hadn't told him about David and me, mostly because, like David, I needed time to think about what it meant and what I was supposed to do.

"Did you think that it would escape my notice?" he questioned in a calm tone, but I could feel the way the room vibrated with the dominant aura he was throwing out. My wolf gnashed her teeth together in my mind, she didn't like this male. I stiffened as I fought her urges to snap and snarl at him for trying to make us submit.

I bit the inside of my cheek. "I wasn't trying to hide anything, I swear, Alpha Aaron. I just thought that with the way things were..." I looked around the room. "I was pretty certain it didn't matter all that much. He already has someone beside him, and I had no plans to come between that." The words tasted sour on my tongue. They cut at my heart, reminding me that I was taking second place to my mate.

"But David did come to see you, didn't he?"

I didn't quite appreciate the interrogation. I couldn't figure out why he cared if his son had come to see me or not. We were mates, after all. Did he expect we would be able to ignore the bond?

I felt my gaze narrow slightly in suspicion. "It seems you already know the answer to that question, *Alpha*. Or else, I doubt I would be standing here." My tongue got carried away.

Alpha Aaron flashed me his teeth in a sneer, a growl rumbling from deep in his throat that had me regretting my tone immediately. Wyatt stepped forward, head bowed, and neck stretched in submission. "I apologize, Alpha. She is still a pup in a lot of ways. She doesn't understand how things work just yet." I turned my face toward my cousin in silence mortification at his humbled display.

"But she will learn," he snapped, losing that bit of calm he had before.

"Aaron," Luna Victoria spoke his name in a tone that urged him to control his temper. I watched his muscles flex for a moment before he forced himself to relax. They seemed completely different than they had a couple of days ago at the pack meeting. They had greeted me with kind eyes and friendly smiles, but now they were treating me like a problem to be solved.

"You know, Scarlett, when I was a young man, a neighboring pack was attacked by rogues. They came through in the night and decimated their numbers. By the time we arrived to help, it was too late. The dead were everywhere. I'd never seen anything like it."

I couldn't figure out why he was sharing this story with me, but I stood quietly and listened.

"We spent most of the day searching for survivors. By noon, the stench of death and decay was overwhelming. I had given up hope that we would find anyone alive, but about that time, I heard a gentle cry from a nearby house. I found a girl not much older than five hiding in a toy chest in her bedroom."

He shifted in his seat, a faraway look in his eyes for a moment. "She must have crawled in there not long after the attack broke out. She had these big brown eyes, I remember them to this day. She stared up at me like I was her savior. When I tried to move her, I noticed the way her stomach was bulging, unnaturally so. She had suffered some kind of trauma that was beyond repair. I knew that in the back of my mind, but still, I pulled her out of that chest and carried her out of that house. I wanted to save her.

"My father knew as soon as I brought her to him that she wouldn't survive. It came down to letting her suffer or putting her out of her misery. 'For the good of the pack, we sometimes have to make hard choices,' he told me before he snapped her little neck."

I flinched at the finality of his story. I wondered who I was being compared to in the tale, was I the little girl who would not survive? Had I been brought here to be put out of my misery?

"I cried as I buried her under a tree next to the rest of her pack. My father put his hand on my shoulder and told me something that I've never forgotten, 'Remember, it's the pack, then us."

He repeated the motto again, looking in my direction with a heavy gaze full of past torments, "The pack, then us."

"I want to hear you say it, Scarlett." Alpha Aaron commanded in a voice much too calm. I shifted uncomfortably where I stood. My tongue was thick in my mouth as he held my gaze, leaning forward in his chair. "Say it."

The eyes that had looked at me with kindness and warmth a few days ago were now as hard as steel. I straightened my back as my wolf pressed her will on me. It was strange to have a complete connection with her. Her thoughts were intermingling with my own. Right now, I understood that she didn't like being told what to do, but I also knew even if she had reached maturity, in terms of being able to mate, she was still a juvenile in her thinking. It would be years before she would even be capable of contemplating taking on a seasoned wolf like Alpha Aaron.

I licked my lips as I lowered my eyes to my hands that were clenched tightly together in front of me. "The pack, then us," I repeated the mantra back to him. The words tasted foul in my mouth.

"Do you understand what this means?" he questioned, satisfied for the moment with my obedience. I nodded my head. I wasn't quite sure what it meant to him, but I could make assumptions.

"This is what good leaders remember when they must make the hard decisions, Scarlett. This is what my father taught me, and a lesson I passed on to my son." He leaned back in his chair. It creaked loudly under the shifting of his weight. I lifted my face to meet his gaze again as his mate gave his shoulders a squeeze as if needing to show her solidarity with him.

"It's always the pack first, then us. Everyone and everything must become our wants and needs."

"You want to be a good leader someday, don't you?" His question made me sick to my stomach, but I nodded my head finding it hard to find words. My head bobbed back and forth, feeling like a hundred pound weight on my shoulders.

"My son wants to be a good leader, too. But to be the leader this pack will need when I step down, the pack will need someone just as strong and capable to share the burden with him." I could deduce he did not believe I was up to par with what he believed were good leadership qualities. It was true that I couldn't imagine myself leading anyone, but if the Goddess had paired David and me together, there must have been a reason for it.

As if on cue, the door to the small office burst open, and the person in question entered. David came into the room with his head hanging low, like a man with a death sentence. Alpha Aaron pushed up from his seat, motioning for his son to come closer. He peered in my direction for a second as he passed, unable to hold my gaze for long.

"David, you know that this is for the good of the pack as we already discussed this morning. It's not what is wanted, but it is what is needed." We both flinched at his father's words. I had already figured out the current trajectory of our path.

I wondered if this was the life that my parents had envisioned for me when they had prepared to bring me into the world. Rejection was not something that was done lightly. The act itself was painful for both parties and could result in deadly consequences. Didn't anyone care that this could possibly kill me?

"Please..." I couldn't help but plead for my own case. This is not what I wanted. I wanted to be given a choice in the matter. I wanted the chance to see if I could be the leader they doubted I could be.

David met my gaze with a pained expression of his own. "Father, perhaps..."

"What is our motto?" Alpha Aaron interrupted before he could finish.

"Father, I—"

Alpha Aaron let out a rumbling growl. "What is our motto, David?"

I watched David stiffen, his jaw clenching tightly. "The pack, then us," he repeated the horrible mantra, something I was certain I would never forget until the day I died.

"Then you know that this is about what is best for the pack." His father's tone demanded respect and obedience. Before this moment, I believed that the Alpha was an infallible force. Whatever he said was truth and law, but standing in this room, all I saw was a selfish man who used his power to do as he saw fit.

"David, you don't have to do this," I said with a shaky voice, attempting to reach through the training his father had indoctrinated him and into the heart of my mate underneath. He looked as though he was lost in an internal struggle. It was clear he was being torn in opposing directions.

"Put the poor girl out of her misery." Luna Victoria commented with a somber expression. She didn't look like she was enjoying any part of the situation she was in, unable to make eye contact with me.

David turned to me with regret burning in his gaze. "Forgive me, Scarlett." He offered it like a soft prayer as he sucked in a shuddering breath.

I shook my head in disbelief. "No, wait."

But he was already speaking the words, sealing our fate forever. "I, David Matthew, reject you, Scarlett Ramsey, as my mate and future luna of this pack. I free you from our bond and the ties that hold us together. You are free to do as you wish."

The fire spread through my chest, and my knees grew weak as I struggled to get air into my lungs. Wyatt reached out for me, but I pushed him away. My wolf was whimpering in my head, her pain only amplifying my own. My legs gave out, and I collapsed to the ground, trying to breathe through the endless ache. I felt like someone had hollowed me out, and I wasn't sure if any part of me remained.

I dug my fingers into the carpeted floor beneath me as I tried to remain tethered to something. I could only imagine how weak I looked prostrated before them. I slowly lifted my face to find David leaning against his father, hand pressed to his chest above his heart. It was the only sign that he was effected at all by the rejection.

Strong hands were gripping my shoulders and pulling me off the ground. "Come on, Scarlett," Wyatt's gentle voice whispered to me. My legs were weak as I tried to stand up, stumbling slightly. "Don't worry. I have you. I'm going to take you home."

I was in a complete daze as he ushered me away from my shattered future.

One week, that was how long I stayed locked away in my room. No one came to visit me. No one tried to contact me. No one tried to console me, not that they could have. It was simply me and the four walls of my bedroom… the four walls that had seen me through some of the toughest nights of my life. They were with me again through another loss, a loss that felt too great to recover from.

The first couple of nights, I had spent tossing and turning and waking up screaming in agony in sweat-soaked sheets. I passed through the worst of it into a state of emptiness. I would go through the motions of being alive, but I felt dead on the inside, full of the decayed remains of who I had been.

I knew that Wyatt was worried about me by the way he looked at me every time he brought me something to eat and took away the untouched plates of food he had brought me before. The days passed by the same: the sun would rise, and the sun would set. I would fall asleep only to be surprised that I was there to greet it again in the morning.

The pain became more manageable with every new day as I fell into a new state of being.

"This came in the mail for you," Wyatt greeted me as I came down the stairs one morning. I crossed the room to grab the sealed envelope he was holding in his hand. My eyes scanned it quickly, noting the insignia in the corner.

I feel my heart pulse in my chest for the first time in weeks as I tore open the letter with shaky fingers. A sigh of relief passed through my lips as I unfolded the paper hidden inside, reading words of acceptance.

In my hand was my ticket to freedom.

03

Scarlett

Two Years Later

I stood behind the counter tapping my finger against the hard, polished surface impatiently as the woman tried to decide whether or not she wanted to order her coffee decaf or not. I was seriously one mocha frappucino away from blowing my own brains out. I sighed softly as I continued to watch the woman as she mumbled through her options. I knew I was just being irritable from my lack of sleep, and my wolf was antsy to go for a run because It had been at least a week since I had let her out to roam.

The problem was there was no sufficient space for me to do so in the city safely and getting out to the woods was a good hour's drive. It was hard to find the time between school and work to make that drive. In my more frantic moments, when I had first moved here, I briefly considered going to the dog park a couple blocks from my apartment building, but I doubted that would go over well with the humans *or* my wolf.

"You know what, on second thought," the woman began, and I felt my teeth clench together a bit harder, "I'll just have a tall chai tea latte."

I gave her my best-practiced customer service smile while inside I was visualizing myself jumping over the counter and strangling her with my bare hands. There was a rumble of agreement from my wolf at the thought. I quickly tapped the corrected order into the electronic screen. "Will that be all, ma'am?" I asked in an overly sweetened voice as I lifted my gaze. She smiled and nodded her head as I gave her the total, completely unaware of how close she had come to physical danger. I let out a sigh of relief when she gave me the exact change before she turned and walked away.

I sagged away from the register, wiping my hand across my forehead. My eyes drifted to the clock on the wall. There were only three hours left until my shift was over. I was going to have to make the drive out to the wildlife preserve, despite the mountain of homework I had sitting at home waiting for me. If I didn't, I was likely to go berserk on some helpless bystander for looking at me the wrong way.

"Scarlett?" I heard the manager, Frankie, call out my name. I bit into the side of my cheek as I reminded myself to keep my attitude in check. I needed this job to keep paying for the awful apartment I was renting. I had ditched the apartment the pack had provided for me a week after moving to the city. I didn't want any connection to the place and people that had so brutally destroyed my heart.

I turned toward his office door to find him standing there with a firm look on his pudgy face. "Can I talk to you for a moment, please?" I nodded my head, but internally, I was groaning. When someone asked you if they could talk to you, it was never a good thing, at least in my experience.

"Carter, watch the register for me. I'll be right back," I said to the new girl while she was mixing up some fresh coffee. She smiled and gave me a thumbs up, and I did my best not to roll my eyes. I frowned as I made my way into the cramped office space and took a seat in the hard chair across my manager. He eyed me in a way that I'm sure wasn't work appropriate, but he was harmless in the fact that he had never tried to touch me. If he had, he would have been met with quite the surprise, and a swift bite on the ass from my wolf.

He leaned back in his chair. "So I got a call." I tensed up at his words. I felt my heart clench at the thought. I had a strong feeling I already knew where this is going. "It was from a detective David..."

I almost laughed at this, *almost*. A detective? He couldn't have thought of anything more original?

Frankie continued, "He gave me his direct number and asked me to have you call him back when I saw you again. He said it was an urgent matter that requires your immediate attention."

I tried to keep myself from grimacing. The moment I had been dreading since I was given permission to leave pack territory was happening. I had done everything in my power to cover my trail, hoping that I would be forgotten, but it couldn't be that simple.

"Is there something going on that I should know about, Scarlett? Problems at home or school?" he questioned, raising a brow. Humans were so nosey. They seemed to thrive on drama. I weighed the answer to his question in my mind. *Now that you mention it, Frankie... Why yes, there is. My ex-mate won't let me go, even though he rejected me and mated someone else. Oh, what? You didn't know werewolves existed? Well, this is awkward.*

I put on a tight-lipped smile. "Not at all. I had problems with a boyfriend a while back. Must be about that. Restraining orders aren't what they used to be," I replied shortly.

He gave me an awkward nod and cleared his throat. "Well then, I'll give you a moment in here to call him back. For the future, you should really consider getting a cell phone, Scarlett. The work phone isn't meant for private matters," he added with a hint of judgment as he got up from behind his desk and slid a piece of paper with a phone number scribbled across it in barely legible handwriting.

I glared down at the number, waiting until he was out of the room and the door was closed before I reached for the phone. The phone rang a couple times before I heard the subtle click of the line turning over.

"Hello? Wyatt speaking..."

A wave of nostalgia rushed through me at the sound of the familiar voice. It took me a moment to register the fact that he was answering David's personal phone.

"Wyatt, why are you answering David's phone?" I couldn't help asking the question. My reason for calling was suddenly lost in my curiosity.

"Scarlett? Is that you?" He sounded surprised to hear my voice. Probably because in covering my trail, I had cut my ties to everyone. They would have been forced to betray me, and I didn't want to put them in that position. Obey their alpha, or protect their friend. It was an impossible choice.

I leaned forward. "It's me, you big idiot. Have I been gone so long that you forgot me already?" I teased him, wanting to cut through the emotions of the moment.

There was a heavy silence followed by a long exhale. "Scarlett, I'm so glad you're alive." I could hear the relief in his voice. "I thought you might be dead. I've missed you. You have no idea how good it is to hear your voice." I bit down hard on the urge to explain why I did what I did because I knew deep down he already understood my reasons.

"Where are you? Are you safe?" These were the questions I had expected.

"I'm safe. I'm going to school and working hard to pay for a terrible studio apartment. Oh, and by the way, the truck you loaned me is a real piece of shit. So thanks for that."

He let out a soft laugh, and I found myself smiling a real smile for the first time all day. My wolf seemed less stressed out. That part of all shifters was always happier with companionship. Our wolves weren't meant for lives of solitude.

Talking to Wyatt reminded me of home, my real home. I missed the mountains I grew up in. I missed the house I grew up in. I missed the familiar things that brought me comfort. The longing in my heart surged to a crescendo. It was a mistake to return David's call. I should have left things alone, but my impulsive nature had led me astray as usual.

He let out another long sigh of relief. "That's good to hear. Real good."

I closed my eyes tight. "How are things for you?"

"They're good. I am going to receive the title of beta soon. The ceremony is being held this weekend." I always suspected that he would be the one to succeed the position. My father had trained him well, after all.

"That's great, Wyatt. The pack will be better for it," I replied honestly.

"Thanks. It'll be hard work, but I love it." I could hear the pride in his voice. "David has been doing well since he stepped into his father's shoes." The moment of connection was lost at the mention of *his* name. The reason for my calling in the first place sucked all the life out of me.

"Speaking of David, could you put him on the phone, Wyatt?" I asked in a calm voice. I'm too calm, and I know it.

He paused as if calculating what his response should be. "He's busy with Eva, at the moment."

The sound of her name sent a sharp pang through my chest. I tried to fight off the last images I had of them together at the announcement ceremony, but they flooded my brain. My wolf growled loud in my head. She didn't quite understand that we had been rejected and that there would be no happy ending for us.

I clenched my hand tightly around the receiver. "I don't have time for this game, Wyatt. He called me, and I'm returning his call. Either he talks to me now, or he never talks to me again. You've got ten seconds to put him on, or I'm hanging up." I snapped, no longer in the mood to chat. I would have never spoken to any of them like that before, but I had been on my own for two years. The fact that I didn't have to answer to anyone changed my perspective on everything. It gave me the opportunity to mature and make my own mistakes without someone breathing down my neck.

They thought I was going to come back after college was over. That was the only reason I had been allowed to go in the first place. That, and the fact that they, David's parents, were afraid that I would ruin their plans to make our pack great again. They couldn't trust that the connection between their son and I had been severed enough to keep him focused on the female of their choosing. The moment I left, I had promised myself that I was never going back to that place if I had anything to say about it. I would live in hiding if I had to, but I was never going back.

Wyatt was silent for a moment, lost in surprise once again. "Uh... Yeah, hold on real quick." My heart began to race as I realized I was about to talk to my mate. Scratch that, my ex-mate, and I hadn't done so since he rejected me. I felt my palms start to sweat.

"Scarlett," his voice rang through the phone, and the ache in my chest grew as though the rejection had happened yesterday.

I clenched my teeth together for a moment before speaking. "How did you find me?" I needed to know. I didn't care if I came off as disrespectful. My anger towards the situation wouldn't allow me to act any other way. Respect was earned, and he had done nothing for me to respect him.

There was a pause. "I contacted a nearby pack, they did some looking into the matter of our missing she-wolf," he replied, not giving away much in the way of information.

"I have permission to be here, David," I snapped at him, reminding him that his father had helped me arrange things to be the way they were.

"It's been two years." The tone of his voice became sharper. "You haven't checked in once. That was not part of the arrangement, and you know it." His tone was clipped, even slightly angry. I knew he would be angry that I hadn't stayed in contact as I had promised his parents, but then again, no one tried that hard to get in contact with me until now. I had hoped that was a sign that they were letting me go my own way.

I could only assume this was his way of giving me space after everything that had transpired between us. The guilt of the rejection had probably kept him at bay for a while before he could no longer ignore the need of his wolf to search for me. It didn't matter that he had his chosen female. She would never be what I was to him. "You gave up the apartment that my father rented for you, and you didn't leave a number for anyone to reach you at or a change of address. Nothing. You vanished into thin air without a single word. I spent a lot of time and money tracking you down, Scarlett." His words sent a shiver through me. This wasn't healthy, and it certainly wasn't right. He had bound himself to another female, but still, our connection lingered like a broken radio signal.

"Yeah, there was a reason for that, David. I didn't want you to reach me. I didn't want to be found. I wanted to be left alone. The only reason I'm calling you now is to tell you to not to look for me anymore. Be satisfied knowing that I'm alive," I said dryly, knowing that I was pushing him closer to the edge with my attitude.

He let out a warning growl through the phone, but it didn't have the same effect it would in person. "You are still a part of this pack. I'm your alpha now, and you *will* respect me. You have been allowed more freedoms and leeway than anyone else. Perhaps more than you should have, by the ways things have gone."

"I didn't ask for the special treatment, Alpha!" I snapped back at him, using his title to mock him.

"I didn't have to let you go, Scarlett. I could have stopped you from leaving." He pushed it in my face. Reminding me that, as Alpha, he had the power to control my life as long as I remained connected to the pack.

"Yeah, but you did let me go, didn't you? You had a choice, and you chose," I said harshly. We both knew I wasn't talking about my little sabbatical anymore. I heard his breath hitch a bit, and I could tell my words had an effect on him because a faint familiar sting bloomed in my chest. I pushed the pain down.

"Scarlett, I'm—"

"Save it," I interrupted. I could tell he was going to apologize, but I was so exhausted by all the apologies he had given me. They didn't take away what had happened. They were only pathetic attempts to soothe away the pain he caused.

I rolled my eyes at him through the phone. "Look, is there a reason for this call, David? Other than to remind me of my position in life?" I said, feigning boredom as I tried to ignore the need to apologize for my behavior. The wolf part of me only knew the order of things; the alpha sat above everyone and required our complete obedience. Disrupting that order was often met with punishment, that was, at times, severe.

I could tell that I was getting under his skin, but he reigned in his anger. "Yes. There is a reason." He was all business now. "We are having a pack meeting this weekend. There are important matters and changes happening that the whole pack needs to discuss and hear about. You are still a part of this pack, so I expect you to be there."

"No," I said without hesitation. I wasn't going to go back there. I knew if I did, I would never be allowed to leave again. He wouldn't allow that. His wolf wouldn't allow that. I would be forced to spend the rest of my days watching as he shared, what was supposed to be our, future with someone else.

"Excuse me?" His voice rumbled a little.

"You heard me. I said no, David. I won't come home this weekend, next weekend, or ever again. Consider this my resignation from the pack." *And from you*, my mind added. I could feel my body shaking as I came to terms with what I had just said to him. David let out a loud growl that made my wolf whimper inwardly. She wanted to submit, but my pride would not allow it.

"If you don't come home, then I'll come to *you*. I'll drag you back kicking and screaming if I have to, Scarlett. That's a promise." His voice was shaking with rage at my disrespect.

I smiled, feeling a sick kind of satisfaction at causing him such distress. I looked at it as karma for breaking my fragile, young heart before it even had time to dream of a future with him. "Best of luck trying to find me. Goodbye, David."

"Don't you dare hang—"

I hung up the phone on him. The phone rang again in the span of a few seconds. I knew it was him, but I ignored it, pushed up out of the chair, and strode toward the door. I only had an hour, maybe a few hours at most, to get ahead of David and the goons he was going to send to fetch me. I needed to get home, pack up what I could, and disappear.

As I exited the small office, I was bombarded with the elevator tunes and the sound of customers chatting. The noise did nothing to calm my racing heart. I was still high on the adrenaline rush of telling David off. I spotted Frankie leaning against the back counter, ogling poor, unaware Carter and her ass as she took care of the customers.

He must have seen me as I exited his room because he straightened up and turned towards me. "Is everything okay?" he asked. I nodded my head before I reached behind me and started undoing my apron.

He watched the movement with raised brow. I unwrapped it from my body and put it down the counter with a tight-lipped smile. "I quit."

04

Noah

My body felt strained as I splashed water from the stream up into my face, hoping to clear my mind. I had been wrestling with my wolf all day after I spent the night tossing and turning in restless sleep and bad dreams. The control I normally had was in short supply. My patience was growing thinner with each passing day as I searched to get some actual information on my brother's whereabouts. I had been led on a wild goose chase for the past two years. Every time I thought we were getting close, the trail would run cold, and we would have to start over from the beginning.

"Captain Ryder sent me to let you know we're ready for you, Alpha Noah..." One of the warriors approached me, making sure to not get too close.

My wolf had a thing about space. Most of the people in my pack understood this and gave me a wide berth whenever I was around. I pushed up to my full height, turning to face the younger warrior. He quickly dropped his gaze to the ground, the scent of his fear wafting over me. I hated the sour stench that it left in my nose, but I was used to it.

I patted him gently on the back as I passed by, hoping to calm his nerves. He had nothing to fear from me. He wasn't my target. He followed close behind me as I made my way toward the voices.

Ryder stood in the small clearing, arms crossed over his chest. I looked over his hardened expression, noting the scar that curved around his head. He had the rogues line up in a straight row, knees pressed to the earth. Their bodies were already beginning to heal from the beatings they had certainly been given at his hands. His hunting party had been very fruitful, which was fortunate because my wolf was hungry for blood and I was ready to feed the beast.

I walked slowly down the line, taking in the scent of fear and rage that poured from them. "I'm not feeling very merciful today, but you tell me where my brother is, and I'll make your deaths quick... If not..." My lips pulled upwards into a sinister grin. "Well, I'm sure I can come up with creative ways to loosen your tongues."

One of the rogues got to laughing, which started the lot of them howling like a pack of hyenas in no time. This was the same response they gave every time, without fail. They never ceased to disappoint me with their predictable responses. I glanced toward Ryder knowingly, giving him a nod of approval. He was already pulling out his weapon of choice, a silver whip that he kept with him during our hunts. He enjoyed a little torture before the kill.

He let it spring from its coiled position before he cracked it towards his target. It wrapped around the throat of the ringleader, cutting his laughter short. Ryder yanked hard on the whip, taking away all the slack.

I watched the show with slight amusement. The rogue choked as he fell forward, using his hands to catch himself before his face could greet the ground below him. The stench of his burning flesh was filling the air. I looked around the group of rogues who stared at their comrade with pale faces. "Now, let's try this again. Which one of you wants to tell me where my brother is?"

The silence was deafening as they watched their leader writhe under Ryder's unrelenting nature. He and I were cut from the same cloth, one that had spent more than a few days in the fire.

I glanced toward the captain of my warriors, and he pulled the whip back, freeing the rogue. I watched as he coughed and gagged.

"You and your followers are traitors to your father's cause." He snarled as he lifted accusing eyes toward Ryder. My wolf peered out with teeth bared at the mention of my father. He had happily helped me rip my father to shreds not long after we reached maturity.

The rogue's bloodshot eyes flipped back to me. "You're fighting a losing battle, *Alpha*." He mocked my title, his voice still hoarse. "As we speak, your brother is out there leading others into the new age. An age of our evolution."

I knew first-hand what their radical form of thinking brought. No longer wolf and man dwelling together in harmony. It was a fusing of the two into a monstrous form.

"Oh, I know all about your evolution. With its unimaginable power comes the insatiable blood lust. The need to feed... a hunger that never goes away. That won't be our ascension, it will be our extinction." His eyes narrowed at my words, this was not a wolf. This was a sheep well-trained by my brother.

"Your little mate thought the same thing before Kellan got a hold of her, but she learned the truth didn't she? They all do once he shows them what true power is..." The warriors under Ryder's command let out low warning growls at his words. They didn't like to be reminded of the loss of their luna, a person who had been far better than any of us.

This rogue was poking at the wrong wolf, taunting a beast more feral than most. My vision grew red for a moment as the beast pushed at the cage of my control, testing the limits. I ran my tongue over my teeth, canines lengthening under the stress of my darker side.

"That was a really stupid thing to say. These rogues never learn." Ryder commented under his breath behind me, knowing exactly what was about to happen.

I kicked out my leg toward his head, enjoying the sound of bone crunching as it struck, and the rogue fell onto his side in pain. I watched the blood run down his face and soak into the earth. I knelt down in front of the broken beast, tilting my head to the side as I examined my work. Dark eyes stared up at me full of hatred. "Kellan is going to come for you."

"That certainly would make this all a lot easier." I quipped back before I reached out, grabbing his broken nose between my fingers and squeezing. He screamed as I pulled him up to his feet. He stood before me bloodied and beaten, swaying slightly.

"Hey, Ryder," I said as I held the gaze of the rogue. "How many people do you think it takes to deliver a message?"

There was a short pause. "One, Alpha." I could hear the smile in his voice. He was already on the same page as me. I released my grip on my prey, turning my back to him for a moment. My wolf poked at the surface, frothing at the mouth with his desire to taste blood. He was becoming as uncontrollable as he had been before I met Claire. I let out a small sigh of frustration as I spun back around, slicing a clawed finger across the rogue's throat. Blood sprayed out, raining down on the earth and appeasing a bit of the beast's hunger.

"Then there were only three," Ryder proclaimed behind me.

"Who will be the one to get away, and who will become food for the crows?"

They looked at each other for a moment in slight confusion before scurrying to their feet. I watched them with amusement as they shifted into there beastly forms, racing off into the trees thinking they would be able to escape the same fate. Around me, my warriors tensed and strained to keep control over their wolves that wanted to hunt as the blood of the dead rogue only added to the frenzy.

Ryder stepped up beside me. "Fruitless, again..."

I pulled my shirt off, wiping the blood from my face with it. "No, I got more than enough information." His brows furrowed as he turned his face in my direction. I knew my brother was building his ranks, scrounging at the bottom of the barrel, seeking out the weaker packs. Now I knew he was planning to come for me again. He thought taking my mate would break me, but all it did was make me a colder creature. I had nothing to lose now, and since I was going to hell anyway, I planned to drag him there right alongside me.

"Happy hunting, boys!" I threw back my head and let out a howl towards the heavens. The sound of bones cracking and shifting, followed by vicious snarls from my warriors as they took off on the hunt, breathed life into my beast who lived in the darkness of my broken soul.

05

Scarlett

This was the second town that I had stopped in since I started my life on the run. I was tired, hungry, and extremely irritable. I knew the last part was because of my wolf. She was pissed at me for not waiting around for David to come and pick me up. It didn't matter how many times I told her that he had rejected us and had mated someone else, she wouldn't give it up. I guess that was how a mate bond worked. Even with a rejection, it could never be completely severed unless one of us died or we both completely bonded to other people, which David would never let happen if I stayed under his thumb.

I sighed as I jumped out of my cousin's beat-up truck, slamming the door behind me. A clean break from David and the pack was exactly what I needed if I wanted a shot at happiness. Perhaps, I could find another pack to take me in as a prospective member, or maybe travel the world and see all that it had to offer. Whatever I decided to do would be fine as long as it kept me out of David's reach.

I walked towards a small diner, the idea of sinking my teeth into some delicious food compelling me forward and pushing unfavorable thoughts of David to the back of my mind. I pushed the door open and entered the cool air-conditioned space. The familiar smell of grease and the sound of a tiny bell announcing my arrival brought a wave of nostalgia and homesickness.

The girl behind the counter looked up and greeted me with a friendly smile. "Just take a seat wherever you like, and I'll be right with you." I gave her a small smile in return before walking over and taking a seat in an empty booth. I scanned the room out of habit, noting where all the exits and people were in case I needed a quick getaway.

The diner was practically empty minus an old man at the counter reading the paper and enjoying his coffee. A single mom sat at a table trying to keep her two kids from jumping around like a pair of crazy monkeys. There were dark bags under her eyes, and her lips were pulled into a tight line. I didn't envy her position, but my wolf let out a small whine. She wanted to have pups. She wanted to carry her mate's future inside of her, but that was never going to happen. Not after everything.

I let my head fall back against the seat and released a heavy sigh when I knew, for the time being, I was safe. I closed my eyes, giving myself a moment to relax for the first time in seventy-two hours. I had pushed myself to the limit trying to put as much distance behind me as possible. I had made sure to cover my trail, doing my best to avoid any pack territories.

Most packs weren't keen on unannounced visitors, especially when the constant threat of rogues continued to increase over the years. Most Alpha's now required visitors to carry official pack papers with them, stating what pack they belonged to, their reason for the visit, and how long they would be staying. I remembered having to fill out all the paperwork when I left for the college in the city. I wasn't even going to be on their lands, but because the possibility of crossing over a boundary line had existed, I had been forced to follow the guidelines to avoid accidentally starting any pack wars.

"What can I get for you?" a sugary voice danced over me. I opened my eyes slowly and turned my head towards the direction of the voice. The waitress had bright blue eyes and cornflower colored hair pulled back into a bun at the nape of her neck. She reminded me a lot of a small town girl on one of those Lifetime channel movies.

"Could I just get a cup of earl grey tea to start," I asked with a faint smile as my eyes looked at her name tag, "Brittany?"

Her body seemed to bloom with happiness. "Coming right up." She turned from me with a bounce in her step. I frowned as I watched her walk away, thinking she was way too happy to be working in this place.

The sound of a roaring engine had me turning my attention to the large window beside me. I watched a sleek black car pull into the parking lot, and I immediately got an anxious feeling in the pit of my stomach. From the looks of the other cars in the parking lot, this car was way too fancy to be normal.

I watched as a group of bulky guys exited the vehicle that seemed much too small to hold all of them. The way they carried themselves set me on edge. Their gazes seemed predatory as they scanned the parking lot, making their way toward the front door.

The one near the head of the group had his dark hair buzzed short, a long scar curving from his right ear to his temple. He was shorter and bulkier than the male on his left-hand side. The taller one had a boyish look to his face, and his lips were lifted up in the corners like he was on the verge of smiling. Out of the bunch, he seemed to be the most approachable, but from the movements of his body, I figured he could carry his own in a fight.

I studied the two bringing up the end, twins. They were talking back and forth with excitement. The taller male was turning his head slightly back towards them and made a comment that had the twin on the right grimacing and shoving him hard from behind while his brother laughed at his expense. I must have been watching them for too long because the scarred one turned his face in my direction with a deep frown.

I looked away quickly from the window and sunk lower in my seat, not wanting to draw attention to myself. When I heard the bell on the door chime, I stiffened in my seat. The scent of shifters wafted toward me as the air circulated around the room. This was definitely not what I needed right now. I didn't know a lot of the packs this far from my own, but I could tell by this group that there must be one very close by. That, or I was already on their lands. Which could've gone badly for me because I didn't have permission to be there.

My wolf stirred at the presence of the other shifters, a small rumble echoing through my mind. She was *very* territorial. It didn't matter if the space belonged to her or not. If she was in it, she saw it as hers. It was a quirk that made things quite difficult for me at times. Perhaps not answering to an alpha or pecking order had gone to her head.

The lovely Brittany greeted them as sweetly as she had with me and invited them to find their own seats. I knew immediately they were going to go for the large corner booth which just so happened to be a booth behind mine. I immediately cursed myself for picking this seat. *Okay, Scarlett, you know how to mask your scent for short periods of times. It will be fine*, I thought to myself as I forced my wolf deeper within. It wasn't an easy thing to do, and she fought me as I pushed her. It took most of my concentration and will to get her to submit to me.

I leaned my head back and closed my eyes, trying to look as relaxed as I had earlier. I sensed them as they passed by, and it was hard to keep my wolf locked within. I was taking in shallow, short breaths to keep their scents from overwhelming her. When I felt certain all of them were behind me, I opened my eyes. I needed to get out of here, quickly.

I started to rise up out of my seat just as Brittany decided to return with my tea. She shot me her smile. "Here you are."

I bit my lip as I stared down at the steaming mug in her hand. I didn't want to be *that* customer, but I couldn't risk staying. "You know what, I actually just realized that I'm late for an appointment."

Brittany's smile never wavered. "Oh, don't be silly. If it's a money thing, don't worry about it. It's on the house." She gave me a friendly wink as she set the cup down in front of me. *Great!* She thought I was some kind of pauper or something. I tried not to roll my eyes as I readjusted in my booth, knowing I couldn't leave now. It would seem odd.

"Thanks," I said solemnly.

"No problem!" She smiled brightly before she turned and walked toward the shifters behind me.

I stared down into my tea, secretly wishing that the ground would open up and swallow me whole. It would solve all of my problems. My wolf began to stir in me, and I knew that I couldn't hold her back for much longer.

The door chimed, and I looked up toward the door to see another male coming through... one more shifter, one that I hadn't seen coming. His eyes roamed the room, and our gazes met. I saw his eyes widen in surprise and I felt my stomach drop. The secret was out, he knew.

A charming smile spread over his lips as he casually strolled toward my table, ignoring his friends, who I was sure were the ones sitting behind me. I tried to keep my face impassive as he eased himself down into the seat across from me. My wolf growled deeply in my head at another shifter entering her space without invitation. I clenched my hands into tight fists under the table as his friends started making noises and comments at his behavior. They obviously didn't realize what he had about me and thought he was making a move on a random out-of-towner.

He wasn't a bad looking guy. His brown hair was a little shaggy, and his eyes were the color of dark chocolate. "I didn't know we had anyone coming through the territory today. Noah never mentioned anything to me. I'm Dane." He introduced himself like I should be pleased to be meeting him.

I kept my face expressionless as I pushed myself up from the table. "Well, I'd like to say it was a pleasure, Dane," I commented, getting ready to make my great escape.

He reached out and grabbed my wrist in his strong grip. "Where are you running off to so quickly? Afraid I might bite?" He wiggled his eyebrows playfully.

I tried my hardest not to growl at him as I pulled my arm free from his hold. "No, but perhaps you should be afraid that I might," I said dryly. Amusement ran through his eyes as he pushed himself up to stand in front of me. I swallowed hard when I realized exactly how much bigger he was than me. I regretted sassing him immediately.

"Ryder!" he called out, never taking his eyes off of me. "Did Noah say anything to you about a visitor coming through today? 'Cause he seems to have failed to mention it to me."

I peered over my shoulder toward the booth, eyes meeting the hardened face of the scarred shifter. I watched his eyes narrow as he looked me over. "Noah isn't expecting anyone." I felt my heart rate skyrocket as the diner seemed to grow very still and silent. The amusement on Dane's face began to fade as they all began to realize that I didn't have permission to be on their territory. Ryder pushed up from his spot, followed by one of the twins.

I shifted on my feet, anxiously. "Well, like I said... it was such a pleasure, Dane." I turned and made a quick break for the door. I didn't try to hide the fact that I was running.

They already knew that I didn't belong, what more could've been done at that point other than running away?

My heart was thundering in my chest as my feet hit the pavement, the chime on the door echoing behind me. If I could just get to my truck, and hit the gas until I was off their territory, then I would be safe.

"Rogue!" a deep voice shouted behind me, and I pumped my legs harder. I wasn't a rogue, but it wasn't like I was going to sit down and try to explain that to them. I was an outsider with no identification other than a human ID in my wallet. It was necessary to blend in with them.

I rounded the back end of a black SUV parked next to my truck, pulling the keys from my pocket, only to come to a sudden halt at the sight of a large man leisurely leaning against the car as if he hadn't a care in the world. His scent pulled at my senses and had me backing up quickly. I needed to find another way to escape. This was an alpha male, and the one person I should want to avoid at all costs.

"Headed somewhere?" The voice that came out of this male made me want to shout *'there is a god, and he's spoken to me.'* It had my knees on the edge of turning to putty.

He turned his gaze in my direction, nailing me in place with a pair of bright blue eyes that had my wolf pulling towards the surface. His pupils dilated, and his brows furrowed in slight confusion as if he had been expecting something or someone else. I felt my body begin to tremble, my chest tightening as if I couldn't catch my breath.

He pushed himself away from the car and started walking towards me slowly. I was unable to run, move, think, or breathe. It was as if he was my whole world at that moment.

He was the only thing I could see, and the only thing keeping me planted to the ground. *I've felt this feeling before... When was that?* I thought to myself as I continued to stand in shock. The feeling was so familiar yet unnamable.

"Alpha," a deep voice rumbled from behind me. That had me shifting slightly, regaining control of myself as the fog of shock evaporated. I threw a look back over my shoulder to find that I was surrounded. Dane and the man I had heard them call Ryder were at my back. The other shifters slowly crept in around the edges, blocking all possible routes of escape.

"What should we do about this rogue?" Ryder questioned with a dark look in his eyes that sent a shiver of fear through me.

I gritted my teeth as I turned back to the alpha. "I'm not a rogue."

He was staring me down as if contemplating the truth of my words before looking to the males behind me, "Take her, *quietly*. You've already drawn enough attention to us chasing her in human territory." His words had me tensing up, and my wolf growled loud in my head as the males moved a step closer.

"But I'm not a rogue." I hissed in frustration, "Listen, I'm not trying to cause any trouble. If you just let me go, I'll be on my way, and I promise I won't come back." I was practically ready to beg them to let me go quietly.

He held my gaze. "I know you're not a rogue. If you were, you would have been the stupidest one to date to come willingly into my territory."

I felt my mouth fall open at his simple response. If he knew I wasn't a rogue, why didn't he simply have his men escort me to the boundary line of his territory and be done with? There was no reason for anyone to be harmed. While I was distracted by his overwhelming presence, one of his men snuck up behind me.

I heard the sound of loose pavement shifting to my left. It had me turning quickly around, only to be met with fingers pressing in on the pressure point on my neck. I stared into a familiar pair of dark-chocolate eyes as my body went limp and my world faded to black.

It was the sound of voices arguing back and forth that pulled me back into consciousness. I groaned as I felt the ache in my neck and tried to lift my hand to touch it, only to find that I couldn't move my arms. My eyes slid open, and I found my wrists tied to the safety bar on the back of a passenger seat. I turned my head to find trees whizzing by outside, sending my pulse skyrocketing as I realized the situation I was in.

"You know, it wasn't very nice of you to run off like that without even telling me your name," a familiar voice spoke to me. I turned my head to see Dane sitting casually in the seat next to me. His lips were bent upward at the corners as if he found the situation humorous.

I glared at him. "How about you go to hell? But first, before you do that untie me and let me go." I growled as I yanked at the fabric holding me prisoner. Dane gave me a sheepish smirk, a challenging light reflecting back at me in his murky eyes. "I don't know how they did things in whatever place you came from, but I do what my alpha tells me. He says I'm supposed to keep an eye on you, and that's what I mean to do." He waited for me to challenge him, maybe even wanted me to.

I sneered in his direction as I continued to work at my bindings. "That's the problem with most of you. You never question what you're told. You just follow blindly like sheep instead of wolves. You get lazy, you get fat, and you get dumb." My wolf pushed toward the surface as my anger and stress levels rose.

He eased himself back into the seat, completely relaxed. "Maybe your problem is that you've never had the guidance of a true alpha. There are lots of wolves out there that like to play at the title these days. You seem like someone who needs a real leader." His words poked at the feelings I had kept buried for a long time, feelings I had about my previous alpha and my ex-mate.

My lips turned downward into a deep frown. "I don't need anyone else to lead me. I can lead myself just fine."

He chuckled, "So it would seem." His eyes moved over me with amusement. I growled in frustration, frantically pulling at the fabric, jerking the seat back and forth like a maniac.

"Chill out, would you?" One of the twins snapped from the front seat. "This car is my baby. If you break anything in it, I will break you!" I glared at the back of the rounded head in front of me, purposefully tugging harder at my bindings. The twin in the passenger seat twisted around with a harsh snarl, eyes narrowed into dangerous slits. "Don't test me." I pressed my lips together in a tight line, contemplating whether or not I should test him.

"I wouldn't suggest it, he's not as nice as I am," Dane remarked coolly from his seat beside me.

I looked at him with a huff. "Where's your alpha? I want to speak to him right now! This kind of treatment has to be against the law." I growled.

"You'll see him soon enough, but I would be careful about that attitude of yours. I might like my women feisty, but I think you'll find that he doesn't," Dane replied. I bit my tongue, visualizing how satisfying it was going to be when I strangled their alpha to death with my bare hands for having them kidnap me without a true reason. Maybe I would let my wolf chew on the leftovers after I was done with him. She rumbled her agreement at the thought, the closest she could come to laughter.

"Now, how about we start over? I'm Dane, and you are?" he asked, leaning forward in a manner that was slightly condescending as if I was some child to be talked down to.

I gave a small growl before spitting toward him in anger. "Screw you, asshole!" I shouted, pulling frantically again at the fabric.

I watched a glob of saliva run down his cheek for a moment before he reached up and wiped it away. He inspected his hand for a moment before flipping those dark eyes in my direction. "Well, that was uncalled for. I was trying to be nice."

"Nice?" I sneered. "You tied me up and kidnapped me, which is illegal by the way!" I yelled loudly for everyone in the car to hear. I had hoped to leave their ears bleeding.

"Did anyone see us *kidnap* you?" he questioned with a lifted eyebrow.

My sneer dropped into a deep frown. I had no idea if anyone had seen them take me. Certainly, the people have seen me run out of the diner, and my truck was probably still sitting untouched in the parking lot. This unfamiliar pack of shifters probably would have thought about all of this and came up with some logical story to tell the humans. Humans were more than happy to explain away things, even things they had seen with their own eyes.

"I'm a bit curious, though, to know why a female is running around out here on her own. A little dangerous, don't you think? You got family expecting you? Maybe a mate running around out here somewhere? Should we be expecting him?" he questioned me. I knew this was some kind of interrogation. They still must have believed I was a rogue, or at the very least working with them. His question caused a familiar ache to bloom in my chest at the thought of David, which only made me angrier.

"For both our sakes, I hope not," I replied dryly, taking him by surprise. I hadn't noticed until the silence that the car had stopped moving and was parked outside a large house... or maybe mansion was the correct word for it. My old pack house couldn't even measure up to this one. I didn't even try to hide the fact that I was surprised.

The driver got out of the car as another man approached the car. His blond hair was shaved short like Ryder's. Perhaps, that was simply how all their warriors were made to look. His gaze shifted to where I was sitting in the backseat as the rest of the group started to talk heatedly to each other. I looked away from them toward Dane, who was watching me silently with a thoughtful expression on his face.

"Yes, but not for rogues," he supplied.

My lips twisted up in frustration. "You know that I'm not a rogue." He had made it clear to me that he did.

"Do I?" I watched him cross his arms over his chest.

I narrowed my eyes. Before I could question my own actions, my hand was cutting through the air toward him and catching up speed. I slapped him hard across his face. The force of my strike had his head snapping quickly to the side. I could feel the sting on my palm as well as shock waves of something else. I gasped as I pulled back my hand toward myself in surprise.

His body started to quake as he turned his face back toward me. His eyes were completely black as his wolf battled for control. I swallowed hard at the sight, shifting back a step as he reached out with both hands and gripped my arms. His touch sent my senses into overdrive. Part of me wanted him to pull me closer, and another part of me wanted to run screaming for the hills.

"This isn't possible," I said aloud. "I already found my mate."

He lifted me off the ground by a few inches, drawing his face closer to mine. His lips parted, showing the tips of his pointed canines. "So have I, but this is still happening. You are mine whether you want it to be or not," he said through his teeth, acknowledging our unspoken connection. His words sounded oddly pronounced by the fullness of his mouth. I knew I had made a mistake attacking an alpha as I had. His wolf certainly wasn't happy.

I stared up at him in shock for a breath. As I came back to my senses, I repeated his response over again in my head, and I started struggling. "If you already have a mate, then you can just reject me."

He raised his eyebrows at me, not at all put off by my struggling. "Reject you? What type of person rejects their mate? Even if I didn't want you, I would never reject you." I stopped moving immediately and went back to staring at him with wide eyes.

His eyes slowly faded back to blue. "Now… if I put you down, are you going to try to run away again or can I expect you to behave?" he asked me with a serious tone. Unable to process what had happened, and against what I actually wanted to say, I nodded my head blankly. He stared at me for a moment longer before he put me back down and took a step back.

Dane rushed toward us, having caught onto what had happened. "I apologize, Alpha Noah. I should have kept a better eye on her." He bowed his head and stretched out his neck in submission, looking for forgiveness.

Noah made a sound in the back of his throat as he looked away from me toward Dane. "It's fine. I can handle it from here. Take Murphy and check in with Ryder about the perimeter details. This morning's *issue* has set me back on schedule." Dane lifted his face, glancing in my direction with a dark look. I frowned when I realized I was the issue he was referring to.

When Dane's eyes roamed over my body, I remembered I was standing there in a state of undress. I growled at him as I covered myself the best I could with my arms. He smirked before he turned and walked back toward the blond warrior.

As if also realizing I had been standing there half naked, Noah lets out a long sigh of exasperation before he lifted his shirt up and over his head. I tried to keep myself from staring at his body, his wide chest dusted with dark hair that trailed down his lean stomach, disappearing out of sight. He held his shirt out toward me. "Here. I don't need every unmated male looking at you. It'll only complicate matters for me."

I accepted it begrudgingly with a mumbled thank you. As I pulled it on over my head, I immediately found myself overwhelmed by his scent. It was a mix of melted snow, pine needles, and masculine musk. I found myself inhaling a little deeper, unable to resist the urge. I peered up at him to find him watching me intently. I looked away from him quickly when I noticed the ghost of a smirk on his lips.

"Come. We can go somewhere a little more private to talk." He turned his back to me and started walking away, expecting me to follow. I rolled my eyes. It was just like an Alpha to act that way. Still, I followed him as he led me into the large house.

I stared at Noah's back as he led me down long hallways. I couldn't help but notice how his muscles flexed slightly everywhere my gaze trailed. It seemed he was very aware of my presence behind him, but he didn't say anything as we passed his pack and they bowed their heads. I tried to keep my head held high as to not look weak in front of them.

He turned and opened a door, leading me into a small office room and closing the door once I was inside. I looked around curiously. "So you have a pretty big house, don't you?" I questioned as he moved around me toward his desk.

"Yes. Well, my pack is quite large," he said in a no-nonsense voice. I looked at him, trying to figure out how it was possible that I had been given another mate. I had never heard of anything like this happening before. Perhaps, I was an abnormality in the system.

"How many people are in your pack?" I asked, trying to ease the tension between us. He looked at me with curiosity, probably wondering where I was headed with this line of questioning.

He turned his attention to some papers on his desk, fiddling with them. "I have roughly six hundred wolves under the protection of my name. The main pack, however, is about three hundred." He looked back at me, and I did my best to keep my mouth from falling open. This guy had to be a serious alpha if he had that many wolves in his pack. I mean, there had only been about a hundred wolves in my old pack, give or take a few.

"That must take up a lot of your time," was the only thing I could say in response to the information he had given me. It's not every day I met someone who had so many lives under their care.

"Yes, it does." He didn't really seem like the talkative type. His responses were often short and to the point. I stared at him blankly as I waited for him to say anything else, but when he remained silent, I ground my teeth together in irritation.

"So, where is your other mate?" I asked with a hint of attitude, "Because I have a feeling she won't be too happy about you bringing me here, and honestly, after the morning I've had, I really don't want to deal with a jealous wolf."

His eyes turned cold. "There's no need for you to concern yourself with that. She's dead."

06

Scarlett

I felt shocked by his words. All I could do was stare at him, unsure of what I was supposed to say to that.

"I'm... sorry..." I said softly, feeling awkward.

His blue eyes fixed themselves on me as I squirmed with unease until he looked away. "It's fine. It's in the past. Where is *your* other mate? I don't imagine he would let you run off unattended." His voice sounded tense at mentioning the fact I was possibly connected to someone else. I knew how possessive wolves were over their counterpart, and alpha males were known to be dangerously so.

I walked over, taking a seat in one of the plush looking chairs in front of his desk, "He's alive..." I watched Noah tense at my words. "But he rejected me and mated someone else." I gloss over the words quickly, pretending they don't cause a searing ache in my chest... pretending that I don't still recall the image of David holding Eva's hand.

His fingers tightened around the edge of his desk. "He rejected you?"

"It's a boring story that I'd rather not go into at the moment," I say with a shrug. I had gotten very good at pretending I didn't care. Humans had a saying that you 'fake it 'til you make it.' I figured that if there was any truth to it, I could fake indifference until I actually felt it. "It's in the past, as you said, but if you must know, he's the reason I ended up here. I was running away from him and my old pack. So there you have it. Not a rogue."

His eyes narrowed slightly at my words, and I could tell by the way his lips twitched that he was planning on asking me more about this. I was thankful when a knock on the door brought his possible interrogation to an end.

"Come in," he yelled in annoyance.

I heard the door as it creaked open. "Sorry, Alpha. I didn't mean to interrupt."

"You weren't interrupting anything," I responded for him, making his eyes spark with anger for a moment, but he didn't say anything.

I turned my body in my chair to find a young girl about fifteen years old standing halfway in the doorway. She looked like she was ready to bolt away at a moment's notice. I could tell by the way she kept her eyes focused on the ground that she must be one of the low-ranking members of the pack. I couldn't smell a wolf on her. She peeked up a little in my direction with curiosity in her eyes, and I couldn't blame her. I was an outsider.

"What do you want?" Noah asked with a stern voice. I looked at him with a frown. He certainly needed to work on his social skills.

I turned back to the young female and smiled at her warmly, mostly to piss him off. I corrected his question. "I think what he means is, what can he help you with?" I felt Noah's hot gaze bore holes through the side of my face, but I kept my smile intact and pretended like I didn't notice.

She looked up, focusing her eyes on me with shock and curiosity. I supposed it wasn't every day that someone corrected the alpha. That was probably half of their problem. I waited patiently for her to say something, raising my eyebrows a bit.

As if coming back into herself, she blushed brightly. "Oh... sorry... Right, Alpha Harvey called while you were out and said he wouldn't be able to make it this week but that he was going to be stopping by near the end of the month. I was wondering if you would like us to prepare a welcome dinner for him and Luna Rose when they set a date."

Noah mumbled under his breath for a moment, clearly annoyed by the situation. "Yes, yes. You and the other Omega's should prepare something." I looked at him as he pinched the bridge of his nose in frustration. She bowed her head and didn't say anything more as she took her leave, looking back at me one last time before she disappeared, closing the door behind her.

There was a long silence before I decided to ask him what I wanted to know. "So you said you wouldn't reject me. So what does that mean for us exactly?"

"I'm not sure, but I don't plan on claiming you either," he said in a rush of words.

I narrowed my eyes into slits. "I didn't say you did, and I don't want you to. So you can relax, big guy." I pushed myself out of the seat with an even breath. "I guess we can part ways and forget this whole business happened, then."

"Wrong. You will stay here where I can keep an eye on you." I found myself surprised by his words, having thought he would agree to go our separate ways and pretend we had never met. He moved toward me in slow steps, devoid of any sign of his wolf or anger. It was a perfect mask to cover any indication that he had ever felt a thing.

I pressed my lips together in a hard line. "And if I choose to leave?"

His gaze locked onto mine. "Not an option."

My eyes narrowed. "So I'm your prisoner?"

"You're not a prisoner. You're a guest," he corrected. "*My* guest. I will make sure to leave one of my men as an escort so you can move around as you wish without disturbing the members of my pack."

"But I can't leave?" I questioned again with a more sarcastic tone. I should have expected as much from an alpha. They were all the same. The lightness of his eyes began to swirl onyx as I poked at the beast underneath. He leaned in toward me so that we were level with each other. "You will not be leaving, ever, as long as I have anything to say about it."

I stared up at him with my mouth slightly open, in shock by his words. I quickly snapped it shut as a rush of anger flooded my veins. "By some fluke of the universe, we may be mates, but let me make one thing clear: you don't own me.

Nobody owns me. If you think for a minute I am going to bow down to your wishes, you better think again. If I want to leave, and I do I am going to leave one way or another," I said as I crossed my arms over my chest defiantly.

Noah's eyes began to darken as he leaned in his face closer, and the heat of his breath swept across my face. I began to question my decision to open my mouth. "You're playing a dangerous game." He reached out and grabbed a strand of my hair between his fingers. "If I tell you to do something, you will do it, or you will be punished. Mate or not, I am the alpha. I will not take disrespect from anyone." His voice was deadly calm.

"So then, I am your prisoner." I pointed out with a sneer. I caught the way his eyes drifted down to my lips for a millisecond.

His jaw clenched tightly in frustration from our repeating conversation. "Look at it however you like. It doesn't matter to me," he said. He pulled back, giving us both more breathing room.

"I'll send someone to collect you and take you to the room you'll be staying in. I have other matters to tend to, and I've wasted more time than I wanted." He didn't give me a chance to argue as he moved across the room.

"Your name?" he questioned as a second thought, glancing back at me over his shoulder.

I held his gaze with a heavy glare. "Scarlett." I spit it at him like a curse. He didn't say anything more. He turned and strode away through the door, leaving me alone in his office.

Twenty minutes later, I was glaring at the sturdy back of one of the twins as he led me to my own private prison chamber. He had told me that his name was Braydon. He wasn't very talkative, in comparison to the other version of him that threatened to break me if I broke his car.

I let out a small growl to myself when I walked smack into Braydon's back when he decided to stop abruptly. He turned and looked down at me with a raised eyebrow. I took a step away from him while giving him a suspicious look, wondering if he had done that on purpose.

"This will be your room while you're here." He reached out and opened the door to the room. I peered inside the room for a moment, not waiting to be prompted to enter. The room was a beautiful shade of purple, and the bed was fit for a queen. As I did a little twirl, looking around the space, I couldn't help but smile a little. "Wow." This was definitely a heavenly torment.

"You like it?" I heard Braydon ask me, but I ignored him, too busy at the moment inspecting everything to be bothered. I moved across the room to a door and opened it with curiosity. Behind the door was a large bathroom that had a deep tub that looked large enough that I could swim laps in it. Next to it was a fancy shower with frosted glass doors as if a pool-sized tub wasn't enough. I let out a tiny laugh as I walked back into the room to find Braydon still standing in the doorway. "Do you like it?" he asked again.

"I love it, but I feel like this might be a little much for a prisoner." I motioned my hand around the space. "Before now, I was living in a tiny studio apartment where I had to call the landlord every other day to fix something or other. Now *that* was torture."

He shook his head, lips turning up with amusement. He was trying to keep a smile at bay. "I'll be outside the door if you need anything else." He closed the door behind himself.

I stood motionless for a moment, staring at the door, before I slowly began to look around my room. It was a beautiful space, but a part of me wondered if this room had been empty until now, or if someone had been forced out to make room for me. That last thought made me feel a little guilty, so I quickly pushed it away as I made my way back into the bathroom, letting out a tiny sigh at the sight of the big tub. "Hello, beautiful," I said with a grin.

Honestly, it felt like I had died and gone to heaven being able to relax after days of being on the run. I sat in the bathtub, soaking in the warm water, until my fingertips began to wrinkle. I didn't have any other options but to put back on the clothes I had been wearing before. If I was going to stay here for any amount of time, I was going to need my truck and all of my belongings.

"Listen up, knucklehead twins," I said with a growl, throwing my hands onto my hips as I stared down the twins who had helped in my kidnapping. I had been kept in my room for three days, and I had already come down with a serious case of cabin fever. "I'm not going to stay locked up in this room for another second. As nice as it is, I want to stretch my legs and get a good look around my new prison." They had been unwilling to allow me to the leave the space. Apparently, they weren't my 'babysitters' as Braydon's evil twin, Murphy, had said.

"Alpha ordered us to watch you, and that was all. We're not here to be your personal tour guides." Murphy snapped in my direction, not willing to look me in the eye. I personally found Braydon the more approachable one of the two of them, but that wasn't saying much. My lip curled up in annoyance. I was two seconds away from giving them distinguishing features.

"I think I can handle it from here, guys," I heard a feminine voice behind me. I looked over my shoulder to see a darker-skinned girl standing there. She was exotically beautiful, and the look in her eyes told me she had been through things that made her tough. That, and the small scar that ran across her cheek.

"Sorry, I'm late. If you'll follow me," she commanded as she turned and walked away.

I hesitated for a moment before I turned and followed after her, walking quickly to fall into step beside her. "I'm Scarlett, by the way." I glanced back over my shoulder at the twins and stuck out my tongue rather childishly. Murphy narrowed his eyes and sneered at me. That guy was a serious stick-in-the-mud. I had no idea how Braydon handled spending so much time with him.

My new escort peered at me from the corners of her eyes, which seemed to sparkle with amusement at my introduction. "I know who you are," she replied.

I looked at her with a frown. "Noah sent you?" It wasn't bad enough that I had guard detail. Now I had a babysitter. He clearly didn't trust me, which meant he wasn't a complete idiot. I had told him I would leave, and there was no way to stop me. Obviously, he was doing his best to prove me wrong.

She chuckled softly as we turned a corner into a long hallway. "I'm Nadia. Noah may have sent me to keep you company, but it doesn't mean we can't get along."

"More like he sent you to babysit me," I muttered sarcastically, feeling overwhelmingly annoyed.

Nadia laughed a little more. "He's a man. An alpha, to be exact. You'll have to excuse his overbearing ways." I found a smile spreading over my lips at her statement.

"You must be speaking from experience?"

"My mate is the Captain of Noah's warriors. Sometimes, he can be far worse than the alpha," she stated plainly as she raised her brows and rolled her eyes playfully. We moved into a large room that reminded me of the foyer at my old pack house.

I sincerely liked Nadia, and we had only met five minutes ago. I never really got the chance to spend time with my own pack before David's rejection sent me running for the hills. The only friends I had ever had were of the human variety. I felt a stirring of excitement at the thought that I might find a proper place among my own kind, and with people who would understand me. I smiled at her brightly. "If all the women around here are like you, then I think I've come to the right place."

She laughed as she turned us toward a door. "I'm one of a kind, Scarlett. Most of the females around here are in need of some actual leadership. You see, ever since Luna Claire died, some females thought it was their right to be in charge.

Trust me, you'll find out for yourself what I'm talking about." She pushed the door open and motioned for me to enter.

The door led to a large kitchen. I looked around in wonder as I watched women bustling around the space, prepping and preparing meals for their pack. I recognized the familiar face of the omega who had come to Noah's office earlier that morning. She stood at the kitchen island, chopping up some vegetables.

"Oh, it's so nice of you to finally join us, Nadia," a tall blonde-haired beauty spoke with sarcasm as she turned in our direction. Her eyes roamed in my direction. "And who is this?" Her tone of voice had me and my wolf standing at attention.

"You don't smell like the pack." She sniffed the area around me slightly. "You reek of humans." She made a disgusted face.

Before I could give her my smart-ass response, Nadia heaved a sigh. "This is Scarlett. Scarlett, this is Gretchen. You'll have to excuse her as she's supposed to get the stick from her butt removed pretty soon."

I tried to contain my amusement as Gretchen's mouth opened slightly and then snapped shut, her brown eyes narrowing into tiny slits. "What? Now you're going to try to act tough because of your new friend here? Remember what happens to little wolves that get in my way, Nadia. Wouldn't want to scar your other cheek, would we?" she taunted with a sneer.

Nadia tensed next to me before letting out a tiny growl. "We can go again if you want. I can show you what I do to cheats."

Gretchen growled back at her, and I realized that, unless someone did something, they were going to have a full on battle in this kitchen.

I reached out and put my hand on Nadia's arm. "Why don't you show me more of the house?" I suggested.

Nadia relaxed slightly but kept her eyes on Gretchen. "Of course. Follow me." I let go of her arm, watching her walk on ahead of me. When she was a good distance away, I turned my attention back to Gretchen, narrowing my eyes.

"You don't know me yet. Hopefully, you never have to know me, but let me be perfectly clear about something..." I spoke to her in a low tone to make sure no one else could hear, "If you want to keep yourself looking as perfect as you look right now, I suggest you consider changing your attitude." I held her gaze for a moment before I turned to catch up with my babysitter.

Nadia smiled brightly at me when I reached her. "You're seriously my new favorite person." She patted me roughly on the back. I chuckled a little as I looked back towards Gretchen, who was bossing around some girls working at the stove. "So I'm guessing she's one of the people you were talking about earlier?"

"She definitely would be, but she's not the one you should look out for," Nadia commented.

I turned back to her with a raised eyebrow. "Oh?"

She nodded her head. "It's Delilah that's the ring leader around here. She definitely thought Alpha Noah would promote her to Luna after Claire's death, if you know what I mean?"

I could definitely understand what she meant, but I didn't want to think about that at the moment. I peered out a window as we passed by it, admiring the far stretching wilderness. "Do you think we could go outside?" Nadia gave me a wavering look as if she wasn't sure it was the best idea, but she finally conceded with a nod of her head.

07

Scarlett

"Scarlett, this part is off limits," Nadia said in a soft voice as her eyes scanned the horizon nervously.

I pressed onward. The scent of honeysuckle clogged my senses, and I watched as sparrows flew high into the cloudless sky before dipping low into the tree line on the other side of the clearing. My wolf was pacing endlessly in my mind. She wanted to run. She wanted to chase the wild beasts. Her urge to hunt was strong.

"Why is this place off limits? This is within your alpha's boundary, isn't it?" I questioned, glancing over my shoulder at her.

She gave me a pinched look with a furrowed brow. "It is, but we've had trouble with the rogues in these parts recently. They don't let any of us come this way without escorts."

"Well, aren't you my escort? Come on," I said as I stepped over the marked ground—a warning to outsiders, from the alpha and other males, that they would meet trouble if they came this way. I felt a shiver of excitement crawl up my spine with every step I take further into the danger zone, and further away from Noah. This was my chance to get away.

"I don't think this is a good idea, Scarlett. Noah doesn't want any of us wandering too far from the house." I heard her call out to me in a tense voice.

Nadia didn't follow after me, she only watched me with a stern expression as I moved deeper into the trees until I couldn't see her anymore. I was sure she was going to go back and tell Noah what I had done. I had gotten a taste of pack life and, while a part of me wanted that, I wasn't inclined to stay put.

I began to strip out of my clothes, not caring where they fell. I smiled to myself as I let the shift take me, bones resetting and molding themselves into a truer version of myself. My wolf shook out her black coat of fur, digging her large paws into the dirt and feeling the vibrations and energy in the world around her.

She watched a rabbit race from one shrub to another. Instincts took over, and she yipped with excitement before running off. The scent of her prey prompted her in a small game of chase. The young rabbit didn't stand a chance.

The sound of a twig snapping behind me pulled at my consciousness. Something was off. My wolf's ears perked up, twitching as she listened carefully to the space around us for danger. Another snapping twig made her ears press back against her skull.

She danced from foot to foot, sticking her nose into the air, trying to catch a scent. She was doing her best to assess the threat. A small whiff was all she needed. The stench of tainted meat hit her nose, and a round of snarls erupted from the surrounding shadows. My wolf lowered her head in anticipation, the fur on her back bristling up instinctively. Low, threatening growls rumbled from her chest in warning to the beast waiting in the darkness. There was a moment of stillness before a large clawed hand reached out of the shadows. A rogue stepped out of the shadows, its fur the color of rusted metal.

It stood like a monstrous beast, locked into some mangled form of wolf and man. It had been a long time since I had seen one, but it was not something I could ever forget. My wolf wasted no time in leaping forward and snapping her teeth at the beast. It hunched forward and let out a ferocious snarl, spit spraying my wolf in the face as it did.

The rogue stretched out one of his clawed hands, and my wolf twisted to the right and caught the creature as it pulled back. The taste of blood filled up her mouth, dripping out to the earth, as the two beasts struggled. The rogue grabbed hold of her front leg, whipping her off. The pain radiated up her back as she hit the ground, and I knew the leg was broken. The beast rushed toward her, crowding in over her, and pushing in on her chest with a massive clawed hand.

She caught a flash of white out of the corner of her eye, turning her head as Noah leaped through the air at the beast that towered over her. He caught hold of its shoulder, forcing it to rear back and reach with a clawed hand to pull itself free. His wolf's golden eyes seemed to glow in the growing darkness like beams of salvation. My wolf pulled herself together, ignoring the pain in her injured leg.

Two more wolves made their way out of the trees, charging toward the rogue with their teeth bared. They worked together, nipping and snapping at the fumbling monster, as Noah took it to the ground, his white fur stained with blood.

His fur gave way to naked flesh. "Shift!" He snarled down at the beaten rogue, commanding it with the power only an alpha had. I let out a small gasp as the bones in my injured leg shifted back into my left arm and tried to reset themselves as I took back control of my body. I watched in awe as the rogue twisted and shook as its body shed its beastly form. I had never seen anything like it before.

Noah snatched the young male off the ground by his arm, smiling at him in a way that made my blood run cold. "You came to the wrong place, little wolf."

Dane stepped up behind him. "Let us take care of this one, Noah. You worry about the girl." He nodded his head in my direction. Noah looked like he was struggling with himself for a moment over which was more important. Dane placed his hand on his shoulder, giving it a squeeze.

Noah let out an angry growl before he tossed the young rogue away, turning his bright eyes on me. I couldn't help but shiver as I took in the feral alpha before me. My heart trembled in fear for the first time since I met him. He stalked towards me with long, powerful strides, and no one attempted to get between us.

His gaze held me prisoner as it roamed down my body in a quick inspection. His eyes narrowed when he noticed the way I was holding my arm protectively to my chest. "You risked your life because, like a child, you seem to think that my rules don't apply to you. What if we hadn't come, Scarlett?"

I let my head fall slightly in shame. The guilt tasted like acid on my tongue, burning my throat as I swallowed it down. "I didn't think—"

"That's right, you didn't." His anger was a potent force that smothered me. I gritted my teeth together, wanting to lash out at him, but I held my tongue. He was right this time. Something worse could have happened. Noah let out a heavy sigh. "Come on. I'll take you to Doctor Owen. That arm needs to be set right before it heals like that."

I peered up at him, and he held my gaze for a moment. Concern flashed in his cold eyes before he turned away from me.

08

Scarlett

"What did I tell you about knocking before you enter a man's home, Noah?" The old man growled in annoyance from an old reclining chair as Noah and I entered the small cabin. There was a pause of unanswered silence followed by the old man's heavy sigh as he grabbed his cane and pulled himself up from his seat. "Well, come in and close the door behind you! You weren't raised in a damned barn."

A high-pitched whistle pierced through the room, and my heart threatened to jump out of my chest in surprise. I watched the older male as he leaned his weight on the cane, dragging his left leg behind him. He was grumbling to himself under his breath, clearly annoyed by the intrusion. My eyes followed his movements with curiosity.

"It's impolite to stare. Didn't your parents teach you anything, girl?" he muttered as he turned off the fire under the kettle. I felt my cheeks flame at his sharp reprimand as I diverted my gaze to the ceiling, feeling it was the safest place to look at the moment. The heavy thump of his cane against the hardwood floorboards echoed through the small space, allowing me to know exactly where he was. "What brings you to my humble abode, Alpha?"

"Scarlett here ran into some trouble with a rogue. I need you to set her arm for me, Owen," Noah replied as he moved us deeper into the small house.

"Well, since you already came all the way here, go ahead and take a seat." Owen's voice dripped with sarcasm as Noah pulled out a chair for me at the dining room table. I sat down in it, feeling slightly awkward. I didn't like the fact that I was caught between two ornery men.

Owen approached us, and Noah stepped away to create room for him. For an older man, he still had a nice face. He seemed like the serious type, with his bushy eyebrows furrowed and lips drawn down into a frown. His gray eyes narrowed as he reached out with his free hand, grumbling under his breath as he looked at my arm. "Seems you've seen better days. You're lucky to still have all your limbs, girl. Rogues are nasty buggers."

My eyes roamed from the doctor to Noah, who stood with his back to us. His gaze was focused out the window. I wondered what he was thinking about and if it was about the young rogue his men had taken.

Owen's eyes drifted back to mine, calling my attention again. "Tell me, what kind of nice girl goes running off on her own?"

I looked away from him to the ceiling as I let myself settle deeper into the hard seat. "Maybe I'm not a nice girl."

"I'd say that the rogue who found you would agree with you on that," he said as I lowered my eyes to see his lips turn up in one corner. This pack doctor was interesting, to say the least.

"Ow!" I let out a growl as Owen set my arm without warning. He met my gaze for a moment before he got up, using his cane to support his weight. "Looks like you'll live to fight another day." My eyes focused on his limp leg as he readjusted it, unable to help myself.

"It was a bear."

I pulled my eyes to his, brows furrowing. "What?"

He shook his head as if I was an idiot. "That's why this leg ain't good anymore. The damn thing nearly ripped it off. Luckily for me, my sweet Abby had a thing for cripples." His frown lifted in the corners for a moment like he might smile before he turned and hobbled away.

I flexed my hand, checking the good doctor's work. "What are you going to do to that rogue?" I asked Noah. I wanted to know.

The silence was heavy as he turned around, his blue eyes focusing on me. "Question him, dispose of him, and whatever else I feel I want to do with him. Maybe hang him like a trophy in my office." I felt a shiver of fear at how easily he talked about these things without even flinching.

Owen returned to the table. "Think it'd start to stink after a bit don't you, Alpha?" He slammed a canister down while looking towards me. "For the pain," he said.

I reached out for it with my good hand, popping the lid. The scent that hit my nose was awful. I looked up at him with a frown. "Talk about stink. What is this stuff?"

"Best just to take it and ask fewer questions." He gave me a pointed look. No doubt his words carried a double meaning. I let out a huff and rolled my eyes at him.

"Whatever you do, whenever you do it, I want to be there," I found myself saying as I turned my eyes on Noah, ignoring Owens blatant warning. I wasn't sure I did actually want to be there, but I knew I wanted to understand the man before me... even if only to have more of a reason to curse his name.

He held my attention with an expression that gave away nothing to what was going on beneath the surface. "You want to see so badly? Then I'll show you. Let's go, Scarlett." The way he said my name was like he was spitting something awful out of his mouth, but I tried not to take it to heart.

The ride back to the pack house was a quiet one. Doctor Owen had put my arm into a makeshift sling to keep it from moving around too much while it healed. I followed Noah through the house and down a set of stairs into a dark room. One solitary light hung from the ceiling, illuminating a door. My sensitive ears could pick up the sound of angry voices. "What is this?"

"The basement," he replied as he opened the door and motioned for me to enter. I gave him a look as I passed him into the room, my body alert for anything.

The rogue that attacked me was hanging from chains in the ceiling, arms raised over his head. He looked like he was barely out of his teen years. There were barely any real muscle mass to him. His body was swollen and bruised, evidence of the treatment he had been receiving. Ryder stepped away, blood dripping from the cracked skin of his knuckles to the cement floor. Dane stood back in the corner of the room as an overseer, not really taking part.

The scent of the blood was overwhelming, making my stomach churn a bit. This wasn't just a basement. It was a torture chamber. How many other rogues have been brought into this room and died on a floor stained with their fallen comrades' blood?

Noah stepped forward toward Ryder. "He gave you anything?"

"Not yet..." He looked up into the kid's face. "But he will. They always do." The rogue spat down at him in defiance, missing Ryder as he stepped back out of the way.

Dane moved out of the shadows in the corner. "This is no place for a lady." He gave me a smile, but it didn't reach his somber eyes.

"She wanted to see, so let her see," Noah spoke up before I could, silencing anything else Dane or I might have to say on the subject. I didn't know what I was supposed to do. Part of me was horrified by the sight taking place before me.

Noah moved towards his men with dominance flowing from every step. "Lower him."

Ryder unhooked the support chains keeping the rogue hoisted. The kid slammed into the hard concrete, his flesh slapping against hard stone and coughing out some of the pain from the impact.

Noah squatted down in front of the crumpled body. "You're a pretty, young kid. Freshly turned. Tell me what pack did they recruit you from?"

"Go to hell..." He coughed in Noah's direction, blood spilling from his mouth. He definitely wasn't in the best shape, perhaps from a punctured lung.

Silence took over the room, and the tiny hairs on the back of my neck stood on end as I watched Noah run a finger through the blood that has begun to coagulate on the floor. He reached out and grabbed the boy's face, smearing red fingerprints across his cheek. "We're already there, can't you tell?"

I could smell the sour stench of fear as it swept through the room. The kid had nothing on the alpha before him. "You're a traitor. They told me about you... about all the things you did."

"So then you know what I'm going to do to you?" he asked in a low voice, cold and detached. The kid looked away from Noah to me, his soulless eyes burning through my mind. The beast inside him was hungry for flesh, probably mine from the look of it. Rogues were bottomless pits of hunger. That was the price they paid for more power.

A loud snap of bone had him arching his back toward the ceiling as a horrible howl of pain passed his mouth. His arm was twisted at an abnormal angle in Noah's hand. "Don't look at her." He snarled. "I'm the one talking to you. I'm the one asking you questions."

I was breathing just as heavy as the kid now. His body shook with adrenaline as it tried to fight off the pain. "If you're going to kill me, then kill me, but I'm not going to tell you shit!"

I could see Noah's lips curve upward. "Death is a reward you haven't earned. Tell me what I want, and I'll give you what you want." Another snap of bone echoed through the room followed by another hollow scream of pain. "Until then, there's still a lot of bones left for breaking. And if we run out of bones, I'm sure there are some organs you don't need all that much."

My stomach knotted at the horrible thought of this continuing. My wolf, however, felt no such sensation. She thought only by instincts. She watched with curiosity, wanting more blood. It was always a matter of weak and strong. This alpha was strong, and that rogue was weak. The sick and the weak didn't last long in the wild. They were picked off fast. Too bad I didn't function in her world of simplicities. It might have made this new revelation much easier to stomach.

There was more silence as Noah waited for a response. When the rogue chose not to speak, more bones were broken.

Snap. "That looks painful…"

Crack. "There, now you have a matching set…"

"Eenie meenie…" *Snap.* "Miney Moe." *Snap. Snap.*

The screams were endless, and they clawed at my sensitive ears. I fisted my hands at my side to keep myself from covering them. I could see that the kid was breaking slowly. His determination to keep his lips sealed was failing, the more his body failed to block the pain.

"Please!" he yelled. *Crack.*

It all came to a stop. All I could hear was heavy breathing. "What was that?" Noah questioned, leaning in closer. The kid was sweating, barely hanging onto consciousness. "Please… no… more," he whispered through heavy breaths.

"Tell me what I want," he said in a stern tone, full of warning that if he didn't, the pain would continue. There was only silence until Noah shifted forward. I didn't know if I could watch this anymore.

"Alpha Randall..."

Noah eased back at the kid's admission. He stared down at him for a moment with a small look of pity before rising back up to his full height. I didn't know what this information meant, but from the serious looks on the faces in the room, it certainly meant something. Noah turned his back to the broken body on the ground. "He's all yours," he said to Ryder as he walked toward me. My heart froze in my chest at the words.

"You said you would give me what I want if I told you! You said!" the boy screamed as Ryder began to hoist him back up. The pain must have been unimaginable as his broken bits rubbed together.

Noah looked over his shoulder. "I lied."

I felt like I was going to be sick. "Just kill him! You got what you wanted!" The words fell from my mouth in a rush. I couldn't be silent anymore. They all looked in my direction with surprise as if they had completely forgotten they had an audience. Noah's cold eyes met mine, his lips pressed together in a tight line. "You want to give him mercy? Then give him mercy, but he won't get it from me." He stepped to the side, giving me a straight and unhindered path to his prisoner.

Those soulless eyes were barely open, but I felt like they saw deep into my soul. I sucked in a breath, my feet guiding me towards him. I tilted my head back to look up into his face. "Thank you... Thank you..." he whispered down to me.

The words sunk into me and burrowed into my churning marrow. My wolf rose up within me, her golden eyes flashing, as her claws ripped through flesh as I pushed them through his heart. The warmth of his blood rushed over my chilled skin, staining my hand.

I pulled back, letting it fall limply to my side. The boy's blood was dripping from my fingertips as I turned around to find Noah staring at me, his eyes burning with unknown emotions.

09

Christa

I watched from the side as men from the pack battled with each other in their war forms. They weren't allowed to stop until they had spilled blood. As Father often said, 'one who has never bled is weak.' The metallic scent of blood hung heavy in the air around his territory. The soil had been stained from years of warriors turning their bodies into the perfect weapons for a war that had never come. Father stood tall beside me, arms crossed over his chest. His dark eyes were focused on weeding out the weak ones from the pack.

Thorton approached father with precise steps. "Alpha Randall…" He bowed his head though I could see from the grimace on his lips, he believed himself above the gesture. My wolf bared her teeth in his direction. She didn't like this male, something about him smelled wrong like the bitterness of a poison. I couldn't deny the fact that sometimes, his eyes lingered on me longer than they should, and it made my skin crawl. Father had taken no notice of it, or if he had noticed, he pretended not to see because he liked him well enough. Thorton had won the right to sit at Father's table.

Father turned his face. "Your training seems to be doing well. You should be pleased with yourself. I'll pick the best ones from the bunch. I want them to give Noah a good show at the trials this year." My ears perked up at the mention of the young alpha who had become like a king in these parts. I had only seen him from afar a couple times, but the way father cowered behind closed doors because of him, pleased me to no end.

Father gave Thorton's shoulder a rough squeeze before he stalked forward toward the warriors, stripping out of his clothes as he went, assuming his war form. He rushed forward, his red fur laced with silver patches due to his age. I took in the bald spots that littered his shoulders and neck from years of fighting.

"You look beautiful as usual, Christa." Thorton's eyes burned into the side of my face, but I refused to look at him. Instead, I focused on Father and the battling wolves. They were like furred gladiators as they wrestled each other to prove their worth and value. They fought to earn father's favor. Thorton inched closer to me, but I pretended he didn't exist. I didn't want to let him think he had a chance with me.

I clenched my hands a little tighter, doing my best to keep up the facade that I was an unassuming female, just as Father wanted me to be. Men are more, women are less. That was just the way the Goddess made things, or at least that was what father had to beat into me as I grew up. Now, I knew how to hold my tongue. This was the part I had to play to survive.

"Thank you," I said quietly, biting back any other words that might try to slip free.

I let out a tiny breath when I felt his gaze leave me momentarily. Thorton was watching as Father battled with his men, testing their limits for himself. Father held his own, but I could tell from the way he favored one side over the other that his age was beginning to get to him. It wouldn't be long before he would need to find an heir to his throne. He would never willingly pass his title to me though I was his only true heir. He carried me like a burden on his back, waiting for the moment when I would hopefully bring him some honor by mating to an alpha. In father's world, a female could never lead at the head of the pack.

Thorton moved yet another step closer to me. His scent soaked into my skin purposefully, a way to ward off other weaker males. It was a sort of claim. My stomach knotted up at the action. He reached out with his hand, brushing his fingers across my arm. The touch made my skin crawl in discomfort, but I showed nothing on my face.

I turned toward him with a tiny scowl on my lips as he held my gaze. "I can smell the fire that is building in you. It gets stronger every day." I knew he was referring the fact that I would be going into heat soon. I knew how it affected the males during the mating season. I had seen how the aggression poured from them as nature took its course. The animal fought for the need to find the strongest female to carry their young, mate or not.

"I don't think the alpha would find your attention to me appropriate, Thorton," I said with a forced timidity. Inside, my wolf was snarling her threats. She was ready to sink her teeth into his flesh. He glanced in Father's direction. A pair of warriors had decided to take him on at once, giving him a good run for his money. They were making him flex every ounce of alpha power.

"Of course, I meant nothing by it, really. I just think you should consider the fact that your father might not be able to keep the other males away when the time comes." He had been sniffing around Father's throne since he joined our pack. He was trying to win it simply through gaining his favor though I had seen him fight and knew he could be a strong contender if things went another way. I stood up a little straighter, turning myself to face the male beside me.

I reached out toward him, placing my palm against his cheek in mock affection. Appearances were everything. I kept our gazes locked. "I appreciate the concern, but I don't need an alpha to keep them away. I can do that all on my own." I let my wolf push towards the surface. Her claws poked through the tips of my fingers, gently probing the soft flesh of his cheek. Thorton's eyes widened as he took in the true glimmer of the beast that lived within me, the devil that I was supposed to keep caged. My lips twitched with the urge to smile, but I held it back. My mask would remain intact.

Father let out a victorious howl behind us. He had kept his throne, at least for another day. I pulled my hand away, admiring the small beads of red I left behind. I would enjoy my marks while they lasted. They were a testament to my strength and mercy. Thorton's eyes darkened as his wolf rose to the challenge I presented. He held himself together as his nostrils flared slightly from his contained anger. "Soon, you might feel differently about that Christa."

"I doubt it," I said back without emotion.

Father approached us, slightly out of breath. "You've done very well with them. Very well, indeed" He clapped Thorton on the back with a smile. The only time father ever really smiled was when he bled, when he overcame the challenge he faced.

Father's eyes fell to me, and I could see the slightest disappointment in them. He wished I was a boy and told me so on many occasions. Instead, I stood like a beacon to the world of his weaknesses, a sign that the Goddess hadn't blessed his line with a true heir. Our family pride would die with him, and nothing could please me more than that.

I lowered my gaze to the ground, returning to the meek female I was supposed to be. My wolf growled at my thought. Given a chance, she would challenge my father for her birthright. I personally would rather watch his pack come to ruins before I ever tried to take it from him.

"I expect you at dinner tonight. We have much to discuss the future," he spoke to Thorton as if I weren't there. The words caused me to tense up, but I tried to keep my mask of indifference securely in place.

"Christa, go see to the warriors. We don't want them too bruised up for trials."

I bowed my head. "You fought well, Alpha. I'll take my leave now," I said the words just like he taught me. They always left a sour taste on my tongue, but I knew it was all a game. If I wanted to survive, I had to play it right. I also knew the rules were subject to change depending on the players, and someday, I planned on being a major player.

I was not born to cower before men. I was born to lead them.

10

Scarlett

I kept myself locked up in the room that Noah gave to me after everything that I had seen. I wanted to be away from the others, away from *him*. He made sure that food was brought to me, but I ignored the offerings. All I wanted to do was fade into the darkness that surrounded and bound me, to slip into the black abyss. I should have never gone into that basement. That was a mistake. I couldn't unsee what I had seen. It felt like a part of me had been swallowed up by the new reality I had been shown. I burrowed myself deeper into the blankets, recalling the conversation that transpired after the rogue attack.

My skin burned as I scrubbed relentlessly at my hands, hot water steaming up the mirror. I could hear my gentle pants and broken sobs as I tried to get the blood off them. There was no peace in my heart, not even after trying to convince myself that I had done the right thing by ending the rogue's life. I had never killed anything in my entire life other than small game.

"You can stop scrubbing. The blood is gone." Noah's *gravelly voice drifted over the sound of running water. I tensed up as I glanced at the reflection in the foggy mirror to find him leaning one shoulder against the door jamb, arms crossed over his wide chest. He didn't look like he was suffering any second thoughts about what he had done. It was more like this was something he did every day, like it was as easy to him as breathing.*

I licked my lips, tearing my eyes away from him to the pink water that was slipping through the drain in the sink. I continued to scrub my hands bitterly. "The blood will never be gone. I can't believe you put me in that awful position."

"You made that choice."

I felt a growl rumble out of my chest. "What choice? There was no choice. I wasn't going to let you torture him for your sick amusement."

I could feel the shift in the room as his wolf rose to the surface. He stepped into the bathroom, chest pressing into my back. "Look at me, Scarlett." *His breath was hot against my ear. I gritted my teeth, keeping my eyes cast downward. My wolf was not happy about the predator at her back, her fur bristling up. He reached up and grabbed hold of my face with his bloodied hand in a firm but far from painful grip. I let my eyelids slam shut as he tilted my face up.* "Open your eyes."

I shook my head slightly, and he tightened his grip. "You wanted to see, so see. Open your eyes and look!" *The snarl in his voice caused the hairs on my arms to rise. My eyes peeled open slowly as he forced me to look at our shared reflection.* "This is what I am. This is what you are. The more you fight it, the more it will hurt."

I glared at him through bitter unshed tears. "You're a monster. I am nothing like you."

He didn't look hurt by my words as if this was something he has already accepted about himself. "You have no idea how right you are about that."

Our gazes remained locked on one another. "But don't blame me because you don't like what you see. Nothing has changed. I was born a monster, and I'll die a monster. Accept it or don't, I don't care. If it's too hard, then look away. Bury your head in the sand and die an ignorant sheep." His words burned through all my barriers.

"I'm not a sheep." I could hear the subtle quake in my own voice. I had seen and experienced the harshness of the world that we lived in. I had never been sheep, nor could I ever be one.

He pulled back slightly, releasing me from the firmness of his grip. I sucked in a sharp breath as we continued to stare at each other through the reflection. "Good, then stop worrying about the blood. You'll be a lot bloodier before this is through."

"Before what is through? What are you trying to do?" I felt calmer now and steadier on my feet. Somehow, his manner of being and words had settled the storm that had been raging in my thoughts.

His eyes were as cold as ice. "I'm going to end what my father started once and for all by sending all of his followers to oblivion."

I furrowed my brows at his words. "Your father?"

He took another step away from me. "Some knew him as Alastair the Butcher." That was a name I have feared since I was a young girl, a name that dredged up memories of the day I had I lost my mother.

My eyes opened wide as I shook my head in disbelief. He gave me a shallow smile full of pity as if he knew what I was thinking. "Some things we don't get to choose." How apt his words were.

I gripped the edge of the sink, trying to maintain control of my spiraling emotions. "What more can your father do to us? He is long dead and buried. The rogues that remain now are nothing but scavengers." This was something everyone knew. The news of his death had spread in every direction. It was the end of the terror we had all lived in.

"Do I look like a scavenger to you?" His question confused me.

I turned to face him, my lips pinched into a tiny scowl. Noah lifted his hand into the space between us, popping out a set of razor sharp claws. "I was born to take up his crown. I had the weakness beat out of me. I knew the hunger. I knew the power. Still, I betrayed all of that when I met Claire because she was supposed to be my salvation... a gift of redemption to me from the Goddess." I could feel the churning of his emotions through our bond, enough to make my stomach knot up.

He clenched his hand into a tight fist, driving his claws through the tender flesh of his palm. I watched the fresh blood trickle down along the tiny spaces between his fingers, dripping onto the tiled floor. "My brother was always jealous of our father's favor in me. He wanted the crown for himself. He was so angry. He kidnapped her... took what was mine and perverted it. Then he turned her loose on the people she loved.

I did what was necessary, freed her from the hunger and the pain I knew she was in. In the end, she thanked me."

I was able to go a week without eating before Noah had enough. His wolf wouldn't let his mate wither away. The bed dipped under the weight of another body, causing me to stir from my restless sleep. I opened my eyes slowly, blinking through the haze. I found Noah sitting on the edge of the bed looking down at me with furrowed brows. There was so much intensity burning in his bright eyes.

He released a heavy sigh before turning his face away. "Clean yourself up then come downstairs. There're some people I want you to meet." His voice was full of gravel like he was more animal than man. I watched his hand clench into a fist at his side, jaw muscles twitching. I could tell he had more to say, but I didn't want to hear it. I didn't want his apologies. I had a lifetime worth of apologies. I wanted to be left alone to wallow in the life that I had been given.

My eyes narrowed as sadness turned to anger. "Why don't you take that other female? Delilah, I think that was her name. I'm sure she would be delighted by the invitation. Personally, I don't want to be anywhere near you." I didn't feel the need to be shy and hide my nakedness as I threw back the covers, rolling out of bed.

I could feel his eyes burning into me as I disappeared into the bathroom, catching a quick glimpse of the girl in the mirror. She looked like a poor imitation of the person I used to be. There were dark rings around my eyes. My once vibrant red hair was now a dull and tangled mess around my head. There wasn't much fat on my body as my bones showed through a thin barrier of flesh.

I caught Noah's reflection in the mirror. I could smell his desire for me in the air. I could practically taste the spice of it on my tongue. The pull of the bond was trying to force our bodies into alignment with it. I turned my face away, not wanting to have another confrontation. "You should leave. I wouldn't want to keep your people waiting," I said.

"I will be waiting for you in the foyer, Scarlett. If I have to come get you, you won't like it." He growled before turning and leaving me to my own devices, not accepting my denial of his company as an option.

When I came back to the bedroom, I found a pair of clothes laid out for me. They fit much looser now that I had lost most of my curves and body weight, but it was nothing some proper meals couldn't fix. I did my best to keep my head held high as I made my way through the corridors of the house. It had a rather light and airy design to it, something I had a feeling was a touch of his dead mate. I couldn't imagine the stone cold alpha choosing this on his own. Something darker and cave-like would be more up his alley. A couple of people passed me, but they kept their noses to the ground, not even bothering to acknowledge my presence.

I found Noah in the foyer as he had promised, his gaze trekking my movements as I stepped into the open room. There were a couple of people in the room talking to each other in happy tones, and when I tried to get a look, Noah invaded my space, becoming the only thing I could see.

I tilted my head back to make sure I was looking into his eyes. I still found myself struck by the odd icy color of them. They were so unnaturally clear. He pulled me to his side, pressing his hand into the small of my back. His fingers danced over some exposed flesh near my hip thanks to the baggy pants. I swallowed hard as my body threatened to lean into the sensitive touch. "Get your hand off me. I know how to walk," I hissed under my breath as he pushed me forward, making me walk closely beside him.

He clutched me tighter, ignoring my wishes. "These people are very important. All I ask is that you try to behave yourself while in front of them. Hate and fight me all you want, but do it later." He growled quietly at me as we fell short before an older couple who were talking happily with Dane. He spotted me nestled up beside Noah and flashed me a toothy grin. "Alpha Noah..." He bowed his head slightly in a formal greeting.

The couple turned around with friendly smiles. The older woman, whose hair is deep, fiery red, uncurled herself from her mate and embraced Noah. Her cheek pressed to his as she inhaled his scent. This was the way I remembered my parents greeted close friends. It was a custom from the old way our people used to do things. "Oh, Noah, It has been too long." She pulled back, stepping nearer to her mate. She glanced in my direction, eyes focusing on his hand which was gripping my waist. Her eyes the color of finest jade twinkled with merriment. "Who is this? A new member of your pack?"

Noah cleared his throat, hand falling from my waist. He stepped forward and bowed his head low. I found myself stunned by the sentiment, not sure exactly what was going on.

"Alpha Harvey, Luna Rose, please forgive me, but this is Scarlett, my mate." The sound of his strained vocal cords rubbed against my ears painfully. My heart felt heavier as I began to realize why he must have been asking for forgiveness. These important people must have been Claire's parents.

My breath fell short. I stood like a statue as I took in the couple before me. The female leaned into her mate, and he offered her the comfort she was seeking. With his other hand, he reached out and gripped Noah's shoulder. "You do not need to ask for forgiveness, son. Rose and I are happy to know that the Goddess has blessed you doubly." Alpha Harvey turned his gaze in my direction, giving me a small smile as if he was looking at a ray of sunshine breaking through the clouds after a heavy rain.

11

Noah

The way Scarlett looked to me with a quiet anger had me biting my tongue hard. From the moment I laid my eyes on her, my whole world had shifted on its axis. Before that, everything was pointing me to a singular path, and that was to avenge Claire, for only Claire had mattered. That was the only thing that kept me moving forward in the months after her death... simply knowing that at the end of that path, I would be able to redeem myself one way or another for what my sins had caused. Now, I was a man divided.

I flexed my hand, trying to ignore the impulse to touch her again. I don't think Scarlett understood how alluring she was to both man and beast. She was a fragile-looking beauty with what seemed to an unbreakable spirit. It did set my alpha instincts on edge that she constantly challenged me, but deep down, I felt a strange pride knowing the small female had the potential to be a true luna, something my pack was lacking since Claire's death.

Rose leaned her head onto Harvey's shoulder. Her eyes are bright with curiosity as she looked Scarlett over, noting the wrap around her wrist. "What happened to your arm, dear?" I found myself clenching my hands into fists at my side, chest rumbling from a swallowed growl. She could have died. The thought alone made my chest tighten painfully.

"Ryder, Noah, and I found her in the woods. She was trying to take down a rogue all on her own," Dane spoke about the feat with enthusiasm.

"My, my! That is something, isn't it?" Rose said as her gaze locked with mine momentarily.

Scarlett shifted on her feet, a nervous response to the attention, I thought. "It's not as exciting as other people are making it sound. It was either me or it. I chose myself." I could feel her agitation through our bond as it continued to strengthen. I couldn't deny the urge to touch her. The impulse to support her was simply too strong. I reached up and placed my hand on the back of her neck, probing gently with my fingers. The brief touch of velvety flesh against my callous palm sent hot desire leaking into my bloodstream. It had been a long time since I've been so overwhelmed. I wanted to feel more of her. The call of our bond was simply too powerful.

I heard the low rumble in her chest as she cast a side glance in my direction. It was a clear warning that she wasn't going to put up with my constant touching. I let my hand fall away from her, getting control of myself once again.

"Who can blame you for that? I certainly would have chosen myself as well," Rose replied with a soft laugh. She pushed away from Harvey, holding out a hand toward Scarlett. "Come, you look like you could use something to eat."

Scarlett looked at me like she wanted me to save her from the encounter, but I knew Rose wasn't going to be turned away that easily. "Let's leave the men to discuss their business." She pulled Scarlett under her arm, not waiting for a dispute as she guided her away. I watched as she cast me one last look over her shoulder, her eyes narrowing before she disappeared.

A strong hand slapped against my back. "I do not envy you, Noah. She's got those teeth sharpened for you," Dane chuckled with amusement. I turned my face toward him with an agitated sneer. "Do you want me to break you?" He didn't lose his smile even as he took a step back, his hands raised.

"She is beautiful and strong, it seems," Harvey commented, "You will be thankful for this blessing in the coming days. The Goddess is certainly showing you her favor in this war." The seriousness of his words was not lost on me, though. I was not sure it was a favor that she was showing me. Perhaps, this was an omen of a repeating future, a constant hell that is meant for me. It was possible that the sins of my past were too great.

I crossed my arms over my chest. I needed to put my focus on the things that mattered in the end. "What has Knox turned up in his hunting? Anything of value?"

Harvey gave me a look that betrayed pity for a moment. "He said it looks like Kellen has fled to the northern area. He left one of his betas in control of the southern rogues while he's away."

I felt the familiar frustration I always had when things turned cold. The constant game of cat and mouse was taking everything I had left to give. I could see that my pack was beginning to suffer under the weight of it all, but I couldn't let it go. I had to see this through to the end. I let out a sigh, pinching the bridge of my nose. "Well, did anyone tell you what the hell he's doing in the north?"

"No one seemed to know," Harvey responded with an equally exasperated sigh.

"Well, then let's put a fire under the pot. I say we turn away our attention from Kellen for the time being and focus on finding this beta and his stronghold. Someone has to be helping to hide it. I guarantee, if we focus your combined might on that, it will flush Kellen out," Dane added into the conversation. He was a great strategist, thanks to the training his father had forced him to endure in attempts to build an alpha out of him. He had been a replacement for the true heir he had lost.

Harvey looked from Dane to me with raised brows, and I could see he was waiting for my agreement. He may be an alpha, Claire may have been his daughter, but he followed my lead on this. He understood that this was my battle to fight, with his support, of course.

"Alright, we'll try things your way, Dane." I crossed my arms over my chest. "Harvey, I trust you can handle getting word to Knox about the change of plans."

"Rose will be happy to have the boy home. He has been gone too long for her liking," Harvey said as I gave him a small apologetic look.

I already took one of their children. I had tried to talk the young alpha out of joining us. He was the only heir Harvey had to take up the mantle when the time came, but he fought his father for the right to join us and won. I couldn't blame him. He wanted to be the one to avenge his sister. He blamed me for her death, of course. I was the one who took her life in the end, after it all. So I accepted his anger happily. It was just another nail in the cross I had to carry.

12

Scarlett

There were a couple of females in the kitchen when we entered, most of them older. They looked in our direction, lowering their eyes and bowing their heads in respect. "Luna..."

Rose gave me a side glance before pulling away from me. "Smells wonderful in here, ladies. Your food always leaves my belly full and my mouth watering for more. Noah is lucky to have such wonderful cooks in his pack." She was playing her role perfectly. She was giving these people the attention and value they deserved. I watched the way their chests swelled with pride from her simple words of acknowledgment.

Rose grabbed an apple from the basket of fruit sitting out on the counter and rubbed it against her shirt. "You'll be going into heat soon enough, Scarlett. I can already smell it on you. Will this be the first time?" she questioned.

My cheeks rushed with blood at her sudden words. I glanced at the other females, but they kept their head down while they worked, pretending they hadn't heard anything. I licked my lips and nodded my head. "I matured a little later than most girls." It felt weird talking about this with a complete stranger, but she didn't seem bothered by it.

"Claire always wanted to be a mother. She would have been a good one, too," Rose said. A sad smile played on her lips as she stared down at the apple in her hand. "I remember the day we found out she was barren. She cried for hours." I knew that in days past, a barren womb was seen as a bad omen. It was supposed to be a sign that the Goddess was bringing an end to a bloodline.

"That never seemed to bother Noah one bit." She laughed softly as if recalling a funny memory. "I'm sure he still would have taken her if she had three legs, a snaggletooth, and a face only a mother could love." I tried to ignore the way my ears burned as she talked about the two of them. My lips pinched together in a tight smile, but I didn't tell her to stop. Claire was here first. I was simply a stranger that the Goddess had brought into their lives as an afterthought.

Rose took a bite of her apple, tilting her head in my direction. Her eyes searched mine with curiosity. "So tell me about yourself, Scarlett. Where did you come from? You're clearly not from a Southern pack." She changed the topic as if she figured out how awkward I felt talking about Noah and Claire.

I held her gaze. "That obvious?"

She leaned back into the counter. "Most Southern females are too soft to take on a rogue alone. Most aren't often trained in their war forms. Wherever you come from, they clearly have a different code."

My lips twitched as I recalled my home and the life I had before. I looked away. "My father was a fine warrior. He taught me everything he knew. Life in the Northern mountains is different, harsher in some ways."

"The North is a beautiful place. Nothing compares to that fresh mountain air." I lifted my eyes to hers in surprise. She gave me a knowing smile. My wolf could sense the power in this woman. I was certain this lady had seen her fair share of battle and violence over the years.

"From one former Northern woman to another." She leaned forward and pressed her cheek to mine. I took in her scent, deeply. "A nice show of teeth will be enough to keep most of these females in line when they start thinking a little too highly of themselves."

Rose didn't choose to share any more advice with me. Instead, she chose to talk about the Southern packs, sharing information about who is in control and of what they controlled. It didn't matter if the pack was Northern, Southern, Eastern, or Western. Land and power would always be important. Alphas rose and fell. Packs were won and lost over it.

"Noah is considered a king by most in these parts." Her words weren't a surprise. I wasn't sure how far his arms reached, but I had seen enough at this point to know he was not playing at anything. He was a true alpha.

I knew she was sharing all of this with me to help me catch up as to what I have inherited from her daughter. She was trying to prepare me for an unwanted throne. "Most of the Southern alphas are loyal to him. Only Alpha Randall remains a stand-alone force, but last I heard, Noah was working out some kind of deal to sway him. It's really only a matter of time, but don't you mind any of that, you'll likely be preparing for your young."

She reached out and rubbed her hand over my flat stomach. I didn't want to spit on the kindness she was showing me by telling her that would happen when hell froze over.

Instead, I excused myself from Luna Rose's presence, feigning exhaustion, but not before an invitation to their welcoming dinner was extended to me. I had no desire to go to the dinner, but I knew that I had no choice in the matter. I didn't want to be anywhere near them. It was too awkward to pretend, knowing everything I did.

My relaxing was brought to a stop when there was a knock on the door. "Yes?" I called out.

"Luna?" I heard a voice squeak out from the other side. I rolled my eyes as I pulled myself off the bed and padded my way to the door. Apparently, news had traveled fast after Noah's proclamation this morning.

I pulled the door open with a sigh. "It's Scarlett," I corrected her.

"Wha-what?"

I found a young girl maybe only slightly older than the omega I met several days ago, stumbling back from the door and nearly tripping over her own feet.

I tried not to laugh. "My name is Scarlett. I'd rather you call me that." The girl kept her head bowed, and her eyes fixed on the ground, making me roll my eyes. "And you can look at me. I'm not going to turn you into stone or breathe fire."

She looked up slowly, clearly nervous. "I apologize for disturbing you, Luna. I mean, Scarlett." She corrected herself quickly with a wince as if preparing for something awful. "Alpha Noah instructed me to help you get ready for this evening before I escort you to the dining room."

I smiled at the girl warmly. "What's your name?"

"My n-name?" she stammered out her question with cheeks that are clearly turning red.

I leaned into the door. "Yeah, you know that thing your parents gave you so people could call you something other than *hey you*?"

She scrunched up her nose. "My name is Janie."

"Well, Janie it's nice to meet you. Sorry, you got roped into helping me out. You probably have loads of other things that you'd rather be doing right now," I said, teasing her a bit.

She quickly shook her head back and forth. "It's an honor to be able to help you, Luna. I mean, Scarlett."

I looked her over one more time before shrugging my shoulders. "If you say so."

I spent the next thirty minutes letting Janie be my personal stylist. When she handed me a shimmery material, I looked at it with raised brows. "What's this?"

Janie, who had become much more relaxed, let out a small giggle. "It's a dress."

"Oh, right. I've heard of those, but I have never really seen one," I joked though it was true I wasn't much of a dress girl. I had spent most of my life in jeans and t-shirts even before I left my old pack. The thought of my old pack caused me to think of David. I frowned as a small ache rushed into in my chest. It had been a while since I had thought of him, I realized.

"Are you okay?" Janie asked with a concerned look on her face. I quickly pushed the thoughts away, not wanting to dwell in the past a moment longer. I smiled at her. "Of course, I was just thinking how angry Noah would be if I showed up in jeans." She scrunched up her face, and I laughed as I pushed her out of the bathroom so I could get dressed.

I had to admit, the dress was beautiful, and it fit me pretty well. Not perfectly, but close enough. The white material actually made my skin look tan, which was nice since I never looked tan. It came just above my knee, but it was backless, the right amount of reveal.

When I opened the door, Janie's brown eyes widened at the sight of me. "Wow!"

"That good, huh?" I winked as I did a tiny spin, the bottom of my dress flowing with the twirl. She smiled at me before holding one of her hands out. "Here." I looked and saw a pair of silver strapped high heels. I stared at them blankly before shaking my head. "No way. I am not wearing those. I will break my neck—"

"But Alpha—"

I held up my hand to silence her. "Oh, I'm sure I know what Alpha Noah told you," I said. "But I'm not wearing those." I reached down and grabbed my converse. "I learn from other people's mistakes. Cinderella should've worn converse." I joked as I finished tying them onto my feet.

Janie led me through the maze that was Noah's pack house. I was starting to think someone was going to have to draw me up a map or get me a GPS if they didn't want me to get lost every time I left my room when she stopped outside a set of large double doors.

She gave me a reassuring smile before she opened the door for me. I walked through, only to come to a stop. The room was huge. In the center was a large table that looked like it could sit at least fifty people comfortably. It was decorated with beautiful chinaware and fancy glasses. It seriously looked like something you'd see in a castle for a king's feast. There was quite a lot of people in the room, and most of them had already managed to form small cliques, laughing and talking with one another. Only those closest to the door seemed to take notice of me. I smiled at them sheepishly as I moved further away from the door.

I bit my lip as I looked around the room searching for Noah. I felt completely out of place. It didn't take long for me to spot him in a small group near the far side of the room. He looked handsome in his dark suit, like the enchanting devil I had discovered him to be. I felt my temperature rise a couple degrees as I continued to watch him. Alpha Harvey and Luna Rose stood with him, chatting happily. I started to make my way toward the group when a tall brunette walked up and put her hand on Noah's shoulder, laughing at something Alpha Harvey must have said.

I felt anger ripple through me, and I grabbed a drink off a tray nearby. A group of people gave me wary looks as I threw my head back and chugged it. I slammed the empty drink down on the tray while glaring at them. "What?" I snapped as they turned away from me, moving a couple feet in the opposite direction.

More people seemed to notice me as I moved through the room. The sound of Noah laughing had me pausing. I noted the brunette was practically latched onto his side. I clenched my hands into fists at my side, my nails digging into my flesh. The pain kept me from charging across the room and ripping her off him.

"Jealous?" a familiar voice whispered into my ear.

I turned to see Dane standing there, shooting me a knowing smile before he looked towards the group. I cleared my throat. "He can do whatever he wants with whoever he wants. I couldn't care less," I said, trying to sound relaxed.

Dane let out a laugh. "I'll be sure to tell Delilah that. She'll be very happy to hear that."

So that was the girl Nadia had warned me about. I watched as Delilah leaned in and whispered something into Noah's ear. I felt my anger spike to an uncontrollable level. I had to hold back a growl that wanted to erupt out of me.

Dane held out a glass of alcohol in front of me. "Looks like you might need this." I took it from him, shooting it back before holding it out toward him.

He chuckled as he took the empty glass from me. "Shall we?" He held his arm out for me like the gentleman I know he was not. I looked at him before I slipped my hand through the opening in his arm. "If you ever tell anyone about me being jealous, I'll kill you."

Dane only laughed as he led me with steady steps toward the group. He leaned his head towards me when we were almost within touching distance of them. "She's got nothing on you. There's no need for you to be jealous." He winked at me as I turned my face. I couldn't help the small smile that spread over my lips.

"If you think kissing my butt will make up for kidnapping me, keep up the good work, but you've got ways to go before I forgive you."

Noah looked in our direction, his eyes meeting mine almost on reflex. I felt the rush of the mate bond, and the urge to go to him was overwhelming. I let go of Dane's arm and took a step forward, stopping myself when I heard a feminine giggle. My eyes looked toward where Delilah was snuggled against him, and the spell of the bond was broken. Delilah was saying something to Luna Rose. I looked at Noah again. This time, my eyes narrowed into a glare before I looked away from him as I approached the group with Dane at my side.

"Alpha Noah, Alpha Harvey, Luna Rose..." He bowed before lifting his head with a charming smile. Harvey nodded his head, and Rose smiled at him affectionately before reaching out and giving his arm a little squeeze. Her green eyes moved over my dress and down to my feet before meeting my eyes again with an amused smile.

Dane cleared his throat, looking toward Noah warily as if not sure what to do. I looked away from him quickly to Noah and Delilah, feeling my anger spike anew. I put on a fake smile. "Alpha..." I bowed my head before I lifted it back, meeting his dark gaze though he said nothing. I turned to Delilah while maintaining my smile. "And you are?" I asked in a cheerful voice.

She looked me over, snorting a little when she noticed my sneaker-clad feet. I tried to keep my wolf reigned in as she met my gaze. "I'm Delilah." She pleasantly put her hand out for me, but I knew it was only to look good in front of everyone. She had no desire to shake hands with me, I could tell by the look in her eyes. I smiled as I put my hand on hers, but I didn't hold my wolf back as she released her dominant vibes.

"It's so nice to meet you," I said as I watched Delilah squirm and clench her teeth together before she looked down at the ground away from my gaze.

She pulled her hand from my grasp quickly as If I had burned her, and I felt triumphant, and so did my wolf. Dane chuckled beside me, understanding what had happened. He leaned in. "Play nice, Luna," he whispered to me. I peered up at him with a mischievous smirk. "I have no idea what you mean. I am being very nice."

A faint growl echoed in the group, causing Dane to take a step back from me. I turned toward Noah to see him looking at us with a dark gaze. He cleared his throat. "Scarlett, would you mind having a word with me for a moment?" he asked, but I knew it wasn't truly a question. It was a command he expected me to obey.

I shrugged my shoulders. "Whatever you want, Alpha," I said, slightly mockingly as I was unable to stop myself. His eyes flared, but he said nothing. He only unwound Delilah from his side and held out his hand to me. I looked at it for a moment, wanting to take it, but I know what would've happened if I did.

I smiled as I moved past him, ignoring his hand. Served him right for letting some girl cling to him like that. Not that I cared. No, I *didn't* care one bit. He growled at my defiance but came to my side. "Are you trying to piss me off, Scarlett?" My name on his lips sent a shiver up my spine.

I peered up at him. "I'm always trying to piss you off, Noah. That's never going to change." He scowled at my words.

I looked back over my shoulder toward the group and found Delilah glaring in my direction. "Your company is lovely. Do you normally bring your whores to these events or is this a new thing? I just want to know what to expect."

Noah grabbed onto my arm and pulled me to him, so we are pressed chest to chest. "Watch the way you talk about people in my pack. I don't appreciate you insulting them."

I glared up at him. "I apologize, *Alpha*."

He growled in my face before he closed his eyes and breathe in deeply, trying to calm himself down. I felt guilty for a moment but pushed it away when I remembered how Delilah had been touching him and how he had let her. It begged to question the type of relationship they had.

He opened his eyes again. "Scarlett," he said my name softly, "can you please behave tonight? At least while Harvey and Rose are around?"

I stared into his eyes for a moment, letting out a sigh as I relaxed my body into his hold. "Fine. If it's that important to you, but on one condition."

"What?" he asked, his voice tense.

"Make sure that Delilah keeps her hands to herself," I said.

I watched his eyes widen for a moment. "Are you jealous?"

I clenched my teeth together. "No!" I could tell he didn't believe me, though.

He held me tighter to his body as he lowered his head so that his lips were near my ear. "Don't worry, Scarlett. I can assure you you're the only one I want." His lips lightly brushed my ear, causing my cheeks to burn as he pulled back and released me.

"I'm *not* worried or jealous. I just don't like her," I said quickly.

"Whatever makes you feel better." I growled in frustration at his comment as I walked away from him to the group who seemed caught up in their own conversation. Noah came up beside me. "What are you wearing on your feet?"

I smiled to myself. "What? These?" I lifted my leg and wiggled my foot back and forth. "They're just my glass slippers."

He shook his head disapprovingly, but I didn't miss the small smile that passed over his lips. "You're going to be such a pain in my ass."

I laughed at his comment. "Definitely." It was easy at this moment to forget everything that had happened… to forget that I had found my second chance at a mate, to forget that I had witnessed him torture a rogue who I, in turn, was forced to kill, to forget that he was the son of the man that caused the death of my mother. It was easy, but at the same time, it felt like there was still a huge chasm between us that I would never be able to cross.

Dinner had been wonderful, but I was happy when it was time for everyone to leave because I was more than a little tired. Harvey and Rose had said their goodbyes and promised to return soon. When it was finally just Noah and me alone, I stretched my arms up over my head and let out a loud yawn. "That was fun," I said, looking back at him. I found him staring off into nothing with a serious expression.

"Hello? Anybody home?" I asked, snapping my fingers in front of his face.

He shook his head and looked in my direction. "I'm sorry, did you say something?" His tone sounded flat.

I started to roll my eyes but stopped myself. "No, it was nothing. Well, guess I better head off to bed," I said to him, teetering back on my heels with my hands locked together behind me.

He watched me silently for a moment. "Do you still feel for your other mate? The one who rejected you?"

His question took me by surprise, so much so that I almost fell back on my butt before I caught myself. "Why? I mean why are you curious?" He looked away with a shrug of his shoulders.

I watched him carefully for a minute before I asked my own question. "Do you still feel for yours?" His body tensed up, and I immediately regretted asking. I could see that he was still hurting, and no matter how much, I didn't want another mate. I didn't want to be the reason he was hurting.

"Sorry," I said softly, looking down at my feet, "I shouldn't have asked that."

There was a moment of silence between us before a heavy sigh. "No, you had every right to ask that question after what I asked you." Noah shoved his hands into the pockets of his suit pants.

"I don't feel anything for Claire anymore. The moment she died, I didn't feel her anymore." His voice sounded choked. "I feel only the absence of her. It's not as bad when I'm near you."

I looked up at him in surprise, and I know my cheek must be red from how hot they felt. He wasn't looking at me, but I could see that he was tense. Maybe he was worried that I planned on rejecting him. Personally, I knew I could never do that to another person. Not after knowing first-hand how it felt.

I looked away from him towards the ceiling. "I don't know which is worse, having your mate die or having them reject you." When I turned my gaze back at him, our eyes met. He was looking at me with an unreadable expression to which I gave a sad smile before I looked back to the ceiling.

"I can still feel my connection to David." Noah released a deep growl, but I ignored it because It was an expected response. "But it's only a connection of pain. That's all I feel when I think about him. When he bonded to someone else, I thought I was dying. My wolf was gone for a while, and I could barely function, but eventually, everything became bearable. I assume that's just how life and loss work."

I found myself startled when Noah stood suddenly right in front of me, hovering over me. I went to take a step back, but he reached out, placing his hands on my shoulders to hold me in place. His eyes were completely black as he stared down at me. "I can take that pain away, Scarlett." I noticed the flash of his canines as he spoke to me. The sight of them caused my heart to speed up.

I tried to pull out of his hold when I realized his wolf was more in control than he was. "Noah, stop. What are you doing?" I questioned.

"I'm claiming what is mine!" He growled at me before he lowered his head to the crook of my neck. His nose pressed into my skin for a moment, followed by the sharp probing of his teeth as they pressed against the sensitive flesh.

I sucked in a sharp breath as I began to struggle a little more frantically. "Please, you're not thinking clearly," I whispered. He squeezed my shoulders, and I winced slightly before I stilled myself in his hold.

"I've never been clearer." His voice rang loud in my ear as my breath caught in my chest. "I won't lose you too, Scarlett. I'm sorry, but I can't," he said before his teeth pierced through the flesh of my shoulder. I let out a painful cry into the empty room. I felt like my body was on fire and it was getting hotter by the second. My mind was in a whirl as our bond began to pull and shift our souls about. I could feel a pressure inside it as if something else was trying to invade my space. There was yet another presence taking up residence in my body. I opened my mouth and let out another whimper as I felt the pressure burst inside me.

Suddenly, I could feel Noah there, in the back of my mind, his thoughts and instincts influencing my own. He had gone and completed one part of the mate bond. He had done it without my consent. He had made it so I could never be without him.

"You son-of-a-bitch," I said aloud. "I'm going to kill you." I felt my body growing heavy. I was teetering on the edge of oblivion. The act of his claiming had zapped all of my energy. He held me closer to his body as if he was trying to comfort me, but that only made me angrier. I remember growling before I fell into the darkness that had been waiting to take me away.

13

Scarlett

I stirred in my sleep, and the movement of my body caused a dull ache throughout my body. I felt like I had been out all night drinking and now I had a terrible hangover. I did note that I was laying down on something soft, which I assumed was my bed, but I couldn't remember getting into my bed. In fact, I couldn't remember much of the previous night after the dinner. It all seemed to be a blur in my mind. I felt a throb of pain go through my head as I tried to recall how I came to be in my bed. I groaned to myself as I slowly opened my eyes, blinking a couple times as they adjusted to the sunlight streaming in through the window.

I heard movement near the edge of my bed. I turned my head to find Janie curled up in a chair. I stared at her in confusion, wondering why she is sleeping in a chair at the foot of my bed. When I tried to sit up, I fell back into the mattress, the ache in my body too much as it turned into a small burning sensation. My motions seemed enough to rouse Janie from her sleep. She blinked a couple times as if trying to remember where she was before she jolted upright. "Oh, you're awake, Luna. I mean, Scarlett," she proclaimed almost as if she believed I would never wake up.

I gave her a weird look as the fire in my body slowly dulled. "Yeah, that's usually something people do when they sleep. I'm more curious about why you're camped out at the foot of my bed."

"Right!" she said in a serious tone like a soldier. "I was told by Alpha Noah to watch over you until you woke up, and when you do, I was supposed to give you these." I watched her reach into the pocket of her jeans and fish around. "Oh, wait, wrong pocket..." she said to herself, switching her hand to the other pocket. "Here we are." She pulled out two blue tablets and held them out toward me. I hesitantly opened my hand and let her drop them into my palm. I looked at them. "What are these? Tylenol?"

"I'm not sure. My father gave them to me." She shrugged. I shifted my gaze, staring at her blankly for a moment. "He's the pack doctor," she said as if that would put me at ease. This timid girl was Doctor Owen's daughter? I stared at her a little harder, beginning to see a small resemblance to the ornery man.

I looked back down at the tablets in my hand before I opened my mouth, throwing them in. I would have given anything to relieve the feeling in my body, which was beginning to grow increasingly more uncomfortable and hot by the moment. I let out a loud sigh as I nestled back into the pillows.

"Can I ask a question?" Janie asked.

"You just did," I replied as I closed my eyes against the throbbing pain in my head. She grew quiet, and I let out another sigh. Clearly, people around here had no understanding of sarcasm. "What's your question, Janie?"

"Is it incredibly painful to be marked?" She sounded like a girl asking if it hurt to lose your virginity.

I chuckled, "I wouldn't—"

I felt my good humor quickly dissipate as my eyes popped open. I looked at Janie who was looking down at me expectantly, waiting for a reply. I swallowed hard against the onslaught of emotions that ripped through me. Memories of last night were racing through my brain. I moved my hand to my neck and shakily touched the spot, wincing at the tenderness. So that wasn't a terrible nightmare. It happened. Anger and disbelief rolled together to create a perfect storm of emotions. I was going to kill him the next time I saw him.

"I'm sorry if it's too personal. You can just pretend I didn't ask," she said, shyly shaking her head.

I took in a slow breath, trying to calm myself down. "Why do you want to know?" I asked, trying to turn the conversation away from things that would upset me any more than I already was. She tucked some of her hair behind her ear. "It's just that I found my mate. He doesn't know yet cause I've been hiding from him. It's just that I am afraid…"

It sounded very much like my own story, the one that brought me to this place. I sat up a little straighter. "What are you afraid of? Is your mate a bad person?"

She looked at me with big eyes and shook her head. "No, at least he doesn't appear to be. It's just that I'm afraid he won't think I'm good enough." She bit her lip. I understood her feelings completely as I had been rejected by David. I was surprised to find that I didn't feel the familiar ache in my body when I thought of him. I waited a moment, but when nothing happened, I couldn't help but feel a strange relief. After two years, I was finally free from the burden of his rejection.

"Scarlett?" Janie called me.

I looked at her, shaking my head clear of my thoughts. "Sorry, you were saying?"

"What if he rejects me?" She continued to nibble anxiously on her lip.

I gave her a reassuring smile. "I doubt he'll reject you, Janie. Only an idiot would reject their mate."

"I don't know. I'm not very strong or smart. He's so popular, and he's so important to the pack. I doubt anyone would even notice if I wasn't around," she said with her head hanging low.

"You're wrong. I would notice," I said to her.

She looked up at me with raised eyebrows. "You're just saying that. You don't even know me."

"That's true, but then again, you don't really know me either," I said. "You've been very kind to me since you met me, Janie, and you didn't have to be. I think you just don't give yourself the credit you deserve." She seemed to warm up at my words, and I could sense her wolf stirring proudly at my praises. I knew this had to be the power of a luna. Lunas were supposed to look out for the pack, to protect and nurture them like only a good mother could.

I looked at Janie when I saw her body tense up out of the corner of my eye. "What's wrong?" I asked before there came a knock on the door.

"Luna?" I heard Dane's voice on the other side. Janie was looking at the door frantically then dropped to the ground, and to my amusement and surprise, pulled herself under my bed. It didn't take me long to put two and two together.

I cleared my throat. "Yes?"

"May I come in?" he asked.

I could smell Janie's anxiety and frowned. "Janie, you have to calm down, or he'll know you're here. I promise I'll keep your secret for now, okay? But he's going to find out, eventually."

There was a small span of silence before she whispered back to me. "Thank you, Scarlett."

"Do you have to?" I asked back even though I know Noah ordered him to come here to check on me.

"I'm sorry, Scarlett, but the alpha has asked me to check in on you personally and to give you some more medicine." His last words are all the encouragement I needed.

"Come in," I said as I feigned exasperation. He slowly opened the door and poked his head in as if he was afraid there might be a fire breathing dragon inside. I tried not to smile with amusement as he entered the room with such caution and care. He came to the foot of the bed but stopped short, tilting his head to the side as he breathed in deep. His eyes darkened, and he scanned the room with a pinched look on his face.

"Is something wrong?" I asked, trying to pretend as though I have no idea what is happening.

"Who else was in here?" he asked me clearly, forgetting his initial reason for coming to my room.

I tilted my head to the side thoughtfully. "I don't know. I woke up alone, but there was some Tylenol on the side table. Could have been anyone."

His lips pressed together in a firm line. He turned to leave the room, but I cleared my throat. "You said you had medicine for me?"

"Oh, sorry." His voice was hoarse as he marched over to the side of my bed. He reached into his pocket and pulled out two blue tablets, just like the ones Janie had given me not long before. He set them down on the side table. "I have to go report back to the alpha, but I will return shortly to check on you," he said with assurance, and I smiled softly.

"Okay, but only if you bring me more of those magic pills."

He stood motionless by the bed for a moment, and I felt myself growing tense. *Please do not look under the bed!* He looked down at me. "Are you sure you don't remember anyone else being in here? Maybe you woke up for a moment and saw something or talked to someone."

I felt slightly guilty keeping him from his mate, but I wanted to protect the small friendship I had built with her. I gave him an apologetic smile and shook my head. "No. I'm sorry."

"If anyone else comes in here, let me know. The alpha was clear he wanted to minimize the people coming in and out of here, so anyone else that wants to visit will need authorization," he said to me.

I rolled my eyes at him. "Yes, sir! Now run along back to Mr. Alpha. I'm suddenly very tired and bored with this conversation." Dane paused for one more minute before he turned and left the room, clearly much tenser than when he had entered. I waited a minute or two to make sure he wasn't going to come back and demand I tell him. I could tell he knew I was keeping something from him, but because I was the luna, he didn't want to press his luck.

"It's safe to come out now," I said dryly.

Janie popped up beside my bed a couple seconds later with her cheeks tinted red and her breathing heavy. "Thank you so much, Scarlett."

I stared at her for a moment longer before I sighed and looked away. "He's going to find out soon now that he knows your scent, Janie. He is going to do everything in his power to find you, which is quite a lot considering he's the beta."

"I know! I don't know what to do. I want to be with him, but I'm afraid. Please, just keep my secret for a little while longer, Scarlett. I'll do anything." She pleaded with me. The sound of her voice made my heart ache. I might not feel the sting of David's rejection, but that doesn't mean I forgot the feelings that had tormented me for so long.

I looked back at Janie. "He is not going to reject you, Janie. If he even thinks about it, I'll cut his balls off and give them to you as a trophy."

She scrunched up her face in disgust and then lets out a small laugh. "I appreciate the sentiment, Scarlett."

"Good, now you better get out of here before he comes back," I said, quickly wanting to be alone. I was feeling the strong urge to sleep. I thought it was part of the blue pills. She nodded her head and rushed from the room.

After the initial pain of the claiming left me, all I felt was the extreme need to get out of my bedroom, but Noah had posted the knucklehead twins outside my door again. Only this time, he had ordered them to make sure I stayed put until he could have a pack doctor look at me and make sure that everything was okay with me. Even thinking about that idiot was pissing me off. Not only because he has forced his claim on me, but also because I felt the need to see his stupid face, a direct effect of the forced claim.

I growled in irritation as I pulled myself out of my bed to shower. The soothing sensation of the warm water helped to calm my nerves a bit which were on edge because my wolf wanted very much to be near her mate. I hadn't seen Noah since he had bitten me, and it was actually a smart move on his part because the human side of me seriously wanted to kill him. I stayed safely tucked away in the shower until the water began to have trouble staying warm.

I walked out of the bathroom and straight to my closet which had magically been filled with clothes. I was sure I had Janie and Nadia to thank for that. I grabbed a pair of jeans and a plain t-shirt, throwing them onto to the bed. I dropped my towel only to have my ears met with the sound of the door opening. I turned quickly to see Noah standing in the doorway of my room, eyes glued to my body.

"Shit!" I snapped as I snatched the towel back up from the ground, quickly wrapping it around myself. I glared at him. "What the hell, Noah? Don't you knock before you enter someone's room?"

His eyes remained glued to me. "This is my house, and you are my mate. I don't have to knock."

I grabbed a pillow from the bed and chucked it across the room at him. "You're a bastard!" I snapped. He shrugged his shoulders as if he couldn't care less.

"How are you feeling?" he asked as he set the pillow down on the small loveseat and made his way toward me.

I backed up, holding tightly to my towel. "I'd be a lot better if you weren't here and if you hadn't claimed me without my consent, but other than that I'm peachy," I replied sarcastically.

He stopped at the edge of my bed, his eyes meeting mine. "We both know you don't actually feel that way, Scarlett. Your wolf has been calling for me to come be near you." His eyes darkened a little at this, and I frowned. He was right. My wolf was much happier now that Noah was near us but I, on the other hand, was much more unhappy. The pull toward him was undeniable, but it didn't mean I loved the guy. Hell, I didn't even really like him, but my wolf wanted him more than before now that he had marked me.

"Yeah, well, who's damn fault is that?" I spat at him.

He ignored my attitude. "It's only going to get worse. Since your previous mate missed out on the opportunity of claiming you, I know you don't understand fully, but you're going to want to be around me all the time. It's going to make you snappy and moody when we're separated for too long, but after the bond is completed, your wolf will be more at ease."

I pointed a finger at him. "That will happen when hell freezes over! Is that why you came here? To try to proposition me? Cause if so, don't let the door hit you on the way out or do, I don't care." I raised an eyebrow as I positioned my hands on my hips.

He remained silent, observing me for a moment, before he smirked. The emotion seemed somewhat forced, though. "I wouldn't dream of that. I only came to see for myself how you were doing. Clearly, you're feeling much better since you are back to your usual self."

"Usual self?" I questioned.

"Yes, usual as in obnoxious, loud, and childish."

I glared at him as I ground my teeth together. "Oh? As opposed to you who's boring, stifling, and uptight?" He lost his smirk, and I smiled, feeling satisfied by his reaction to my comeback.

The knock on my door pulled our attention. "Alpha? Luna?"

"Yes, Murphy?" Noah questioned back, keeping his gaze fixed on me.

I let out a huff of air before snatching my clothes from the bed and walking into the bathroom to get dressed, slamming the door behind me. I threw on my clothes quickly before making my way back out into my room where I found Noah seated on the edge of my bed waiting patiently. He watched me closely as I moved around my room. "Are you going to sit there and watch me all day? Don't you have anything better to do with your time?" I asked him in annoyance.

"Am I intimidating you?" he questioned as his lips turned up into a small grin.

"Hardly." I scoffed. "You do dark and broody pretty well, but I've had more practice being a hard-hearted bitch. So if your objective was to intimidate me, you're going to have to try harder than that."

His smirk grew a little wider at my words as if he truly found them amusing. "Duly noted."

I stood there staring at him, trying to understand exactly what he was still doing in my room, when he pushed himself off my bed and walked towards me. "You know, I forgot what it was like to have a mate. I'm not sure if I like this feeling or not."

"You should have thought about that before you claimed me," I said out.

"Do you have a response for everything I say?" he questioned dryly.

I shrugged my shoulders. He stood silently, regarding me for an awkward moment. I turned away from him. "So what did Murphy want?"

"There was a small issue with rogues near the eastern border of my territory. He is holding one of the rogues he caught for questioning." *Holding a rogue for questioning?* I flinched as the memory of the rogue in the basement flashed in my mind. Questioning my ass. Holding it for torture was more like it.

"Does this happen a lot? I mean, the rogues invading your territory," I asked, turning back toward him.

"Lately? Yes." He looked me over as if he was trying to reach through the bond to figure out was I was thinking. I didn't want him to know what I was thinking because I was certain it wasn't something he would like to know.

"Well." He looked away from me, his movements stiff. "I should probably head out. I'd feel better if you remained in your room until I have the proper time to show you around myself since you seem to have a hard time listening to the rules. We don't need a repeat of last time."

"You mean you want me to stay locked up for longer?" I asked, my wolf and I feeling irritable at the thought. Noah lifted his hand and scratched the back of his neck. "I'll send someone to take you outside for a run if you'd like—"

My lip curled back into a sneer. "I'm not some kind of pet."

His eyes darken at my attitude. "You will stay in this room unless someone is with you. You don't know your way around, and you haven't proven that I can trust you yet. Until then, this is the way things will be, Scarlett." I wanted to throttle him.

"You—" I found it hard to put my words together. I was so keyed up. "You really piss me off, you know that? I'm your mate, and you're treating me like some kind of problem that needs to be solved. Please, get out of my room. I have nothing more to say to you," I found myself saying calmly.

"Gladly," he replied coldly before turning and walking away from me. My wolf was begging me to chase after him, but I stay rooted to my spot. Maybe I was being difficult, but he still had a lot to learn about being a mate. When I heard my bedroom door slam shut, I let out a breath that I didn't even know I was holding.

14

Scarlett

Noah and I hadn't spoken to each other since the day he came to my room, and it has been close to a week since that happened. My wolf had been pining for Noah, but I knew he wasn't going to answer her call after the things I said to him, and honestly, I was happy he has stayed away.

I appreciated the silence of my room of which I had become a willing prisoner. I was sitting, reading a book that Nadia had given to me during a visit, when a knock on my door came. "Who is it?" I called out, not bothering to look up. The door opened without another word.

I lifted my gaze to see Dane entering my space. I frowned at him. "I could have been naked you know."

He chuckled. "If only I could be so lucky."

I narrowed my eyes. "What do you want?" I snapped the book close. He made sure to keep his distance. Noah must have sent him here. "I only wanted to see how you were feeling."

I looked away from him. "What you mean to say is that Noah was wondering how I was feeling and he sent you to check up on me because he was too afraid to come see for himself," I said in a bored tone.

"That obvious, huh?" Dane teased playfully.

I looked up at him to find him grinning. "You know, you're making it incredibly hard for me to sulk and that's annoying since that's all I want to do right now." He moved closer to me with confident steps, taking a seat on the couch next to me.

I stared at him openly. "Feeling brave, I see."

He looked down at the book in my hands. "What are you reading?" He changed the topic.

"Some crappy teen romance Nadia lent me." I turned myself, so I was facing him on the couch. "Are you planning on being here long? I have other things I need to do today like pace, pout, and pace some more. All of which will be much more enjoyable to do without someone watching me."

Dane held up his hands in surrender. "Don't kill the messenger."

I narrowed my eyes. "Why not? I've heard it sends a message." Dane quickly scrambled off the couch and moved a small distance away from me, which had me fighting the urge to smirk.

"Look, Scarlett..." Dane's playfulness was gone. "I know you don't know Noah like the rest of us and he hasn't really made a good first impression..."

"You think?" I said sarcastically.

Dane gave me a look. "He isn't the monster you think he is. We all have done things we aren't proud of, but I've never once questioned Noah's love for Claire or his loyalty to this pack. He cares about all of us. He just doesn't know how to show that all the time. It probably has something to do with his past. I'm not trying to persuade you to forgive him for anything... All I'm saying is maybe you could try to understand him a little and see where he's coming from."

I turned away from Dane with a tired sigh as I pushed up of the loveseat. "You're a good beta, Dane, but it's complicated. This relationship between Noah and I shouldn't even be possible. We both already had true mates—"

"But it did happen," Dane interjected. "I know some part of you wants to make this work, Scarlett. Even though you're putting up a hard front, I saw how upset you were at the dinner when you saw him with Delilah. You wouldn't have reacted that way if you didn't want this in some way. All I'm asking is you try to make it work here, not only for Noah... but for the pack. We need you just as much as he does."

I looked at him and studied his expression for a moment. I knew he was right. A part of me did want to make this work. It was my second chance at something I should have had from the beginning but was denied to me. I had no idea if Noah and I could ever have a true mate relationship, but we could at least work together for the good of this pack. I closed my eyes and let out a sigh. "Fine. I'll try, but I'm not promising anything."

"That's great news!" Dane exclaimed as I opened my eyes to see a truly happy expression on his face. It warmed my heart that he cared so much about his alpha and this pack.

"How would you like to get out of this damned room?" Dane asked me, still smiling.

For some reason, I felt like there is something else going on. "What you trying to do?" I asked as I eyed him suspiciously.

He shrugged his shoulders. "I guess you'll have to come with me and find out."

I have never been one for surprises, but I would bite if it meant I could get out of this room. "Fine, but just know I still haven't forgiven you for the whole kidnapping thing." I gave him a pointed look.

"How long are you going to hold that against me? It's not like I knew you were Noah's mate at that point. He had yet to reveal that information to me..." he said in exasperation.

"That kind of makes it worse, don't you think?" I teased.

He moved toward the door. "Come on, grouchy pants." I smacked him on the back of the head as I passed by him, going through the door he opened for me.

"What was that for?" he asked as he fell into step beside me.

"You know what it was for," I said in a clipped tone.

Dane showed me around the pack house shortly before he took me outside to a small enclosure which turned out to be an indoor garden. It was so peaceful and beautiful that my earlier anger toward my mate was forgotten. I wandered around a bit, taking in the splendor of it all. Whoever made this place must have loved it very much. I took a seat on the bench and closed my eyes, letting myself relax for a moment, "This was

Claire's place?" I questioned, but in my heart, I already knew the answer.

Dane came and sat down on the bench next to me. "She used to have me escort her here all the time mostly when she wanted to think or when Noah was making her mad." He elbowed me on the last part.

"Oh, so it's not just me?" I teased as I opened my eyes once again, amazed by all the colors around me. Dane chuckled but didn't say anything else in response.

It felt strange being in Claire's special place like she might appear at any moment. This was Claire's world out here, the last remnants of her that existed outside of memories. It was my only way to learn and understand her truly without prying into painful memories and feelings. I could tell that Claire was a kind and generous person. I bet even when she was mad at Noah, she probably never said a mean thing to him.

I frowned and let out a sigh. "She was perfect for Noah." It wasn't like I was pitying myself, just acknowledging the truth.

Dane took a moment to respond probably trying to figure out a safe response. "She was. She was the light to his darkness. Before they met, Noah was a dangerous man, but even a hardened rogue couldn't help but love her. That's just the power she had." I nodded my head and looked at him to see a small smile on his lips.

I watched the smile slowly fade into a painful grimace. "When she came back. That light was gone. Noah tried to save her. For weeks, he had her locked up in hopes that he could help her get back to this side, but she didn't have the strength it required. Noah blamed himself. He thought it was something he deserved for all the terrible things he had done before Claire came. No matter how deep his love for her was... there was no way to bring her back. He did what none of us could do and set her free from the darkness before it truly ruined her."

"That's a mighty poetic way to say he killed her," I said solemnly.

"That was almost three years ago. At first, I was afraid he was going to turn rogue again. He had these horrible nightmares for a while, but after months, he slowly began to come out of that. The light in his eyes was gone, though. He was a hollow man. I think he would have gone rogue again if it hadn't been for the pack and his loyalty to us." It was painful to hear about what Noah had endured after Claire's death.

Dane shifted next to me. "When we ran into you, that was the first time I saw real emotion in him since Claire. It was even more of a surprise when he told me you were his mate. He was obviously upset and confused, but I thought it was a second chance, a way for him to become the man he used to be... the man we all came to love." I turned to Dane and looked at the sad expression on his face, and it broke my heart.

My heart felt the crushing weight of knowing that my mate had killed the woman he loved. That he had tried to save her and had watched her become what he had once been... that his pack was mourning not only the loss of their luna but also their alpha. My wolf whimpered inside of me at the feelings rushing through me, and I felt her urging me to go to Noah and to apologize for the things I had said, but I stayed sitting, knowing he would not welcome anything like that from me.

I let out a small, heavy sigh. "And then the Goddess went and made us mates? What a joke."

Dane nudged me with his shoulder. "Maybe because you're exactly what he needs now. You have a fire in you, Scarlett. Sure, it's not that warm light that Claire had, but that's not what Noah needs now, or what this pack needs. We need that all-consuming fire inside of you to burn away all the pain and sorrow that's left behind. Your courage and strength, that's what we need."

I shook my head. "Trust me, I'm not a strong as you think I am."

"I have seen first-hand what rejection of a mate looks like, Scarlett. Most wolves turn into hollow shells and die out. Yet you were rejected, and here you are, alive and well. Perhaps you aren't giving yourself enough credit." He nudged me again, and I smiled at his attempt to cheer me up.

I turned my head towards him. "Noah is lucky to have you by his side."

Dane let out a laugh. "You remind him that next time he throws one of his fits and threatens to put me in the dungeon for the rest of time."

I turned away from him. "Thanks for bringing me here. I can see why Claire loved it so much." In my heart, I felt like she was there with me and she wanted me to help Noah. The truth was he was lost and confused right now. He didn't want me to get close to him because he was afraid. Of what, I wasn't exactly sure anymore.

I let out a determined sigh and pushed myself up off the bench. "I think I know what I need to do now."

Dane got up and stood next to me with an amused expression. "Oh, yeah? And what is that?"

"I can't tell you. That would ruin all the fun," I said as I walked away from him toward the exit. He caught up to me quickly and playfully pushed me to the side as he passed by. Dane reminded me of my cousin. Being around him gave me a sense of familiarity and comfort. The fact I was hiding what I knew about his mate made me feel guilty, but I promised Janie I would keep her secret.

"What are you thinking so hard about?" Dane's voice broke through my thoughts. "You look like you're plotting something."

I walked out the door he was holding open for me. "There is something you need to understand about women, Dane. We are always plotting something." I patted his shoulder lightly. As I walked away, I felt a fire in my heart set alight with a new determination. I was going to help Noah, Dane, Janie—all of them. I was going to try to bring this pack back from the dead, and maybe along the way, I would find myself too.

15

Scarlett

It was another week before the dreams came... before our bond took hold of my mind because of Noah's claim.

I could feel the breeze rustling my hair as I chased after Wyatt. He turned around every couple of feet to wave me onward with a bright smile on his face. The trees stretched into the sky, high above the dense fog that cloaked the top of the mountain, looking like giant wooden pillars holding the world in place.

"Hurry up, Scarlett..." His childish voice floated through the air. "Over here."

I went after his voice, but I could no longer see him. The world grew darker around me as I moved deeper into the woods. My eyes roamed the shadows as paranoia began to blossom in my chest. Something hung off in the shadows, just out of sight.

"Wyatt?" My voice quaked as I pushed myself onward though my steps were more hesitant now. The only response I received was the whistling of the wind through the leaves overhead. There was a heavy silence that had me holding my breath as I waited like a sheep for the slaughter. Wyatt's loud shout of terror made me tense up and spin around to find myself staring into the eyes of a monster, its eyes glowing red.

Its teeth were long and jagged and stained yellow as drool dripped from its open and panting mouth.

"Run, Scarlett, Run!" I heard my mother shout, and my little body began to move, my legs carrying me away from the beast who let out a fierce howl of a hunter. As I ran away, I tripped over my feet and tumbled down.

Down, down I fell. I fell through unending darkness, giving rise to the terror in my mind.

The next thing I knew, my feet were planted on solid ground. A rough hand gripped the back of my neck, forcing me to take unwanted steps forward. The presence at my back seemed to radiate pure malice. It had my stomach churning, and I leaned forward expelling its contents.

"Stupid little bastard!" A deep voice growled into my ear, making my body shiver with fright. The fingers were burrowed through my hair, pulling hard until my neck snapped back at an awkward angle.

The familiar crystalline eyes of my mate stared down at me though it was a face of a stranger hovering before me. "I'm going to beat the weakness out of you. No heir of mine is going to cower at the sight of blood." He smiled down at me like a hungry predator with his canines extended.

Suddenly, I stood in the shadows watching as an audience to a boy as he took blow after blow from a silver whip, the tiny cries for mercy slowly dwindling into nothing, until he no longer cried out. He was silent and unmoving. My fingers twitched with the urge to reach out for him, and my lungs inflated with the urge to scream for his relief, but I could do nothing but watch. Darkness encroached on the scene, slowly swallowing us all.

I was drowning in it as it pulled me down deeper and deeper. Bloodcurdling screams lurched me out of the shadows. My feet were moving quickly over the earth as I ran, not knowing what exactly I was running from or towards. I saw a break out of the tree line and stopped when I saw my pack in complete disarray. There were rogues coming from every direction, cutting through women and children as they tried to flee.

My mother rushed out of the crowd towards me with terrified eyes. She grabbed onto my hand and began to pull me away from the terror-stricken crowd. "Come on! This way!" I let her pull me along, tripping over my own feet as my concentration was diverted toward the killing happening around us. People I knew were falling prey to monsters before my very eyes.

She stopped pulling me, and I turned my attention to find myself staring at the man and the young boy. He was smiling at me with sharp teeth, his hand resting on the shoulder of the child he had beaten. The boy was staring blankly ahead with cold, lifeless eyes.

"There's only one thing left to do before you're ready to be my heir... to kill your weakness," the monster said to me.

I found myself staring into his glowing eyes as I grabbed hold of my mother and killed her as I had the rogue. She fell down at my feet, eyes clouded and void of light. Terror rushed through me as I realized what I had done. My hands were covered in her blood.

I backed away quickly, tripping over my own feet. I hit the ground with a thud and turned my face to the side, only to find myself staring into the clouded eyes of a beautiful girl with fiery red hair, lying dead beside me.

"You killed me. This is your fault. You killed me!" Her face morphed into my Wyatt's then my mothers, over and over... different faces professing the guilt that dirtied my hands. I couldn't handle any more. My mouth opened and screams poured from my lips. Over and over, I screamed. I lifted my bloodied hands to my ears, not wanting to hear any more. I tried to close my eyes, but tiny fingers held them open.

The little boy's face was hovering over mine. "Look! You have to look! Kill the weakness!"

"Wake up Scarlett—" Noah's voice called out for me, but the demons in my subconscious held me captive. I could hear my own terrified screams echoing back to me, but I couldn't open my eyes. I couldn't look away from the horrifying scenes that were rushing through my mind.

"Scarlett!" he growled my name with his alpha tone, jolting me back into reality. I was still screaming as my eyes snapped open to find his face inches in front of my mine. I reached up with my hands, hitting him like a crazed woman. His eyes glowed bright in the darkness of my bedroom, just like the monster from my dreams. He took a couple of hits from me before his hands grabbed onto my shoulders, anchoring my arms to the bed.

I struggled against him as he pushed me deeper into the pillow-topped mattress. "Enough!" he bellowed, enough to cause my body to be still as bitter tears fell from my eyes.

"Please, I don't want to see anymore. I don't want to look anymore."

His expression softened slightly as he stared down at me, holding my body in his rough hands. These were his demons, spilling into my mind through his claim while we both were unaware. I didn't know what to say or do with what I had seen. All I knew is that I didn't want to see anymore. It terrified me that I could be sown together with a monster because what did that say about me? Only that I was just as monstrous as he was, just better at hiding it.

I watched as his jaw muscle twitched and tightened as he clenched his teeth. He understood what had happened though I couldn't figure out what he was thinking as easily as he could read me. My mind was becoming an open vault to him as our bond strengthened. I felt sorry for him for what I had witnessed. I now knew some of his deep hidden secrets.

He turned his face away from my gaze as if it burned him. "I'll be outside the door if you need me." He released his grip on me and stood up. My eyes followed his movements as his feet carried him away from me and toward the door where he paused. "Whatever you saw, Scarlett, it would be to best put it out of your mind, and I'll do the same. Some things are better left buried."

I lay on the bed, staring up at the ceiling, as the moonbeams danced within the shadows, carving out the silhouette of the trees outside. There was a lonely feeling in my stomach as I stared up at them. Rolling over, I grabbed a pillow, hugged it to my chest, and wrapped my legs around it like another person in the bed. My body was as uncomfortable as my mind.

Noah's scent drifted in under the door. He had taken to guarding my bedroom that night as he promised. His wolf was the dominant one with strong instincts, and he wouldn't let me go unguarded after the nightmarish episode we'd shared. It was annoying, but I knew it didn't matter how much I fought him on it, he was going to be there no matter what. I let out a small groan as I burrowed my face into the pillow, finally finding the sleep that had been eluding me.

Morning came with a different feeling as the house seemed to be full of life and excitement. The usual suspects received me with full smiles when I turned up in the dining room to see that the seat at Noah's right was already empty. A plateful of food was set out in front of it. I hesitated for a moment in confusion before Nadia smiled in my direction, waving me over.

I shuffled toward the table, watching Noah stiffen slightly as I took my seat. He continued to eat his food silently, his knife and fork scraping the bottom of the glassware. The table was full of the lively chatter of his pack, and I couldn't help being curious about the excitement.

"How did you sleep, Scarlett?" Noah's voice cut through all the noise.

I let my eyes trek over his face. His icy eyes met mine, and his brows lifted as he waited for a response. My childish heart wanted to ignore him and pretend I never heard him, but if I wanted to win this power struggle between us, I realized that might not be the way to do it. I grabbed a piece of toast, taking my time to answer him.

I chewed slowly. "I slept fine, I guess. There was this awful stink that made it difficult at first, though." I took another bite of my toast, my face blank as I met his stare. He knew I was taking a jab at him.

"Really?" Nadia joined our conversation, turning her face toward Noah. "Maybe you should send one of the omegas to check it out. Maybe a mouse got inside again and died in a vent."

I enjoyed the slight twinge of pink that rose in his cheeks. I couldn't help being satisfied with my small victory. A large group of pack members flooded into the dining room, looking like they had been out training. Dane was in the lead. He had a bright smile on his face, and his hair was damp with sweat. His eyes were focused on the table, giving me a wink as he passed to take a seat on the other side. He was getting too much enjoyment out of the awkward tension between Noah and me.

Delilah separated from the group. A smile was on her lips as she sauntered towards the table. Her hand touched Noah's shoulder as she passed, eyes meeting mine momentarily, before she continued onward to find a seat with some of her friends. My wolf growled threateningly in my head at the female. She wanted very much to take her by the throat and put an end to her.

"Don't mind her too much, Luna. Her bark is a lot worse than her bite," Dane said to me under his breath, having noticed the interaction.

I forced myself to focus on my food, pretending that it didn't matter at all. I shrugged my shoulders as I took another bite of my toast. "I'm not worried about her. Never was, never will be."

"That's the spirit." Dane let out a small chuckle as he filled his empty plate with food. I could see that Noah is watching us out of the corner of my eye, looking a little stiff. I purposefully inclined my body toward Dane's, bumping my shoulder against his. If he was going to let other females touch him, then I should let him feel the burn of jealousy as well. "What's with all the excitement? Did I miss something?"

Dane turned his face in my direction like I was completely daft. "It's time for the Trials."

I lifted my brows in confusion. "And those are?"

I lifted my brows in confusion. "And those are?"

"You Northern wolves," Ryder commented from across the table with a snort and a small disapproving shake of his head.

Nadia smacked his arm, clearly not pleased by his attitude. He gave her a deep frown in response. I was beginning to think perhaps he was always like this with everyone. Nadia rolled her eyes before turning her attention back to me, leaning forward. "The Trials is our way to show which pack is the best. Kind of like a week of the Olympic Games. There is always a giant party at the end. That's my favorite part, to be honest.

Seeing old friends and my family is nice, too," she added as an after-thought.

"Sounds interesting." I had never heard of anything like this before.

"It's a way to vent out aggression between packs, to settle our disputes without actually going to war. There is a real enemy out there, and fighting amongst ourselves over things like land and power is what they want. It makes us weak." Noah joined the conversation. I swung my gaze at him, remembering our conversation, remembering the rogue. He held a serious expression as he got lost under the weight of his inner thoughts.

Dane knocked me playfully with his elbow. "Don't let him fool you with that. He plays the serious alpha card well, but in truth, he is just as excited as the rest of us to knock each other around." He looked at Noah with a teasing smile. I peeked over at him to see him shaking his head as he lifted his glass to his lips. I didn't miss the way they twitched upward as he took a drink.

"These Trials are even more important than the last. Alpha Randall is hosting. He's also the only person who has yet to show support for the war against the rogues," Ryder commented. I remembered the name because it had fallen from the rogue's lips, and I had seen the way the three of them had reacted to it.

Noah leaned back in his seat, looking like a king on his throne. "Yes, well, it's something I'm planning to rectify. Our talks have been slow-going but productive, and I feel positive that he will come to see things our way after the recent affairs." He shared it so openly where other members of his pack could hear. This took me by surprise. Usually, alphas kept business matters only between those they deem to be in the 'know.' Then again, from all the things that Noah had done, he had proven to be a bit unorthodox in his ways. However, those same ways seemed to have brought him a great amount of influence and power, so perhaps there was something to it.

"Maybe you should have brought him to your basement. I bet that would have sped things right along. You could have eenie meanied the agreement right out of him," I said as I took a drink. Noah gave me a sharp look that said I needed to shut my mouth. So there were some things that are still meant only for the few. His torturing was obviously not something his pack mates knew about. I wondered what they would think of their beloved alpha then.

Dane threw back his head and let out a boisterous laugh, causing a couple of pack members to look in our direction. I turned my head, with a look of confusion. He gave me a hearty clap on my back while looking at Noah. "A woman with a sense of humor! The Goddess did bless you ten times over."

16

Scarlett

Alpha Randall's lands were set up like a military fortress. The smell of blood hung fresh in the air as we unloaded from the cars. Noah tossed a look in Dane's direction who, in turn, moved closer to me. Obviously, it was some silent order of protection detail. Just more alpha male bullshit as far as I was concerned.

I gave him a look, and he returned it with a toothy smile. "You know the deal. Gotta do what the alpha says."

I rolled my eyes, following after Noah. "Yeah, I know the deal." I grumbled under my breath as I sped up my steps, so there was some breathing space between us. I didn't need to be protected, and I was more than willing to make that point if Noah didn't get his head out of his ass. A large group of males stood to greet the incoming members, bowing their heads respectfully toward Noah as he approached them.

There were different scents of visiting pack members. They scattered about, greeting one another. There were families reuniting after time spent apart. There was a feeling of happiness in the air, but there was a twisting in my stomach. My wolf was uneasy, and I couldn't explain the reason for it. All I knew was that she hadn't led me astray yet. I was going to keep myself alert, nevertheless.

A male sniffed at me as I passed by, pushing past my comfort bubble. My wolf lunged toward the surface with a fluidness that surprised even me. My head twisted on my shoulder, and I snapped my teeth inches from his face. He flinched slightly but didn't retreat as I expect him too. He was clearly a young male looking to prove himself in front of the other males, only he had picked the wrong person to do that with.

My chest puffed up more as a threatening snarl rumbled out of me. "Do you have a death wish?"

He flashed his own set of pearly white canines, more than happy to meet my challenge. Mating season was dangerous, and I was getting my first taste of it. I could feel that we had a small crowd building around us.

Luckily for him, Dane pushed his way through. He pulled the young guy back by the collar. "This one has already been claimed, but you're welcome to fight for rights to her if you want. Alpha Noah is right over there." He nodded his head toward Noah who stood watching the scene from afar, arms crossed over his chest.

He quickly backed down, lowering his eyes to the ground in submission. I couldn't imagine many males wanting to challenge Noah. He radiated a dominance that was not easily matched. My wolf, however, felt unsatisfied with the outcome. She wanted to sink her teeth into some flesh. She hadn't left a single mark on her challenger. I pushed back against her, wrestling her back into the cage of my mind.

Dane released the young man, who scurried off quickly, easing his way into the current of bodies.

"I had it handled." I growled in annoyance as I walked away from him. People in the crowd stepped out of my way as casually as they could. I knew my wolf was too close to the surface. Her dominance was leaking out into the world around her.

Dane caught up to me easily. "Killing someone isn't handling it. That's just making more problems."

"I wouldn't kill him," I mumbled.

He gave me a look that said he didn't believe me. I turned my face to hide my dark grin. "Maybe seriously maimed, but not killed."

"Right..." he said in mock agreement as he ushered me to Noah, who stood proudly in front of another alpha male.

"That's Alpha Randall," Dane whispered to me under his breath. I let my gaze turn more scrutinizing. He was much older, probably closer to my father's age if only he was still alive. He was definitely past his prime. He had gray hair spotting his temples. He still seemed to be in fairly good shape, but he might find himself in trouble in a contest with a younger alpha. His face was pulled together in a deep scowl of condemnation. He obviously thought highly of himself, more so than he probably should have.

My gaze shifted to the tall female who stood behind him. Her shoulders were hunched forward, and her eyes were focused on the ground. She looked unassuming at first glance, another weak female, but from the tension in her muscles, I could see she was pretending to be less. She was dampening her true self for some unknown reason.

Dane must have noticed where I was looking. "That's his daughter."

"And his son? Is that the one next to her?" I nodded my head toward the younger male that stood beside her. He was clearly a warrior as his hair was kept shaved close to his head plus a scar running up from one eyebrow to the top of his forehead. He held a firm pose of dominance, one that rivaled the alpha.

"Alpha Randall has only one offspring." He pointed at the male "That is Thorton, their newly appointed captain who seems to be doing quite well for himself by the look of things."

He guided me to Noah's side, making sure that I was squeezed between the two of them. The alpha regarded the two of us with a narrowed gaze, looking as if he was put off by our appearance. Noah placed his hand on the small of my back, the heat of his palm burning through the thin cotton shirt I had thrown on. I pressed my tongue to my teeth to keep myself from snapping at him to stop touching me. I also tried my hardest to ignore the urge to incline my body in his direction. The pull of our bond made my body long for more of his touch.

"Alpha Randall, you've already have met my beta." Dane bowed his head respectfully.

Noah stepped closer to me, his scent sinking into my skin in a soft claim. He obviously wanted to keep the other males away after what had happened earlier. "This is Scarlett, my mate." He seemed to struggle with the last word, but he got it past tight lips. All eyes seemed to focus on me. I could almost taste the scrutiny in the air. My wolf paced back and forth in my mind with her chest puffed up proudly. She wanted to prove to everyone how worthy she was of her position and title

"Interesting choice to make after I offered you my daughter as a replacement luna. This female looks sturdy enough, I suppose. What's her breed?" I tried to keep my mouth from dropping open with surprise at his words.

Noah didn't seem to react though I noted the slight tensing of his muscles. "And I appreciated the offer. Christa is a beautiful woman with, I'm sure, many admirable qualities that would make her a great luna, but she has a true mate out there, and I'm not him." He sent a smile at the tall blonde, and I had to keep myself from growling as jealousy ripped through me.

"As for her breed—"

I stepped in, unable to hold my tongue. "I don't know anything about breeds, but I do come from a Northern pack, Alpha, if that's what you mean." My voice dripped with irritation.

Alpha Randall clicked his tongue at the roof of his mouth. "The Northern packs produce strong warriors, but most of their wolves are much too wild. They have a hard time taming the beast within, and the possibility of madness runs deep with them. The Northern pack women... Well, I can say I don't envy you, my friend," Alpha Randall told Noah while casting a small disapproving look in my direction. My wolf flattened her ears and flashed her teeth. She was more than willing to show him how wild and untamable she could be.

All the while, Noah was as stiff as a statue, doing his best to keep his own beast in check. "That might be true, but I've always enjoyed a good challenge. I've tamed much larger beasts." Randall let out a hearty laugh, losing his tense form and scowl as he clapped Noah on the back. It was something that he allowed, but from the darkening color of his eyes, his wolf did not appreciate the contact.

"Come, let's talk in my office. The other alphas are here already." He motioned for Noah to follow him into the dreary-looking house.

"Christa, why don't you show Noah's mate to their room. Let her clean up before the festivities. I'm sure Noah will want her looking proper when she stands beside him at the opening ceremony." His comment had me gritting my teeth. I took a small step forward, thinking about how easy it would be to attack him with his back turned to me. An alpha outside of his prime against a young luna would be a fair match. A hand grabbed hold of my arm in a firm but gentle grip. I swallowed a growl as I turned my gaze to see the tall female. Her blonde hair was swept up into a neat bun at the nape of her neck. It was the fire that burned in her eyes and the dominance that leaked out from her touch that made my wolf settle down instantly.

Everything became clear to me. She was the alpha's heir, a wolf much stronger than my own even in her most fury driven state. Female alphas weren't unheard of, but they weren't extremely common either. In days past, when most packs still followed the Old ways, they were often killed at birth or cast out into the wilderness to test the validity of their inheritance. If they survived and returned, they could claim what was always rightfully theirs. In a world that praised and lived dutifully under the guidance of the Goddess, the men still often believed themselves more than their female counterparts.

She gave me a sly smile. "If you'll please follow me, Luna," she said, letting go of my arm.

Noah leaned in closer to me, pressing his lips to my forehead. We were both stiff as statues as tingles rushed through us at the touch. "Behave yourself. I'll come for you before the ceremony." I clenched my hands at my sides as he whispered the words against my ear. I knew this was only a show.

Noah lingered a moment longer than necessary before he stepped back and turned away from me. He entered the house without saying anything more. Dane winked at me before he followed after Noah.

17

Noah

The room is full of the overbearing stench of alphas. My wolf was pacing uncomfortably under my skin, itching to be released from the cage of my flesh. It has been too long since I gave him the opportunity to hunt and satisfy his hunger, a mistake on my part. Harvey greeted me with a small nod of his head as I made my way across the room to take the empty seat next to him. "Where's Knox? I thought you'd be showing him the ropes before you pass the torch."

Harvey crossed his arms over his chest. "He's running a little late. He should be here by the opening ceremony. There was a situation he needed to handle first." The implication of his words was not lost on me, but now was not the right time to discuss our private matters.

Randall took his spot between his trusted friends. Most of the alphas in this room have been around a lot longer than me and have earned the respect of others in the room. Still, I could easily stamp them out if I wanted. They knew this as well, which was why they never turned their noses up in my presence.

Randall cleared his throat. "Let's get down to business, gentlemen. I don't want to keep the masses waiting any longer. Any matters that need to be addressed will be dealt with now. The floor is open." The air in the room became tenser. Everyone was trying to figure out who would be the first to speak. It was always a power trip for alphas no matter the occasion. It was a surprise any of them ever accomplished anything.

For the next hour, I sat silently and listened to them gripe to one another about land and power, who had it and who wanted it. They wanted to complain about things that mattered so little, especially when there were real matters that needed our attention, things that they would happily ignore if I gave them the choice. They would be wading through the blood of their dead pack mates if it wasn't for me keeping the rogues back from their gates. They really had no idea, these good ol' boys, just how much danger they were in.

When I couldn't handle anymore mindless bickering, I chose to interrupt. "We found another rogue that had wandered onto my lands, a young kid. He tried to take out one of my own. He was too far gone to be brought back. He had to be put down." I turned my gaze toward Alpha Randal. "Before he died, he told us he had been taken from your pack, Alpha." I watched as his face pulled into a deep scowl, his eyes a deep obsidian as his wolf pushed at him.

"Well, he must have lied! You know how rogues are, Noah, half mad with the hunger." He sneered, eyes looking around the room to gauge the faces of his friends. He was hoping they didn't believe the words I was saying. It would make him look weak.

I remained calm as I crossed my arms over my chest. "I've dealt with a lot of rogues in my life, Alpha. They might be mad, but that doesn't mean that they don't speak truth. If it's evidence that you need, I could send someone to fetch his head for you. It doesn't matter to me." That seemed to make him tense up further. I knew I was poking at the old wolf. Honestly, I was hoping I would finally get him to see reason and make him lend us his warriors in the incoming war. His warriors were renowned for being the best trained out there, which made his small pack a formidable ally to have.

"Are you trying to make a joke out of me?" He snarled in my direction, flashing his teeth in warning. Harvey uncrossed his arms, foot shifting slightly forward. He was ready to fight by my side if Randall decided to step out of his line.

I waited for a breath before responding. "I meant nothing by it. I am only trying to point out that you are not immune to the disease. You might want to think about weeding through your men because it's likely one of them is working against you. It only takes one of them to rot a pack from the inside out." We had seen it happen with several of the smaller packs, rogues infiltrating their numbers until there was mutiny and a sliver of what was left. I would hate to see it happen again, especially with a pack full of useful and trained warriors.

"You would know about that rot wouldn't you, Noah?" he questioned, not backing down. I may have poked at him too much. He moved closer. "How do we know that you aren't the one creating these rogues? Fabricating all these tales of woe, trying to win us over. You get us to give you our loyalty and men while secretly, you take everything for yourself." He tried to weave his assumptions into logical thoughts to get the other alphas to doubt me.

The beast in me turned its attention toward the alpha who was brave enough to step up to him. I was sure that the entire room could feel the change in the air. I quietly observed Randall. He may have been a challenge in the past, but time had affected his body and mind.

"I am not the enemy, Randall." I rose up from my seat, taking a step toward him as my arms slip to my side. My chest was puffed out. "I am the only one trying to save you from your own demise. The real enemy has already found its way into your flock. I have proof of that even if you don't want to acknowledge it. All I'm saying now is that I'm willing to help you if you are willing to help me. This is the last time I'm going to make an offer to you. Take it or don't, but you won't say another word against me. My patience only stretches so far."

The other alphas remained silent. They have already pledged their allegiance to me. Alpha Randall was the only one who continued to play games, trying to get me to give him more than simply the protection of my name and the guarantee that his pack would remain untouched when everything was said and done.

He took a step away from me before turning his back. The beast in me saw the act as disrespectful. You didn't turn your back on someone you perceived as a threat. You only did that to someone you had little to fear from. I narrowed my eyes, clenching my hands into tight fists at my side, to keep the beast in check. The damned fool had no idea what he was doing.

"I'll take my chances, Alpha Noah. Now, if there is nothing else to discuss." He waited for a beat when no one spoke. "I conclude this summit. I look forward to seeing you all at the opening ceremony tonight." The flow of bodies in the room shifted. Some chose to leave while others chose to stay and speak with one another. I was one of the first ones out of the room. Rage was burning deep in my chest. I had been so certain that I could get him to agree.

Dane was waiting for me as I exited. "I'm guessing from the look on your face that things didn't go well?" A growl of irritation rumbled out of my chest. I felt incapable of words at the moment.

Harvey called after me. "Noah." I stopped and turned my face in his direction, watching as he closed the gap between us. "Randall is a complete fool. He always has been as long as I've known him. Don't let it get to you, son. You've done everything you can."

I gritted my teeth, knowing he was coming from a good place. "I know."

He reached out and gave my shoulder a squeeze. I swallowed the urge to growl, the beast was far too agitated at the moment. It didn't matter that I knew I had done all I could, innocent and good people were going to die because of one man's pride. I could feel the storm clouds building up just out of sight. Something was coming... something that couldn't be stopped now.

"Father." I turned my head to see Knox standing in the distance, his green eyes practically glowing with scorn as they caught my gaze. He still had a lot of hatred in his heart toward me. He and Claire had been very close growing up, and he blamed me for not protecting her better.

As if sensing the tension between us, Harvey gave my shoulder another squeeze. "Don't worry. He'll come around once he gets through his grief. We all have our own ways of processing what happened. It's easier for him to blame you then accept the truth."

I gave him a small nod, watching as Harvey walked away to greet his son, the heir to his small empire. Knox gave me one more look before he turned, letting his father lead him away.

18

Scarlett

Christa walked quietly beside me, keeping her head low. I didn't even know if she realized she was doing it or if it was the years of training to make herself purposefully lower than she was. I could feel my irritation spiking at the thought of her suffering at the hands of idiot males, suffering as I had suffered. "You don't have to do that around me. I know who you are and what you are," I said.

She glanced in my direction, the corners of her lips lifting a bit. She raised a hand and pointed in the direction of a couple of males of in the distance. They looked like they had been out training, bodies covered in sweat and blood. "It's not for you that I am doing this. It's for them."

Her hand fell back to her side when they looked in our direction, her eyes lowering to the ground. "It's better that I let them think I'm not a challenge. It's an attack they would never see coming. It's my advantage over them. I'm the one with the high ground."

She used her body to guide our path into the opposite direction, away from the men and toward a couple of smaller housing units. "There is a time for everything, Luna. Right now is a time for patience. I've heard good things come to those who wait, and I've been waiting a long time."

She thought like a warrior. She was clearly someone who has been trained in the art of war. She was playing for the long haul, and she had her strategy all planned out. Christa had all the makings of a brilliant leader. She really was born to be an alpha.

Maybe her father had been right about the Northern packs. We lived in an untamed and wild place. We weren't brilliant strategists. There wasn't time for that. We played a game of survival not of politics.

I felt a little uncertain of myself as I looked around at the people we passed by. There were lots of different pack members from all over, moving in and out of the houses. They bowed their heads respectfully at us. They understand the need to respect the hierarchy even if they weren't from the same pack as us.

"Sorry, I'm just not used to all of these politics and customs. Things are a little different where I came from." I felt uncomfortable with all the eyes on me, but my wolf is basking in it. That was something that had never changed from when I was a young girl. I didn't like to be the center of attention. I was much happier blending into the crowd, but apparently, fate didn't care much about what I liked or didn't.

"I think different is good. Different is sometimes exactly what people need," she replied thoughtfully, and I found myself holding back the urge to smile.

"I think this thing between us could work out very well." I patted her arm, testing the limits of her wolf and her friendly nature. I wanted to know if that was real or forced because I could always use another ally. She gave me a look of amusement as if my words struck her in a funny way. She stopped us outside of one of the housing units. "This is where the other alphas and their mates are staying."

Whatever she was going to say next died on her lips as Delilah exited the building, turning around to finding me standing there. I felt surprised, but my eyes narrowed in suspicion. Her face showed her surprise for a moment before a cocky smirk spread over her lips. "Hello, *Luna*," she said in a mocking fashion as she walked toward the two of us.

I clenched my teeth together tightly yet kept myself as controlled as possible. "Hello," I said back, but it came out as a growl. Delilah flipped her hair over her shoulder and looked at Christa. "What's with Jolly, the green giant? Feeling the need for a bodyguard? Afraid someone might try to challenge you for your position?" Her eyes fluttered back to me. She clearly thought she should be the one leading alongside Noah.

Christa was looking toward Delilah with a nasty sneer on her face, but she remained quietly standing beside me. I was certain Delilah had no idea how outpowered she was at the moment.

"I'm not afraid. Anyone who wants to challenge me for the position is welcome to..." I said in a calm, even tone as I watched her eyes flicker with surprise for a moment. She was trying to rile me up, trying to make me afraid. I stepped in toward her. "I'd never back down from a good challenge... though whoever challenges me should be prepared to lose."

I watched her stiffen at my words, and I only continued to smile. "If I decide to have mercy and not eat the scraps of you that will be left when I'm done, you will have to show me the respect I deserve as your Luna." I twisted the words around on my tongue, spitting them out at her like knives.

She flashed me her teeth, her wolf rising to the challenge. "You're a prop. You've earned nothing!"

Christa leaned forward. "You remember what I said earlier about patience?"

My eyes remain focused on Delilah. "Yes."

"Now, is not the time for patience. Now is the time to make an example of this wolf," she whispered into my ear like a devil on my shoulder, giving my shoulder a firm squeeze before stepping back. Her actions spoke louder than her words. I had her blessing as an alpha, as a female, and as an ally.

I gave a toothy grin, my wolf salivating with her hunger to tear through flesh. "I am going to enjoy this."

A small group has gathered around us, unable to resist the urge to watch. Delilah and I were stripping out of our clothes in a hurry, not caring where they landed. She was the first one to shift, a large reddish-brown wolf standing in her place.

I jumped at her, smiling as my skin gave way to fur. My wolf snapped her teeth together in warning, only inches away from connecting with actual flesh. Delilah's wolf answered in kind. She wasn't going to back down. This only roused my wolf's frenzy for blood. My wolf wasted no time, going straight for a killing blow. Delilah's wolf moved forward a fraction of an inch, and teeth sunk into her shoulder.

Blood filled my wolf's mouth, and I know the real fight has begun.

They were both pushing their dominance, body crashing into each other over and over. I knew my wolf was playing with her prey, tiring her out before she finished with the game. She was proving a point to everyone, solidifying her position beyond the claim of her mate.

Delilah's wolf was huffing and puffing, leaving herself open for more attacks. My wolf decided she had enough with the game, latching onto her challenger's throat and dragging her down to the ground. She struggled, trying to dig her claws into the soft parts of my wolf, but she was already prepared to bleed for her cause. She would rather die than give up.

Delilah's wolf finally conceded, falling still in submission. My wolf bit down harder. She was going to leave her mark on this female. She was going to make her an example to anyone else who dared to challenge our position again.

When she was satisfied, she released her grip. Delilah shifted back into her human form, still lying prone before my wolf. She looked defeated, but there was still a fire of hatred burning in her eyes. My wolf snapped at her face, and she flinched, lowering her gaze.

My wolf strutted around her defeated challenger, looking on to the crowd that had gathered, waiting for any more challengers, but none came.

I pulled back on the reigns, and her fur gave way to my flesh once more. I stood in the center of the circle proudly. Christa stood in the back with a sly smile on her lips. Beside her, Noah and Dane stood.

I wondered how long he had been there and if he had been watching the entire time. His eyes were drinking me in as he moved through the crowd. I felt my muscles tense up as he drew closer. If he tried to correct me, I would not be able to control my reaction or my tongue.

He slipped off his shirt and held it out to me. I reached out and took it, quickly covering myself

He glanced down at the defeated female at my feet for a moment before reaching down and pulling her off the ground roughly by her arm. He flashed his teeth at her when she peered up at him from under her curtain of hair. She cowered before him, a soft whimper falling from her lips as she turned her head to expose her neck in a sign of submission.

"You will remember your place in the future Delilah," he warned her.

"Sorry," she mumbled as he released her.

He turned his icy gaze in my direction. "I told you to behave yourself, Scarlett. Why is it so hard for you to do what I say? Until you are an actual member of my pack, until our pack brand is somewhere on your skin, attacking anyone could be seen as an outright act of war. If you value your life at all, you will mind yourself while you are just a guest."

I gave him a hardened glare, and for a moment, my wolf rose toward the surface, her anger turned toward him. As if sensing this, he let out a low rumbling growl that had her rethinking the outcome of that choice. I noticed the way Delilah puffed up a little out of the corner of my eye. I turned my attention toward her to find a smug smirk playing on her lips.

I swung my gaze back to Noah, our eyes meeting in a silent battle of wills. "I guess I better go clean this blood off me. I would hate to make you look bad at the opening ceremony and prove Alpha Randall right about Northerners being a bunch of barbarians." I turned my back to him and walked away.

I let them all have my back. It was a meaningful show that I didn't see any of them as a challenge. My wolf and I had proven ourselves and would happily do so again.

19

Christa

I approached Noah slowly, the aura seeping out of him was overwhelming and intoxicating. He had so much power for one wolf. He watched as Scarlett disappeared inside the house, leaving the chaos of her battle behind her, much like a storm that came and went. He turned his head, his lips pulled up slightly in a sneer. His wolf recognized the threat I presented at his back. I held up a hand and gave him a small smile that I hoped would soothe his beast's ruffled fur.

It took a moment for him to recognize who I was. Once he did, I watched his expression soften. "Christa." He gave a slight incline of his head to greet me.

I tilted my head as I peered past him to the front door. "Alpha Noah, you've chosen well by taking the little Northerner as your Luna. With some time and training, she will do well by you and your pack."

He snorted. "I didn't choose this. If I had a say in the matter, Claire would still be the one beside me. No, this was all the Goddess' doing."

I felt my lips turn down at the words. I couldn't even begin to imagine what suffering he went through at the death of his mate. Everyone had heard the rumors about what happened to her, and that was why the South had united behind him, fearing the same might happen to them if they didn't. Well, everyone but Father, *the stubborn fool.*

"Well, the Goddess works in mysterious ways, Alpha. Who knows her true mind? No wolf that I've yet to meet. We are all pawns in her greater schemes. We just have to trust that she leads us well," I replied.

He let out a humorless chuckle, turning his face so that he was looking directly at me. "Your mother was from an Eastern pack, wasn't she? A priestess of the moon?"

My cheeks rushed with heat. "She was." Though the truth was, she was still serving them as their holy mother. She hadn't died in childbirth as father led everyone to believe. Father had never claimed her completely. He had only kept her long enough to put a pup in her belly. When she had me, and I turned out to be a girl, he sent us away. We went back to the east where she raised me until my mother realized I had the alpha instincts. After that, she brought me back with a simple message—that he raise me or she would tell everyone what he had done.

"Her family has taught you well." He forced a smile. "But I don't need to know the Goddess' mind. I'm but a tool of righteous vengeance, and where she leads me, none should go."

He looked past me to his beta, giving a nod of his head. "If you'll excuse me."

He walked away from me, heading into the house after his mate. I stood amongst the thinning crowd for a moment before taking my own leave. I headed to the woods, wanting a moment to myself away from all the madness of the Trials.

In a few hours it would be the opening ceremony, and for a week, I would be forced to play my weak female role more than usual. I needed time for myself, and so did my wolf.

I followed the most deserted path toward the area of father's territory that was less secure. I wasn't concerned about anyone attacking me. They would be dead before they even had a chance to break skin. I stripped quickly, folding my clothes and leaving them under some foliage.

The shift was painful. It always was for me whenever I had gone too long in one form or the other. I bore the burning and breaking. The pain made me stronger. When my wolf was free, I let her take control. I hung back in my consciousness, letting her lead us wherever she wanted to go.

She ran far and hard. There wasn't any game for her to hunt, but she still played with birds that landed on the ground, stalking them and sending them flying high into the trees howling with excitement. It had been a long time since she was this happy.

I felt something stalking us through the shadows, but my wolf didn't seem to be concerned with it. I, however, felt differently and took back control of my body. I led us toward the nearby river where I could rinse myself clear of my alpha scent and sweat.

I stood alone in the river, letting the water wash away the grime from my skin. Father's rule was that I had to be at the edge of his territory if I wanted to let my wolf lose. He wore me like his shame, and perhaps, I was meant to be just that. Maybe I was the Goddess' punishment for not taking his mate the way he was meant to. The wind rustled the leaves overhead, and my wolf picked up the scent of something else in the air, an intruder to her space.

I spun around quickly with lips pulled up. I flashed my canines in warning as my eyes caught a pair of vivid green ones.

My heart became still in my chest. My wolf knew who this person was to us. I didn't hide myself in shame. I had done that enough in my life. I could never hide from the person whom the Goddess had tied my soul to. I let my eyes have their fill of him as I memorized all the lines of his face.

He was tall and sturdy. He had wide shoulders and powerful looking legs. His hair was the color of burning sunsets and just long enough that the breeze rustled it. He was an alpha male. It was easy to see from the way he carried himself as he took steady steps toward the water's edge. There was a mischievous light in his eyes as he squatted down, touching the edge of the water with his fingertips.

I tilted my head, letting my hair fall over my shoulder. "Were you following me?"

"I smelled something interesting. I didn't know I was following you per se." He reached up and scratched the back of his neck as if he felt a bit shy or uncomfortable. I lifted my brows at his explanation, trying to suppress the urge to laugh at him.

I waded closer to him. "Why were you wandering around in the woods, then? Other than to creep on unsuspecting females..." I couldn't help my desire to tease him a bit. My spirit felt light for the first time in a very long time, and my wolf wasn't lost in her usual anger.

His face turned red. "I wasn't creeping on anyone."

"Of course, you weren't," I said with a smirk, rising up out of the water. His eyes followed my movements.

"You still didn't answer my question, though."

He swallowed hard, unable to hide the way his eyes brightened with desire as he took in the sight of my body. I knew I had nothing to be ashamed of. He forced his gaze toward the sky, and I smiled to myself. I was glad to know that he had respect for females, even if the female, in theory, belonged to him.

"I was making sure that the boundaries were as secure as they claimed they were simply out of my own curiosity." He peeked in my direction, greens eyes holding mine, as I wrung out the wetness from my hair. I wasn't sure if he was lying, but I knew he wasn't simply curious about Father's boundaries. His answer was too vague to tell what was truth and what was something else. I didn't care much if he was plotting against Father, though. I would happily point out his weaknesses if he asked me.

"I can assure you that Alpha takes the protection of his territory seriously. The threat level is minimal. You can report that back to whoever sent you out here." His brow furrowed a bit at my words, and I knew for sure that it had something to do with Father. This young alpha male must be an ally of Noah's.

He took a step closer. "You are Alpha Randall's daughter?"

I lifted a brow. "Does it change anything if I am?"

He tilted his head in mock thoughtfulness before meeting my gaze again. "Nope, just means it'll be easier for me to find you tonight."

I found that I didn't want to think of not being in his presence, but at the same time, I felt a fluttering in my stomach at the promise of seeing him again. I tried to suppress my smile, not wanting to seem too eager. "I should get back before Alpha sends someone looking for me."

He didn't try to stop me and only gave me a small smile before stepping back to give me the space I needed to go. As I passed him, he reached out toward me. His fingertips brushed the ends of my hair. "I'll find you again."

I peered over my shoulder at him. He tapped his finger on his nose. "I'll remember that scent until the day I die." My cheeks heated at his words.

I turned my back to him. It was time to go back to pretending. "See you around."

"Knox," he called his name out to me, and I smiled to myself.

"See you around, Knox." The name sounded perfect on my lips. Maybe the time for patience was over. Maybe the Goddess was finally rewarding me for my steadfast devotion to her plan for my life.

20

Scarlett

I was coming out of the shower when Noah entered our shared room, something we were going to have to discuss because I refused to share a bed with him. That was simply not going to work for me at all.

I didn't hide my body as I crossed the room to gather the clothes that Nadia had helped me to pack before coming here. She gave me some of her nicer outfits to borrow.

I noticed the way Noah's eyes followed the droplets of water as they rolled down my body and dropped to the floor. A soft rumble came from deep in his chest, and I knew the beast inside him hungered for me as any mate and healthy male would. My own wolf would have been happy to lift her tail for him. Personally, I didn't want any part of that. I wasn't looking to have my soul broken by another alpha male.

"Is there something you needed, Noah?" I questioned as I slipped a thin cotton dress up my legs and the tiny straps onto my shoulders. It was a little loose in the chest. I still have very little to offer in the breast department which was disappointing. I watched as he sat himself down on the edge of the bed, facing me. His legs were spread apart, and I found myself glancing at the apex of his thighs. He had such a powerful body, and his scent was so much stronger than usual. Everything seemed to push us toward each other despite our misgivings about the match.

"Alpha Randall is not giving me the support from his pack," he spoke his mind, sharing his frustrations with me like a true confidant. This surprised me, and I was sure that shock was written on my face. I didn't expect him to reach out toward me like he actually cared what I thought about him or what his pack did. He was such an enigma at times that I wasn't sure if I would ever understand what was going on inside his head.

I turned my back to him, hiding my face. I swept my wet hair over my shoulder. "Help me with this zipper? It's a bit tricky." I would let him wait a moment before I would share my thoughts with him.

I heard the creaking of the bed as he stood up. His footsteps were heavy as he came to stand behind me. His fingertips glided over the bare skin of my back, causing goosebumps to rise to the surface. He slowly drew up the zipper. I knew that I was tempting him, but he deserved some suffering after what he had put me through over the past couple of weeks.

"What do you want me to do about that, Noah? You have more than enough men for your war, don't you think?" I stepped away from him, heading back into the bathroom to fix my hair.

He followed close on my heels. "Numbers won't matter if none of them know how to fight against the rogues. We need his warriors, Scarlett. Most, if not all of them, have been training since they were young pups in their war forms as well as in their skin. I don't have the time or patience to train all the men from the other packs."

I met his gaze through the mirror as I braided my hair. "Then perhaps you need to think of a new strategy. Why not find one warrior willing to help you teach the other packs? Maybe give up some of your lands to convince him."

"You want me to give that jackal some of my land? He hasn't earned it, nor would he know what to do with it." His alpha instincts rose to the surface. I knew that for any alpha, land meant power, and to give even an inch was a huge deal, but sometimes it was necessary.

The pack, then us. The mantra that had ruined my world suddenly seemed to make a little more sense to me, and I hated that.

I rolled my eyes as I spun around to face him. "What is more important to you? Your land or justice for your dead mate?" I knew I had him trapped with my words. It was cruel, but it was necessary evil needed to help him see things more clearly. I did my best to keep my expression blank.

He rubbed his hand over his chin, playing with the couple days growth that had taken up residence on his face. "Fine. I see your point, but he would try to cheat me if I went to him with this deal. He would give me his worst warrior."

That I could believe. I had only just met Alpha Randall, but he didn't strike me as an honorable man.

I focused my eyes on his, feeling for the first time since we met like he was looking at me as his equal and was ready to heed my advice. "Then take what he has already offered you." Noah's eyebrows drew together in a look of slight confusion over my words. I let out a small breath. "Make a trade, some of your land for his daughter."

"His daughter? What the hell am I supposed to do with another female?" He seemed slightly annoyed by my suggestion, running his hands through his hair. I came to stand closer to him. I reached out and pressed my hand to his chest. I gritted my teeth against the pull of our bond. The growing threat of my heat was becoming a slight concern in the back of my mind.

His eyes fell to where my hand rested, but he didn't step away. I knew I had all of his attention. "She has been raised by him. She's his only child... his heir even if he doesn't recognize her as such. She has spent her days in his shadow, watching as he trained his warriors. She'll know the techniques. She could be a great asset to you." I could tell that I had the wheels in his mind turning.

"And when Alpha Randall returns to the Goddess, if you treat his daughter well, I'm sure Christa will be more than willing to negotiate the return of the land you gave to her father to secure her into your care." I was more than certain this would be true. Christa probably would be willing to do a lot more than that if she could get her freedom which I was also trying to secure. Killing two birds with one stone.

He stepped closer to me. "You are as clever as you are brave. Your other mate truly was a fool to reject you, Scarlett."

I held his gaze for a silent moment. "All men are fools. I don't expect much."

I stepped away from him, letting my hands fall to my sides. "Also, if you think your pretty words will win you a spot on the bed beside me tonight, you thought wrong. You can find yourself a comfortable spot on the rug to lie down because the bed is my territory." I didn't wait for his response before I made my way around him and out of the bathroom. I slipped my feet into a pair of sandals, looking as put together as I could.

I could feel his eyes on my back, but he said nothing.

"I'll wait for you outside."

I walked silently next to Noah. His hand was resting on the small of my back, guiding me through the gathering crowd that was headed toward the opening ceremony.

I tried my best to ignore the flames that were licking over my skin from the small contact of our bodies, but it was hard. I clenched my hands into fists, poking my nails into my palms in hopes of using the dull pain to distract myself from his touch and intoxicating scent.

"I think I can walk by myself," I muttered under my breath when I couldn't take anymore. When I tried to step away from him to create more space to breathe, he pinched the material of my dress, keeping me from going away from him. A warning growl rumbled out of my chest, which he answered in kind.

"You will stay by me where I can keep an eye on you. This is may be a friendly gathering, but that doesn't mean I trust everyone here," he spoke to me in a low voice, words meant only for me to hear. I watched as his eyes scan the flow of the crowd. No one got in his way. They made sure a small path was always clear for us.

I glanced around at all the excited faces. "What do you think is going to happen to me, Noah?" I leaned away from him, trying to get as much space as he was willing to allow me at the moment. "I'm pretty sure I am more of a threat to them than any of them are to me."

He gave me a look that said he had more to say on the matter, but before he could form a response, Dane appeared out of the crowd and came to stand on the other side of me. "Noah," he greeted.

Dane turned his playful smile my way. "Scarlett. You look really nice." His eyes worked down the length of me. I felt Noah press his hand harder into my back as if he needed to stake his claim more firmly, the only outward sign of his rising irritation.

Dane leaned in closer to me, close enough that our cheeks almost touched. "That's an interesting perfume you're wearing." He breathed in my scent. I knew Dane was trying to poke at the beast on the other side of me, trying to get under his skin and break through his stubborn walls.

Noah glanced in his direction, flashing his teeth in agitation. "Don't push it." The words sounded more guttural than human. a good sign that Dane was accomplishing what he was trying to do. Noah sped up his steps, leaving Dane to bring up the tail as his laughter filled the air around us. I casted a dirty look over my shoulder. His harmless flirting was not wanted nor needed at the moment.

The clearing was set up with a large tent full of tables and food. In the center, there was a large pyre of burning wood, the smoke funneling upward through the trees. It was quite the sight to see, so many people gathered together in one place, the differences of packs and land boundaries set aside. If only it was always so simple, but our inherent nature made it impossible for things like this to last. Noah moved us toward the edge of the tent.

I spotted the familiar face of Alpha Harvey who was standing next to a younger-looking version of himself. The only difference was that his hair is red like his mother's.

Harvey greeted Noah with a pat on his shoulder. "Son." His eyes roamed to me, and he gave a small bow of his head. "Luna Scarlett, good to see you again." I bowed my head back but kept my lips sealed tight. I didn't really feel as though the title was necessary considering Noah didn't treat me as such.

"Knox," Noah greeted the tall red-headed male. He gave Noah a strong look of aggression, locking up his jaw tight. I felt a wave of confusion over the response. Clearly, there was some kind of bad blood between him and this young alpha. Harvey let out a small growl in his heir's direction. The tension between everyone was palpable.

Slowly, Knox bowed his head, his body stiff. "Noah."

As if she sensed the awkward tension, Rose appeared out of the crowd, approaching our small group with a smile. She squeezed in between the men and embraced me, pressing her cheek to mine. She held me firmly. "It's good to see you again." She pulled back but placed her hands on my shoulders as she took me in. "You're looking healthier. Noah must be taking better care of you." She gave me a wink.

I gave her a tight-lipped smile but said nothing. I didn't want to make her think there was something happening between Noah and me. She embraced Noah next, giving him her cheek. My wolf is not happy that another female was putting their scent on his skin. Mated or not, she doesn't feel a difference. I pushed the feeling back because I knew the difference. I knew that Rose was happily mated and was no threat to me.

As Rose pulled away, a smaller female charged out of the crowd, her red hair flowing behind her. "Noah!" She called out to him with childish excitement, getting his attention just as she launched herself into his arms.

My wolf reared her head. Her claws poked into the soft flesh of my palms. Noah glanced in my direction over the girl's shoulder as if sensing the danger she was currently in. He gave a subtle shake of his head. His eyes spoke the word 'behave' loud and clear.

He set her back down on her feet. She pulled back, glancing in my direction with curiosity, not even realizing how close to danger she was moments ago. Noah cleared his throat. "Clarissa, this is Scarlett."

Her eyes widened with recognition at the sound of my name. She stepped forward embracing me. Noah's scent still lingered on her. "I've heard so much about you from my parents. You're a lot smaller than I thought you'd be," she joked as she pulled back. There was a bright smile on her lips.

As I look at the lot of them, it didn't take long for me to piece together that this was his mate's entire family. I gave them a small smile. "Is there anyone else I should know about? Any more of your family I've yet to meet?" Noah looked as uncomfortable as I felt. Rose and Clarissa laughed, taking my question as a joke.

At this moment, the world felt at peace. Everyone was enjoying each other's company. The dangers of the past and fears of the future didn't exist. Yet, at the back of my mind, there was an unsettling feeling. I couldn't tell if it belonged to me or if it belonged to Noah. Our bond tangled together our emotions more these days thanks to the mark on my neck.

It was the familiar yet horrible howling sound that echoed over the sound of the gathering that made my stomach clench up with dread. My eyes tore to the tree line just as rogues in varying sizes and conditions ripped into the clearing. They were destroying everything and everyone in their path.

Chaos broke out around us as people began to flee in every direction, trying to escape the warpath of the hungry rogues. The terrified screams of females and desperate shouts from warriors and alphas as they tried to protect their pack mates drifted around me like the crescendo of a thunderstorm. My thoughts were scattering and breaking apart as I was completely absorbed in the mayhem.

It reminded me of the nightmare. It was surreal. Noah grabbed my hand, pulling me away from the chaos.

He shook me out of my haze. "Move! Now!" he commanded to everyone. We were all moving together as a small group with the males barricading us females into the center to protect us.

I felt a small hand grab mine, and I turned my gaze to see Clarissa clinging to my hand. Her mother was two steps in front of us. My wolf wanted me to let her loose. She wanted to get her teeth into something. I didn't share her sentiment, however. Standing up to one rogue was fine, a hundred of them was a completely different thing.

The men got us to the tree line safely, but it seemed like the rogues are coming from every direction. I watched as a girl tried to flee from one rogue, shifting into her wolf, only to be met by another rogue on the other side. I watched in horror as it ripped into her throat, spilling her blood into the earth. Noah turned to me with the dark eyes of his wolf. "Keep moving. Stay with Rose and Clarissa."

I felt the urge to reach out to him. Suddenly, the thought of being separated with him felt wrong. He reached up and grabbed my face in his hands. "Do you understand?"

I nodded my head. "Yes."

He released me, turning his gaze to the others. "Let's go."

Harvey gave Rose a quick kiss before they disappeared back into the chaos. I had never seen anything like this before. I didn't know how to process it or if I could. I simply turned my back and started moving again. My feet carried me deeper into the woods and away from the madness happening around us.

Rose was right beside me with Clarissa holding tightly to her hand. She might only be a couple years younger than me, but at this moment, she seemed like a lost pup. I could hear the sound of howls and screaming, but I tried to focus on the sound of my own breathing. The need to survive helped me keep my composure.

The shift in the air came on swiftly, causing the hairs on the back of my neck to stand on end. A rogue charged out of the shadows at us, tackling Clarissa to the ground and ripping her free from her mother's grip. Her shriek of terror filled the night and pierced my eardrums. It was trying to drag her back into the darkness to finish her off. Clarissa clawed at the loose dirt, trying to catch anything to grab onto.

A flash of gray came from the trees, ripping the rogue off the helpless Clarissa. Rose rushed quickly to her daughter, pulling her off the ground and tucking her behind her back protectively. My eyes were trained on the large gray wolf as it tore into the rogue, teeth scraping against bone. It didn't stop until the beast was nothing but tattered pieces of meat and fur.

The wolf turned toward us, blood dripping from its fur. I flashed my teeth in warning. My wolf could only see threats at the moment. I watched closely as gray coat gave way to skin. Christa stood before us breathing heavily. Her body was riddled with small wounds that were already healing. "Come on! Follow me." She moved past us into the shadows of the trees. I didn't wait to be told again. I followed after her, even surer of my choice that she would be a great asset to Noah's war if we survived the night.

21

Noah

There was chaos in every direction. The beast inside me was chomping for release. I was being torn between my instincts to protect my pack as I swore to do as their alpha and my instincts to chase after Scarlett to keep her safe from the danger.

The chaos left me with little room to waver as I watched a rogue go for a fleeing female. It had its teeth buried deep in her leg as it was dragging her across the bloodied earth. She screamed, her fingers digging into the ground. The beast took control, launching me forward, my skin giving way to fur.

It caught the rogue by his throat, severing an artery. Its blood seeped into our mouth and rained down on the helpless female below. My beast bit harder, not letting up, until it heard the snapping of bone, and its prey fell limp.

The female trembled as she peered up in deep fear. The beast could smell the fear dripping out of her pores. It found the sour stench annoying, but her eyes were glassy moss like my Claire's had been. The beast rumbled out a growl at the thought of our dead mate. He didn't like it when I thought about her. He forced images of a small, red-haired beauty with eyes like fire into our mind.

"Get out of here! Now!" Dane screamed to her, and that seemed to break through her trance. She scrambled off the ground, dragging her bad leg as she tried to run as quickly as her body could go. She followed others as they fled into the woods, following the instructions of the warriors leading them.

Dane met the beast's gaze for a minute before heading back into the thick of the chaos, shifting into his own wolf. He was one of the few ones who knew how close to the edge of sanity I sat. Sometimes, I thought he was waiting for me to snap and finally lose control of the beast that Claire had helped tame.

My thoughts turned quickly as the beast asserted his presence, focusing on the task of eliminating the threat. It was a bloody mess, a massacre on a whole new scale.

In the end, we stood victorious with most of the rogues dead or fleeing. The victory didn't feel like much of a victory as my eyes took in the sea of dead. Females, children, and young warriors, all lost.

The sound of yelling caught my attention, and I turned toward the commotion as Dane and the others approached.

Thorton came at his Alpha, knocking their chests together. "If you had listened to Alpha Noah, this could have been prevented. All of these people died because of your pride. You're a fool. You're no longer fit to bear the title of alpha."

Randall puffed out his chest, growling. "Step down, Thorton."

Thorton snarled. "No, you step down." A challenge had been issued, one that no alpha of his position would have been able to ignore. The rest of us watched as they shifted into their wolves, clashing together.

"This is madness. Now is not the time for this bullshit." Knox stepped forward, intent on breaking it up, but his father held out his arm, stopping him in his tracks. He turned his gaze toward Harvey in confusion.

"Let them have each other's throats, son. It's not like they can make matters any worse than they already are. If we're lucky, things may even turn in our favor if Alpha Randall loses."

Dane clicked his tongue off the roof of his mouth. "Ever the strategist." He seemed to agree with Knox about the timing of this challenge.

Harvey glanced in his direction with a dark gaze. "Someone has to be."

"We'll see," was all I said as I watched the two wolves tear into each other. When one would get the upper hand for a moment, the other would turn the tides. The tension in the pack grew, the more the two fought.

Alpha Randall began to show signs of fatigue, the small wounds he got from the fight with rogues becoming more serious. Thorton was tiring the old alpha out, coming up close and fast before backing away. He was making him work harder than he had the strength for. All of us understood that it would take a miracle from the Goddess above for him to win, but still, he fought until he was sagging into the dirt and panting hard.

There was no other option but death for the defeated alpha. Thorton's wolf went for the kill with swift precision. Teeth tore through meat and flesh, severing his spine. He continued to rip into him until his head came loose. The new alpha dropped his trophy, throwing his head back as he howled in victory.

There was silence among the remaining warriors of the pack. Then one by one, they knelt down, stretching out their necks in acknowledgment and submission to their new alpha. There was no time to mourn what has happened. Randall would become just another name to add to the list of those that had been lost.

Thorton approached them one at a time, waiting for any challengers, but none came. His wolf released control, and he became a man once more.

I was the first to separate from the crowd, approaching him slowly. He stood up a bit straighter as I came to stand before him, making sure there was a fair amount of space between us. My eyes fell on the head of the previous leader. I warned him that there would be consequences. This was how it was, this was how things were done between us. It was kill or be killed.

I lifted my gaze to meet Thorton's. "I hope you will learn from Randall's mistakes and be wiser with the power you've been given." I reached out my hand. This would be my last offer to this pack. Either they had seen the light or they would fade into the darkness.

Thorton narrowed his eyes into a focused gaze. "Alpha Noah, I know you want me to give you my word that we will help your war, but I can't. I need my men here to help rebuild and protect whatever is left of our pack." I could feel the tightening of my muscles. The beast was still hungry for violence. He was never quite satisfied.

I clenched my hands into tight fists. "You're making a mistake. You will have nothing left of you don't—"

Thorton stepped up to me, chest bumping against mine. "This is my pack now, and I'll decide what is right for them," he interrupted me.

I stepped in a little closer, pressing our chests firmly together. I was alpha born, and he was not. I could easily remove him from his position with a snap of my jaw. He didn't look like he was going to back down, which surprised me, considering most would have.

A heavy hand pressed into my chest, separating the two if us. "I think this conversation can wait for later. Perhaps, after we've mourned our dead," Dane spoke reason to the both of us. His tone was one full of reprimand. I pulled away from his touch. The beast was unsettled by the contact and was still on edge. It was too full of aggression to recognize friends from foes.

I eyed Thorton for a moment longer. "You're making a mistake... one you will regret later."

"I guess we'll see, won't we?" he replied as his lips twitched upward slightly before he turned his back to us. I watched with a heavy glare as he approached some of his warriors. Dane had to drag me away from the scene. The beast was fighting for control of my body. It wanted to kill the imposter alpha.

"You can't go around trying to kill anyone who goes against you. It does little to help in the making of alliances, and right now, we need all the bodies we can get," Dane told me under his breath. I growled in annoyance. Civility has never been a gift I possessed.

"Diplomacy won't serve us very well either if everyone ends up dead," I said, breathing heavily. My eyes roamed over the death that surrounded us. This wasn't the work of the Goddess reaping justice. This was the work of my brother reaping his vengeance. He was still one step ahead of us at every turn.

I clenched my hands into tight fists. "We need to find my brother's beta. He is the one responsible for this attack under my brother's orders. Of that, I am certain. When he is found, I will be the one to deal with him. I will be the one to take his head." I marched away, needing a moment to myself.

22

Scarlett

Christa led us through the trees without trouble. It was clear that these were her woods and that she had traveled them many times before. I was doing the best I could to keep up with her long strides. Clarissa was still clinging to her mother who was doing her best to console her and keep her quiet in case there were more rogues lurking this deep in the woods. My wolf was on high alert, the sounds of the nighttime creatures had her growling out in warning. Her aggression made my skin crawl with anticipation. I was ready to shift at a moment's notice.

"Where are you taking us?" I asked when I realized we were moving deeper and deeper into the woods and further from the chaos. I felt conflicted over leaving so many behind to fend for themselves, but I trusted that the Noah and the others were doing everything to give them a fighting chance.

She cast a look over her shoulder. "A safe room. Alpha had them planted all over the territory. I thought he was paranoid in his older age, preparing for a war that was never going to come. I guess he wasn't as paranoid as I thought." She got a hardened look in her eyes before turning her gaze from me to Clarissa.

"She needs to be quieter, or she'll draw them straight to us," she said before she turned her face away, picking up her speed. She pushed branches out of her way, letting them snap back. A couple of them almost whipped me in the face by accident. Clarissa seemed to become more frantic at the sound of a loud howling in the distance. I found my wolf couldn't take any more of her sniveling, knowing she was putting us all in more danger.

I spun around to face them both. "Do you want to die?" My eyes fixed into a hardened stare as they pulled up short. Clarissa looked anxious at my quick reactions. "I know you're scared. We're all scared, but you need to get yourself together." I snapped.

Rose flashed me some teeth, clearly not liking the way I was talking to her daughter. A mother wolf would always be protective of her pups. I ignored her. I wasn't looking for a fight. "You're still alive, but others aren't so lucky. Be thankful." Clarissa sucked in her lip, silencing her whimpers. I held her glassy-eyed gaze for a moment longer before I turned away, feeling the heat of Rose's gaze on my back.

Christa had stopped walking and was hunching over near the ground. I watched as she began to dig around in the foliage, revealing a hidden hatch. She yanked it open with a small grunt. "We'll be safe in here."

We waited inside the safe room in silence, all of us lost in our own thoughts. I didn't know how long we stayed down there, but when the hatch opened again, we all stiffened up only to relax when a warrior dropped down into the hatch. "The territory has been secured," he said it to us in a formal tone.

We followed the warrior back to the clearing. A somber feeling hung in the surrounding air. The closer we got, the stronger the smell of death became.

The space was full of death. I tried not to cringe as I stepped over and around bodies that had yet to be moved or claimed. The rogues had come and gone like a storm, leaving only destruction in their path.

The warriors were taking care of the dead, doing their best to sort them according to their packs to help make it easier for their families to find them. Some people were already finding their loved ones, weeping and screaming out their pain. It made my heart burn with recognition. Emotions I kept buried deep churned within me.

I felt *his* gaze on me before I saw him. My skin tingled as if his hands had touched me. Our eyes locked across the distance as I planted my feet solidly on the ground, clenching my fists at my sides. Noah came to me, his eyes searching every part of me. I found my own eyes doing the same thing, unable to stop myself.

A part of me needed to be certain that he has made it through the storm unscathed. He glanced toward Christa who stood at my side wearing some rags that she picked up from the safe room. "Thank you for watching over them, Christa."

"No thanks required. She watched over herself," she replied quickly as her eyes searched the crowd. "If you'll excuse me." She took her leave, heading into the crowd of survivors.

He watched her walk away with a look of regret. "What's wrong?" I questioned him, knowing something was eating at him. There was something that he hasn't said, something he wanted to say.

He turned his eyes back to me, searching my face again like he needed to memorize all the lines before he turned away. "Alpha Randall is dead."

"Good riddance. He was an idiot. His pack will be much better off without him. We all will be better off without him." I believed everything I was saying. I knew I should feel sorry for Christa and her pack — without an alpha to lead and protect them, they would be easy pickings for anyone looking for a little more power — but I didn't.

"He was killed by the captain of his warriors. He was challenged, Scarlett," he said it more tensely. My mind processed this new information which sent dread racing up my spine.

"Why didn't you say that first?" I snarled at him. "You just let Christa walk into her own death sentence! You know what happens to the defeated alpha and their bloodline!"

He flashed me his own teeth, eyes darkening as his wolf made itself known. "If I interfered, I was risking war and gambling the lives of my pack for one person. If anyone is to blame... if anyone signed her death warrant, it was her own father."

I stared him down with hard eyes, chest heaving under the force of my contained anger. I knew in the back of my mind that he was right, but my heart didn't want to concede. It wanted to rage against all the systems and customs of our world. I wanted to curse the moon and the Goddess that created us.

"I am not going to stand by and do nothing. She saved Clarissa's life, and that is a debt owed. If they aren't going to repay it, then I will." I turned away from him, only for him get a hold of my arm.

I let out a vicious snarl, but he remained calm, holding me steady. "I didn't say I wasn't going to do anything. We just need to be smart about the move we make, Scarlett." I could hear the urgency in his tone, trying to get me to yield to his judgment of the situation.

I pulled my arm out of his grasp, and this time, he didn't try to stop me. "If she dies, Noah..." It was a warning with intention. What intention? I wasn't quite sure. I just knew that I couldn't let anything happen to that female.

"I won't let any more people die today. I swear to the Goddess above." I couldn't smell any lies coming from him. Still, I wanted more assurance. I had little faith in the good intentions of others, especially those who the Goddess had tied to me.

"I don't care about the Goddess above. Swear to me on something that matters. Swear to me on Claire." I knew I was being harsh, but it was the only way I knew I would believe him.

His eyes narrowed, pausing for a moment. "I swear on Claire that no one else will die today."

I turned my eyes away from him, finding Knox and his father in what looked like a heated debate with Thorton. Christa was positioned behind them.

"I hope your plan is a good one," I mumbled under my breath, giving Noah the benefit of the doubt.

He grabbed my hand and pulled me along beside him. I tried to pull away, but he held on tighter. "A united front is a strong front," was all he said to me. A justification for himself and me.

23

Christa

There were many wandering around in dazed confusion, searching the wounded and dead for their pack mates and loved ones. The sight tested my resolve. Before, I had been forced to watch men bleed for hours in the hot sun in the name of strength, and I had spent years on my knees, praying in my mother's temple. It was a drastic change, one side of me trained to be a peacemaker and the other born to be a war monger.

The Goddess always has a plan, child, that was what mother had said to me many times. *She is blind to nothing.* At this moment, thinking that the Goddess allowed such a thing tested my resolve.

I stopped to help a female who was trying to drag one of the dead. Her eyes were empty as tears spilled from them. I bent over and grabbed the body's legs, the body barely recognizable. "Let me help you," I said in a soft voice. This was not the voice of an alpha. This was the soft voice mother taught me.

The female let out a sob as her knees almost gave out, but she forced herself to remain upright. This male must have been very important to her. Mate, father, or brother... I was not sure which, and I was sure it mattered little.

"Alpha Thorton has requested your presence," a warrior said as he approached me with a stern expression. The female I was helping glanced between us, lowering her gaze in submission. My mind had to recalibrate itself to the news I was just given. I shouldn't have been surprised, but I was.

He had taken Father's life and took the title that should have been passed on to me. This pack was now under his thumb. Not that I cared. They had never wanted me, and I had never wanted them.

I let the warrior lead me to Thorton. He stood in the center of the now controlled chaos, conducting the warriors. He was already settling into his title. I wondered how long he had been plotting behind my Father's back. How long had he been waiting for the perfect opportunity to strike? He must have sensed us as we approached because he turned his gaze in our direction. "Christa," he greeted me with a dark look in his eyes.

I could feel the eyes of the pack on me, burning into my back as I moved forward. All I could see was the dead placed in a line. There were rows of them. My eyes searched the faces that had, only hours ago, been alight with life. This was something I would force myself to remember. This was the burden of failure and a burden an alpha must carry.

I felt stiff as I came to a stop, lifting my gaze to his. "Thorton," I greeted him, trying to keep the growl out of my voice. My wolf was dangerously close to the surface, unsettled by the world around us.

His eyes sparked with new knowledge. Now that my father was gone, he must've felt the truth surging between us — of who and what I truly was. "That's Alpha Thorton now." He wasted no time correcting me.

My wolf snapped her teeth in his direction as I narrowed my eyes slightly. I knew he could feel the dominance pouring out of me, filling up the small space between our bodies. I gave him silence for a single beat of my heart. "Alpha Thorton," I corrected myself. What did it matter to me if I called him alpha? Just because I called something by a name, didn't make it so. Still, I watched him puff up at the words coming from my lips.

His mouth dropped down in a mocking frown. "You know the customs."

"I do," I replied with a calm voice. I did know well that in accordance with old laws, the defeated alpha and all his bloodline were often killed so that no more heirs could be produced. It was a way for the conquering alpha to make sure the power remained in their hands and their future heir's hands.

Thorton crossed his arms behind his back, tempting my wolf to take her best shot at him. "If you bow now and pledge your loyalty me as your new alpha, I'm willing to overlook the old ways. I do not wish to kill you. I do not blame you for your father's choices." His words were like sweet poison. I could see how they would twist the minds of the weakened pack. They made him seem like the hero, but I was not as simple-minded as them.

My body was rigid and my mind was uncertain about how to proceed. I could kill this wolf. I knew it, my wolf knew it, but I did not want the power he now held. I also knew my wolf would never let me bow to someone below her. He flashed me his teeth when I remained unmoved. "This is the only time I will make this offer. Think wisely. Do not follow down the same path your father did."

I held my head up, lifting my chin. "I will not bow to you, or anyone else. I was born an alpha. You'll only ever be a pretender." He reacted quicker than I expected him to, grabbing hold of my arm and yanking me forward. His teeth snapping inches from my face in full aggression.

My wolf pushed against my skin as she tried to gain control. Her claws pricked through my flesh. Before I could respond, I was pulled back away from Thorton. I knew who was touching me by the way my body responded, and my wolf calmed down. Knox positioned himself in front of me, snarling harshly. "Touch her again, and I'll rip your throat out myself, alpha or not."

Another male charged forward. I could feel he was another alpha. He had a similar build to my mate and the same eyes. My mind connected the dots quickly. This male was his father. He looked wary of the situation, glaring at his son. "What the hell are you doing?"

Knox was completely focused on Thorton. "He is threatening my mate. Even after everything that has happened..." My face became heated at the sudden announcement in front of all of these people. We had only met a few hours before. I thought we would have had a little more time to get to know each other before we began to share that information with others.

Thorton's eyes blazed with hatred. "She is a part of this pack. She is the last remains of Randall's bloodline. You should be thankful I didn't kill your *mate* the moment I saw her again," he said these words with all the authority his new position afforded him.

Knox's body began to quake, and his grip on me grew tighter as his wolf pushed for control. Knox's father stepped forward, understanding the explosive situation we were all in. "Perhaps, we can figure out something on the girl's behalf. I understand your concern, but the female belongs to—"

"You understand nothing. She *belongs* to the pack. She pledges her loyalty, or she dies." Thorton interrupted with a powerful sneer plastered across his face. Knox snarled loudly. I could feel the shifting of bones as his wolf fought harder for control. My wolf snapped her teeth in Thorton's direction in support of her mate's aggression.

I gave Knox's arm a squeeze before I pulled away, stepping around him. "Enough," I spoke firm and clear. The males cast their attention in my direction. "I won't bow." Thorton took a step forward. His eyes narrowed into angry slits, but I didn't turn away.

"If you want to challenge me over you own pride, go ahead. I won't stop you, but neither will I spare you from my wolf." He seemed a little uncertain now, glancing between the three of us. My calmness over everything seemed to only add to the uncertainty swirling in his eyes. I had found his weakness.

I took another step forward. "I have no desire to lead or be a part of this pack." I was speaking the truth that had been burning in me since the day mother returned me to Father.

"If that is the truth, why not banishment?" Noah's voice echoed above the whispers of the onlookers. We all turned towards him. Scarlett was at his side, their fingers intertwined and their hands locked together.

"Noah..." Scarlett hissed his name under her breath, clearly not pleased by his suggestion. I, however, saw the reason in his thought. It would maintain the peace of all the packs, and no one else would have to die this day. My wolf was not in favor of this choice. She would rather fight and prove herself then concede. The human side would always understand things deeper than instinct, and right now, I had to lean on my own understanding.

I straightened my back, keeping my eyes focused on the trees behind the chaos. "I accept banishment."

"What?" Knox sounded surprised, but I had already made up my mind, and nothing and no one would change that now. Thorton was looking at our small group with a sneer. He wasn't pleased by this outcome, but I could tell he was going to give into it. His gaze met mine, full of dark hunger and rage. "Banishment it is."

He snapped his fingers to get the attention of nearby warriors. "Escort Christa to the post, and someone fetch me the whip."

Knox snarled and lunged forward. His father was forced to hold him back. Noah had to release Scarlett to grab hold of him on the other side. "I'm going to rip your fucking throat out the first chance I get, you fucking bastard."

The warriors stepped up in my direction with grim expressions. They didn't look like they wanted to do this, but they must do what the alpha says. The dead were behind me and the early morning sun was rising before me, peeking out from behind the mountain.

I didn't have to be forced to grip the post like the others before me had. I spread my legs and grabbed hold of the wood, splinters poking at the tender flesh of my palms. Everything was my choice now, and these scars I would bear forever because I chose to bear them.

The bodies were beginning to be burned. The smell of them drifted into my nose as the wind carried their ashes away back to the moon. I stood in the midst of the flames, a small circle of onlookers to what was transpiring. Thorton came to stand before me, making sure our eyes were locked. "I'm choosing to banish you from these lands and this pack. Let it be a show of my mercy that you were allowed to keep your life. If you or any of your offspring should return to these lands, I will not spare a single life." He nodded, and the warriors tore the material I was wearing open, revealing my back.

Thorton held my gaze as if he was waiting for me to break or tremble, but I stood firm. "Strike true, Alpha Thorton." My word made him clench his jaw tightly.

My wolf stirred anxiously under my skin, wanting to fold me inside of herself and handle this situation the way she saw fit. I closed my eyes at the sound of my mate's vicious snarls. I knew Noah and his father would keep him prisoner, and I was thankful for that. I needed him to respect my choice, but I also didn't want him to be hurt by it either. A part of me prayed to the Goddess that he would look away.

I knew what was coming.

Crack.

The sound was met by a fierce snarl from my wolf. My skin screamed as the silver barbs tore into it, ripping and pulling again and again. I dug my fingers into the post, nearly splintering it in half from the strength of my grip.

Crack.

Crack.

"Enough!" a deep voice bellowed, and the pain came to an end. My ears were ringing, and my mind was foggy as I opened my eyes.

"Get her!" I recognized that the voice belonged to Noah.

My knees gave out, and I sunk into the dirt. Scarlett was the one who came to me first. I didn't think Knox could be trusted to come to me at the moment. She was looking at me with a pained expression as her hands caught me as I fell over. "Everything is going to be okay." Her voice sounded gentle and melodic. I closed my eyes and drifted into the darkness.

24

Grace

I stared at the dirt that was embedded deep underneath my nails. The incessant dripping of the rain spilling through the crack in the small window above me was beginning to make me tense. How long had I been here now? Two months or two years? Time was completely forgotten in this prison.

I was a caged beast, kept like a pet. My wolf paced back and forth in my mind. She was hungry—hungry for flesh, for blood. She snarled loudly with her need, her fur bristled up. I clenched my hands into tight fists in my lap before unclenching them, flexing the joints and muscles. *Soon*, I thought to her.

"I tink I'd like a nice warm bath. Giv'em my left arm fer one," Patrick commented, breaking through my internal thoughts, his accent sounding like a familiar melody. The poor wolf had come from across the sea, banished from his land. I often wondered what he had done, but I never asked. I tried not to get attached to the other prisoners because they never lasted long.

"I'm startin' tae offend myself."

I didn't say anything to him. I just kept my gaze focused on my hands and my dirty fingernails.

"Great company yer are. Like talkin' tae the wall, but at least the wall talks back," he mumbled as he shifted around. The chains on his ankles rattled as he did. I peeked over in his direction to see him lifting Nolan off his lap and setting him on the ground beside him, peacefully asleep. When the rogues had brought him back, he was screaming. A completely inconsolable mess. Patrick had held him. He had rocked him back and forth as he hummed songs from his homeland until he had quietened.

The stench of the rogues hit my nose long before I heard the key turned in the door. My skin itched with desire to shift, but the silver kept my wolf bound tightly in the cage of my skin. The door opened slowly, creaking. The sound collapsed under the rumble of a growl that echoed out of my chest. It was the only warning I would give to the intruder.

I launched myself forward. The chains that were wrapped around my ankles kept me from getting far. My claws were out, and I was flashing my teeth like a rabid beast, snarling loudly. The rogue they sent in first nearly shat himself, scrambling backward and almost tripping over his own feet, only to have Patrick rush at him from the other side, snapping his teeth with a toothy grin. The others outside the room roared with laughter.

Kade kicked the young rogue in the back as he entered, making him fall to his knees. He scrambled to right himself yet fell over instead. "Get yourself together, boy." He stepped over the terrified mess on the floor. His eyes roamed over me, and I flashed him my teeth, snapping them together.

"You're so very scary... little Gracie," he said in a mocking tone, clicking his tongue off the roof of his mouth. I watched his every movement closely, noticing every subtle twitch of his muscles. I wanted to bathe in his blood. I wanted to feel the warmth of it as it rained down my flesh.

He stayed just out of my reach. "Kellan sent me to retrieve you," he said as if he was exasperated by the fact that he was at the beck and call of someone else, yet here he stood to do someone else's bidding. He knew his place, and he knew it well.

I gave him a toothy grin. "If he wants me, let him come and get me himself." My wolf was greedy for violence. She was howling with her desire to wreak havoc in the world.

Kade let his eyes wander over me again, lingering in some places that made my skin crawl with disgust. This male wanted me for himself, but my neck was still angry from the marks that his leader had left on me.

Kade gave me a bitter smile with his canines elongated, filling his mouth. "You should be happy that I'm the one he sent, little Alpha. The others would have taken liberties with you. They only see you as our alpha's whore pet." I snarled at his comment, stretching myself forward as far as the chains would allow. He was still too far for my claws to reach. His eyes sparked with amusement at my folly. "Save your strength."

"I'm going to kill you." My words were guttural as my wolf tried to make herself known. It's was a promise we intended to keep.

He lifted his fingers to his mouth and whistled. The high-pitched sound irritated my ears. A couple more rogues flooded into the room, eager to please their captain. "Get the others out of here and load them up. We need to get to our new location," he ordered while still holding my gaze.

Patrick was edged in next to Nolan, flashing his teeth protectively as if it was his own young. He had grown quite attached to the pup whose eyesight had been ruined because of the experiments their Frankenstein doctor liked to conduct on the prisoners. My own body was littered with scars from the torture, but my face was never touched. All my limbs remained intact, unlike most prisoners I had seen flow through. I was Kellan's little pet after all. I had an image to uphold.

One of the rogues got too close to Patrick, and he grabbed hold of his head between his hands, releasing a window rattling growl as he drove his clawed thumbs into his eyes. The blood sprayed out across his face as he smiled like a madman. "Got me dat warm bath, after all, young one." He laughed hysterically like he was having the time of his life. The rogue hung from his thumbs like an ornament off a tree. The smell of blood had my senses tingling and itching for more.

I watched as another used his buddy as a distraction, coming up from behind while Patrick was focused on the dying rogue in his hands. He stabbed a syringe into the back of Patrick's neck. I watched as he dropped his toy and twisted around, swiping out with his claws. He caught the rogue in the face, but it was barely a flesh wound, something that would be forgotten. He staggered before dropping to his knees. The liquid silver worked through him quickly. Once he was down, the other rogues moved quickly toward Nolan. All the while, Patrick was growling, unable to stop them.

There was only a subtle twitch of his hand that warned me that Kade was up to something. I had only a moment to try to brace myself as he charged at me. His body slammed against mine, knocking me back into the wall. My head banged against the concrete wall so hard, I saw stars. The devil inside of me took control of my limbs. The devil had me snapping my mouth shut on his shoulder though I was trying to get his throat. My every intention focused on killing him. His blood coated my mouth. The bitter tang was almost as refreshing as spring water.

I felt the sharp prick as the needle pierced through my skin. I had fallen for the same trick like a fool. I growled in protest because I had failed again.

"I will get out of these chains someday, and when I do... there will be no escape, no mercy... only death." I howled violently, spit flying from my mouth into Kade's face as the liquid silver began to course through my veins. The echoing roar of my wolf grew more distant until I could barely feel her at all. I sagged forward, my body weakening to the state I could no longer hold myself up.

Kade caught me in his arms. "I look forward to that day, little Alpha."

25

Scarlett

Knox never went far from Christa's side, and he wouldn't let anyone into the room, except for myself and Doctor Owen. I think the only reason he let Owen into the room was because he threatened he would turn him into a new throw rug for his cabin if he didn't let him do his job. It was hard to tell if he was bluffing or not. I was betting on not.

"You better stop growling at me, boy," Owen remarked as he began to undo the wraps he had put on Christa's back. She had been in and out of it for a couple of days. He had pumped her full of his 'special' pills that kept her from feeling most of the pain. I couldn't say I wasn't curious to know what made them special, but I didn't have the stomach to ask.

Knox quickly cut the growl off in his throat, but his lips were still pulled down in a deep frown. I watched Owen intently, noticing the way his hands shook. His joints were swollen. It was probably arthritis. I could see his age was catching up to him. Soon, he wouldn't be of much use as a healer. I wondered if Noah had noticed this or if he was too consumed by his desire for vengeance to notice anything or anyone else. Owen looked up in my direction as if sensing my thoughts. His eyes narrowed, and I stood up a little straighter, just like I would when I was a young girl and my father caught me doing something I shouldn't.

"Look smart, girl." My wolf snapped at his comment, and I clenched my teeth to keep from growling at him like Knox had been. He motioned for me to come to him. "My daughter Janie is busy with the others, but I need someone who can help right now. So make yourself useful if you're going to be in here." He cast a quick glance in Knox's direction with a firm gaze as if daring him to say something about it.

He kept his mouth shut, his body stiff as a statue made of stone. I pushed away from the wall by the door and approached the bed slowly. I knew how mates could be irrational at times, especially alphas. Their wolves were stronger, and so were their instincts. They were more prone to violent acts, and I had seen enough violence in the past couple of weeks to last me a lifetime. He watched my movements closely and carefully, flashing me his teeth in warning, a warning that I understood clearly.

I turned my back to Knox as I came to stand on the opposite side of Owen. I was showing him that I had no harmful intentions for his mate by making myself weak to his possible attack. A sign of good faith on my part that I hoped he hadn't misunderstood. Owen stared between the two of us for a moment longer as the tension in the room settled down again.

"Undo the bindings on that side. They might stick, so you'll just have to pull them up." I pursed my lips as I did what he said, pulling back the strips of cloth he had used to bind the wounds when we had first arrived back at the pack house. The ointment that he was rubbing onto the open wounds had a pungent smell that made me want to gag. I forced myself to breathe through my mouth, holding myself together the best I could. "Once Janie gets here, she'll take over the care of Alpha Randall's daughter. She has the healing touch that this female needs."

"Is she going to be okay?" Knox jumped in, voice more guttural as his wolf remained close to the surface.

Owen glanced up from his work with a scowl. "She's still breathing, ain't she?" He sounded offended that he would even ask such a thing, grumbling under his breath as he finished up the task of putting on fresh ointment. He wiped his hands on the bloody shirt he arrived in. "This should help to lessen the scarring, but it won't take them away." He tossed a fresh roll of gauze in my direction.

I caught it with one hand, looking at him curiously. "Wrap her back up." He pointed down to Christa. "I've got to get back to the wounded. Some are much worse than this female."

He grabbed his cane that was leaning against the nightstand beside the bed, hobbling across the room and out the door. I didn't waste time wrapping her wounds, doing it as carefully as I could. I didn't want to wake her from her medicated sleep.

Knox moved in closer, standing beside me and watching me carefully as I worked. I could tell that he was going to be a strong alpha once he came into his own completely. My wolf was in agreement with my thoughts. She may not care for many people, but she respected the strength she sensed in the young male.

"Do you want to help me?" I asked him as nicely as I could, peering up at him from under my lashes. He didn't meet my gaze. His eyes were focused completely on Christa.

"I don't want to hurt her."

I found his words endearing. *If only all males could be as honest about their feelings as Knox*, I thought bitterly. I reached out and grabbed his hand, not waiting for his permission. He stiffened, growling at me, but I ignored him as I placed his fingers to the end of the gauze and made him hold it to Christa's skin for me.

I watched as Christa's body seemed to relax more even in her current state. The connection between the two of them was strong. I let go of his hand and continued to wrap her, noting how his thumb traced small circles over the small patch of untouched flesh.

A calm silence took up root between us as we worked together. "You know, Claire would never have been able to stomach this." My ears perked up at the mention of Claire while, at the same time, my heart cringed. I wondered if I was a painful reminder of what had been lost. My insecurities were telling me I was a poor imitator of the one who used to walk these halls.

"She could never handle blood." He let out a half laugh. "She was always the sensitive one out of the three of us. She'd always been thin and sickly growing up. She was weak in the ways that counted most in our world. You're nothing like her." His words were harsh, both on his sister's behalf and on my own. I tried not to let them affect me. I tried not to let them settle in too deep where they could hurt me.

"Well, things are different in the North. The weak ones never live long. They usually get picked off early on. In some packs, if pups seem to have a weak aura, the mothers will leave them out for the bears to take." I could feel his gaze burning into the side of my face, and I turned to look at him. His green eyes were full of emotions.

"Thank you for helping with Christa." I pulled away from the bed, turning my back to him as I set the gauze away. "It's good that you aren't like her. I mean, like Claire." I peeked over my shoulder to find he had already returned his focus to his mate. I felt my lips twitch with the urge to smile at his comment, but I didn't.

A knock came on the door, and Knox let out a growl. "Send him away." I knew who he was talking about. I knew who was standing on the other side of the door by the way my body sang as his scent drifted in, tickling my senses.

I made my way toward the door, but before I could reach it and tell him to leave it open, our eyes locked for an instant before he looked at Christa on the bed. His blue eyes were full of the weight of his own regrets and sorrow. I had to force away the gnawing feeling in the pit of my stomach. Our bond was trying to suck me in under the flood of his raw emotions.

"What are you doing here?" Knox growled, coming to stand at the foot of the bed protectively and blocking Christa from Noah's view. I expected Noah to lash out, but he didn't.

Instead, I could taste his guilt on my tongue. The terrible bitter tang of it made me want to gag.

"I just wanted to come and check on her myself. Make sure she was healing well." He sounded calm, almost gentle. This was a whole new side of him I had yet to see, and I found jealousy swirling around in my mind. How could he show everyone else such gentleness but never me?

Knox snarled viciously. "The reason she's here at all is because of you! All of this is your fault!" I watched as his wolf reached out for control of his body. Knox charged forward at Noah, completely enraged. Noah did nothing to block or stop him. He was blindly accepting the brunt of Knox's anguish and rage. Years of it that had been bottled up to be tasted for this exact moment. He grabbed hold of Noah's shirt, yanking him forward. "If Claire had never met you, none of this... none of it would have happened! She would still be here. Those innocent packs wouldn't have been attacked." He knocked him hard across the face with his fist. The sound of bone cracking echoed through the room. The scent of blood only seemed to incite the frenzy of Knox's wolf.

His wolf ascended to the forefront, and he lost all rationality. In its place was a beast raged: an alpha male looking for retribution. I watched as he sunk his canines into Noah's neck, going for the kill. Even then, Noah didn't fight him though I knew he could. He was simply submitting himself to Knox's wrath. He was willing to accept his own death, perhaps even hoped for it.

My wolf rose as our bond began to pull at the seam of my being. The instinct to protect my mate, true or not, was too heavy to ignore or shove away. Noah's eyes met mine over

Knox's shoulder, and the weight of his guilt rushed over me, making my limbs heavy.

I pushed myself away from the bed and rushed towards Knox from behind. "Enough!" I yelled over his loud growls. I watched him bite down harder, sinking his teeth in deeper. This was definitely going to leave a mark on him if it didn't kill him. My wolf pushed harder to be free, snapping her teeth. Her claws were popping through the tips of my fingers. "I said, enough!" I grabbed onto Knox's forearm, clawing my fingers in deep.

The sudden pain must have been enough to shock him back into sanity because he released Noah. The smell of his blood flooded the room. It covered Knox's mouth and the front of his shirt. He looked a little shocked as he stared at his handiwork. Noah was pale, blood running from the deep wound at his throat, soaking his shirt, and falling to the carpet.

I found myself at his side, helping to bear his weight as his legs weakened under the loss of blood. Our eyes lingered on one another. "You're a damn fool," I said through clenched teeth. My stomach felt nauseous at the thought that I could have lost him. I could have let Knox kill him and be free to go on as I had wanted, but yet my soul stirred for someone who was a little more than a stranger to me. His pain was my pain. We weren't as different as I wanted to believe we were.

I lowered us to the ground, unable to hold his weight. I was quick to press my hand to the wound at his neck. His eyes were focused on mine the entire time. "Don't let anyone punish him..." I knew he was talking about Knox. "Th-that... I deserved that."

I growled lightly at his words. "Fine. I'll make sure nothing happens." He relaxed at my agreement to his wishes.

"What happened?" Janie's voice carried across the room, and I looked over my shoulder to see her standing in the doorway in shock at what I was sure was quite the sight. She moved into the room quickly, making her way to Noah and me.

She paused when I tightened my grip on him, giving her a good show of my canines. She slowly lowered herself to her knees, so we were on the same level. "Scarlett, you know that I am not going to hurt him," she said calmly in a friendly tone as she tried to suppress the aggression and anxiety of my wolf. She glanced at Noah, inspecting his condition from afar. He was growing paler, and his eyes looked unfocused.

"He needs help. I can help him if you want, but you'll have to step aside and let me work. I want to help him, Scarlett." There was an urgency and pleading in her voice. I loosened my hold on him, lowering his head to the carpet that was now stained with his blood.

I scooted away, and she moved quickly to his side, working on him. "You're a damned fool," she muttered under her breath. I couldn't help the twitch of my lips at her comment. She had seemed so reserved and quiet up to this point, but being the mate to the beta meant she had something special. She also had Owen for a father.

I pushed myself off the ground, looking toward Knox who watched Janie work. The anger rushed through me quickly. "Feel better?" I questioned as I moved towards him. "You could have killed him, and for what? Because you think he's the reason you've lost things? You think he's the reason we're all suffering?" I pushed Knox back, snarling at him.

"Wake up! Noah has continued to do what's needed to be done. Did what I'm sure no one else, not even you could have done. So maybe stop blaming him for the sins of others. He may not be a perfect, but he's not the one to blame."

26

Scarlett

Noah was sleeping in his room. I didn't want him to be put in my bed. I didn't want his scent in my sheets or lingering on my flesh. It was hard enough to resist the growing strength of our bond. I didn't need to have him soaking his intoxicating scent into my personal space. As it was, I had to shower after every time I was in the same space as him.

I sat in his room in a chair next to his bed, watching over him because my wolf wouldn't allow me to do anything else. Her constant urging had been too much for me to ignore. I knew he was going to be fine. He didn't seem like one to be taken out by some young alpha. Plus, Janie had reassured me over and over, as if she thought I was concerned. I wasn't, but I didn't have the heart to tell her that.

My wolf may have been thoroughly displeased by the current situation, but I was simply a bystander, an outsider trying to understand what had led to this moment. So here I sat glowering in Noah's direction, upset over my inability to ignore our bond completely.

My eyes drifted to the nightstand, boredom and curiosity driving me to poke around through his things. I opened the drawer, finding a couple of scraps of paper. They looked like letters that had been read over and over again, most of the words smeared and unintelligible. I shifted the small stack before finding the jackpot hidden underneath them. There were a couple of overturned frames. I pulled one out, flipping it over in my hands, and found a beautiful female staring back at me.

Her red hair and mossy green eyes sparkled with a subtle mischief, and it told me exactly who I was staring down at. I could feel a shifting of something in my stomach, a bitter feeling that I've felt before, a feeling that was hard to forget. I forced myself to linger in the sensation, glancing in Noah's direction.

He doesn't belong to you, I reminded myself. He belonged to this female, and her to him. They were true mates even if I was here now. We would never be what they were. I set the picture up on the nightstand, closing the drawer.

I took up my position at his bedside, resting my chin on my knees as I balled myself up in the chair. I must've nodded off for an hour or so before I awoke to the deep sound of Noah groaning. The sound sparked up every cell in my body, rattling me out of my sleepy state. I lifted my head and turned my face in his direction as he opened his eyes.

He let out a breath that sounded almost like disappointment as if he had wished he wouldn't have woken up. The thought had my wolf flashing her teeth. She didn't appreciate his willingness to give up. She saw it as a weakness. I, however, understood the feeling more than I wished to acknowledge.

"Have you been here with me this whole time?" he asked me as his eyes found their way to mine.

I cleared my throat as my cheeks heated. "Not the whole time..." I lied as I looked away from him. I didn't need him to think I was going weak-kneed for him because I wasn't. *Nope, I definitely wasn't.*

"Right, you had to sleep at some point," he commented dryly, voice cracking. I got up and walked into his bathroom, filling up a cup near the sink with water before returning to his bedside. I reached out to help him lift his head, but he flashed me his teeth in a powerful sneer.

I stared down at him with hard eyes, contemplating throwing the water in his ungrateful face for a moment before deciding against it. "Fine, do it yourself." I slammed the glass down on the nightstand. I plopped myself down in the chair, watching as he stared up at the ceiling. He let out a heavy sigh before rolling over, wincing as he reached for the glass. He froze when his eyes connected with the picture of Claire I put back on the nightstand. "You went through my things?" His question was dripping with anger.

"She's beautiful," I said, not denying what I did.

He growled as he snatched the picture off the nightstand and hid it back in the drawer with the others. His gaze swept in my direction. It was dark and malevolent. I could feel his anger at me and at himself. He was tearing himself in two. The wolf in him was ready to move forward, but he wished to linger in the past. I turned my eyes away from him, pulling my knees up to my chest. I wanted to leave the room, but my wolf was crawling under my skin. She wasn't quite ready to retreat back to our territory just yet.

"Is this what you were like before you met, Claire?" I asked after several minutes of silence. I noticed him stiffen out of the corner of my eye. He didn't say anything back to me, so I figured that was one area of his life he didn't want to talk about. I opened my mouth to say I was going to leave, but his voice cut me off.

"No, I was worse. She made me better. She saw what others never saw. Everyone thought we're born heartless, but we weren't."

He was staring down at his hands. "Even rogues are born with some bonds. Rogue mothers are always bonded with their children. It's impossible for it not to happen. They are allowed to keep the bond with us until we mature to an age where we don't need them to sustain us. Then the bond is broken. I was five when my father forced my mother to break her bond to me."

I felt my heart clench at the thought of a tiny Noah being forced to endure something like that. He looked up from his hands. "She wouldn't do it. I'm not sure why I was any different than my brother to her, but she refused to do so. My father was so angry. He brought her in front of the entire pack and forced her under the threat of killing me to break the bond. The last thing my mother ever did for me was save my life."

I swallowed the pain lumped in my throat. "I'm so sorry, Noah," I said in a raspy voice. His eyes met mine. They looked vulnerable for a moment before they turned cold again.

"After that, I was taught how to be a proper rogue." He looked back down at his hands.

I could tell Noah wanted to shut down the moment we were having, but I wanted to reach out a little. "My mother..." I started, and his eyes went back up to mine "She died during a rogue attack. I was playing in the woods with a couple of other kids from the pack. My mom was nearby, watching over us as she gardened. I remember that it was a particularly beautiful day." I closed my eyes as the memories flashed through my mind, and I smiled slightly, thinking of my mother in her garden with her giant, dorky sun hat.

"My house sat near one of the boundary lines, but it had never really been an issue before that day. A group of rogues crossed over into our territory. I remember my mother tearing through the woods to reach us. She tried to lead us back to safety, but we didn't make it far before we were cornered. She turned into a crazed animal and attacked those rogues without a second thought. She fought to protect us all. The last thing my mother ever did for me was save my life." I met his gaze, and the air between us sparked up with all sorts of emotions, but the most prevalent was understanding. We may have come from different worlds, but we could understand each other. It gave me a little hope that we weren't so different from each other, after all.

The moment we shared ended as quickly as it started. His eyes turned cold as he struggled to sit himself up, and I didn't offer to help him again. "You can leave now," he said in a commanding tone. He didn't want anyone to watch him as he fumbled. I could tell that he was afraid of being vulnerable, especially with me around. So I chose to stay and continued to watch him if only to show him that I wasn't going anywhere.

He let out a vicious growl of frustration, knocking the glass of water off the nightstand and onto the floor in his fit of rage. He fell back into his pillows, breathing heavily. Soon, that became the only sound in the room. All of a sudden, the door to the room flew open, and I turned around to see Janie rushing in. Her eyes were filled with concern. "Is everything okay in here?" She moved toward the bed. "Do you need help, Alpha?"

"Don't help him," I remarked in a cool tone. If he couldn't take my help, he was going to get no help at all. Noah needed to learn that.

She glanced in my direction. "What?"

I slowly turned my gaze from Noah to her, staring her down. "I said, don't help him." She gave me a look of confusion. I could tell she was torn between helping her alpha and listening to me.

Noah cast a look in my direction, and my skin heated up everywhere his eyes touched, rolling over me from head to toe. Our gazes locked, and I watched as he pulled himself together, pushing against whatever pain he felt until he was sitting upright in his bed. He was no longer the fumbling male he had been moments before, he was the alpha that everyone saw and respected.

Noah turned his face away from me toward Janie, and she flinched back under his gaze, bowing her body deeply towards him. "Alpha, I'm sorry if my presence offends you. My father asked me to help him. I wanted to lend my talents where I was able. I'll leave as soon as things are under control." Now, it was my turn to be confused by her words.

He quietly assessed her for a moment before letting out a heavy breath. "Stop bowing, Janie." She lifted her head slowly.

"I am happy to see you helping around here. This is what you were born to do, after all," he said in a tired voice. I noticed the way her body stiffened at the words, and I had a feeling there was a deeper meaning to everything that was transpiring, but I wasn't going to pry.

She bowed again. "Alpha."

She rose again, turning in my direction to meet my gaze. I tensed up as she bowed her head in my direction. "Scarlett, if you need anything else, I'll be back to change the bandage in a couple of hours." With that, she left the room with stiff movements. I watched her as she disappeared through the door, closing it behind her.

"Don't mind her," Noah said, and I turned my attention back to him. He had his head leaned back against the headboard. He closed his eyes as he let out a tired sigh. "She blames herself for what happened to Claire."

"Seems to me that a lot of people blame themselves for things they can't control. It's a waste of energy that would've been better served elsewhere," I said in response, sitting down in my chair again. He opened his eyes and looked at me with a curious light in his icy eyes like I was a puzzle he wanted to figure out.

I pushed up from my chair after a moment of his silent inspection and grabbed the glass off the floor. "I'll get you something to drink." I walked away from him, trying to ignore the way the bond pulled us into each other's gravity.

27

Scarlett

"What's got everyone in a rush this morning?" I asked Nadia as I came into the kitchen, still wiping the sleep from my eyes.

She turned to look towards me with a nervous smile. "The Holy Mother showed up this morning. We weren't expecting her, and with Noah out of commission at the moment, everyone's a little on edge" She whispered under her breath as she glanced around the room, watching as the other females worked hard to prepare a meal fitting for the surprise guest.

I had heard of the famed woman who had been chosen by the Goddess. How she had special sight that allowed her to have visions of the future, and how she had the divine wisdom to council the alphas when in need. Honestly, it wasn't something that many Northern pack had chosen to put much stock in. We believed in things that we could see and touch for ourselves. No superstitions or ghost stories. The other packs still believed in some of the old ways. The Goddess' maidens were one of them, apparently.

I tried not to roll my eyes. "Oh, makes sense, I guess."

"How are you feeling this morning?" she asked with concern.

"Like I could kill someone if they so much as look at me in the wrong way." I heard a gasp of someone nearby and turned to see a woman ushering herself away from my vicinity. I stared after her. "But that's a normal feeling!" I called after her in annoyance. Sure, they could live with a reformed rogue as their alpha but couldn't handle some poorly timed sarcasm.

Nadia let out a small laugh. "Ignore them. I'm just happy to hear that everything is going well. After everything... Well, it's good to have good news." I understood that most of the pack was still mourning the loved ones they had lost in the attack at the trials.

"Oh, look who we have here," a voice chirped, and I turned to see Delilah and Gretchen entering the kitchen. My good mood was suddenly lost, and the edginess crept back in. "Looks like someone forgot to put the trash out."

Delilah looked at me, her eyes flashing darker for a moment, making it clear that she was willing to go for another round. Which did surprise me a bit. After the beating that I gave her and her wolf?

"How are you feeling today? A bit roguish, *Luna?*" Delilah mocked as she grabbed an apple out of the fruit bowl on the counter. She took a bite out of it with a teasing smile. I had to hold my tongue to keep from lashing out at her, not wanting to give her the satisfaction of another fight. She had submitted physically, but I doubted she would ever truly submit unless Noah forced it on her.

Gretchen stood beside her with a similar look of superiority. "You know, perhaps that's what the alpha sees in her. Maybe she reminds him of his hay days with all her uncultured behavior." I growled at her words, and she made sure to meet my gaze. "But just remember he's already found his true mate. You're just a replacement."

Delilah laughed at her comment, skimming her eyes over me. "A poor imitation of a luna. Come on, let's go before she gives us rabies or something." They smirked at each other before they left the room.

My wolf was ready to track the two of them down and make an example of them. As if she knew this, Nadia placed her hand on my arm, and I turned to her with a harsh growl, my wolf more in control than I was. I quickly pulled back on the leash. "Sorry."

She gave me a wary smile. "Don't worry about it. I would have felt the same way. They're idiots. I'll talk to Ryder--"

"No!" I cringed at the loudness of my own voice. "I mean, no. I don't need anyone to fight my battles. Thank you though."

"If you say so," Nadia replied. She didn't look all that convinced, and I was certain that she was probably going to talk to her mate regardless of my wishes. She was the motherly type, but that also made her the meddling type at times, as I was learning. Still, I was happy to have her as a friend.

"Well, I think I'll take a look around. See if I can't spot this infamous, Holy Mother." I teased. I couldn't help myself. I was a bit curious about what she looked like. I wanted to see for myself if she glowed like I had heard people talk about or if she had eyes in the back of her head.

I wandered through the halls, lost in my own thoughts. Most of those thoughts were either centered on Delilah or Noah, both of which left me completely vexed. When I became aware of the world again, I found myself standing outside of Noah's room. I glared down at my feet in frustration. My body had betrayed me. I let out a heavy sigh as I lifted my gaze to the door, staring at it in continued irritation as my fingers twitched with the urge to open the door.

My eyes were eager to see his face again and my senses already hummed with the faint scent of him that was spilling through the crack under the door.

I didn't know how long I stood there cursing the bond and the Goddess who formed it. When the door opened quickly, I found myself surprisingly startled, jumping back away from the door as I flashed my teeth in warning. Noah stood on the other side, his chest heaving. Our eyes focused on each other in a similar hunger, a torment that neither of us could resist no matter how much we may like to.

"Are you just going to stand out there all morning or are you going to come in?" His voice was gravely from sleep, and his annoyance was evident.

I stared at him. "I hadn't decided yet if you deserved my company or not." I snapped at him more from my own frustration with myself.

His eyes narrowed slightly at my tone and choice of words. He looked like he was fighting with himself for a moment. I watched him closely as he took a deep breath before stepping back, creating a space big enough for me to pass through.

I stared at the space, trapped in my own internal dilemma. *Do I give my wolf what she longs for, or do I walk away like I want? Decisions, decisions.*

"I would welcome your company, Scarlett." A powerful shiver raced up my spine and nestled itself at the base of my skull at the sound of my name leaving his lips. I felt my core stir with a primal need for the male before me. I couldn't control the reaction my body was having to him any more than I could the weather.

My cheeks reddened with my embarrassment as I watched Noah's nostrils flare and take in my scent, which was heavy with my mating pheromones. His hand tightened on the door, his knuckles turning white. "Scarlett..." His guttural tone had me meeting his gaze, the dark eyes of his wolf peering out at me.

I gritted my teeth as my body swayed towards him. "I don't think this is a good idea, after all. I think we both would regret being in each other's presence." His gaze was heavy and hungry as I took a step back away from him slowly, knowing that if his wolf was the one in control, he would chase me. That was basic law when it came to predators. Never run, because they loved to chase.

He growled as his body shifted forward, inching a step out of the doorway in my direction. My mind screamed danger while my body screamed out its twisted desire for him.

"No!" I snapped at him, wanting him to know I didn't want this thing that was building between us at the moment. I knew deep down that neither of us did, but trying to make the beast inside him understand that was nearly impossible.

"Go," he said in a low rumble as he lowered his gaze to the ground, pulling back on his wolf. He grabbed onto the wood of the doorway. When he lifted his face again, his features were more angular as the beast pressed harder for release. "Lock your door behind you... Hurry."

My body was shaking as I turned and ran away like I knew I shouldn't, but he didn't leave me with many options. I threw myself into my room and locked the door. I stared at the door for a moment before pushing my dresser in front of it for good measure, not trusting the flimsy lock to keep him out.

Note to self: I should have stayed in bed today.

28

Christa

Fingers were sliding gently over the healing flesh on my back. My body shivered with awareness under the assault of Knox's touch. His scent was like a cocoon around me, sinking deep through the layers of my skin. I was certain he wanted it so that everyone knew that I belonged to him. I wasn't sure I was ready to open my eyes and find out how the world had changed while I was lost in a sea of swirling darkness and images.

"I know you're awake." His voice was a deep rumble. My wolf perked up at the sound of him talking to us. I let out a small breath before I slowly opened my eyes to the world, being greeted by sunlight that was streaming in through the window. I had to blink my watering eyes a couple times before they were fully adjusted to the harshness of the sudden light.

I turned my head slightly in the pillow in Knox's direction, wincing as the motion pulled at my stiff and scabbed flesh. My eyes connected with his and I felt the pull to reach out to him. I wanted to be as close to him as I could possibly get. I fisted the sheets under me to keep myself from moving as my body wanted. He looked as handsome as I remembered. Only there was a seriousness to his gaze that hadn't been there before. All the playful mischief had been absorbed by a darker emotion, one that I was afraid I may have pulled out of him. We continued to stare at each other in silence, his fingers still playing with the bare skin of my back.

"Where am I?" My voice cracked. My throat was dry of lack of use.

His lips pulled together in a tight line. "Alpha Noah had you brought back to his territory. His land was closer than my father's, and you needed a doctor."

I closed my eyes and breathed easy. "I see."

I could almost taste his desire for me on the air. It made me squirm under the covering of the sheets. My body was more than ready to welcome its mate. This was the first time I'd ever felt such potent feelings, and I wasn't sure what I was supposed to do with them. I knew now was not the right time to pursue them, but my biology didn't care about time.

"Christa..." Knox's voice was almost a growl. Pleasure rippled through me at the dominant tone. My wolf wanted this male as much as I did.

"I'm sorry. I can't help it." I gritted my teeth, trying to pull myself together. I felt embarrassed by the weakness of myself and my wolf. This was a trial I had never faced before.

"Don't apologize. I want you." His words brought me into a new cocoon of security. "I want to put my teeth on your skin." His finger trailed upward to the soft spot of my neck, leaving a burning fire in its wake. I opened my eyes and stared up at him from where I laid practically defenseless. At this moment in time, I was completely at his mercy. His mossy eyes burned with an unquenchable hunger that was threatening to consume us both.

He kneaded at the tender flesh, bringing a soft moan from my lips. "I will sink myself deep into you to a place where you will never be able to wash me away. You will be mine. I'm going to mark every inch of you, so the whole world knows who you belong to." He was definitely an alpha male through and through. There was no mistaking that.

My wolf let me know of her agreement with his thoughts. Her delight in him echoed out of my chest in a soft rumble. His eyes darkened as his wolf rose to the surface at the call of his female. "You'd like that, wouldn't you? My claim on you."

My wolf pushed for control, but I held her back, my body shivering. My eyes sought out the unmarked flesh of his neck, my canines aching to break through his skin. My lips part in a pant of excitement. "I'm going to put my teeth to you. No other females will have you. You belong to me." I held his gaze, both of us lost in the pull of our bond.

The moment was interrupted by a knock on the door, and both of us let out a growl of annoyance.

"Alphas?" A soft voice echoed through the room.

Knox peeled his eyes from me, glancing toward to the door with a sigh. "What is it, healer?"

"Someone's here to see Alpha Christa," the slender female with high cheek bones decorated with freckles said softly from the doorway as she opened the door. She seemed to have a sadness in her eyes that lingered and tugged at the frayed edges of my soul.

"Tell whoever it is that she isn't taking visitors," Knox said in a sharp tone. His wolf was making him unreasonable. I didn't blame him, but I didn't need to be lorded over. I've had enough of that to fill a lifetime. My wolf didn't enjoy the overbearing presence of the alpha male beside her even if it was her mate.

The female looked uneasy about his response, eyes meeting mine quickly before looking back to Knox. "Alpha... th-the visitor...she is..." She was struggling with the right words.

"The visitor can come back another time when my mate has had the proper time to heal." He pressed as his lip curled up in the direction of the female. I cleared my throat to cover a small growl of irritation as it swelled up in my throat. "Healer, tell me who is it that wishes to see me?"

I could feel his eyes burning into the side of my face, but I pretended not to notice. I had learned to ignore most things through the years. The female stood up a bit straighter under my attention. "It's the Holy Mother, Alpha."

I let out a sigh of exasperation, knowing this was going to be a situation. "Show her in please."

Her presence was strong, and the familiar scent of moonflowers tickled at my senses. Memories of my younger years flooded my mind. I had spent many of them clinging to mother's robes as she wandered the mountain temple, giving counsel to alphas from near and far and praying to the Goddess that birthed us. The memories of when she sent me back to

Father and the bitterness I felt washed over any good thoughts of her I tried to cling to.

The female bowed low in deep respect of her position as she passed into the room.

"Thank you, healer."

I could feel her eyes on me from under the shadow of her hood. I could only remember a handful of times that I had ever seen mother's face or looked into her eyes. I often wondered if we looked alike or if all of my genes came from Father, which was maybe why she had continually kept a wall between us.

"He is quite the male." Her voice was low. My wolf let out a growl in her direction, feeling very territorial over what belonged to her. "The Goddess has chosen well for you, daughter."

Knox was stood stiffly at my bedside. I knew he was in shock over the news that this woman was my mother. Even though I had been an offspring of an alpha and the Holy Mother, the Goddess had not shown me any favorable treatment. If anything, I was the proof that the Goddess was fair and just. Good or bad, weak or strong, she would treat all her children the same.

"Mother," I greeted her stiffly, rolling onto my side so I could get a better look at her. The tension in the room rose steadily. "I am sorry about Father." It was a lie. I wasn't sorry. I was glad that he was gone, but he had been her mate even if he had never officially claimed her other than as a vessel to carry his heir.

"No, you're not. He was a fool. He was always a fool. I'm surprised he lasted as long as he did." Her words were a matter of fact. I didn't hear a tone of malice or anger. She remained objective even to her own life, even when it came to her own mate's death. I couldn't tell if this was a strength or a weakness, though.

She moved in closer to the bed, the fabric of her robe rustling. "I would like to talk to my daughter alone. If you wouldn't mind, Alpha" She pulled back her hood, a smile on her full lips. She was beautiful even as a woman in her age. Her eyes were crystalline, so clear, one could see their reflection in them.

Knox seemed stunned for a moment before glancing in my direction. I could tell that he didn't want to leave my side, and a part of me wanted him to stay. I resisted that feeling. "It's okay. She isn't going to do anything to me." I looked in mother's direction, holding her gaze. "I would rip out her throat before she could even touch me."

Mother held her smile as her eyes sparkled with a light of amusement at my comment. I wasn't sure I could actually win against her. I had never seen her wolf. I didn't know if anyone ever had, but I wasn't going to back down.

"I'll be right outside," he whispered down at me as his fingers brushed over my bare shoulder, leaving a trail of fire before he walked away. He didn't bow to the mother as he left. Instead, he puffed up his chest and held chin high. I found that the sentiment warmed my insides, and my lips twitched with the urge to smile. He was a fine male, indeed.

"What do you want?" I asked after the door closed, and we were alone.

She lost her smile a bit, moving to my bedside. "I'm here because the Goddess wished for me to come. She sent me terrible visions of the future. It was a surprise to me when I heard that you were here as well."

I started to shift on the bed, so my back was to the mattress, but she reached out and stopped me from moving. My lip curled up in a sneer. My wolf was not happy about being touched.

She didn't seem bothered by the response. She was more amused than anything. "Let me see."

I stared into her eyes for a silent moment before I rolled over, turning my back to her. She brushed her fingers over the raised scars that the whip had left behind. Her touch was cooling and gentle, and it soothed the lingering burn. "You are beautiful, daughter. Strong and fierce, just as the Goddess wished you to be."

"No thanks to you." I snapped. I couldn't ignore the bitterness of her abandonment.

"You're right. This is all thanks to you. I have done as I will always do." She pulled back her hand, "The Goddess leads us all down separate paths. I follow my path as you follow yours."

I turned my face, so that I was looking into her eyes. "And what is the path the Goddess wishes me to follow, Holy Mother?"

There was sadness in her eyes as she reached back and pulled her hood over her head, shielding her face from view again. "Only you can discover that, daughter. I can say this... the enemy is at the door. If you do not help these people, you will all fail. Death is the least of our worries."

29

Scarlett

Noah entered the room with his head held high and his beta and warriors following in behind him. They've been training this morning from the sweaty clothes and red faces. The mark that Knox left on Noah was completely visible, and he wasn't trying to hide it. He wore his shame and failure as a mate forever for everyone to see. I could tell he was happy that he had something other than memories and pictures to remember Claire by. This mark would never fade. He would always remember.

I could hear the soft whispering of the pack as they took notice of the new scar, and it had my back straightening up like a board. I hoped none of them were foolish enough to try to challenge Noah because they would not be met with the same consideration he had given Claire's brother. His eyes met mine across the dining hall, and my cheeks burned as I recalled how things ended the last time we saw each other. I was the one who looked away first, shifting around in my seat awkwardly.

He took his spot to my right at the head of the table, making sure to stare everyone in the eye as he surveyed the faces in the room. He was giving them the opportunity to challenge him if they wanted. Some stared into his eyes a little longer than they should have, and he flashed them his pointed canines, and that seemed to be enough to have them remember who was alpha.

Dane took up his usual seat on my left side. "Good morning, Luna." He gave me a smile, but it wasn't as carefree. His shoulders were drawn up tight together, and his forehead was slightly creased.

"Good morning," I greeted back. "Did something happen?"

Dane let out a heavy sigh, reaching up to rub at his temple. "I found my mate."

I choked on my breath, turning to face him. "That's good."

"Yeah," He sighed again.

Dane stiffened as Janie entered the room. His eyes betrayed him as he watched her movements intently.

"She's your mate." I was happy I didn't have to worry about keeping the secret anymore, but from the way he was reacting, a part of me wished that it had remained unknown for a little while longer.

"She is," he said in a guttural tone, his wolf close at hand. He was trying to control himself from taking what was his. I wondered if David ever felt the pull to me like the male beside me felt for his mate. I wondered if he struggled with himself like this or if it was easy to throw me away for Eva. I wondered if Noah felt the pull between us like I did, or if it was easy to ignore it because I wasn't his true mate. I wasn't Claire.

"You don't want her?" I questioned him, wanting to discern the truth of the situation for myself.

He growled at the question, turning his gaze toward me in complete seriousness. "I want her. Wanting her is not the problem."

He looked back in her direction, and I followed his attention. She finally turned her eyes in his direction. She was the first to look away, focusing back on the people surrounding her.

A small growl rumbled out of him as his wolf scratched at the corners for release. "It's complicated. I'm just trying to give her the space she wants and treat her like she is any other wolf."

"But she isn't like any other wolf," I replied. I understood the sensation. Then and now, it was the same. David was now like any other wolf to me. I didn't feel any lingering sensations for him. Noah had seen to that the moment he had claimed me. He was now more than he deserved to be, but I couldn't change that. My body and soul would bear his claim until his last breath or mine.

Dane let out a heavy sigh. "No, she is not. She is so much more."

I reached out and grabbed his hand, giving it a squeeze under the table. "In the North, there's this saying, a long winter brings a longer summer."

He chuckled a bit. "Who knew Northerners could be so philosophical?" I let go of his hand and shoved him away from me. I knew he was teasing me, trying to divert the attention away from the topic of his mate.

I crossed my arms over my chest in mock annoyance. "We're not just a bunch of barbarians, you know?"

"If you ask me, the world needs more barbarians and fewer politicians. Alphas of the old ways lean too much on politics, they forget that they're wolves, but when you're trying to fight a war, sometimes, you have to play the game laid out before you." I tilted my head in his direction with a stir of curiosity. Noah was lucky to have such a strong and cunning male to be at his right hand. There was no question in my mind if he was loyal to Noah or if Noah valued his opinion. The bond between the two of them was clear.

Noah began placing food onto my plate, no words leaving his lips. The action was more than enough. The fact that he was doing it in front of his pack was sending a message. It was showing them that he accepted me and my place in his pack. He was giving me my portion before taking some for himself. Even more, he grabbed a piece of watermelon from my plate and held it up toward my mouth for me. I wanted to push the plate of food back toward him and tell him that I could take care of myself. I didn't want or need him to feed me like I was a baby. We held each other's gaze for a moment in a battle of wills. I had a choice to make: take the food or bite the hand that was trying to feed me.

I reached up with my hand and plucked the food from between his fingers. I put the food into my mouth, enjoying the flavors as they washed away a small amount of the contempt I felt. I licked the leftover juices off my lips, watching how his eyes followed the movement of my tongue.

I gave him a little show of teeth, snapping him out of his own lust. He met my gaze before looking away, cheeks pinker at having been caught. His body was drawn together in tense motions as he filled up his own plate with food.

We ate our meal in silence. The mood around the table was a somber one. When Noah rose to leave the table, he paused with a strange amount of uncertainty. I looked up from my food, meeting his gaze. "Would you please join me in my office when you're done, Scarlett? There is something I'd like to discuss with you."

His question took me by surprise that I didn't say anything and only stared up at him. Dane nudged me with his shoulder, shaking me out of my surprise. "I am finished now," I said in a rushed tone as I pushed my plate of food away and rose up from my seat. We left the room together, making sure there was enough distance between our bodies that there was no possibility of accidental touching. We both knew our wolves were just beneath the surface, waiting for the opportunity to be together.

"The moon ceremony is going to held tonight. The Holy Mother came here to conduct it for us," he said as we turned down the hallway that led to his office.

"Do you think you're well enough for that?" It felt weird to be talking to him like this as if we were confidants. I peeked over at him, studying the way the muscles in his jaw clenched as he thought over his answer.

"It needs to be done. The dead deserve their dues, so I will find the strength." His words were an echo of his entire character.

He opened the door for me, and I gave him a look. "Don't worry, Scarlett. I'm in control of myself." I hesitated for a moment longer before entering the small space. His scent was stronger in this room. I felt a wave of uncertainty about my own control as he closed the door behind himself.

"I wanted to talk about Christa."

I tilted my head to the side as I crossed my arms over my chest. "What about her?"

"I want her to stay here once she has healed up like we talked about." I furrowed my brow, trying to understand why he was telling me this.

"Okay, what is it that you want from me then?" I questioned, wanting to get to the point.

His lips pulled tight. "I know that Knox is going to be an issue. He isn't going to let me anywhere near her, but he seems to trust you enough." I narrowed my eyes a bit as I began to note where this is headed.

I didn't want to be a part of this war, but it looked like I wasn't being given much of a choice. I moved further away from him. I needed space so he couldn't influence me through our bond. He watched my movements with dark eyes, "You're always running away from me," he stated.

I felt my cheeks rush with heat, remembering the last time I had run from him. "Perhaps it's just in my nature to run when something dangerous is nearby." I suggested and watched his eyes focus on me like they would prey.

"Do you think I'm dangerous?" he asked in a dark tone that made me shiver with a strange excitement laced with fear.

"I don't *think* you are. I *know* you are," I stated.

He moved closer to me a couple of steps. "That's probably one of the most intelligent things you've ever said," he commented, and I resisted the urge to roll my eyes.

"But it's nothing I can't handle," I said as I challenged him.

He lifted a brow. "If that's true, then why do you run away?"

I clenched my jaw together as I stared him down, losing the small amount of good humor I had. "I'm not the only one who runs away." I bit back defensively. He seemed surprised by my words for a moment and quickly masked it as he usually did anytime he showed emotions.

He clenched his jaw tightly and stared back. "I don't want to talk about this. This isn't why I asked you to come here." He sounded frustrated.

"Is it so awful to be around me? Do you hate me that much?" I snarled at him. It was my insecurities speaking, the ones that haunted me in my sleep and in the dark corners of my mind, the ones that had turned me into the person that I was. I only ever wanted to be loved, to be the first choice instead of getting the leftovers.

He reached out and grabbed onto my arms in a strong grip, startling me. He was looking down at me with a dark gaze that said I had gone too far this time. I felt my heart thrash rapidly inside my chest, and I found breathing to be difficult. The last question had been for my own sake.

"I can't do this Scarlett!" He growled down at me. "Every time I'm near you, I think of Claire, and all I feel is guilt! But I can't—"

"What?" I interrupted him, feeling my heart sink in my chest, and my eyes widened in horror. All the memories of the past were flying through my mind. Those words echoed through my head like a thousand knives piercing my soul. "But you said…." I said breathlessly.

My wolf whimpered in my head. She felt the sting of his words as much as I had. He had already claimed us. For us, there would only ever be Noah. The anger took over, and I started to thrash around in his hold. "Let go of me! You're an ass!"

"Scarlett, calm down," he said to me in a cool tone that only made me angrier.

I glared up at him, feeling like I was on the verge of violence. "If you do not let go of me, I am going to rip you apart with my teeth. If you think I'm kidding, go ahead and try me. Find out how serious I am." My voice sounded so venomous, even I was a bit shocked.

"Just shut up and let me explain." He sounded annoyed and not the least bit concerned by my threat.

"No." I snapped. "I told you to reject me in the beginning, but you wouldn't. Instead, you marked me, and now you want to reject me? You really are a heartless bastard aren't you?"

His eyes widened at my words. "I'm not reject—"

I growled loud. "I told you to let go me!" I brought my leg up and kneed him in the stomach. He got knocked off balance and lost his grip on my arms. I turned away from him quickly, but I didn't get far before I was tackled down to the ground.

I tried to get him off me, but he overpowered me with his weight. "Get the hell off me, Noah!" I screeched in frustration as angry tears began to fill my eyes.

"Not until you shut up and listen to me!" He growled into my ear. His hot breath hit my skin, causing gooseflesh to rise.

I gritted my teeth against the sensations coursing through me. "Go to hell!" I growled at him. He growled back as he gripped me and flipped me over so that we were nestled together, chest to chest. His dark eyes stared down into mine, challenging me to fight him more. I glared up at him as my eyes moved over his face. I felt my wolf rushing towards the surface. My thoughts and behavior had put her into distress, and she wanted to get to her mate.

The fear of facing rejection again had me shrinking back in my mind and allowing my wolf to take over to shield me in some way from in the incoming pain. That was a mistake because once I was shoved back and she was in control, she struck with perfect precision. Her teeth sunk into the soft spot of his neck. The bond between us sizzled and snapped until I felt it press in over us.

What have I done?

I took control again, but it was too late. All of his thoughts and emotions were flowing into me as I pushed away from him. He was staring at me with wide eyes, blinking slowly as if he was just as stunned by what had happened between us. I watched as he reached up and touched the bleeding mark on his neck. I felt a surge of disgust and self-hatred, and I wanted to cringe back under the weight of it.

I didn't want to be in his head, just as much as I didn't want him in mine. "Why?" I asked him with a shaky tone. He didn't answer me. He was still in shock. I have brought the alpha to his knees with one bite. Any lingering connection to Claire was being eaten away by my claim.

He stumbled off me, falling onto his back on the ground next to me. I quickly sat up, turning to him in concern. "Noah! I'm sorry. I'm sorry," I found my words spilling out as I looked down at him, but I wasn't sure if they were meant to comfort him or me. His eyes were clouded a bit, and he seemed slightly out of it as he looked up at me, but he didn't say anything. His eyes slowly fluttered shut, and I cursed myself.

There was a knock on the door. "Alpha Noah, the Holy Mother is waiting to speak with you." My entire body tensed up at the words. The door opened to reveal Dane. He looked over the scene with widening eyes. I was sure I must have looked half-crazed.

Dane stepped into the room, moving toward us hesitantly. "Scarlett?"

"I didn't mean to… It just happened. I couldn't control it." I rambled on.

Dane looked from me to Noah who was lying unconscious. "What happened?" he asked me calmly as he moved closer.

"I marked him."

30

Scarlett

I had decided to stay behind in Noah's room long after Dane and Doctor Owen had left. I couldn't stop the guilt that was ripping through me. I ran my hand through my hair as I paced back and forth at the foot of his bed.

The thought of him hating me was enough to make me want to curl in on myself. I knew it was the damn bond, though, because I would have never been that hurt before, and it just made me more frustrated.

I peered at Noah who was laying on his bed. His brows were drawn together in discomfort, and his body was moving a bit restlessly in his unconscious state. I knew it was the bond working its way through him forcefully just as it had done to me. I shouldn't have cared that he was suffering. I mean, he definitely deserved it. Yet, now that it was happening, I didn't feel any satisfaction. I let out a frustrated sigh and walked toward his side of the bed, not really sure what I was going to do.

I stood over him looking down and feeling completely unsure of myself for the first time in a long time. This was my mate, and I had claimed him, which meant that for better or worse, we were stuck together now. I bit my cheek at this thought and almost laughed at myself. I had been trying to escape one alpha only to fall into the hands of another. I bent over, examining him more closely.

My eyes fixated on his lips, and I felt the desire to kiss them. The feeling welled up inside so much so that I leaned in close enough to feel the soft, warm pants of his breath hitting me. I pulled back quickly, my face rushing with heat when I realized that I was about to kiss him. I turned my back to him and put a hand to my heart to try to calm myself down. Great, this had to be part of strengthening the bond, and if that was the case, this was not going to go well for me.

When Noah let out a soft whimper. I turned back to him quickly with concern. He was beginning to move more restlessly in the bed. I bit my lip, rolling it between my teeth anxiously as I watched him. He only seemed to grow more distressed as the minutes ticked by.

I let my instincts take over, and I reached out to grab hold of his hand. Surprisingly, that seemed to help calm him down somewhat. Curiosity took over, and I pulled my hand away from him. The distress kicked up a notch, and he seemed to be almost in a full panic in his unconscious state. I quickly reached out and grabbed onto him once again. "It's okay! I'm right here, Noah," I said to him even though I doubted he could hear me. I brought up my other hand and hesitated for a moment before I stroke his hair lightly.

I wanted to roll my eyes at myself for the fact that I was in this situation, but at the same time, I couldn't help the tightening in my chest at being able to touch him like this. Normally, he was so closed off, and I wasn't much better, but if I thought Noah was willing to be open with me, then maybe I could finally take down the walls I had erected around myself.

I stayed like that for a long time, but eventually, Noah's calm breathing began to lull me to sleep. I decided against my better judgment to take up residence on the bed next to him, making sure to keep our hands locked together. It took a couple minutes to calm down my racing heart, but eventually, I fell asleep.

I didn't wake up again until I heard a loud thud and a flurry of curses. I blinked a couple times and rolled over to see that Noah was no longer in bed next to me. I popped up quickly, my eyes scanning the room nervously until I spotted that the bathroom door was open. I pulled myself off the bed and slowly eased my feet onto the floor. I made my way to the bathroom while chewing on my lips, not sure if he was going to attack me or something for what I had done. I wouldn't blame him. Hell, I would have attacked him if he had been anywhere near me when I had woken up.

I peeked my head into the bathroom to see Noah sitting in the shower with the water pelting down on him, looking extremely uncomfortable. He was still wearing his clothes. His eyes were closed, and his head was leaned back against the tiled wall behind him.

"Noah?" I called out to him. His eyes snapped open quickly at the sound of my voice. His blue eyes still seemed a little unfocused as they stared into mine. I felt my heart jump in my chest, and my stomach was suddenly under attack by a plethora of butterflies.

I broke eye contact with him. "Are you okay? Do you need me to help you? Get you anything?" I rambled out. The sound of quick movements had me turning my gaze back to him. I let out a small startled gasp because he was no longer in the shower. He was standing a few feet from me, soaking wet and staring at me with dark, hungry eyes.

His chest was heaving up and down. "What I need is for you to get out of here." His voice was gruff and husky. My eyes widened in surprise at his words. I bit my lip to hold back the lump in my throat. Noah's eyes caught the movement and focused on my mouth. He let out an animalistic growl and took a step toward me before he squeezed his eyes shut, clenching his hands into fists at his side. "Get out, Scarlett." His voice almost sounded pained.

"I'm sorry, Noah. I didn't mean to," I mumbled. My heart clenched tightly in my chest. I took a step toward him. "Please, don't hate me." I reached out hesitantly and placed my hand on his wet chest. His eyes flew open, and his hand reached up quickly, gripping my wrist in a manner that bordered pain. My eyes widened in shock as the currents of electricity pulsed between us so much more intense than they were before. Noah pulled me closer to him with his free hand and smashed his lips into mine with a hunger that took me completely by surprise.

He growled low in his chest, almost commanding me to respond to his kiss, but this passion felt darker and animalistic. It wasn't making me excited. It was making me feel dominated and scared.

I tried to push him away, and that didn't seem to make him happy because his grip on my wrist tightened, making me gasp out my pain. That sound seemed to pull him back into some form of sanity. Quickly, he was shoving me away from him as if I burned him. I slipped in the puddle he had created, landing on my butt with a thud.

"Shit!" He swore as his body shook. "Are you okay, Scarlett?" He gritted out between his teeth.

I stared up at him in shock but nodded my head as I slowly pulled myself off the ground. His eyes started to grow dark again. "Stop looking at me like that!" He snapped at me. I flinched back at the strange bipolar behavior that was taking place.

"What's happening?" I asked.

"Get out of here, Scarlett." He took a step further away from me, leaning his body against the wall.

"Tell me what's going on. I'm sorry about what I did, but let me help you." I didn't like the way my voice cracked. It made me sound weak. It made me feel weak. It made me feel like I was the old Scarlett before David's rejection had poisoned me.

"Just get out. Please..." He sounded like he was in agony and that made my wolf whimper inside of me, causing me to feel unsure as to whether I should stay and help him or respect his wishes and leave. As I stood there debating with myself, the hungry look returned to Noah's Gaze. I took a couple steps back, and his eyes followed my movement. He had the look of a predator who had prey set in its sight.

"Run, Scarlett," Noah said aloud in a raspy voice. "Don't let me find you."

I stared at him in disbelief and confusion. "Noah."

He forced a smile to his lips as beads of sweat began to line his forehead. "It's going to be alright, Scarlett. Just run."

I didn't wait to be prompted again. I listened to what Noah said and took off out of the bathroom and across his bedroom. I opened his door and bolted down the hallway. I had no idea why I was running, or what I was running from, but when I heard a loud roar come from Noah's room, my body began to move faster.

Dane came barreling around the corner at me, almost knocking me down. He caught me quickly, his eyes full of concern. "Are you okay?"

I nodded my head as I pointed back towards Noah's room. "Something's wrong with Noah."

He got a look in his eyes as if he knew something about it, something that I wasn't supposed to know. "Don't worry. I'll handle it. Go find Nadia. Stay with her and don't leave until I come get you." He let go of me and took off towards Noah without saying anything else.

Noah

I could feel Scarlett in my skin, burying herself deep into my soul. I wanted to fight it off, but there was no way to put out the fire of her claim as it burned through me. I could feel what remained of Claire turning to dust within its consuming hunger.

The longer I stared at her, the more my anger faded. I could have let her go when we first met. I could have pretended that there was nothing between us, but I was selfish. My wolf's hunger for the female he knew was his had gotten the better of me. My own anger and confusion had caused me to lose control and stake my claim. That had been our undoing, the point of no return.

She was nothing like Claire. Scarlett was more, so much more. I could see that now without the haze of Claire. It was as if this was the first time I had truly seen her since I laid my eyes on her in that parking lot.

Scarlett had been forged into a powerful wolf through her own trials. Claire hadn't faced much in her life. She had been gentle and pure, easily corrupted by the darkness of the world we lived in. It made me feel disgusted with myself to be thinking so poorly of my dead mate. She was the one who had saved me, the one who I had promised my heart and soul to.

I was disgusted by how badly my body wanted Scarlett, even knowing I would be breaking my promises to Claire. Confusion, anger, and sorrow filled me up. She has taken the last of what had remained of Claire from me. The things I have chosen to do killed her all over again.

My door burst open, and Dane and Ryder rushed in with tight expressions. The beast and my humanity danced for control as my vision turned into a haze of red. I let out a feral snarl. The beast wanted to gorge himself on them.

"This is going to hurt," Dane said before charging at me. He knocked me back into the wall, plaster cracking from the force of our bodies

I snapped my teeth together like the rabid beast I had been, pushing back against Dane. I could taste blood on my tongue, but I couldn't tell if it was his or mine. I couldn't stop myself. My control was gone. Deep down, a part of me didn't want to stop.

The beast was strong, but its hunger was stronger. The perversion of my past, the taint in my blood, had never gone away. It had only been kept contained. It was always looking for a release, whispering to me in the recesses of my mind, feeding on the darkness of my soul.

Ryder came at me from the side while the beast was distracted by Dane. He knew the hunger. He had been with me from the beginning even before Claire. He held onto me tight. "Noah."

The beast had more control. It was trying to break free from his grip, growling and snarling. "Noah!" Ryder snarled in my ear as Dane got up from the ground, adjusting his broken nose. The madness began to recede enough for my vision to clear. I took in the mess that I had created.

I felt shame as I tried to break from Ryder's grip. My body was tense. The beast lurked just beneath my skin. "Basement... Take me to the basement," I mumbled between my teeth before the beast broke my control again.

31

Scarlett

I sat on the couch in Nadia's room for the past several hours, trying to think about what could be wrong with Noah. It had been such a confusing situation, but it didn't feel as though he was trying to push me away the more I thought about it. It was as if he was trying to protect me from something as if he had been trying to protect me from himself. I could hear Nadia and Janie whispering to each other over by the door where they had been standing most of the time I had been in here.

I think they were afraid I was going to bust out of there and try to get to Noah, and while a part of me was tempted, I had to admit that even I wasn't that reckless. I peered over at them as they continued to whisper to each other. Nadia was talking in very harsh whispers and Janie was wearing an expression that said she wasn't very happy about whatever she was being told.

I felt my eyes narrow in suspicion. "What are you two whispering about?" Nadia's body tensed up at my question, and Janie spun on her heels to face me as she forced the tense expression on her face to relax. "It's nothing important." She shrugged, but my gut told me she was hiding something.

I opened my mouth to refute her statement but shut it when the door opened. A part of me hoped that it would be Noah, but I felt my heart sink when Ryder stood in the doorway with a serious expression. His eyes connected with mine. "Would you please come with me, Luna?" he asked, but I could tell it wasn't a request. Dane had told me to stay here until he had returned, but it was possible that he sent Ryder to get me.

Nadia and Janie looked at me with anxious expressions, but I ignored them as I pushed off the couch and moved toward the door. "Is this about Noah?"

Ryder said nothing and only looked at his mate and Janie for a moment before addressing me again. "These things are best discussed in private. If you would allow me to escort you." I pursed my lips together but didn't ask any further questions as I allowed Ryder to lead me from the room. I had a heavy feeling in my chest that whatever I was about to learn is going to be something unpleasant.

I decided to focus on something else as I was led through the house. Ryder was clearly the stoic type of person, which was odd to think considering he was mated with Nadia who was so lively, but I supposed I didn't know Ryder that well. It took a moment for me to realize that we were headed toward the basement. I wrapped my arms around myself as a strange feeling settled in my stomach. I caught Ryder looking at me out of the corner of his eye for a moment. "Do not worry too much, Luna," he said in a calm tone. "Dane is quite good at making sure no unnecessary harm comes to Alpha Noah during these moments."

I peered at him. "These moments... do they happen often?"

Ryder didn't say anything for a moment, and I figured that he was not going to give me an answer. "It's hard to say. Alpha Noah keeps many things to himself but after the passing of Claire, yes. This has happened many times," he answered honestly. I bit the inside of my cheek as I digested his answer.

I gasped when I felt a warm hand wrap around my clenched fist. Ryder gave my hand a squeeze, but he didn't venture to look at me. "You have to be strong for your mate now. No matter what you see, think, or feel... this is your mate, and you are the only one that can help him properly. Do you understand what I am saying?" He looked at me, pulling us to a sudden stop.

I stared back into his intense gaze, feeling as though perhaps he understood something of the darkness that laid in Noah's heart. "You were a rogue," I stated rather than questioned.

Ryder said nothing to confirm or deny it. "Do you understand?" he repeated his original question.

I swallowed. "Yes, I understand."

"If you want to leave at any time, just let me know, and I will take you away immediately," he said more softly.

I swallowed and looked past him to the door behind him, knowing that whatever was beyond it was not going to be pleasant. "Open the door." I hadn't been back to the basement since the day I had seen them torturing that rogue.

Ryder let go of me and opened the door, standing to the side so I could enter. I registered the door closing and Ryder's presence behind me, but I focused on the sounds of struggling.

My steps became more rushed as I got closer to the bottom. My eyes adjusted to the dim lighting in the basement room. My breathing came to a halt when I saw Dane breathing heavily as if he had been wrestling. His eyes peered up towards me with a small look of surprise and then looked at Ryder with narrowed eyes. "What are you thinking to bring her here?" He growled angrily as he stood up straighter.

"Why did you come down here? Didn't I tell you to wait until I come and get you?" He growled at me.

Ryder stepped forward. "Oh, stop your growling. I tricked her and brought her here because she needs to know."

Dane looked absolutely furious. "That wasn't your place to make that decision, Ryder. Noah didn't want her to know."

"Well damn Noah and what he wants! He's always been an idiot when it comes to matters like this." He spat out. "As his mate, she has the right to know, and even you can't deny this."

"And I planned on explaining it to her!" Dane hisses. "But not here and not like this!"

"She doesn't need your pretty words to comfort her. If she is going to be his mate, then she needs to see first-hand exactly what she is dealing with. You know it, I know it, and even Noah knows it." Ryder said harshly. He had seemed like such a quiet man before, but now it was clear that stoic way of being hid something much more volatile.

"Can you both stop acting as though I'm not standing right here," I whispered in frustration as they both stared each other down. "What is it that I need to see?" Dane looked from Ryder to me with his jaw muscles clenching and unclenching. I could see he was still contemplating what he should do.

"You're an impulsive idiot. I hope Noah hands you your ass on a platter," Dane said to Ryder.

Ryder snorted. "I have no doubt that he will."

Dane shook his head and ran a hand over his face before looking back at me with a tired expression. "Are you sure you want to know?" I stared at him, feeling uncertainty in myself for a moment, but I shook the feeling away. If I was going to be his mate, then I needed to know who he was, and it was clear this was a big secret.

I nodded my head and took a step forward, but Ryder reached out and caught my arm. I looked at him with surprise as he turned his face toward me. "Remember what I said." I nodded my head as he released me.

I stood before Dane, not venturing to look anywhere else, afraid what I would see. He stared down at me with a hard gaze before turning his face toward the cell. I knew he was telling me to look without saying it, but I couldn't find the strength to look. What was I going to see? Would I be afraid of my own mate? Would he be a man? Would he be a monster? So many thoughts raced through my mind. I squeezed my eyes shut and took a deep breath.

Come on, just look, Scarlett! I growled at myself and forced my eyes open, turning my head quickly to look into the cell. All thoughts flew from my mind, and I stood motionless staring at Noah. There he was, chained, stuck in some strange half-shifted state his dark eyes trained on me. I had never seen anything like this before. My disbelief was bringing me closer to the bars of the cell as my eyes rake over his body.

His arms were stretched over his head, and I could see that his fingers were more like claws. His face was strangely furrowed as if it had tried to take its wolf form but had stopped short. His lips were peeled back in a snarl, revealing his elongated canines that could rip through flesh if he had wished to use them.

"What is this?" I asked, my voice barely above a whisper as I kept my eyes trained on him.

"This is what it looks like when a man is at war with himself." Ryder has come to stand beside me on the other side.

Dane snorted bitterly, clearly upset that he had brought me down here. "You would know, wouldn't you?"

I cringed at his words but didn't dare to look at Ryder. "How come this happened? I know Noah was a rogue, but he beat that, didn't he? I mean, Claire helped him come back, didn't she?"

"The stories are true. Once you go rogue, there is no going back, but that doesn't mean you have to be the monster. All Noah did and has done is gain control over his wolf's more violent and bloodthirsty urges, but his wolf will always remain on the feral side," Ryder stated matter-of-factly.

"Then you're saying that when something sets him over the edge, he becomes like this?" I motioned with my hand toward Noah.

Ryder chuckled darkly. "Noah is always on the edge. He'll always be on the edge, but luckily, he has anchors to keep him from falling over. Before you, it was Claire, then it was the pack they started together. His killing her was like cutting the rope that tethered him. He was hanging on by a thread, then you showed up and threw him another rope."

I nodded my head, taking in the words he was telling me and trying my hardest to understand. "So this is what you meant earlier when you told me that I had to be strong for him regardless because I'm the only thing keeping him from falling over the edge."

"Aye." Ryder put a hand on my shoulder.

"Would he hurt me when he's like this?" I asked, feeling my throat grew tight.

"I couldn't tell you. I would never want to hurt my mate, but even I don't have that kind of self-control when I'm like that," Ryder said softly. My eyes scanned over him, realizing that he had admitted to being a rogue wolf once as well. I turned my face away quickly to look back at Noah. "I want to go in there."

"What?" Dane blurted out.

"You heard me. I want to go in there with him." I wasn't sure what I was going to do once I was inside, but I was trusting my gut.

"No way! I'm sorry, Scarlett, but I will not risk your safety like that. There is no way to know what Noah will do when he is like this. He wouldn't forgive himself if he hurt you." He stopped short when I turned to look at him with a determined stare.

"I take full responsibility for myself. Now open that door. Please don't make me command you," I said firmly. Dane looked like he wanted to argue with me more, but when my gaze didn't waver, he sighed in defeat.

"Noah is going to kill me when he gets out of here," he grumbled under his breath.

He stepped around me and unlocked the cell door. He pulled it open and looked away in anger at my choice. I said nothing to him as I made my way to the door, taking a deep breath before I entered. I heard movement behind me, and I looked over my shoulder to see Ryder had followed me in but stood close to the door. "Just in case," he said. I gave him a small smile before turning back to Noah.

He hung very still, his chest heaving up and down from the strain I was sure it took to keep himself from going completely wild. He watched me with his predatory gaze. It seemed as though he was analyzing every move I made. I would have been nervous about this if he wasn't chained up. I held up my hands in a surrendering position but kept my eyes locked on his. My skin seemed to tingle with every step that brought me closer to him. The closer I got, the more I could see him and the more I was in awe of him.

He stared down at me as I stopped a few feet away from him. I realized that I wasn't afraid of him as I had thought I would be. He was neither a man nor a beast—he was a monster. Yet, my heart thundered in my chest as it did whenever he was near me, and that was how I knew that it didn't matter to me what Noah was... because he was mine, for better or worse.

I reached out slowly with a curious hand, wanting to touch him. He moved quickly, lunging forward and growling into my face as if to tell me to stay away from him.

"Scarlett!" Dane called from the door.

"It's fine. I'm fine," I told him calmly. I remained frozen, staring into his darkened gaze. "I'm not afraid of you."

His breathing became more ragged as if he was the one who was afraid of me. I gave him a soft reassuring smile. "I won't hurt you," I whispered before I continued stretching my hand out forward. His lips pulled back, revealing his sharpened teeth in a threat, but I didn't stop. When my hand came into contact with the hot flesh of his chest, the shocking sensation was immediate, and it made him growl loudly, straining against the chains.

I took another step closer to him so I could feel his hot breath on my face. "It's okay. I think I understand now," I whispered to him. I understood why he had pushed me away so much. He was afraid I would run from him. He was afraid that he would hurt me.

He brought his face closer to mine, keeping eye contact with me. My wolf was whimpering inside of me at the intimidating gaze, and for the first time, she wanted nothing more than to submit under the weight of it. I swallowed hard against the urge. He turned his head a bit so that his face was almost nestled into the crook of my neck. I remained motionless, not wanting to startle him in any way. I felt his tongue touch my skin, and my eyes widened in surprise. His canines scraped against my flesh sending a shiver racing down my spine. "Mine," he growled low into my ear. The statement made my knees feel like jell-O, and I stumbled back away from him in a small shock.

His eyes watched me, and I knew he understood everything that I had said. My heart was racing wildly in my chest, and I felt a heat wandering over my skin. His pupils ate up his iris as he strained against the chains. He snarled viciously at me.

Ryder grabbed onto my arm. "I think that's enough for today. No need to test his self-control anymore."

Noah let out a loud roar at the sight of Ryder touching me. Ryder quickly released me. "Get out of here," he hissed.

I continued to back away, and out of the cell, though my eyes were still trained on Noah until at last, I turned away and booked it up the stairs and out of the basement with Noah's roar following behind me. I flung myself out of the door, slamming it shut behind me and leaning against it. My heart was still beating erratically in my chest at everything that had just happened. I didn't know why I was running away. I wasn't afraid of what he was. I knew deep down, he would never hurt me. No, I was afraid of something else entirely. I was afraid of what he had made me feel and how deeply I had felt it.

I hadn't left my room for a couple of days, except to eat. I had a lot on my mind. It was not only the secret that had been revealed to me in the basement, but also the fact that I could feel the symptoms of my heat coming on stronger with each moon rise. It wouldn't be long now. I nibbled on my lip, the thought driving up my anxiety over my current situation.

When the knock came at my door, it was a soft and unassuming sound, a whispering embrace that shook the air around me. I burrowed deeper into the comforter on my bed, trying to block out the echoing of Noah's doubt and uncertainty. They clawed at my raw heart. I had too many of my own fears and doubts at the moment to handle his.

"Scarlett." His voice was smooth like honey. My mouth turned dry with the desire to have another taste of him.

"I just want to talk. Give me a chance to explain myself. I promise not to touch you." His voice was soft and coaxing, nothing like the harsh tones he had used on me before. It was hard to believe that a big, powerful alpha was standing on the other side of my door at the moment. He waited for my verbal response, but when he got no indication one way or the other, he made the choice for me. The sound of the door knob twisting bounced off the walls and cut through the silence of the room.

The moment his eyes landed on my blanketed form, I stiffened up. It was like there was nothing between us. His gaze fell over me like warm currents, clinging to my flesh like fresh water from a hot spring. I tightened my hand into a fist around the comforter. I was doing my best to ignore the effect his proximity was having on me.

I lifted my eyes to his face. He looked worn down. There were dark bags under his eyes, and his skin was flaxen. My gaze traveled from his face to his neck, greedy to get a look of the spot my teeth scored him. It looked like he had tried to claw it off in desperation unsuccessfully. The skin around it was red and angry.

All of my hope that knowing his secret would bridge the gap between us left me at the sight of the guarded look in his cold eyes. I gave him a quick look of pitiful disappointment before I turned my back to him completely, fixing my eyes on the blank wall across the room. The silence hung heavy between us. The tension was like a tightening vice. I wondered if there would ever be a time when we would stop pushing and pulling at each other or if we would end up tearing each other apart because of this bond.

The mattress dipped down as he sat himself down on the edge, careful to make sure we didn't touch. "Before you, there was only Claire. I never desired anyone else before her. I had no idea I could feel anything other than the desire to hunt, to kill, and to feed." I knew he must be talking about his time with his father, about his time living as a rogue. It still seemed odd to me that he had been able to recover from such a state, but here he sat. Perhaps not recovered but rehabilitated.

"But now my body wants more, again. My body hungers for your body." I tightened my thighs together.

The bed creaked as I felt him leaning in closer to me. "I want to touch you so bad, it's like a gnawing hunger, but my mind is disgusted by the thought. It's hard not to see it as a betrayal to the woman who saved me, who loved me when I was only a monster." His words pulled at the scabs on my heart. Hadn't I shown him that I could do the same thing? Or had that meant so little to him?

He made a pained noise in the back of his throat. We were both being crushed under the weight of our bonded souls.

Our hearts were crashing against each other as they tried to synchronize their rhythm. "This need, this desire we feel for each other is only because of the bond. If you had been given a choice, would you have chosen me, Scarlett?"

I had no answer for him. I didn't think there was a right answer to his question. The icy hand of rejection was slowly suffocating me. "Is that all you wanted to say?" I asked as my throat clenched up with the urge to cry. I knew he could feel the pain circulating in my chest.

"Scarlett..." he said my name gently like he was going to try to comfort me. That turned my pain into anger. Something inside of me snapped.

I sat up quickly, my hair falling around my face in a mess. "Stop. Don't say another word." I could feel my lip quivering as I did my best to hold back my tears. "I just want you to go. I don't want to be anywhere you are right now."

He stared into my eyes with those cold sapphires of his. They reminded me of the ocean, the way his emotions ebb and flow through them. I swallowed my feeling down as they surged and swelled with his. "Let me make this easier for you, Noah. I won't bother you anymore because I don't want to know what you're thinking or feeling. I don't want know anything more about you." He let out a small breath as he gave into my request for him to go, pushing up from the bed.

When he reached the door, he paused with his hand on the doorknob. "I'm a ruined man, Scarlett, and now I've ruined you too. I'm sorry for that." He sounded full of regret. He was choking on his remorse for me, for the both of us. It only made my stomach twist up more.

He left, and I sunk back into the bed, my tears falling freely. He didn't know that I was ruined long before I met him. I was used to the feeling.

32

Grace

Strong fingers worked at the knot at the back of my head for a moment before the blindfold was removed from my eyes. A snarl erupted from deep in my chest. The devil inside of me needed a fix of violence and blood. Kade hovered over me with a wicked grin on his face. The smell of death and rot that hung around him burned in my nose. "Rise and shine, little Alpha. Welcome to your new home."

I blinked a couple times to push away the blurry vision as I looked around the room. It was a lot nicer than the dirt-padded cellar I had been kept in before. *What a considerate upgrade.* It only took me a moment to notice that my previous companions were missing in action, and I was the only guest in this particular room.

I was laying naked with my wrists and ankles were chained to the steel bed frame. I pulled at them, testing their strength. My wolf snapped her teeth in frustration as she rushed back to the forefront of my consciousness.

I growled at him as my lip curled up in a show of sharp, monstrous teeth. He only gave me an amused smirk. "Don't worry. I've made sure you got preferential treatment, being Kellan's whore and all. You have a room all to yourself with a nice meal each day. *Alpha* Thorton has been quite accommodating."

He nodded his head to the rogue just out of my sight, but I could smell it. "He even had a welcoming gift made for you. It might be a little snug since he didn't know your size." The rogue's hands were trying to pull something down over my face as I fought with them, nearly taking off his finger. It was a muzzle made of silver, and it burned as it settled over my mouth. I was growling low in my throat, baring my teeth behind it.

"Guess you'll have to drink those meals through a straw." Kade laughed as he turned his back to me. He followed after the other rogue, turning off the light as he left me alone in the room. The darkness was welcoming and familiar to me. I lay still on the bed, listening carefully to the world around me. I noted all the different sounds and scents.

I tapped my clawed finger against the frame, counting the number of steps I heard the guards take before I couldn't hear them anymore. There came a clank of metal on metal from the wall near my head. My wolf growled at the sound. It irritated our ears. It came again, and I tilted my head up toward it in annoyance.

"Aye, young one? Yer alive in there?" Patrick's voice echoed through the wall. I let myself settle back into the bed, not responding. As far as anyone needed to know, the Grace that had been taken from her parent's house had died long ago. I didn't know who I was anymore, other than a beast that my circumstances had created. Someone who had been forged in the fire and made sharper and more dangerous than before.

The clanking came again. "The wall is still better company," he stated before he started singing a song from his old country. I rapped my knuckles against the steel frame if only to shut him up so I could have my silence. I heard his light chuckle, and then there was nothing. After that, I dozed in and out of sleep for a while, the silver keeping me weak.

It was when a particular scent of festering rot drifted into my nose that I came to completely. I turned my face toward the door, waiting for *him*. He had stayed away longer this time, but his sickness would never let him leave me for too long. The door swung open, and I squinted against the sudden light, his shadow darkening the doorway. I could smell there was another wolf with him. His stench was softer. He was a newer member.

Kellan came into the room as the other Alpha hung back by the door. I barred my teeth at him as deep, rumbling growls echoed from my chest. He didn't seem put off by the show, his hand stroking over my leg as he came in close enough to touch.

I jolted up against the restraints, snapping my teeth in his direction. He gave me a toothy grin. "I've missed you, my queen. Those Northern women are wild enough, but not nearly as wild as you." His claws scratched at the surface of my flesh. Just a little more pressure and they would poke right through.

I stared at his throat through narrowed eyes, watching the vein in his neck pulse. The movement was subtle and calm. I wanted to sink my teeth into that spot and tear the life-giving vein open and see how calm it was then. My wolf rumbled her agreement, her mouth fixed into a feral wolfy grin. She was the devil inside of me.

His eyes grew darker as his beast rose to the surface. "I've hungered for you." His claws pierced through my flesh, cutting deep. I could feel the blood rushing from the gash and running down my leg. The soft drip of it as it splashed to the ground was a pleasant serenade.

His other hand dipped between my legs, and I flashed him my teeth, snapping them at him while I pulled at the restraints. "When your heat comes, I will make sure to put a pup in you," he said with a satisfied smirk. The other male at the door turned his face away from the scene. He looked uncomfortable with watching. He was not like the others that usually came with him. This alpha would not last in the world that Kellan was carving out for himself. He was too soft.

Kellan waited for the blood loss to take effect, to take more of my strength with it. He had them keep me in silver chains because he knew that without them, I would have his throat. All of these beasts were nothing to me.

"David, if you're not going to watch, you can go wait for me in my office with Kade and Thorton." He called out to the alpha in his company. The alpha named David hesitated for a moment as our eyes connected.

He looked away from my gaze. "What are you going to do to her?" he questioned. He must be a new rogue. The hunger hadn't yet replaced his veneer of humanity.

Kellen tensed up. "What does it matter? You've got your own female to worry about. Now go." He growled. That was all it took for David to leave. *What a spineless fool.*

Kellan stared down at me with a look mingled with contempt and desire. I watched his teeth elongate and his face became more angular as the beast sat just beneath the surface. I couldn't do anything to escape or block his attack. I could only wait, knowing exactly what his next move would be. It was always the same.

He lunged for my throat, knocking my head to the side with his elbow. Even though I knew I couldn't do much, I still growled and snapped my teeth at the air like a rabid animal. The muzzle was keeping my attacks from being effective.

His teeth scored my neck, marking me. Our minds tried to meld together. My devil growled viciously. Neither of us liked when his sickness slipped in through the cracks. It confused my wolf, and she did not like tricks. The effects of this bonding would fade in a couple days. It never stuck because I was not his to claim but until then, it was like a snake slithering around in my head.

He rocked himself against me, letting me feel the heaviness of his desire as it pressed into my leg. He bit harder as I thrashed against his body, against the restraints. He liked the violence, rage, and hatred.

He fumbled around with his jeans, undoing them. His manhood landed heavy against my thigh. It made my skin crawl, and my wolf snapped her teeth together viciously. I knew what was coming. The first time it happened, I cried for hours. Now, I just focused on my rage. I let it carry me to some place far away, a place where I was the queen of ashes and bones, a place where the world burned in the wake of my vengeance.

He plunged into me, lifting a hand to my throat. His palm was calloused, and his grip was strong as he squeezed, cutting the flow of air to my burning lungs. I could hardly breathe. My vision was fuzzy, but he made sure I remained half-aware of what he was doing. He wanted my hatred, and I was more than happy to give it to him. He grunted out his pleasure over and over, the sound echoing off the walls. I stared up at the ceiling above me with my hands clenched tightly into fists at my side. My body was stiff as a board.

My wolf was watching from inside, her rage building like a consuming fire. We were of one mind that this male would die by our teeth. Once we get freed, we would come for him. He wasn't the one we wanted most, but his blood had to be spilled. It would be spilled if only to satisfy my own hunger.

33

Dane

Janie sat alone under the tree with an open book in her lap. The way the sun hit her skin made it look like she was glowing. I could feel the wolf rising under my skin. I wanted her. My wolf wanted her. It was hard to pretend otherwise, but she seemed eager to avoid me. I was surprised when I found her. She wasn't what I was expecting. I remembered her, only I remembered her as Claire's little friend, not the graceful female I had found. Maturity had done her well, *very* well.

It had also turned me into a tongue twisted fool, and now, she was under the impression that I was somehow ashamed of her and that, I didn't want. She had made it clear she wanted me to steer clear of her. I have been trying to respect her wishes, but the wolf could not be denied.

The breeze sent her scent in my direction, and I inhaled it like a drug. I couldn't get enough of it. She smelled like the air before a storm, potent and charged with life. My feet paced toward her without an active thought telling them to move me.

She lifted her face, and those dark eyes looked in my direction as the golden streaks in her chestnut hair reflecting the light of the sun. My heart clenched in my chest. It was hard to breathe. Those eyes hold my whole being captive. I'm a prisoner to her every movement, *a willful captive.*

I made sure not to get too close to her. "How long do you plan on avoiding me?" I couldn't help asking. I needed to know.

She tucked some hair behind her ear. "I'm not avoiding you. I was thinking maybe we could sit down and talk when I had more time. I've been helping my father with all the healing members. It's hard to find free time." My heart grew hopeful at the words that she was speaking to me. I moved a little closer to her. I noticed the way she stiffened at the movement, angling her body so that she was leaning away from me.

My hand clenched into a tight fist, and I shoved it into my pocket to hide it from her view. "I know that Noah must be happy to have an extra hand around here. Especially with the mating season coming up, a lot of females are going to need care."

Her lips twitched at my comment. "I'm sure Noah will be happy about that." Her tone is flat, but her words held more meaning.

I didn't know what more to say to her. There was so much lingering between us. She turned her face back to her book after a moment.

"Janie." I couldn't stop my craving for her.

I noticed the whitening of her knuckles as she clutched the book tighter. My presence was having an effect on her. "What?" Her tone was no longer flat. I could hear the slight fluctuation of her vocal chords, an indication of hidden emotions trying to seep out. She was afraid. I could sense that much through our fragile bond. I wanted to know what I could do to ease her fears, how I could get her to accept me.

"I'm glad I found you." Those weren't the words I wanted most to say, but they're the ones that slipped from my tongue. I didn't want to push her away when she was almost in reach.

She turned her face toward me again, giving me a small smile. "Me too."

I wanted to ask her if I could touch her, just one touch. Instead, I shoved my other hand into my pocket to keep myself from begging for it. I gave her a small tight-lipped smile in return. "Guess I should let you get back to your book."

She held my gaze as I took steps away from her. I wondered what she saw when she looked at me, if she felt the pull of the bond as much as I did.

I forced myself to turn my back to her and go back inside the house. My skin crawled with the desire to look back, but I didn't. I wanted to respect her choice the best I could, giving her the space she wanted until she could come to me on her own.

I came in through the kitchen side door, expecting it to be empty at this time of day. I was surprised to find Scarlett standing alone in the kitchen, staring out the window toward the woods. She has been avoiding everyone for the past couple of weeks ever since Ryder had brought her to the basement. I figured that Noah had gone and done something stupid. Her hair was hanging loosely down to the middle of her back. It had grown out over the past couple of months. I remembered when we met, it was only at her shoulders.

"What are you looking at?" I came up behind her, curious to see what had captivated her attention. My eyes were instantly drawn to my mate. I gritted my teeth as I cast my gaze to the trees quickly.

Scarlett sighed heavily. "Freedom." Her word caught me off guard as she turned those dark eyes toward me. I could feel the power radiating out of her. She was like a raging fire looking to consume everything in her path. She always met everyone's gaze without shame or remorse, a true wolf through and through.

"I saw you talking to Janie." She gave me a knowing look.

I felt the tension in my shoulders. "Yeah."

She didn't look away from me. Her eyes burned into me, agitating my wolf. He didn't like that she was showing dominance over him even if it is unconscious.

"You need to make your move," she started, her voice full of emotion, "or you should reject her." The last statement seemed more provoking than what she actually thought.

I couldn't stop the growl that rumbled out of me at her words. "Never. She's mine."

Scarlett didn't even blink and stepped in closer to me. Her scent tickled my senses, coconut and something sweeter. I could feel my body reacting to the fire building inside of her. She was going into heat. It was putting my mind into a haze, hypnotizing me with a feral need.

My wolf wanted his female, but this female was also strong and could carry his young. She smelled of life, and it was dancing just beneath the surface.

I tried to take a step away from her, but she followed me. "Then stop giving her what she thinks she wants. She will never accept you if you don't change things. Fight, Dane, fight hard." She was breathing heavily as she threw the words at me. She had so much passion behind them. There was a pain buried under the fire in her eyes.

Noah was a fool to leave her so unguarded. Any male could notice her worth. I found myself leaning toward her.

"What are you do—"

Her question was cut short as my lips crushed hers for a moment. I felt nothing but a heavy lust. It was like a fog in my mind as my wolf wrestled for control to be at the female in heat. I pulled away quickly, sucking in a breath. I needed fresh air. I needed to get out of this room. "I shouldn't have done that."

I backed away from her quickly like the room was on fire. "I'm sorry. I'm sorry." She reached up and touched her lips, eyes wide as she stared at me. I thought I might have stolen her first kiss from the look on her face. I found myself colliding with the counter.

What have I done? my frantic brain thought. Noah might kill me if he ever found out. Who was I kidding? He *was* going to kill me when he found out. I felt confused by my own body's betrayal.

"It's the heat." I found myself fumbling over the words. "Your smell... it's too much." And then I ran away.

I had touched someone else's mate. It not like I wanted Scarlett. She was my friend, and she was beautiful, but she wasn't the one that I wanted. Not truly. I wiped my lips with the back of my hand feverishly, trying to wipe away the taste of her. I felt disgusted with myself.

I knocked into a body as I turned the corner in my haste. The touch got my arms lightening up with pleasurable shocks. I could almost cry with relief and despair at the moment, trapped between heaven and hell. The Goddess had to be punishing me for what I had done, swiftly. She had thrown my mate directly into my path at my moment of weakness.

My wolf was ascending in his heated madness, a growl of hunger passed from my lips as I pushed Janie's soft body up against the wall. "You should have stayed outside where it was safe," I said, my voice deep.

I pressed my face into her space, leaning my forehead against her shoulder as I shook with my need. She pushed against me to escape. "Dane, back off!" She froze as I ran my nose up the length of her neck, breathing deep. I ground my hips against her. "I need you, Janie."

I heard her subtle intake of breath and the way her scent bloomed around her, pulling me deeper into the madness. "Dane... calm down." She's tried to coax me back into control, but she had no idea how good it felt to finally touch her. I wanted to let my wolf have his way with her, to take what was ours.

A rumble echoed as my teeth elongated with the fierce need. It was all the mating madness. I pushed myself away from her, knocking my back into the wall across from her so hard, I was sure I had dented the wall.

"Run..."

Our gazes locked, and I could see the concern flickering across her face. I crumpled to my knees as I held onto my humanity by a thread. "Run! And don't let me catch you. I won't be able... to stop myself a second time."

Janie took one step then another, not wanting to turn her back on me. She held my gaze until she couldn't anymore, turning and racing off the way she had come. The moment her back was to me, my wolf took control, skin falling away to fur. He chased after his female with the intent to make her ours forever.

34

Scarlett

"I need you to pack a bag." Noah's words crashed into me as he stood in my doorway, clouding up my room with the heaviness of his scent. I tried to ignore the way it seeped into my skin, marking me as his.

"Why? Where am I going?"

"I have a personal cabin a couple miles from here." He crossed his arms over his chest. The motion seemed stiff as if he was trying to hold himself back. His body teetered on the edge of the threshold to my bedroom. I could feel the magnetic pulse between us as the bond sparked to life as if it was a completely separate entity with its own beating heart. "We will be staying there for a couple of days."

I stiffened up. "I would rather stay there alone." I hadn't forgiven him for what he had said to me. I was still hurt by the way he had disregarded me despite the fact we were completely bonded to one another.

"That is not an option right now," he replied firmly, those blue eyes of his burning into me. They didn't feel like ice anymore. They had become more like dancing flames ready to rage and consume me. I slipped my tongue along the seam of my lips, my mouth suddenly feeling incredibly dry. This was a bad idea. I could feel it deep in my gut. We would not be able to fight off my heat together. It would only consume us.

Maybe he had resolved himself to the inevitability of it, but I hadn't. I didn't want to be a second thought in anyone's mind. I didn't want to be treated as the alpha's whore. I was more than that. I knew my own worth even if no one else seemed to recognize it.

"Don't worry. You'll have the bedroom. I'll be sleeping on the couch." I knew he must have sensed my wariness over the concept, but I didn't know what else I could argue.

I turned my back to him. "I understand. You can leave now." I could feel his internal battle with himself, a push and pull in his mind with his own demons. He wanted to leave, but he wanted to stay.

"Leave," I said in a more commanding tone. That must have set off something off in him because he entered my room. I turned back to face him, not wanting my back to him when he was so unpredictable. He closed the distance between us with long, powerful strides. I felt stressed at his nearness, my wolf rising to the surface ready to fight if that was what was needed.

He pulled me flush against him and wrapped his arms around me. I couldn't stop the sound that came out of my mouth—a cross between a gasp and a moan. I wanted to push him away and tell him to let me go, but my body would not obey me.

He buried his head into my neck. "You let another male touch what is mine, Scarlett. Are you trying to push me?"

I should have known he would know. I was foolish to think otherwise. I shook my head and pushed against him, trying to break through his hold.

"Did you like the way he tasted? Did you want him to taste more of you?" He was holding me so tight that I was struggling to breathe. "Did you, Scarlett?"

"Why do you care? I disgust you, remember?" I struggled against him. I could feel my claws poking at my fingertips as I became more distressed with the current situation I was in.

"No." His voice was guttural. "I disgust me. Never you... not you." I felt confusion over his response. It didn't seem to fit with my interpretation of the things that had transpired.

"God, you smell so good, Scarlett." He wasn't here anymore. He was lost in the frenzy of the heat that had been building in me. His nose pressed into my neck, trailing down to my shoulder. A shiver of pleasure rushed through me under the assault of his touch. I felt my canines filling up space in my mouth as my wolf rose closer to the surface.

"Let me go!" I growled and squirmed more frantically. I bit at him. I could taste his blood on my tongue, and felt his pleasure over my teeth piercing his flesh. He was shaking with his need to have me, to take me. He growled deeply as he lifted me up off the ground and started walking us toward my bed. My anxiety about the situation surged higher. I knew if he got me to the bed, something would happen whether we wanted it to or not because the wolf would take over.

"Noah, please." I pleaded with him. "You can't do this! I don't want to do this! Not like this, not like this." I started squirming in his hold, trying to free myself. He tossed me onto my bed as if I was nothing. My body bounced when it hit the mattress, and my world jumbled around, making my scramble to escape a laughable one. Noah grabbed my ankle and pulled me toward him before his body pressed into mine, pinning me underneath him.

He ground his hardness into me, and I could feel his pleasure rush through me. His hunger for my body was consuming my mind. I stared up into the black eyes of his wolf, and I knew he was going to have me, if not now, *soon*. All I could feel inside myself was the fear of him, of this moment. All my hardiness has been swallowed up, and a glimpse of the dainty, helpless female I was before came through. "Noah, stop. Please... Please..."

I watched as his consciousness pulled back at himself, the haze receding. He closed his eyes and pushed himself away from me. "I'm sorry," he said in a strained voice. I could feel his pain and regret as it ripped through him. He sank to his knees, and I watched from where I lay on the bed, unable to move myself either.

"I'm so sorry. Forgive me... Forgive me." His head was bowed low in shame.

I peeled my eyes away from him. "Please, just go." My wolf was pacing back and forth in my mind. She wanted to go for Noah's throat for what he had almost done to me against my wishes, but she was holding herself back. He bore our claim. Otherwise, I knew she would try to rip out his throat. I knew he could feel her unrest. It must have clawed at his skin.

He pushed up from the floor, taking a step towards me. "Scarlett, I am sorry if I hurt you." He was stumbling for words. "It's my fault you're like this. I—"

My eyes snapped back at him, and I knew they were completely black by the way he stopped talking and stared at me. "If you don't leave, I'm going to end up doing something we both may regret later. Please, Noah, just go." I pleaded with him. There was a long stretch of silence, and I started to panic that he would leave and then that he wouldn't leave. My emotions were at war within me over what I truly wanted him to do. I felt broken, angry, and lost. The bond had me twisted up sideways.

He said nothing else as he left me alone. A part of me was hurt, but I pushed it away knowing it was the right thing to do. I listened as his footsteps got farther away from me as a dull ache took up residence in my chest.

I made sure to shower before I headed down the stairs with a bag full of clothes and essentials I may need for the next couple days. I thought I had an idea of what to expect, but after what just happened in my bedroom, I felt like I was running completely blind.

Noah was waiting near the front door for me. He looked worn down as he met my gaze.

I peered over to see Dane standing back near the corner in the room with his head hung in shame. He wouldn't meet my gaze. There were teeth marks on his body, deep ones on his neck that would definitely leave a scar. I knew they were from Noah, but he said nothing about them. This was the punishment for touching his alpha's mate, but I knew Noah had stayed his hand because they were friends, chosen brothers. Any other person would have been dead. The beast within Noah would have demanded he kill the competition.

The wolf did not understand the complicated emotions of our human forms at times. It functioned in a land of instincts. If it was hungry, it ate. If it was tired, it slept. If there was a threat, it eliminated it. If it wanted its mate, it took its mate.

"We will be back in a couple of days," Noah said to Dane without looking at him, his voice more of a growl. He took my bag from me as I came to stand next to him. Our fingers brushed against each other in the exchange. I stiffened as the shock waves pulsed through me, and he tightened his grip on the handle, wrenching the door open.

The sun was setting on us by the time we settled into his truck and pulled down the dirt path, taking us away from the pack house.

35

Noah

Her scent danced around me as we drove down the road toward my cabin. I had to clench the steering wheel to keep from jumping across the seat at her. I already lost myself in her once. It would be so easy to do it again.

"Did you come here often with, Claire?" she asked me with a curious tone. I gazed intently at her, watching as the wind whipped through her hair. The sun played against her pale flesh so that it almost seemed to glitter. Her veins were visible just beneath the surface. She turned her face in my direction, those dark eyes of hers peeling back the layers and seeing straight into my soul.

I had to turn away from her. "No. I never brought her here. This was my personal sanctuary away from everything and everyone, including her." It felt odd to admit these things aloud to her, but at this point, it wasn't like it was possible to hide the truth from her, and I found out that I didn't want to. It felt oddly nice to share and talk about these things with someone.

She didn't respond to my words. She simply made a small thoughtful sound in the back of her throat. I wanted to know what she thought. I wanted to open the door in her mind and see what was lurking beneath her hard exterior. There was a quiet gentleness in her, a vulnerability that she tried to keep buried under her sharp-tongued remarks. I had seen glimpses of it in her eyes and in her movements. It was something I found myself drawn to like a wolf to the moon.

She shifted on the seat next to me, leaning her head back. I chanced another peek at her to see she had her eyes closed, drinking in the last rays of the sun. I had to force my eyes away from her as the hunger for her reared its ugly head.

"If being around me is such a struggle, maybe you should have sent me wherever the other unmated females are being kept," she said in a dismissive tone that made me bite down harder, my hands wringing the cracked leather of the steering wheel.

"It's fine. I can control myself," I replied shortly as I turned the truck down the road that led back to my cabin.

She snorted. "I think we'd both be fools if we believed that either one of us would have any control over this bond between us." I turned my face to her again to find her peeking one of her eyes open, looking in my direction with a humorless smirk.

I frowned as my gaze swept away from her to the trees that lined the dirt road. "You seem to be able to ignore it just fine." I was envious of her ability to seem completely unfazed by it. Even when I had held her, I had only smelled her womb's readiness and her fear of me.

Scarlett laughed dryly. "That's because I'm used to being burned at this point."

I flinched a bit at her comment. "I am sorry." The words tasted bitter on my tongue, but she needed to hear them. She needed to know I meant them. Only a weak male would not be able to admit when he had failed.

I saw her shrug her shoulders out of my peripherals vision. "Save your words for someone who actually needs them, Noah." I deserved her harshness. These were the consequences of my actions and treatment of her. I hadn't been able to see clearly through the cloud of Claire, that I missed the beautifully crafted creature right in front of me. I didn't think there was any way to undo the damage I'd done to her, but perhaps, there was a way to earn her understanding and forgiveness. I didn't want to spend the rest of my days fighting my mate. There was a real enemy out there, and it was not the female beside me. We were both cogs in the Goddess' cosmic plan, moving things in the direction she wanted them to turn.

She gives, and she takes. I understood that better than anyone.

"You deserve more," I started, admitting the truth to her, "more than me or the other male before me has to give you."

She looked at me with dark eyes full of unsaid feelings and hurt from the past. I could see something swirling in her gaze, but she didn't say anything to me.

The cabin came into view, and I could tell that Scarlett was more aware of her surroundings as she sat up straighter. I felt a warmth spread through my chest as I watched her stick her hand out the window and pluck some leaves from an overgrown branch that was pushing its way out into the path. She rubbed the greenery between her fingers before releasing them into the air. I could sense her love for nature. It swirled around her mind and into mine like a gentle breeze. The feeling was followed by a quick stab of homesickness. I wanted to reach out for her hand and soothe away the sting, but I kept my hands firmly planted on the steering wheel. I wanted her to feel like she was at home here with the pack.

"There is a lake a couple of miles to the east of the cabin," I commented, thinking that was something she would like to know, or maybe the truth was a part of me wanted to please her, to make that warmth in my chest last a little longer.

"Hmm," was the only sound she made as we pulled to a stop at the end of the road. She didn't waste any time, getting out of the truck and into the fresh air. She wandered towards the tree line as I gathered her bag out of the back. I felt a tug in my chest as I watched how wistful her expression was as she stared off into the woods.

"If you're interested, we could go for a run later tonight," I said as I came around the side of the truck.

Scarlett stiffened slightly as she turned toward me, her dark eyes raking over the length of me. "We'll see." Her tone was dry and empty. The beast was pacing back and forth over the thought of running wild with his mate. He wanted to take her in the ways of the wild. I knew she must have sensed the subtle agitation and change in me because she frowned in my direction as I quickly made my way to the door.

I pulled back the welcome mat and grabbed the key that was hidden underneath, exactly where I told Ryder to leave it after I had him stock the place with food. I opened the door for us and dropped her bag just inside the entryway. It wasn't a big space, but it was big enough for the two of us to share comfortably for the time being. The couches and chairs could use a little dusting and the floor a good sweeping.

Scarlett entered the cabin, looking around curiously at the humble space that belonged to me. I wanted her approval desperately, and so did the beast. He wanted to know that he had provided a secure den for his female in her time of need.

She grabbed her bag off the ground. "Is there a lock on the bedroom door?" she asked as she turned her back to me. She was making it known that she didn't trust me to stay away from her. I held my tongue to keep me from telling her that if I wanted to get to her, no lock in the world would keep me out. Instead, I nodded my head. . She walked away from me without another word, and disappeared through the bedroom door. The sound of the lock echoed distinctly in my ears.

I settled into the feeling of regret, doing my best to restrain myself from chasing after her. A few hours later, Scarlett emerged from the bedroom with wet hair and clothes clinging to her still damp skin. It was hard to ignore how the cloth clung to her curves. Her breasts were ample, and her hips were wide. All of her was designed to be held, touched, loved, and devoured. I had to turn my attention back to the food on the stove that I had been preparing for us or else I might lose control again and take her.

"Smells good," she said softly as she moved toward me. My skin tingled with awareness of her nearness.

"I thought you might like something to eat. I'm not very good at cooking, but I've learned a bit from the women in the pack," I replied as she came to stand beside me, looking over my shoulder at what I was doing.

She only stood there for a moment to observe before she moved away. "You should add some salt to that, or it'll be really bland." She left the kitchen without another word or look in my direction. A few minutes later, I heard the sound of her door closing. She had no interest in being near me, and I didn't blame her after all the things I've said and done. These were the consequence of my choices.

Scarlett returned to the kitchen as I was taking a seat at the table. I wondered if she noticed the surprise in my eyes as she took a seat across from me. Her dark eyes wandered from my face to the plate full of food in front of me. I pushed the plate out towards her, and she took the food I offered. I tried not to get lost in the warm feeling as I rose up and fixed myself another plate. I wanted to feed her from my own hand, but I knew I needed to take this thing between us one day at a time.

We ate together in peaceful silence, neither of us trying to bridge the gap. Still, I knew this was a step in the right direction. I finished my food first. My stomach was full, but the hunger was still clinging to me, as it always has.

"How much longer do you think we have?" I asked her. I wanted to prepare myself for what was coming toward us. Claire never went into heat, but I could smell the young that was waiting to be created inside of Scarlett's womb.

I didn't want that to happen. I didn't want any offspring to take up my mantle. I wanted the rogue blight to die with me when the Goddess took me back into her embrace.

She settled her fork against the plate, not looking in my direction. "Maybe a couple of days, at most."

I pushed up from the table, taking my empty plate with me. "I had Janie make up something to help you through it. She's giving it to the other females to help them." I dropped my dish into the empty sink, keeping my back to her. "She said it should help with some of the discomfort."

Scarlett let out a small snort. "What did she make you for yours?" I turned back around at her snide comment. She was looking at me with a smug grin. There was a slight twinkle in her eyes as if she found the thought amusing.

"I guess I'll just have to bear with it," I replied with a forced shrug as I turned my gaze to the window behind her. The sun had set, and the moon had already risen above the trees.

"Would you like to run with me?" I asked her again.

She pushed up from the table, her chair scraping against the floor. "I don't think that's a good idea." She brought her plate to the sink, and I took it from her, our fingertips brushing.

The feeling was electric. We both stood stiffly, staring at one another. I wanted to lean toward her, touch her, taste her. Her eyes became darker, and I noticed the way she inclined her body slightly toward mine.

"Why isn't it a good idea, Scarlett? Do you not trust me?" I tried to keep the desperation out of my voice. This female... *My* female got me ready to get on my knees and beg.

She shook her head and pulled back. "My wolf..."

"She doesn't like me." I finished the thought for her. I had sensed that her wolf had grown angry with me. She didn't like how I had treated her or Scarlett.

"She hates you right now, Noah. She would kill you for the way you have treated both of us, and I don't blame her. You've been cruel. To her, you aren't any better than David at this point," she told me flat out, holding my gaze to make her point clearer. I already knew this.

I dropped the dish into the sink and reached my hand out toward her. "Then let me make amends with her." Scarlett eyed me like I had lost my mind, not even trying to take my hand. I gave her a look, "Either way, you win, Scarlett. If she kills me, you're both free of me, and if she doesn't, then maybe we can talk about a future where we aren't constantly at each other's throats."

She held my gaze before turning away from me. "Fine. Let's get this over with." She walked toward the front door, and I felt the urge to smile. She was already stripping out of her clothes when I stepped outside. I took in the sight of her curves that looked like starlight in the glow of the night. She didn't feel any shame, she never had and nor should she. My female was perfect, every dimple and line that helped create her form.

She let her wolf free with a shudder of snapping bones and shedding skin, revealing her other beautiful but deadly form. I got down on my hands and knees before her wolf. Its teeth were bared as it licked its gums like she was ready to feast. Its dark fur looked like the color of raven wings. She was a fearsome and beautiful creature. The Goddess took extra care to mold her.

She was a perfect luna, one that other wolves would fear or follow. She came closer to me, low growls emanating from her chest. They were meant to be threats that I wasn't disillusioned about. She could follow through if she desired to.

I lowered myself further to the ground, ignoring the agitation of my own beast. He wasn't lower than anyone in his mind. I, however, understood that winning Scarlett's favor started with earning the forgiveness of her wolf.

She came close to me, snapping her teeth together inches from my neck. She was telling me that she could easily take my life, but she was showing restraint. She came again. This time, she nipped my flesh. The sting of her teeth coursed through me, but I remained unmoved.

We remained like this for several minutes until her growls slowly tapered off into silence. I didn't lift my head. I let her make the next move, let her make her choice.

A cold nose pressed to my neck, and I heard her breathe me in. I couldn't help the shudder as my beast rushed to the surface. She let out a small growl when I shifted slightly, and I forced myself to keep still though my muscles were screaming for me to move and my wolf was begging for release.

She pressed her body into mine as she circled around me. I knew she was marking me with her scent. This was a good sign. She was accepting my olive branch.

A warm wet tongue slid over the place she had nipped at before stepping away. I let out a breath, slowly lifting my face to look at her again.

A warm wet tongue slid over the place she had nipped at before stepping away. I let out a breath, slowly lifting my face to look at her again.

Our eyes met, and I took her in again. "You're so beautiful." I reached out slowly and waited for her to close the distance between us. She moved forward one step then another, pressing her forehead against my hand. I pushed my fingers deeper into her fur, rubbing and teasing it.

"You're a strong one aren't you?" I spoke to her wolf in a low voice, admiring all that she had to offer. She met my gaze as she pulled away from my touch, turning her back to me. She moved towards the tree line shortly after glancing back at me.

Her tail began to wag slightly, inviting me to come play with her in the moonlight. I pushed up from the ground and pulled my shirt up over my head. "You may want to turn away," I said.

She snorted at me but didn't look away. I felt my lips twitch up in the corners. "Suit yourself."

I took the heel of my boot and slipped my foot free, the other following suit shortly after. I was giving her a chance to turn away, but she never did.

I pulled down my pants and exposed myself to her. It was not that we hadn't been around each other naked before, but this felt different. I watched as her tail flick back and forth in a slow seductive dance, calling to the beast inside of me.

I didn't try to stop him this time. I let him take control. He shook out his fur as he settled his paws against the familiar dirt. This was his domain. This was his land, and he reigned over it all.

His female watched him as he approached her. He came to her slowly, carefully. Low whimpers came from his chest as if he was looking for a sign that she approved of him.

She brushed her tail across his muzzle, and he came alongside her, brushing up against her fur. She leaned into him for a moment, their scent mingling, before she nipped at his ear playfully. He let out a growl from the startling action, and she lowered herself a bit with a whine, her ears tucked back.

She lifted her face and licked the underside of his muzzle a couple times before he relaxed. She took the cue and rose up, brushing against him as she took off into the trees. I could feel his excitement as he pushed after her, releasing a howl toward the moon. He was eager to hunt this prey.

•

36

Scarlett

It has been a couple days since we let our wolves run together. I could see the great effort that Noah was making to help me feel comfortable with him, but I still didn't know how to feel about the changes in him. I didn't want this to be because of the bond. I wanted these changes to be because he actually felt differently.

I peered around the corner of the kitchen to see his sleeping form on the couch. His hair was hanging down over his forehead in a disheveled mess. The usual tension in his face was missing. He looked completely at ease. I felt a strange pull in my stomach to go to him, but I knew it was the bond.

I turned my back to him, finishing off the last of the tea in my mug. I had been drinking it every night before I went to bed to help with the growing discomfort in my body. I was hoping deep down that it would magically keep the heat at bay. It had done well to hide most of the symptoms and help me get through the days, but the nights were always bad. I slinked back to my bedroom, prepared for another evening of tossing and turning.

I woke up in the middle of the night in cold sweat, my body screaming in a burning inferno. At first, I thought I was ill, but slowly, I began to realize that I must have come into my heat. I pulled myself out of bed, and I stumbled toward my bathroom, needing to find relief from the raging fire inside my body. I didn't know how I made it to the bathtub, but I did. I turned on the cold water and quickly stripped out of my sweat-drenched clothes.

I lowered myself into the cool water with a sigh of relief. After a few minutes in the cool water, I gained more control of my brain. I relaxed my head back against the cool metal, closing my eyes as the water gently rippled around my body from my small movements. I didn't know when it happened, but I must have dozed off while in the tub.

When I came to again, I lazily got up out of the tub and made my way to my bedroom to get some fresh clothes, happy to find that the symptoms of the heat had dissipated somewhat. I grabbed a large shirt from the top of my suitcase, not having bothered to unpack anything. I slipped the cool fabric over my body and crawled into bed again, throwing the comforter off the bed.

I drifted in and out of sleep for a bit. The tea was doing its job but eventually, the fire returned. It ravaged my insides until I couldn't bite my tongue anymore. I was twisted up in the sheets, pulling at them as my body melted away.

My anguished noises must have roused Noah from his sleep because he knocked on the door. "Scarlett?" His voice sounded pained, and I knew he could smell that I was in heat. There was no way to hide that truth from him now. Another wave of fire raced through me, and I arched upward with a loud whimper, squeezing my eyes shut.

"Scarlett, I'm going to call Janie." He sounded uncertain about what he should do.

I gasped for air as the wave receded. "No... don't need. W-won't help." I could feel another wave building up again, and I wanted to sob for it to end. The door opened a crack. I had stopped locking it after the first night. I could hear him as he entered the room slowly like he was walking on eggshells. His scent danced over me, and I snapped my eyes open to find him standing beside the bed.

"Please..." I begged him as I shifted around on top of the sweat-soaked sheets. His blue eyes seemed to glow as he stared down at me from where he stood beside the bed. There was a wounded expression on his face, and I couldn't tell if it was from his discomfort or my own.

Another wave of heat rushed through me, and I squeezed my eyes shut as my back bowed off the mattress. My thighs were rubbing together to create some kind of relief. "Noah," I moaned his name as I opened my eyes again, vision blurry from the unshed tears. "Make it stop. I can't take anymore."

"Okay, okay..." He looked uncertain as he lowered himself onto the bed beside me. I reached out to him quickly, the need to feel his skin on mine overwhelming any logical thoughts. He caught my wrists together with his large hand before I could touch him. He held my gaze as I gave him a confused frown, not understanding why he wasn't letting me touch him.

"I want to touch you, but I can't have your hands on me, Scarlett. I only have so much restraint. Promise me that you'll be able to behave yourself, and I'll touch you," he said, almost like a plea for me to give my word. I nodded my head, licking my lips as he released my hands. I pulled them back to my chest so that he could see them. I was going to keep them to myself. I watched him through a hooded gaze as his eyes raked over the length of my body.

He swallowed hard as he reached out and grabbed the hem of my baggy shirt, slowly lifting it upward. He sucked in a breath when he found that I was completely bare and ready for him underneath it. "You're scent is so strong. You're so ready for me." He growled as he slipped his fingers between my slick fold.

I released a growl of my own at his touch. It eased some of the pressure that had been building up in me over the last few hours. I began to rock my hips against his hand, needing more relief from the sweltering heat that was trying to consume me from the inside out. A hunger that I've never felt before was festering in my stomach. I felt ravenous for something I had never tasted before.

Noah slid a finger further south and into my heated channel. I let out a whimper as a wave of pleasure rushed through me like a storm of ice against the raging inferno. When he tried to get another one in, the pressure built up again. I tried to escape his touch, pushing my heels into the mattress. He placed his free hand against my hips, stopping my poor attempt to escape him.

Our eyes locked. "It'll be over quick. Trust me, Scarlett." The way he said the last words released the tension in my body. I relaxed against his hand. "That's my female," he whispered to me in a soothing tone before he forced the second finger into me. It was blindingly uncomfortable for a couple of moments, but slowly, the pain gave way to pleasure. I followed the movement of Noah's touch, singing my praises loudly. Higher and higher, I was rising, and it felt like I could touch the moon if I reached up my hand enough. He kept up his motions, but relief seemed just out of my reach, and the inferno was beginning to lick at my insides again.

"Noah, please... It hurts. I feel like I'm going to burn out." I didn't know if my words made any sense to him, but there was an urgency in me, an instinct that was screaming I would die if he didn't do something soon. He growled in frustration as he pulled away from me, leaving me in more discomfort than I had started in. I cried out for him, reaching down between my legs to touch myself, hoping it would have the same effect.

"Noah... don't leave me..." I cried out as nothing seemed to fight off the fire.

"I'm right here, Scarlett. I'm not leaving." I turned my sweat covered face toward him to see that he was stripping out of his clothes. My eyes ate up the sight of his naked flesh with a greedy hunger I never knew I was capable of. He wasted no time crawling onto the bed and lowering himself on top of me. The weight of his desire for me pressed firmly into my thigh.

I stared up into his eyes. His beast was fighting for control. "This is the only way. I know what I promised—" He was trying to ease me into this, but I didn't have that understanding or patience right now. I lunged up and pressed my lips into his, silencing his tongue.

That seemed to alleviate any concern or doubt from his mind. He let his nature take over, wrapping his arms around me. His hand reached down between us, and I spread myself open for him. He didn't seem to have the restraint to hold himself back anymore, and he plunged himself into me with one quick thrust.

I let out a cry as the pain of him filling me rushed through me. My nails dug into his shoulder as I held onto him. He let out a ragged breath before leaning forward and pressing gentle kisses to my face as if trying to soothe the sting. After a moment, the pain was gone, and something else took its place, making me ache for more of Noah. I arched my hips up a bit. "Noah..." I whispered his name, my voice sounding needy.

He seemed to understand what I needed because he drew back out of me before pressing us back together again. The motion sent shock waves of pleasure through me, and I moaned at the feeling. I wanted more. Noah answered my hunger with another thrust of his hips, anchoring me to the bed.

"You feel so good, Scarlett." He started to move against me harder and faster. I met him thrust for thrust as the fire inside began to burn hotter until I was afraid that it might consume me from the inside out and burn us both. I whimpered and moaned against him. "Please, Noah." I begged him for what? I wasn't quite sure. All I knew was that I needed relief, and he was the only person that could give that to me.

He pushed us onward, *harder*. Both of us were sweating as the madness of the heat consumed us.

"Let go, Scarlett," he whispered into my ear as his thrusts became greedy and forceful. His words sent me over the edge, and I let out a strangled cry that was swallowed as Noah captured my mouth with his. He gave me a couple more hard thrusts before he found his own release. I felt the bond between us spark for a moment as we clashed against each other.

I could feel the heat leaving my blood and a contented weight in my mind as my wolf let out her own satisfied growl.

The morning after brought a fog of different feelings and sensations. I could hear the soft breathing of Noah on the bed beside me. His scent was thick in the air, and the smell of our union still clung to my skin. I turned my head and peered over my shoulder at him. He was lying close to me, but there was a small space between our bodies. His lips parted slightly, and I could see the subtle movements of his chest.

My wolf rumbled her contentment as she looked at our male. He belonged to her now, both the skin and the wolf beneath it. Noah looked content to remain where he was, only shifting slightly when I got up off the bed.

I walked on tiptoes to the bathroom, leaving the door open a crack so as not to make any noise to wake Noah. I wasn't ready for those eyes to see me or for his words to flood my ears. I needed the silence that filled the air at the moment. It helped calm my anxious heart.

I spied my reflection in the mirror as I made my way to the tub to wash away any evidence of what had transpired between Noah and myself. I paused for a moment to regard the female staring back out at me. Her dark eyes seemed livelier than before, and her dark circles were fading after a night of complete rest.

Her long hair was tousled and roused from sleep and the mating but was full of life. She no longer looked like a shell clinging to existence. There was life starting to grow anew. I turned my gaze away, biting into my lip. I didn't want to think about the changes that were beginning to show in me. It made me nervous about what would happen if Noah decided he didn't want me anymore. What if he rejected me now? What would happen? I would be even more lost than I had been before.

I turned on the faucet to the tub and let the hot water build up steam in the small space. I dipped my foot into the water, testing it before I lowered myself onto its warmth. A sigh passed through my lips as the warmth lapped at my skin, easing away any lasting tension and soreness from the night spent with Noah.

I sucked in a breath before I pushed myself deep under the surface water with my eyes open, watching the way the colors distorted and rippled from my perspective. It was completely different seeing things from this side. The world seemed to make more sense as I felt my lungs began to burn.

I rose up out of the water with a gasp, reaching forward to turn off the faucet before the water could escape the tub. I didn't have to look to know that Noah was watching me. My skin prickled with awareness. I could feel every part of me like a live wire, and I was certain that he could feel it too through the bond.

I turned my face, casting a look over my shoulder in his direction through hooded eyes. He stood in the doorway as his shoulder leaned against the frame. This brought back memories of the past couple of weeks, but this time, those blue eyes regarded me in a new light. They were soft and warm as they traced their way across my skin.

"How do you feel?" those were the first words he chose to speak into the void between us.

I took in his form slowly, drinking in the male that had claimed me as his. He was far from weak with his broad shoulders, wide chest, and scars of past battles marking his flesh. I found my body was greedy for him. One taste and I was already longing for another. I forced myself to look away from him, focusing on the water that kept me hidden from view.

"I feel better." I rolled my shoulders, testing out the tension in them.

He pushed off the frame and moved into the small bathroom, his long legs quickly eating up the distance between us. I found myself sinking in lower to the water, wanting to shield myself from his view. Last night, I had been a wanton woman owning her body but today, I was feeling unsure and insecure in the new territory.

He dipped his fingers into the edge of the water, causing ripples to flow outward, but he didn't encroach any further. I could see that he was testing the waters between us, trying to bridge the gap that has been there since we met a couple of months ago. So much had happened, and so much has been left unsaid. We were strangers whose fates were tied up together in a manner that was never anticipated.

The Goddess had made a mighty joke of us—that was what I thought before, but the more I stared into those blue eyes, the more I felt my previous perception of reality shifting. Maybe there was something else to be gained in our union, something that would have never been found if the choices that had led us to one another had been different.

"I'll go make us something to eat," Noah said after a moment, hesitating before he bent over and placed a gentle kiss on my forehead. I felt my cheeks heat up from the sudden show of affection. He pulled back quickly, almost as if he was afraid that I would attack him, and a couple of days ago, that probably would have been the truth.

I watched with my lips pressed tightly together, unable to find the words to express how I felt. He gave me a lingering look before turning away. "No rush. Enjoy your bath. Join me for breakfast when you're ready," he said as he walked out of the room, closing the door behind himself and giving me the privacy that I was suddenly longing for.

The smell of bacon and maple was what drew me out of the bath. I took my time drying off and dressing, trying to keep my eyes from straying to the bed that was a mess of blankets and pillows. I tried not to think about what we had done in that bed together. I tried not to think about how badly my body wanted to do it again.

I heard a loud pounding of flesh against wood, startling me out of my replay of the previous night's events. I grabbed a sweatshirt as I exited the bedroom, pulling it on over my head. I was curious to know who had the bravery to invade Noah's private sanctuary. I spotted Dane through the small crack between Noah and the door. His eyes drifted to me, and my cheeks flamed with heat, wondering if he could tell what had happened between his alpha and me. Noah closed the door slightly, blocking me from view as if he sensed my discomfort.

"We will discuss these things later," I caught Noah saying as he closed the door, turning to face me.

"We have to go back already?" I wasn't ready to leave the seclusion of this sanctuary. I felt nervous of the changes that had taken place between Noah and I. I couldn't help but be afraid that things would go back to the way they were before we left.

He lifted his face toward me, those blue eyes holding me captive. His expression was soft as the silence between us pulsed with unsaid words. "We can stay for a couple more days if that's what you want, Scarlett. I'm sure that Dane can handle whatever the problem is without me." He was calm as he spoke to me. I could see the effort he was making for me, putting me before the pack. This male was nothing like David.

I wanted to be selfish. I didn't want to share him with anyone else, but at the same time, I wanted to push him away. He seemed too good to be true. I couldn't help but feel that there were hidden motives behind his sudden change. I shook my head. "It's already been a week. The females will be returning to the pack, and Janie will be needing some help with the influx of what I'm sure will be pregnant females. And there is your war with the rogues..."

He moved closer. "That's not what I asked you. Do you want to stay here longer?" he asked with a firmer tone. I kept silent as my mind tried to process everything that had happened.

"Scarlett?" he called my name, wanting an answer, an answer I didn't have. It wasn't that simple. Nothing was simple.

"I don't know. I don't know what I want, okay?" I snapped at him. My anxiety rose as my heart thundered against my chest. I was confused. I needed time to think.

I could feel the sting of my words as they vibrated through him. Neither of us said anything for a couple of heavy minutes. He sucked in a slow breath, standing up a little straighter. "Would you rather I leave you here alone to sort out your mind?"

I stared into his eyes, hesitating for a moment. "Yes." I could feel the confusion and hurt rushing through our bond. He was fighting with himself over what he wanted and how to give me what I wanted. I watched his brows furrow and his tongue swipe over his dry lips as he gathered the right words.

"I'll come back for you in a few days. I'll send someone to come check up on you if I can't come before then." He sounded so certain and full of concern. His words warmed me up in a way that I had forgotten I could feel. I gave him a small smile, an olive branch that I hoped he would notice. His gaze was soft as it drifted over me, but he didn't smile.

The future was such a fragile and uncertain thing. "Breakfast is on the table." I watched him turn his back on me and leave the house, closing the door gently behind him. The sudden emptiness of the cabin had me wrapping my arms around myself for the warmth that had left with Noah. The smell of our mating spilled underneath the crack in the bedroom door, and I found myself regretting my decision not to go with him.

37

Noah

I had to force myself to get into my truck and drive away from my cabin. I could still smell her on my skin. I was glad for that. It helped to calm the beast's urge to turn back.

I was fighting every instinct that screamed for me to hold Scarlett closer and never let her go. The fear of losing her like I did Claire was almost debilitating as I got further away. I looked back in the rearview mirror every couple of minutes until I couldn't see the cabin anymore. I didn't think I would survive that type of loss again, neither me nor the beast. I was already too close to the darkness. I was riding the razor's edge of the reality that I had built.

Scarlett was becoming the new gravitational center of my world. Every second that ticked by brought me closer to her, binding me to her will.

I could recall the taste of her on my tongue clearly. I remembered every curve and line of her body. It was ingrained deep into my mind. She was beautifully crafted by the Goddess, a piece of art that was meant for me to love and admire, but it wasn't her body that I found myself longing to bury myself deeply in. It was the core of her being that I wanted to sink into. It was the only place I could be certain the pains of her past had not sullied.

I was on edge when I pulled into the driveway of the pack house. I could sense the unease that hung in the air as I got out of my truck. I turned my gaze to the sky, but it was clear as day. It was blue as far as my eyes could see. There was no sound, no breeze. There was only a heavy stillness that coated the world. It was like sitting in the eye of a storm.

Dane appeared on the front porch, and Ryder was not that far behind him. They were both wearing solemn expressions. I covered the distance quickly, pushing my own problems to the back of my mind. I was the alpha of this pack, and they needed me to be their strength in times of turmoil.

"What was the issue that you felt unable to handle on your own?" I grumbled as I paused at the bottom of the steps. Dane glanced toward Ryder, and he looked back with an expression that said he wasn't going to be the one to speak first.

Dane shifted before standing up straighter, forcing himself to look me in the eyes. "There's been an attack."

My body froze at his words, and my wolf flashed his teeth, his fur bristling up in his distress. "When did it happen?"

Ryder spoke, taking the heat off Dane. "It happened during the early hours before the sun rose. We were able to save most of the females, but we lost a couple, and the patrol was completely wiped out." His words had my wolf howling in vengeful anguish. These were his people to lead and protect, and he did not take kindly to people coming into this territory and taking what was his.

I clenched my jaw tightly. "Take me to them," I commanded in a sharp tone.

We took the two-mile walk down a dirt path that cut through the woods to the house that we used to keep the unmated females during the mating season. It wasn't a huge house, but it was big enough to house at least thirty girls at a time.

I could see that the females were all congregated together on the front lawn. Doctor Owen and Janie were looking at a couple of them while warriors stood posted as guards. They seemed to be in different levels of shock. Some of them wore blank expressions while others were weeping.

My gaze swept across the front lawn to white sheets soaked with red. I passed by everyone. I needed to see for myself what was done to these innocent females. I needed to see what I had brought upon them. I bent down and lifted the first sheet, and then the second, and followed by the third.

It was getting harder and harder to breathe as I moved down the line. I stared at the massacre before me. Their bodies were tattered pieces of flesh, nothing more than scraps for the scavengers that circled overhead. There were six bodies, six lives that have been added to the list of those who were lost.

I breathed in deeply, the scent of blood thick in the air. "How did this happen?" I could feel my bones shifting as the beast rose with the need to hunt down those who were responsible. I had failed again in my duty as alpha. I should have been here to protect them. My body shook with the force of my rage as it descended over me.

My fist collided with the sturdy oak beside me over and over. I could feel my skin breaking apart, but I didn't care. I welcomed the pain like you would an old friend with a deep embrace. My knuckles were raw and bloody, but that didn't stop the rage.

The strong grip of a hand on my arm was the only thing that kept me from continuing. I turned my gaze to meet Ryder's concerned stare as my chest heaved wildly. He didn't need to speak any words for me to understand that I was dancing dangerously close to the edge. I pulled away from him, unable to bear the weight of my own shame, and spun around to Danc with a heavy growl. "How did this happen?"

I could see the flicker of his wolf rising, but there was deep regret in his gaze. "I don't know, Noah. I had a patrol out here to make sure they were safe. They took out our patrols without a problem. It was too clean. There is no way they didn't know how many men we had out here. They got in and out without us catching a single one."

That did not make any sense to me. There was only one answer that my mind was screaming, and it only brought me more anger. "We have a traitor in our midst." Ryder and Dane seemed surprised by my words, but they didn't argue against them. Even they had to see that it made sense. I watched as their gazes grew darker and more suspicious as they scanned the group nearby.

"I want them found, and I want them brought to me *alive*," I commanded in a low voice for only us to hear. If there was a traitor, I didn't want them to know that I suspected anything of that sort. I wanted to catch them unaware just as they had these innocent females.

"And send someone to my cabin. Bring Scarlett to me," I said in haste. I didn't like the idea of her being anywhere out of my reach with rogues running around on my territory. When no one moved, I struck out at the closest thing to me, another tree. My blood splattered across the ground. "Now! Bring her to me now!" Dane and Ryder hurried away from my side, back towards the trail that brought us to this killing field.

My whole being felt frantic. This had to be my brother's influence. This was what he wanted me to feel. He wanted me to remember the day that stole Claire from me, remind me of my weakness. Only he would orchestrate something so heinous. None of the rogues I had dealt with this far had sought out to do such a systematic attack. They were usually focused only on the hunger and the need to feed it. This was something entirely different. This was a message.

"Noah!" I turned at the sound of a frantic female voice. My beast was on high alert, and for a moment, our mind thought it might be Scarlett. The fear suffocated me with its bony fingers.

Delilah came towards me with tears in her eyes. There was blood splattered across her clothes and face. "Noah..."

Her arms wrapped around me, and she buried her face into my chest. My skin crawled from her touch, but I tried to hold myself together. She had been through something horrific, and she was seeking the comfort of her alpha. I placed my hand on her shoulder tentatively. "What happened here?"

She lifted her tear stained face to meet my gaze, her lips quivering. "They came through the door. Someone left it unlocked." She struggled to get through her words as she recalled the events. I gave her shoulder a light squeeze.

"You're okay now. I won't let anything happen to you or anyone else." I didn't know if I could keep this promise that I was making. "Just explain what you remember."

"They came during the night. The patrol tried to protect us, but they were no match for the rogues. I did what I could to usher the females into the cellar, but I wasn't fast enough to get them all... I... they..." She broke down into a sob, and I pulled her closer. I gritted my teeth as I watched the females consoling each other. "Don't worry. You're safe now. I'll make sure those responsible pay for what they've done." I got my brother's message, and I would respond in kind. Only this time, one of us would be welcoming the abyss with open arms.

38

Christa

My wounds had healed, but my heart weighed heavy in my chest as I stood looking out the bedroom window, arms wrapped around my waist. I might not have the ability to see into the future or commune with the Goddess like the temple maidens or Mother, but there was something unsettling in air.

A storm was forming on the horizon, just out of sight.

I felt Knox's presence as he came up behind me. My body was completely attuned to his. Our flesh were like magnets, pulling us toward each one other. I turned sideways and cast my gaze in his direction. Those green eyes were swirling with desire, but he stayed safely out of reach. "You are looking better today."

I gave him a small smile. "I am feeling better every day." He had been by my side throughout the process, taking his role as my mate very seriously. No one had ever shown me so much consideration in my life. Father had tucked me away, afraid I would be his shame, and Mother had given me away when it turned out I was more like my father than her.

All I had ever truly wanted was to be first to someone, to be loved because I knew that was what I deserved. I knew with Knox, I was his priority and that soothed the pain of the past.

As I continued to watch him, I noticed the way his muscles were drawn up tight. There was something hanging between us, something dead. I tilted my head slightly, examining him closer. "Has something happened?"

He shifted on his feet, tucking his hands into the pockets of his jeans. "Nothing that you should worry about." His words were vague and dry. They didn't give any hint to the truth. They only kept it hidden behind a thick curtain.

I held myself a little tighter. "You don't keep things from me, Knox. I am not a female who needs protecting. Whatever has happened, I can handle it. I am an alpha, the same as you." I lifted my chin a bit higher, my eyes narrowing slightly. I knew that he was fighting with his instincts, but I wouldn't be treated as anything but an equal. The scars on my back were evidence enough of my determination to be seen as such.

He breathed a small breath, giving me a burdened look. "Rogues attacked the females in the safe house. A couple of them didn't make it. The patrol was taken out." I felt my heart pause for a beat. It was only a second, but in that span of time, something snapped in me. The clarity of my mind was almost blissful. I know what needed to be done. I knew what I needed to do.

The path for me was one paved in blood and justice. The Goddess raised me up for this sole purpose, and I could see that now. I wondered if this was what Mother felt when she handed me back to Father, if she knew what the future held for me, if she had seen it in her visions.

"I need to speak with Noah." I moved away from the window with sure steps.

Knox shifted his body so that he was blocking my path to the door. "Slow down a minute. What's the rush?"

"Time isn't on our side," I replied, waiting for him to move out of the way. The truth was that time was already ahead of us. If we didn't take control of the situation, we were likely to be lost underneath the rogue scourge that was barreling towards us.

When he remained in my path, I gave him a look. "What are you doing?"

His chest puffed up. "I don't want you near him. I don't want you involved with any of this." He was trying to assert his dominance.

My wolf growled low. I felt my muscles flex as I asserted my own dominance. "I'm already involved, Knox. I've been involved from the beginning. We all have. This is not something any of us got a choice about."

He clenched his jaw. I could sense his frustration. "Noah will want you to help him. He'll put you on the front lines of this damned war. I can't have that. He's already got enough people to fight for him. Let them handle it, Christa."

I felt my patience growing thin. "I appreciate your concern, but listen carefully..." I took a step towards him so that our chests are almost touching. He was just taller enough than me that I had to tilt my head back to look up at him. "This isn't about you, or me. This is about all of us. We are the alphas. It's our duty to lead our people and protect them. Northern or Southern, what pack we belong to... none of that matters. The rogues don't care about that. They don't discriminate. They only know their hunger."

He held my gaze intently. I knew I had his attention. "I'll be damned if I am going to stand back and watch our people suffer because *you* don't want me to get hurt. That doesn't work for me. Whether you can accept this is who I am or you can't..." I took a pause, feeling my heart racing and my stomach bubbling with doubt and insecurity, but I wouldn't back down.

"Either way, what I choose to do is *my* choice. Now, please get out of my way." I said the last part in a much softer voice. The emotions that were rushing through me making me feel weak.

He held my gaze for another silent moment before moving to the side. I sucked in a small breath before I took my next step. I didn't look back towards him as I made my way out of the room. This could be the end of a future with my mate. I knew well enough that I was not exempt from death, but sometimes, sacrifices had to be made for the good of others. This was the blessing and curse of being an alpha.

I felt a soft wave of relief when I heard the sounds of heavy footsteps behind me. I could feel his eyes as they moved over my body. I sent a silent thank you to the Goddess for gifting me with such a male... one that was willing to stand alongside me even if we were marching toward death itself.

We were in Noah's office, waiting patiently for him to return. Knox stood in the corner, seething with his own anger. He wasn't happy about being in this place. He wasn't happy about my choice, but he kept quiet. I could almost taste his grief and disdain as it saturated the air in the room.

"Will you be able to control yourself?" I asked him seriously.

He shifted slightly. "It'll be fine."

I turned in my chair to get a look at him. "If not, you can wait--"

His eyes darkened, his teeth flashing. "I said it'll be fine, Christa," he interrupted, and I didn't say anything more. I could see that I had pushed him far enough. I didn't need to poke at the beast anymore.

When Noah returned, he was alone. He looked a little startled to see Knox and me in his office, but he recovered his composure quickly. "What can I do for you, Christa? Shouldn't you be resting?"

I folded my hands together in my lap. "I've had enough rest. Your healers have treated me well. Thank you." Noah's gaze shifted from me to Knox in the far corner. The tension between them was thick enough that if felt hard to breathe. I was happy when Noah turned away from Knox. His shoulders were tense, but he was not looking for a fight.

"Then what can I do for you?" he questioned.

I lifted my chin and straightened my back. "I wanted to talk about the army that you've been building yourself."

His eyes narrowed. "What about it?"

"You won't survive this war that is coming, Noah. None of us will if you don't start preparing for the battle," I said with a tense voice. I knew that mother had been right when she told me that they would fail if I didn't step up.

Noah leaned back into his desk with his arms crossed over his chest. "So what are you offering? I assume that's why we're having this conversation."

"Myself."

Knox let out a growl at my words. "Christa—"

I held up my hand to silence him before he could dispute my words. I could feel his anger, but I didn't fixate on it. This was my choice. This was my future, our future that I was trying to secure, a future that must be earned and paid for with blood and sweat. I knew better than anyone how things like this go.

Noah stared me down. He was the leader that these people needed. He was a war machine hidden beneath the veneer of flesh and blood. The Goddess had made no mistakes in the game that she has been playing with all of us. On her divine chessboard, most of us were pawns, myself included. The male that stood before me wasn't simply her pawn.

He was the king, a king that I wanted to serve.

"I will help train the warriors, your warriors. As they are now, they don't stand a chance, but with a little guidance, I can turn them into sharpened blades of silver. My father might have been a fool about many things, but the one thing he knew better than anyone was battle. I studied his every move in case the day came when I might have to challenge him."

Noah looked at me with a skeptical gaze, and I couldn't blame him for that. None of these males had ever seen me in action. They didn't know what I was capable of.

"I accept your offer," he said firmly, reaching out his hand toward me. I noticed the torn and raw skin on his knuckles. I hesitated for only a moment before grabbing his hand, sealing my fate, whatever that may be. A knock came on the door before it swung open to reveal the king's knights. The two of them were wearing hardened expressions. They stepped to the side to reveal *his* queen. Her dark gaze swept over the room and lingered on her mate.

She was the most dangerous piece of the board, the one that could turn the tides of the entire game.

39

Scarlett

The room was full of tension as I entered. Dane and Ryder had explained to me what had happened for it was the only way they could get me to return. Of course, once I found out I willingly went with them.

This pack had become my pack over the past couple of months of me living among them. My wolf saw them as hers to protect or destroy. Outsiders were not welcome in her territory.

My gaze moved from Christa to Knox, who was standing in the far corner of the room. I shoot him a skeptical glance, wondering if he has finally got his contempt for my mate under control. For his sake, I hoped so because if he ever tried to go for his throat again, I was certain my wolf would go for his. She flashed her teeth in his direction as if to reaffirm the thought.

"We are done here," Noah said firmly to Christa and Knox. It was clear that he wanted to be alone with me, but I wasn't sure if I wanted that quite yet. I didn't trust myself not to be influenced by the bond. It happened once before, and it would be easier now.

The two of them said nothing more, and Christa allowed Knox to help her up out of the chair. She gave me a friendly smile as they passed by and out of the room. Noah nodded his head to Ryder and Dane, and they too disappeared, closing the door as they went.

"What did Christa want?" I asked, trying to ignore the tension that was sitting between us. He watched me as I walked around his desk. "She offered to help train my warriors, and I accepted." I nodded my head as I ran my hand over his desk, slowly making my way closer to him.

"Still need time to think?" Noah asked in a low voice.

I let out a small breath. "Things aren't that simple. I mean, how are things supposed to work between us now?" I motioned between us with my hand.

"I thought we could give us a try... take it at whatever pace you wanted. I'm not trying to rush you, Scarlett. I just want to know if you even want this," Noah replied calmly.

"Yes, but obviously, the circumstances are different now that I marked you." And there it was, the giant elephant in the room. It was not him being a rogue or the attack. All of that, I could deal with, but the fact that I had marked him as my mate was the one thing that was keeping me up at night.

"Right, and you don't want me as a mate," he said with a harsher tone. I felt the sting of the statement and cringed that he believed that was how I felt about him. I mean, I had thought like that in the beginning, but I wasn't sure now.

"That's not true," I replied in a softer voice as I kept my eyes focused on the desk.

"We both know it is, Scarlett. There's no need to lie on my account. I'm not going to be upset. I can understand that being mated with someone like me must be quite unfortunate." He still sounded harsh, but I could tell he wasn't angry.

I pulled my gaze from the desk to him. "I am telling the truth. I don't feel the same about you as I did when we first met."

He stared back at me silently for a moment. "And how do you feel about me now?" His voice was strong, but his eyes showed his vulnerability. He expected me to hate him even more after I had discovered his secret. I could see that now.

"I'm not entirely sure myself..." His expression looked sad for a moment, but I pushed onward. "But I know that I do feel something for you that I don't feel for anyone else, and I don't want to lose the opportunity to find out if I can truly be mates with you. I know I've been a brat in the past, but I'll work on that if you promise not to keep any more secrets from me."

We stared at each other for a moment before he subtly nodded his head. "Okay. I think I can work with that."

I smiled at him. "Good."

He closed the distance between us quickly, which made my heart beat nervously in my chest, but I could tell he was not going to hurt me. He stopped a few feet from me. I couldn't stop myself from being pulled toward him. I found myself desiring his touch. I was hungry for it. "So it looks like you got everything you wanted."

His eyes blazed at my comment. "Not everything. Not yet." I knew there was an obvious meaning to them that he wasn't trying to hide. He reached out for me, his arm encircling my waist. "I shouldn't have left you this morning. I should have fought you harder." My defenses were buckling against his assault. "I won't make that mistake, again."

He pulled me closer, and our lips touched in a soul-shattering kiss. I couldn't blame the heat for the need anymore. There were still doubts in my heart, but I wanted to reach for something more beyond the fear. I wanted a chance at a future, a future with the cold-hearted alpha who had taken me.

"I want to learn every part of you, Scarlett. I don't just want to claim your body. I want to claim your soul," he whispered into my ear, and I shivered as I leaned into his touch. His lips danced down the side of my neck to the mark he had given me. He pulled back reluctantly. "When the Holy Mother returns to my territory, I want to brand you as part of the pack."

I stared into his eyes as he waited for my response. I didn't know what to say to him. I have never been branded by my old pack because I had left for college before anything like that could happen. It was a purposeful move on my part. Once you were branded, you could never fully turn your back on the pack.

This was not a choice made lightly, but there was one thing I was certain despite the whispering doubts about Noah and I in my heart—I wanted to become one of the pack. I had come to care for them as if they were already mine.

I gave a small nod. "Alright."

He smiled brightly before gathering me into his arms again, breathing me in deeply as he rubbed his cheek to the top of my head. His excitement was surprising and slightly child-like as if he was afraid I would reject not only him but the whole pack.

I gave him a wary smile. "But first, we should deal with the rogues." His smile slowly faded as if my presence had banished the dark reality from his mind.

40

Scarlett

The weeks passed, and I watched the season change from my window. Everything seemed to be building in a positive light like the Goddess herself was smiling down on all of us.

I decided to see how the warriors were coming along and to see if Christa's influence had made the difference I believed it would when I suggested that Noah try to get her to come to his pack. They practiced out in the clearing at the back of the pack house. The smell of blood and sweat was heavy in the air.

The men were all gathered in a circle, and I could see that two men in the circle were beating on each other like there was no tomorrow. I looked away from the bloody scene and scanned the crowd for my reason for being here. It didn't take long for me to find Noah standing proudly next to Ryder. Every once and a while, the male leaned over and said something to

Noah. I took in a deep breath and lifted my chin a little higher as I walked toward the crowd.

"Alright! That's enough!" Christa yelled, and the fighting stopped. The two men in the circle looked like they could barely keep themselves upright.

"I'm not impressed. You call this fighting? You look like a bunch of newly born pups playing with each other," she said coldly. She was completely in her element, a queen amongst the peons. I came to stand at the edge of the group to listen in. I had expected Noah to notice that I was there, but I guess the other smells were too strong for him to sense anything.

"Alpha Noah..." she said and turned to look at him, "would you like to show these men what a true fight looks like?"

I looked at Noah, and he looked slightly put off, but he nodded his head slightly before he pulled his shirt off and over his head. My wolf rumbled her pleasure at the sight of our mate's strength on display. I felt my cheeks grow hot as images of past events ran through my mind. I licked my lips as I felt my heart beat harder in my chest.

Noah moved to the center of the circle. Christa was wearing a wolfish grin. "Now, who would like to challenge the Alpha?" The crowd went still for a moment and then there was a lot of men trying to get picked to go up against Noah. None of them stood a chance, but that didn't stop them from wanting to fight him.

I decided to take a chance. My wolf was eager to test herself and her mate. My voice called out above all the others.

"I would like to challenge the alpha." The crowd went completely quiet.

The males all turned around to look at me, and they parted like the red sea, giving Noah and Christa a clear view of me at the back of the crowd. She sized me up for a moment before her grin grew wider. Noah's face remained expressionless, but his eyes were locked on me with an intensity that made my stomach flutter with excitement.

A dark grin crept over his lips. "I accept your challenge." I felt a wave of fear rush through me quickly before a strange excitement overcame it. Christa bowed her head slightly in Noah's direction and then motioned for me to come to the center of the circle.

Noah stood there grinning. "Don't expect me to go easy on you because you're my mate," he said to me in a taunting tone. He was trying to get under my skin purposefully, pushing my wolf.

I smiled at him as I got into a fighting stance. "I wouldn't dream of it." He crouched forward, bringing his elbows up a bit, and I knew he was going to take this seriously. I quickly sized him up. In strength, he obviously had me beat. I would never be able to beat him that way, but in speed, I knew I had the upper hand. All I needed to do was move quick, burst and tire him out, and stay out of punching range.

Noah's eyes darkened as his wolf rose toward the surface. "I can see the wheels in your head spinning, but this is a fight you won't win, Scarlett, no matter how hard you try. You should just submit now."

I bristled up at his words. "I wouldn't say all hope is lost. If you want me to submit, you'll have to make me."

"If that's what you want, so be it," he said as he came at me. He moved much faster than I had expected but luckily, my reflexes were much faster. I jumped back as he swiped at me with a fist. I ducked down as he moved forward and punched again. I let my wolf come to the surface so I could tap into her extra strength. I moved forward quickly while I ducked down. I jumped and landed a kick to his stomach causing him to stumble back a bit, creating the distance I wanted between us.

A small smile graced his lips as he met my gaze. "I'm going to enjoy your submission, *greatly*."

"Don't count on it." I growled back before I launched myself at him using as much speed as I could. I became a flurry of kicks and punches. All Noah could do was take the defensive position against me as I backed him toward the crowd. He blocked most of my attacks, but I hit him several times. He got a busted lip and a black eye which of course would heal soon enough.

I was growing tired, and my movements were slowing down. As if he sensed this, Noah pushed forward, forcing me to break away from him and create space between us. My chest was heaving in and out quickly as I tried to catch my breath.

He spat out blood from his mouth as he locked eyes with me. "You are not bad." His words made my wolf puff up with pride. "But you fell right into my trap." My brow furrowed in confusion as I watched him begin to circle around me, but I made sure to never let my back to be to him. We were both grinning like hungry beasts enjoying the chase.

"You let me rile you up, and now you've wasted most of your energy. I've seen what you're capable of, and I know how to attack you now. I've already won," he stated calmly, and I felt my brain sputter to a stop. "So what will it be? Will you submit on your own or must I *make you?*"

I clenched my teeth together tightly. My wolf was telling me to submit. She was satisfied with the strength of her mate, but my own pride wouldn't allow it. I wanted to beat him.

I met his gaze. "If you want me to submit, you're going to have to beat me. Unless you're afraid that maybe you can't." My words sparked a fire in his eyes. He came at me like he had the first time, and I rolled my eyes, knowing I could avoid his moves. I avoided the first punch, then the second. I ducked down. I was going to deliver my move, but when I came in close to him, I caught his smirk seconds before he grabbed my leg as I kicked it out.

"You fell for it again," he muttered before he twisted my leg. He sent me tumbling down. I hit the ground with a thud, and I winced, but I didn't have time to assess the damage. I forced myself upright, but Noah was already waiting for me. He delivered a sharp punch to my face. I tumbled back down to the ground. My cheek burned from his hit, and my body ached everywhere. He lowered himself over me, straddling my body, and the crowd cheered suggestively.

I thrashed underneath him, swinging my arms widely. I wasn't going to give up until all hopes of gaining the upper hand was gone. He leaned back a bit, catching my wrists in his big hands. He pushed them back to the ground, holding them over my head, making it so that our chests are pressed together.

"Get off me!" I growled at him, and I flashed my teeth.

Noah's eyes focused in on mine. "Submit and I will."

The words caused my body to go still underneath him as I stared up into his eyes. I could feel his heat sinking into me, causing a familiar warmth to build in my stomach. Noah leaned his face closer into mine, and there was no way for me to escape. "Submit, Scarlett." His tone of voice was huskier now, and I knew that this was changing into something else.

I swallowed hard. "Only because you beat me fair and square," I said breathlessly.

I let my eyes flutter close as I turned my head to the side, baring my neck to him as a sign of submission. A low growl of approval rumbled out of his chest as the crowds cheered with excitement. I felt his hot breath against my skin. "Soon, you will submit to me completely." He whispered into my ear before he pulled himself off my body. I immediately mourned the loss of his heat, but I quickly pushed away those feelings and peeled myself off the ground.

Christa clapped her hands together in approval as she approached us. "That men..." she paused for emphasis and looked at me with amusement before looking out to the crowd, "is what a real fight looks like. Remember that in the future." I looked around the cheering men as they approached Noah, clapping him on the back in approval of his fighting skills. He was wearing a grin as he accepted their attention, and I couldn't help the butterflies that broke out in my stomach. His eyes met mine for a moment, and the promise of his words echoed through my mind. I quickly looked away to find Christa approaching me with a bright smile. "That was amazing. You moved so quickly."

"But I still lost." I reminded her.

"Yes, but next time, you'll definitely win. I'll help you." I couldn't help but laugh at her words. I felt a strange cramping in my lower abdomen that brought my laughter to a halt. I gripped my shirt in my hand. Something felt off. Suddenly, I felt not quite right.

"Are you okay?" she asked with concern, noting the change.

I nodded my head, not wanting to draw unwanted attention in my direction. "Yeah, just bad food, I guess. Excuse me." I rushed away from everyone back into the house. My stomach was rolling in discomfort, and I pushed past people to reach the bathroom. I heaved all of my food into the toilet as sweat poured off my brow. It happened over and over again until my stomach was empty.

There came a knock on the door. "Scarlett, Are you okay?" I heard Janie from the other side. "Christa, sent me to check up on you. She said you looked a little unwell when you left the training."

I pushed up from the floor, staggering as I moved to the door. I clamped my clammy palm on the door knob, opening it enough for her to enter. My wolf seemed extremely agitated by another presence, flashing her teeth and growling loudly. It surprised me that she was suddenly so aggressive. In fact, she had been more aggressive lately, but I thought it was the stress of everything that made her that way.

Janie's eyes moved over me then towards the toilet that held the contents of my lunch. There was a heavy silence before she turned back to me with more calculative eyes.

"How long has it been since you bled, Scarlett?"

Janie's question threw my world off kilter. I staggered back, catching myself on the edge of the sink. I hadn't bled since I came into heat. I pressed my hand to my stomach. My heart was hammering in my chest. This couldn't be possible, could it? Noah and I hadn't taken proper precautions.

I swallowed the lump of anxiety as I came to terms with what was wrong with me. I should have noticed sooner, but I was too lost in everything else. I was pregnant. There was a young growing inside of me that Noah and I had created together in a moment of passion.

Janie held my gaze. "Well?"

"Not since my heat," I said hesitantly.

She sucked in a breath and turned her body toward the door. We both knew that this was a big deal, for many reasons. An alpha male with a pup on the way usually became much more protective. If Noah knew I was carrying his pup, I was certain he would want to lock me away somewhere. His fears wouldn't allow for anything else. It would ruin all the progress we have made. I wouldn't survive an imprisoned situation like that, and neither would my wolf.

I grabbed her arm in a tight grip. "You can't say anything about this, you understand?"

She didn't look happy about what I was asking her to do, but I didn't care. Now was not the right time to tell Noah that he was going to be a father. His focus needed to be completely on the task at hand. Destroying his brother and the rogues was the most important thing. Creating a safe place for us to raise our young—not just ours but for all the future pups—was all that mattered now.

"You won't be able to hide it for long. He is going notice the changes if he doesn't smell them first." I knew she was speaking the truth.

I shook my head. "I don't need to hide it for long, just long enough... until this whole war is over." She pulled her arm free from my grip, sneering at me as she rubbed the spot I was holding. This was the first time she looked at me in such a spiteful way. I had a feeling she felt anger toward me, probably having smelled my scent on Dane when he claimed her. Maybe some part of her blamed me for the mark on her neck. My lips twitched with the urge to smile. This female was certainly more than she let on. She was definitely a wolf strong enough to be mated to Noah's beta.

"Fine. I'll keep your secret but only because you kept mine," she replied in a cool voice.

I inclined my head slightly. "Thank you."

"You're going to need things." I could see she was already planning and calculating.

41

Scarlett

Janie had kept her word and had not said anything to anyone about what she had discovered. She snuck me vitamins and special herb teas that she said would help with any sickness and support healthy growth. A part of me felt guilty having roped her into my little charade, but I knew it was best for everyone.

I was already feeling protective of my young. My wolf watched everyone around us more closely as the days went by. I knew she was going to start feeling the need to build her den soon, but I was hoping that she would hold back a little longer. I wasn't quite ready to share this secret... not while things were still so uncertain.

Noah and I were still dancing around each other. He liked to catch me in the hallways with small teasing touches, but he didn't smother me. He was giving me the space I wanted to sort myself out. I found myself seeking him out on my own some days, happy to watch him from a distance.

He always knew when I was around. His bright gaze gravitated toward me, and his lips would always turn upward into a seductive grin. My stomach fluttered with excitement. I knew that I was falling for my mate. What started as a slow burn was turning into an unquenchable hunger.

We made sure to always sit together during meals, knees brushing against each other under the table.

Tonight, he filled a single plate and placed it down between us. I watched him with a raised brow as he grabbed some of the meat with his hand and held it out toward me.

I could feel the crowd's eyes fixing on us. They wanted to see a unified front, an alpha pair strong enough to lead them. I held his gaze as I leaned forward, taking the food from his hand with my mouth. A small moan of delight built in my throat as the juices rushed into my mouth. The pregnancy had left me needing to eat more. I found myself sneaking into the kitchen for midnight snacks when I was sure others were asleep.

I watched Noah's nostrils flare up and his pupils dilate as I licked away the leftover flavors on my lips. I wanted him as much as he wanted me. We were becoming as attuned to one another as our wolves were to each other.

"Save it for the bedroom," Dane commented from beside us with a cough. Some of the older mated couples around the table chuckled, and my cheeks blazed with heat. The atmosphere around the pack had become lighter even with war looming on the horizon. We were all simply enjoying the peaceful time the Goddess was giving to us at the moment.

I was happy when I saw Janie shuffling through the door. We had grown closer over the weeks though that might have been because she was the only one I could go to when I was in need "Janie," I called out to her.

She turned her face in our direction, but her eyes betrayed her, going first to the male beside me. She approached hesitantly. "Luna Scarlett," she greeted me formally, and I gave her a small frown.

"Just Scarlett is fine. We're friends, after all," I remarked. I watched the way her cheeks blushed from the recognition.

She glanced in Noah's direction. "Alpha."

He gave her a tender expression. "Janie, why don't you sit with us?" He extended his hand. Everyone needed to know that he was no longer holding onto the past the way he had before. Each day, it slipped further from his fingertips.

Her eyes widened a bit in surprise. "Oh, that's okay. I was just going to grab something quick... Lots of females are in need of my attention." Her eyes met mine for a moment, and I straightened up a bit in my chair.

"Oh, come on, Janie," Nadia said from her spot next to Ryder as her hand rested on the small growing bump on her belly. She had found herself pregnant several weeks ago though from the coloring of her skin and the darkening around her eyes, it was not going smoothly for her. I felt a wave of concern for my friend as she looked at her mate who seemed even more watchful and protective than usual. "None of them will die if you take a small break."

I scooted over, making room for her between Dane and me, purposefully. "Please, I insist."

She eyed the spot for a moment, knowing she couldn't run away as easily as before. Her hand went to the mark on her neck, covering it. Slowly, she made her way to sit down beside her mate who was just as stiff as her. I grabbed the empty, unused plate in front of me and filled it with food before setting it down in front of her.

She looked at me with wide eyes. It was a big sign of esteem, especially from a pregnant female, even though she was the only one who knew the true significance of my offering.

Her eyes grew watery. "Thank you." Her head hung slightly as she picked at the food like a bird instead of like a wolf. I could see this was a small step in the right direction, a step toward her own future. I noticed the weak smile that she and Dane shared between each other before turning away.

Noah walked me back to my bedroom when the moon was high as his fingers brushed the back of my hand every couple of steps. I felt the warmth spreading up my arm while a small smile tugged at my lips. I didn't reach out for him. I still wasn't ready to close the gap between us. There were still tiny doubts whispering in the back of my mind. When I did finally reach for him, I wanted it to be with both hands open and devoid of any doubt.

We stopped at my door. This had become my territory, and he was yet to be invited in even though I knew he longed for me to do just that. Someday, we would share a room or a bed, but not today. Not yet.

He shifted on his feet. "I am going to be gone for a couple of days, Scarlett. Knox and I are taking some of the warriors Christa had trained to the Eastern packs. Alpha Harvey and his men haven't checked in as they usually do, and we want to make sure everything is okay."

I felt a nervous tug on my heart at his words. There was a shadow creeping toward us. "What if it's a trap?"

He gave me a small smile, coming closer but not touching me. "I am sure everything is fine. They are only a couple days overdue. This is just precautionary move on our part."

"You don't know that, Noah. Don't you think that it's all a little... you know." I bit my lip, holding back my doubtful thoughts. I couldn't get over the foreboding feeling in my gut.

"All a little what?" he asked me softly, seemingly interested in my opinion.

I let out a small breath. "That it's all been too quiet? A little too easy?" Personally, it all seemed suspicious to me, but I felt like I was missing some of the puzzle pieces to have a clear picture.

Noah leaned forward and pressed his forehead to mine. "Don't worry, Scarlett. I won't let anything happen, not to you or anyone else."

He thought I was nervous for myself? I tried not to laugh at him. "Just promise me you won't do anything stupid." I pulled back away from him, holding his gaze.

He smirked. "You're worried about me?" There was a teasing element to his question.

I shrugged my shoulders as I opened the door to my room. "Goodnight, Noah. I'll see you when you come back." I teased back, enjoying the dark look of desire that sparked in his eyes. He reached out for me, grabbing my face in his hands and planting his lips to mine. The kiss had me shivering with delight as it shot fire through my veins. I leaned into the urgency of his lips against mine.

When he pulled back, we were both breathing heavily. "When I come back, I hope you'll have your mind sorted out." I could hear the longing in his voice, and I felt it in my whole being. "I don't know how much longer I can hold myself back from you."

My stomach fluttered. "When you come back, we'll talk about us." My words held a double meaning that he didn't quite pick up on.

He gave me a hopeful smile that sent my heart soaring as he took a step back. "That's a reason worth fighting for."

42

Scarlett

The sun rose and set several times and still, there had been no word. I had taken to spending the evening on the porch, staring into the distance, hoping to see a sign of them on the horizon. Christa took up position beside me. "I can smell it on you." I stiffened at her words, hand automatically going to my stomach, but I kept my gaze on the horizon.

Her hand came to rest on my shoulder, giving it a gentle squeeze. "Don't worry. They will return soon, Scarlett." I wondered if she was saying that for herself or to calm her own worries… the ones that put the dark circles around her eyes.

I pulled away from her touch. "I won't spend another sunset out here holding my breath. If they don't return tomorrow, you will take the rest of the warriors and head after them while I have Dane move the pack somewhere safer."

She met my heavy gaze as I swung it back around in her direction. I was the one in charge while Noah was away. I was the one left to protect the pack, and I wasn't going to slack on that responsibility. My wolf had risen to the occasion. I was born to be luna, and I demanded the respect.

Christa nodded her head. "As you wish, Luna."

We head inside together. I wanted and needed rest. I tried to remain hopeful that Noah and the warriors would return during the night, that the moon would guide them back to us safely.

Christa hung back behind me. She rarely left my side, and I had a feeling that Noah had requested that she keep a close eye on me while he was gone. If it wasn't Christa, it was Dane or Ryder lingering around me like another shadow. It had been irritating at first, but now I was used to it.

I was surprised when I rounded the corner to my room and saw a small crowd had gathered near my door. I slowly made my way down the hallway with people turning to see us. I began to get a strange feeling in the pit of my stomach that something was very wrong. I moved faster, and people moved out of my way for me to enter my room. I felt my eyes widen at the sight. My room was completely destroyed. My furniture looked as though Edward Scissorhands had tried to sculpt something out of them.

On my walls were what looked like smeared bloody hand prints, but all that made sense with the dead body lying bloody and tattered across my bed. Christa came rushing into my room and by my side. "Oh, my Goddess." She seemed shocked by the scene. She moved away from me and toward the dead body, but I could already tell from the scent who it was. Gretchen's lifeless eyes were staring in my direction in surprise as if she hadn't seen this coming. I didn't suppose most people see their own deaths coming, though.

Christa came rushing back to my side. "We need to get you somewhere safe, now." She grabbed onto my arm and pulled me from the room and through the crowd. I let her drag me away from the gruesome scene. I was in shock after everything that I had witnessed. My brain was overloaded.

As if snapping back into myself, I said, "I need to see Noah."

"You can't see him right now, Scarlett. You know that," she said back to me as she continued to move us quickly through the house. She was looking around as if she expected the killer to jump out at us at any moment.

I ripped my arm free from her grip. "You don't understand."

"No, I understand just fine. You seem to be the one that doesn't understand the situation. Your mate is preoccupied at the moment. There is nothing he could do to help you, Scarlett. It's my duty to make sure you're safe when he can't. Now, let me do my job." She growled at me in annoyance.

I glared at her. "I can take care of myself. It's not like I need you and Noah to protect me… or anyone else for that matter."

"Someone killed Gretchen. No, they butchered her and left her for you to find as a message. I know you can protect yourself, but this is different than a play fight with your mate. You might be out of your depth on this one. Even I've never seen anything like that." She looked at me seriously as if trying to communicate that she was disturbed by what she had seen. I didn't put up any more of a fight as she continued to lead me through the house

As we came around the corner, we were met with a wicked grinning Delilah with a glass vase in her hand. There was no time to react as she knocked Christa hard across the face before swinging back to hit her in the head. I watched as she hit the ground with a loud thud, completely unconscious.

I had a moment to try to turn away, but she moved quicker than I could process at the moment, clipping me in the side of the head. I collapsed to the ground as my hand instinctively went to my stomach protectively. My world was blinking in and out of the darkness.

She dropped the vase and grabbed onto my hair, pulling my head back. "You took everything from me, everything that was supposed to be mine. I waited patiently. I was there for Noah while he grieved, but then you showed up and ruined everything. Now, I know that I can be more than you if I embrace Kellan's way."

I glared up at her, watching as her features become more angular as another type of beast began to surface beneath her skin. "Don't do this," I said firmly. "You choose this, and you'll never be able to return."

I didn't like this female. Hell, she had been a thorn in my side since the day Noah had brought me to the pack house, but I didn't want to see her turn into one of those beasts. I knew that it would hurt Noah. It would be another name on his list of people he had failed to save.

She flashed me her teeth into a wide grin. "It's already been done."

My eyes widened. "You were the one that killed those females... You killed Gretchen... You're the traitor." I shouldn't have been surprised, but I was. I knew she hated me, but I assumed her loyalty to Noah would keep her in check and that she had some loyalty to her friend.

She laughed in a way that sent a shiver up my spine. "Guilty as charged. I've never felt so much power before. You should have seen the terrified look in their eyes as I cut through them. They never saw it coming."

"You're sick," I growled as I struggled in her hold. She picked up a piece of broken glass and pressed it to my throat.

I felt it prick into my pulsing vein. "It would be so easy to kill you right now," she whispered in sick merriment. My wolf wanted to burst forth from my flesh, but she also wanted to protect our pup. She knew that if she came out, it could kill the young we were carrying. Neither of us was willing to risk that. She and I had grown rather attached to the small life inside of us.

"I want to kill you..." I felt the broken glass dig in a little deeper as something warm trickled down my strained neck. "But Kellan would kill me if I did." She sounded disappointed.

I dug my nails into the ground. "Noah will kill you when he finds you." It was a promise. There was no doubt in my being that he would even think of sparing her.

"Goodnight, Luna." She growled as she slammed my head into the ground. I heard a cracking noise splinter through my skull as darkness became the only thing I knew.

43

Scarlett

When I came to, my body was swaying back and forth. I knew I was outside by the coolness on my skin. Dirt crunched loudly under Delilah's feet. The added strength of turning rogue helped her to carry me as if I was nothing but a feather.

I groaned, turning my head slightly to see a sleek black car waiting at the end of the path. I knew if I got thrown into that car, the chances of me seeing Noah again, of our young surviving, would grow smaller. My wolf wouldn't accept defeat, and her instincts to survive pushed me into action. My head was still spinning, but I shifted my weight quickly. Delilah dropped me, and I saved myself from hitting the ground, catching myself with my hand. My skin scraped across the gravel as I twisted myself around to face the traitor.

I rolled my shoulders, letting my wolf rise to the surface. I growled at her, knowing I was on the very edge of shifting. She let out a violent snarl before she charged towards me. I knew there was no time for me to avoid her attack, so I tried my best to brace myself against it. Her body hit mine, pushing me back into the car. Pain rushed up my back, and I felt like my lungs were screaming. I pushed back against her, bringing my knee up quickly and hitting her in the stomach with as much force as I could muster with the space I had.

She sucked in a breath as she fell back a bit from me, allowing me to squeeze around her. I ignored the pain in my leg as I moved behind her, wrapping my arm around her throat. I had her in a chokehold, and I was not about to let go. She reached back, clawing at me. Her nails were slicing through my flesh, but I ignored the pain. Realizing I was not going to let go anytime soon, she spun us around and started knocking us back against the car again. She kept building the force behind each slam, and I cried out as my arm loosened from her neck.

My body slid down the car into the dirt, my hand cradling my stomach. My back was screaming, and my head was fuzzy. I was at a disadvantage the way I was now.

She coughed a couple times as she tried to recover from her lack of oxygen. I started pulling myself away from the car, trying to get away from her and into the woods. Delilah turned her focus to me with a growl, but I just kept pulling myself toward the trees with determination while my body screamed at me to stop.

"You little..." she hissed as she made her way to me, snatching me off the ground by my hair. My scalp burned and pulsed under the strength of her pull. "Forget orders. I'm going to slit your pretty little throat and watch you bleed to death." She sneered to my face. I started to squirm in her hold as she lifted her free hand to my throat and pressed a long clawed finger to my throat.

A deep guttural growl ripped through the night, making both Delilah and me flinch. My wolf snarled back in my head, and I turned my eyes toward the direction of the person in question. I prayed that it was one of the pack members, but my brain sputtered to a complete halt at the vision before me.

"You would disobey direct orders?" he asked Delilah. She was quiet as she sneered back at him before focusing her attention on me. She let out a growl of frustration before pulling her claw away from my throat. I was still staring at the man near the trees in complete shock. There was no way he could be real. This had to be some kind of hallucination brought on by the knock I took to the head. He focused his attention on me, and I let out an audible gasp

His eyes raked over my body inspecting me. "You're hurt," he commented with slight concern. His deep voice sunk into my brain as it had in the past, but it didn't stir up feelings of longing as it once did. This broke me out of the strange trance I had fallen into. My body started to shake as a deep rage began to build inside me, feeding my wolf. I turned my eyes back to Delilah, and I swung out full force with my arm. My fist collided with her face, and I heard the snap of her nose. She released me with a howl.

"Damn it! Stupid bitch broke my nose!" she hollered as she cupped her hands to her face.

The pain that wracked my body seemed to be the furthest thing from my mind as I rushed toward David, ready to deal out some swift vengeance. I caught him off guard, allowing me to land a kick to his stomach which caused him to fall back into a tree. I lunged forward, hitting him with a quick punch to the face, feeling the sting in my hand.

I was on the warpath. This was a rampage of blood lust and desperation to survive. When I went in for another punch, I was tackled to the ground from behind. My body hit the ground with enough force to rattle my bones. A hand pressed the back of my head, shoving my face into the dirt. "Can I kill her now?" Delilah barked with a bit of sarcasm.

I heard the masculine voice groaned. "No," he snapped, "I deserved that."

I squirmed under Delilah, trying to get her off me, but I knew that this time, I wouldn't be getting another shot. I let out a feral growl as my wolf grappled with the despair and rage. Heavy footsteps made my heart thunder against my chest. "I know you're confused, but don't worry, Scarlett. Everything will work out the way it's supposed to, and then we will be together like we were meant to be."

My eyes connected with David's as he squatted down in front of me. They were no longer the same as I remembered them. The darkness they had now made a shiver of fear race up my spine.

"I will never be yours!" I barked at him.

His tongue clicked off the roof of his mouth like a parent scolding a disobedient child. "I guess we'll see about that." He looked past me to Delilah, nodding his head. She knocked me on the head harder, making sure she did the job right this time.

44

Scarlett

I fell in and out of consciousness for a while, but through my bouts with consciousness, I was certain that I had lost my mind. That was the only explanation for what I had seen. It wasn't possible that I had seen David. He was supposed to let all that go once our bond was completely broken. Once Noah claimed me, there should have been nothing left. Yet, I saw him standing there like a ghost from my past coming back to haunt me once again.

I could tell they had moved me some place far away from wherever Noah was. The separation pulled at my mind and unsettled my nerves until I felt like my wolf wanting to claw her way through my skin.

I tensed up as I felt my grip in reality begin to strengthen. My senses were coming back like a computer that was being rebooted. I could feel that I was laying on something hard and damp. Around me, the only sounds I heard were heavy, labored breathing, but they weren't my own, which meant I wasn't alone wherever I was.

I took in a small subtle breath, trying to see if I recognized any of the scents. Through the smell of mold, blood, and sweat I caught the underlying scent of two, three... no, four other shifters. Two of the scents seemed familiar, but the other two were foreign to me. I slowly opened my eyes, not wanting to alert anyone to the fact that I was awake now because who knew what they were planning for me.

The room was dark, the only light was from a small window near the opposite side of the room. I was lying on the ground in a fetal position in what looked like some kind of a prison cell made out of clear walls. It must've been made of heavy duty glass or some other kind of material of that nature. I scanned through the dark, looking for any kind of guard, but I found nothing, so I pushed myself up off the ground using the clear wall beside me as support. I groaned at the pain that lanced through me, leaning my body into the wall.

I put my hand to my stomach, feeling anxious. It took a moment of concentrating to feel the soft heartbeat of the life inside me. It was a little quick, but other than that, I sensed no distress.

"We were wondering when you'd wake up," I heard Wyatt's familiar voice. "You look like you got dragged through hell kicking and screaming, cousin."

My eyes flickered toward the cell next to mine to see him leaning back against the wall. It was clear from his current state that he had been down here for a couple weeks. He wasn't as bulky as I remembered, and his body was riddled with bruises and cuts. He turned his face in my direction, and I saw the hardened look of desperation swirling in his eyes.

I turned my gaze to the huddled form near him. She doesn't look as I remembered her in my mind, but there was no mistaking. It was her... Eva. She had a pinched expression on her face as she looked at me. "I'm so sorry, Scarlett," her voice shook as she spoke. I could tell from her hunched posture that she was full of regret. "I didn't know. I swear, I didn't know..."

I stared at her, taking in her words. Surprisingly, I found that I believed them. After everything that had happened from the moment I met David, her words made the most sense to me. She was just as much a victim in this whole situation as I was. I didn't know her or her life before she met David and his family. I could only imagine what had led her to them.

"It's in the past." I found myself saying the exact words that Noah had told me when I apologized for the death of his mate. It was true, though. There was nothing any of us could do to change what had happened. Guilty, innocent—it didn't matter anymore. I let out a small breath as she stared at me in her own surprise. I wondered how she had imagined me reacting to the news. I had hated her at one time, but I didn't feel those feelings now.

"I forgive you, Eva. What happened is not your fault. You aren't the one to blame," I said the words in a gentle tone, hoping that it would help her move forward in her own life.

I waited for a moment before I looked to my cousin. "What happened?" I whispered. I needed to understand what had happened to them and to our old pack.

Wyatt was silent for a moment. "David lost his ever loving mind, that's what happened. Everything was fine, and then a couple weeks ago, David started freaking out. He lost complete control of his wolf. It took a couple days before he was able to get some self-control, but there was something off—he was almost too calm after that kind of outburst." It must have been his reaction to our bond being broken. He had never actually expected me to mate with anyone else.

"I didn't know it then, but I guess he had been negotiating with the rogue bastards, but since we're a small pack with nothing much to offer except well-trained warriors," Wyatt paused and tensed his shoulders, "David gave us all two options, join them or die."

"So everyone..." I choked back a sob. They might not be my pack anymore, but I had known most of them my whole life. It didn't matter how much death I had seen or the fact that I have been forced to kill, it didn't make any of this easier. Perhaps, for some people it did, but not for me.

Eva pulled herself up the ground, her legs unsteady as she did. "Not everyone, but they might as well be." Her voice was firmer now as if she had some resolve she hadn't moments before. "Alpha Aaron and Luna Victoria were gone, though. David killed them first."

I sucked in another breath. "Why are you guys still—" I started but stopped when Wyatt let out a harsh chuckle.

"Why we still alive?" He finished the question I had started to ask. I bit the inside of my cheek, feeling a bit sorry that I had even thought to ask something like that.

"I have been asking myself that question since this whole nightmare began. Eva is here because she's pregnant.

They said something about a new generation of rogues." My eyes moved quickly to her to see that there was a swell on her stomach. She stared down at it as she rubbed as a small circle over her belly. I recalled the story Noah had told me about his mother, and a sharp anger surged through me. They planned on forcing her to raise her child until it was old enough to not need her. They would end up killing her in the end. This was just a prolonged death sentence.

"As for myself, I couldn't come up with a good answer until now." His eyes fixed on me, and there was a humorless smirk on his chapped lips.

I swallowed hard as thoughts began to race through my mind. "They plan to use you against me."

"This sucks." Wyatt let out a dark laugh. They were going to pit my ties to family against my ties to Noah and the pack. I could already see it in my mind. It was a genius plan, actually, a well-crafted game plan.

The sound of a heavy door scraping across the hard ground snapped my attention away from my dark thoughts. I watched as soft light flooded into the room and a large mass lumbered into the room dragging a small shadow beside it. As my eyes adjusted to the now lit room, I could see that the large mass was a man about the size of a bear. He was wearing an angry scowl that seemed even more defined by the ugly scar that cut through his upper lip. His eyes were dark pools of black which seemed more intimidating than if they have been glowing red.

His big meaty paw was gripped around the scuff of a small boy's neck. The boy's blond hair was matted and hung around his head like a mop. His clothes were torn and covered in dirt, and his eyes were a pale blue that looked unfocused as they flitted about the now dimly lit room. I could see scarring around the outside of his eyes, telling me that these monsters had purposefully blinded the young wolf. By the scent coming from the boy, I now recognized him as one of the foreign shifters.

The bear of a man practically threw the small boy into the cell beside mine. I growled at him under my breath. My wolf was not appreciating the fact that these monsters were treating a defenseless pup in such a manner. The man threw his gaze at me and smirked as if he had enjoyed my reaction. I wished for nothing more than to rip through the walls of my cell and tear his throat out with my teeth.

Another familiar scent wafted into my nose, and I immediately froze. David strolled through the door with two other rogues at his back. His eyes roamed over the room until they landed on me. I felt like I was standing there with a spotlight fixed on me with nowhere for me to hide. So I leaned against the wall and stared back at him.

He moved away from his entourage and walked toward my cell with confident steps. I watched every step with heavy suspicion. If he thought I was going to let him anywhere near me, he had another thing coming. He stopped in front of my cell. "Good evening, Scarlett. I apologize for the accommodations, but it's necessary. At least until we know we can trust you."

I sneered at him but didn't respond to his greeting. That didn't seem to bother him one bit. His eyes raked over my body as if he is cataloging all of my injuries, of which I had quite a few. His eyes returned to mine after his appraisal. "You seem to be healing a lot slower than expected. We'll have to take you to see the doctor." I didn't want to go to the doctor. If he took me to the doctor, it was likely they would find out the reason for my slower healing. I couldn't have that.

David turned his attention to the men who had come with him. He motioned his head toward Wyatt's cell. "Take him." I watched as they walked to it and opened the door by entering some kind of code into a keypad. I pushed myself off the wall and limped quickly across my cell. Eva tensed up as well, moving closer to Wyatt with her teeth bared.

David let out a sigh as if Eva's actions were an inconvenience. "Make sure she doesn't hurt herself or the pup." I couldn't understand how he could be so callous over his own child, and mate. Even if she hadn't been his true mate, they had bonded.

Wyatt's gaze met mine for a moment, and I saw a flurry of emotions rush through them before he looked away. He pushed himself off the ground. "Eva," he said to her using a voice that was firm, "back down for your pup's sake. I don't need any more deaths on my conscience." She gave him a pained looked as she forced herself to back into the wall.

He turned toward the intruders. "I'm sorry, gentlemen, but I'm not really feeling up to the torture chamber tonight." He rolled his shoulders before he lunged at the man closest to him. He caught him off guard and was able to land a thundering punch to the man's face. The force of the punch knocked him to the ground. However, the other rogue was more prepared, pulling a syringe he had hidden in his pocket and jamming it into Wyatt's back.

"No!" I yelled as Wyatt fell to his knees, his hands slapping against the clear wall between us.

"Bloody hell," he swore under his breath. "Fucking silver... Son of a bitch..." He collapsed forward trying to hold himself up. The man he had punched was pulling himself off the ground angrily. Without a second thought to it, he kicked Wyatt in the face, sending him sprawling across the cold, hard concrete.

All I could see was red as a vicious snarl tore from my chest. I reared my body back before I slammed it into the thick glass partition separating our two cells. The initial crack of my body against the glass caused everyone to switch their attention to me. I didn't stop my attack on the glass. I kept slamming my body into it like a rabid dog in a cage. I wouldn't let them hurt anyone else that I cared about. I was going to kill them, all of them.

The glass shuddered under my assault which seemed to surprise them. I watched the two attackers take a step back away, unsure of what they should do. David let out a growl of frustration. "Scarlett, you have to calm down. You're only damaging yourself further. You're never going to get through that glass."

I pulled back. "Watch me!" I growled back at him as I threw everything I have into it. This time, when my body met the glass, it rattled, and a crunching sound echoed off the walls. The two rogues in Wyatt's cell stared wide-eyed at the clear wall that now had a large crack in it.

"Get her out of there, now!" David yelled, but I didn't let up. I wanted to kill the men who were attacking my cousin. A large hand grabbed hold of my neck, pulling me back from the glass wall. I snarled and twisted around, striking out with clawed fingers. I caught some flesh but was only rewarded with a low growl and a mighty shake that rattled my brain.

"She's like a wild animal," a deep accented voice stated as I was dragged from my cell. Eva's gaze focused on me. She took a step forward, but the rogues in her cell let out a warning growl, and she backed down, but I could see the defiance swirling in her eyes.

"And this is the creature you want to take to your bed? She's likely to eat you once you're done." I squirmed more in his grasp, but my body was screaming from all that I had put it through. I shouldn't have done what I did. I could have hurt my pup without thinking things through clearly. The problem was, I had seen them going for my cousin, and all logic slipped from my mind.

David glared at the man who held me captive with a dark expression before he fixed his eyes on me. "It seems like you still need to learn obedience." His hand reached out quickly toward me, and I snapped my teeth at it, barely missing. The man holding me let out a loud laugh, and David glared at me. His hand collided with the side of my face, shocking me out of my wolf's bloodlust.

His hand came back to my face, and he gripped my chin between his fingers. "You will listen, and you will obey. Do I make myself clear, Scarlett?" A shiver raced up my spine as I stared up into his eyes. I made no attempt to answer him. My words were nowhere to be found. His grip tightened. "Answer me."

"Yes," I hissed out between my clenched teeth.

His eyes searched mine for a moment longer before he leaned forward, pressing his lips against mine. It felt so wrong, and my wolf was rearing back, ready to bite him for putting his hands on us. Bile rose in the back of my throat, but I held it back. He pulled back with a smile. "You taste just like I thought you would" He released his hold on me, and I let out a silent sigh of relief.

"Take her to Kellan," David commanded. "I'll handle the other prisoner since these two idiots," he paused and motioned his head toward the two men still in Wyatt's cell, "are completely incompetent."

I dragged my heels to the ground when the man started to drag me to the door they had entered through. He only chuckled, "Either come like a good little girl, or I'll be forced to take you the way I did the others. I much rather prefer the latter." His words made me feel sick all over again.

Noah would come for me, of that I was certain. Until then, I needed to be smart. I needed to play along with these people and find out exactly what was going on. I anchored myself to the thought of Noah as I walked out of the holding room.

45

Noah

"Where were you, huh? Where the hell were you?" I growled at Christa who was sitting with her hand knitted together tightly in her lap. When she raised her head, I noticed her swollen eye and pained expression. "You were supposed to be watching over her!" My body trembled with the force of my rage.

Janie stood to the side, nibbling on her lip nervously as she glanced around the room. "It wasn't her fault," she mumbled under her breath.

"What?" I snarled at her, causing her to cringe back into the wall.

"Noah!" Alpha Harvey barked, gripping me by my shoulder tightly. "Calm down, son," he said a little softer, almost showing his exhaustion. I clenched my teeth together. I was struggling to keep myself from shifting and destroying everything in sight. He gave my shoulder a squeeze before he removed it and limped over toward his mate. He placed his hand on Christa's shoulder as he did as if to say he supported her.

I spun on my heels and punched the wall hard, trying to let out some of the anger. The wall gave in under my fist, and the plaster cut into my skin. Not that I cared. Knox came charging into the room. His eyes were frantically scanning the faces in the room until they landed on Christa. She was pushing herself out of the chair as she pressed her side. "Noah..." Her voice came out hoarse.

I looked over my shoulder at her with narrowed eyes. "I don't want to hear your excuses."

She took a hobbled step toward me. "She told me that—"

"I don't give a damn what she told you!" I snarled, turning around to face her completely. My feet were carrying me towards her with my wolf barely in check. Her eyes widened a bit in fright, and she took a small step back. "You had one job! When I am not around, you were supposed to protect her." My hands trembled with the need to hurt someone. I clenched them into tight fists. "Yet here you stand, and no one knows where she is! *Where is she*?" I bellowed.

I was suddenly yanked away from her by the collar of my shirt. I spun quickly to see an angry looking Knox. "Don't you talk to her like that!" He growled at me.

My eyes narrowed as I pulled myself free from his grip. "This isn't your business, *pup*." I growled low in my chest as a warning. I was about two seconds away from snapping my fine-tuned control over my more feral urges.

He didn't back down. Instead, he stepped closer to me while puffing out his chest and staring into my eyes. "It's my business if you're going to continue to talk to my mate like that." The room became still. They were waiting for the fight to break out between us. I couldn't deny that the beast was itching for some violence.

I looked away from him toward Christa whose eyes were downcast and cheeks were tinted with a soft blush. I ran my tongue over my teeth as I looked back to Knox. "Mate or not, she failed in her duty which is my pack business. Learn your place... 'cause you really don't want to challenge me right now. You'd lose."

His eyes narrowed at my words, but luckily for him, Alpha Harvey stepped between the two of us, "That's enough." He gave his son a lingering look until he backed down, but I could tell by the look in his eyes that he was ready to challenge me again at a moment's notice. Harvey let his hands fall to his sides with a heavy sigh before he looked at me. "Noah, you can't go around ripping everyone's head off. That is not going to bring Scarlett back or help you find her any faster."

I felt an ache in my chest as if it were a gaping wound. "I can't lose her. I can't..." My voice cracked, and I squeezed my eyes shut to hold back the emotions that wanted to spring free.

Harvey's warm hand came to rest on my shoulder again. "And you won't," he said with a firm voice. I opened my eyes to meet his focused gaze.

"We are going to find her, Noah. I swear this on the love I have for the daughter I lost. We will find her." He gave my shoulder a squeeze, and I felt my wolf relax slightly under his words. "Trust me and have faith, son." I gave him a nod of acceptance as his hand fell from my shoulder.

The door to the room was opened again, and Dane and Ryder came through. Both of them were looking tense as they whispered to each other under their breaths. I moved around Harvey to get to them. "What's the news?" I asked.

Dane looked at Ryder with a subtle glare. "Why don't you tell him?" he almost said sarcastically. Ryder ignored Dane and focused his gaze on mine. "We've caught one of the rogues."

"So what's the problem?" I questioned in a low voice.

"He won't talk," Dane answered with an annoyed sigh. I knew he had probably beaten the wolf within an inch of his life to get him to talk. Dane had come to care about Scarlett just as much as the rest of them, and as my friend, I knew he was willing to do anything to help me find her.

"Take me to him. I'm sure I can loosen his tongue," I said with a hollow smirk. My wolf was welcoming the chance to work some of our anger out on the enemy. Dane looked to Ryder with a skeptical expression, but Ryder returned my smirk with one of his own. "It would be a pleasure, my Alpha." He turned on his heels and marched back the way they had entered.

It didn't take long before the three of us were standing in front of the bloodied rogue. He was chained to a chair with silver, and there were red burn marks where the cuffs rested against his wrists. His head was hanging low, breathing in short, shallow breaths. He let out a choked laugh. "Did you come back to try your hand at torture again, *pup*? You're going to have to try a lot harder if you—" He looked up, his words falling short as his eyes connected with mine. I could see the shock work its way through his body, and that suited me just fine.

"You are..." He seemed to be grasping for words in his shock.

"You made a big mistake of not sharing what you knew," I said coldly as I stepped toward him. He leaned back in his chair as if wanting to escape me. I gave him a wicked grin at the gesture as I came in closer until our faces were close enough that he could feel my breath on his skin. "This will be very unfortunate for you and very fortunate for me."

He glared back at me before gathering some courage as the initial shock of my presence wore off. "You'll be dead before the week is over." He spat at me. I didn't flinch away as the wetness of his saliva ran down my cheek.

I reached up slowly, wiping it away causally. "That might be true, but I guess you'll never know if you were right because you'll be dead before this day is over." I reached out quickly, wrapping my hand around his throat. My claws dug into his skin, causing him to let out a howl of pain.

My eyes scanned his face as he shuddered in my grasp. "Damn, it looks like I missed the vein," I said, tightening my grip.

He started gasping for air. "Wait..." he choked out.

I lifted a questioning brow. "What was that? I couldn't quite hear you." I twisted my hand a bit, making my claws slice deeper.

"Wait!" he yelled out

I retracted my claws but kept my hand on his throat. "Tell me what I want to know, and you might see tomorrow."

My wolf wasn't satisfied with my statement, but at the moment, all I cared about was finding Scarlet.

"I can't. He'll... he'll kill me," he stammered

"Wrong answer." I growled, tightening my grip again.

"You don't understand. He'll kill me!" he said in a choked voice, trying to loosen my hold on him by squirming in the chair frantically.

"You should be more concerned about the person with their hand on your throat killing you!" I said to him in a cool tone as my canines lengthened at the thought of ripping out his throat. He shook with terror before me, and he should because the bloodthirsty thoughts in my head weren't showing a pleasant end for him.

"Now, tell me, where my brother is hiding?" I asked as my body trembled with the force of the beast's hunger underneath my skin.

"Okay! Okay!" he screamed.

I removed my hand from his throat, taking a step away from him. My body and mind entered into a calm state again. He was breathing heavily as he tried to calm himself down. "He is hiding out on Randall's pack lands—a deal he cut a while back. Thorton would take out the alpha, and Kellan would convert more wolves." I listened carefully for any fluctuation of his heart rate, but it stayed steady. He was telling the truth.

I looked over my shoulder at Ryder and Dane who were wearing similar expressions. Clearly, both were surprised by the rogue's revelation.

"That double-crossing Alpha." I sneered. I turned back to the rogue, slashing at him with a clawed hand and slicing through his throat. His eyes were open wide with surprise as he bled out in the chair.

"Alpha," Ryder spoke to me, trying to get my attention.

I spun on my heels, and both of them took a step back from me. The stench of fear from my friends had me snapping back into myself. I frowned as I heard a soft feminine gasp. We all turned to find Janie standing in the doorway with a look of horror in her gaze. Her eyes were fixed on the dead rogue. I could see that she was surprised by the brutality. Her father had seen many things in his years as pack doctor, but she was only just beginning her journey. She still had a timidness to her that made it easy to underestimate her strength.

Dane was looking at her with a pale expression. He wanted to protect her from the truth. I knew the look well enough. I had made it enough times in my life. He stepped toward her. "What are you doing in here?"

She snapped her attention toward him before swinging her wide-eyed gaze at me. "There's something you need to know about Scarlett... something she asked me not to say anything about. I really don't want to betray her... but..."

My wolf was already on edge, and I tensed up. "What?"

She twisted her fingers nervously together. "She's pregnant, Noah."

My knees grew weak at her words, and I felt myself sinking into the ground. She was carrying my pup, *mine... ours.* It made more sense now when she said she wanted to talk when I returned. I could only assume she had planned on telling me the news. I didn't want to have a child, but now that

I knew my mate and pup were out there... I knew they needed me.

How could the Goddess be so cruel to allow this to happen again?

My knees gave out underneath me as the weight of her words crashed down on me. Dane caught me before my knees hit the ground. Ryder came to my other side. "Don't worry, Noah. We will find them. We will," he repeated over and over.

The beast raged within my mind, and I knew there would be blood. I knew it was possible that I might not come back this time, but I was willing to sacrifice myself for Scarlett, for my pup, and for my pack. I wouldn't lose anyone else.

46

Scarlett

The rogue who was escorting me had his hand wrapped firmly around my upper arm in a grip that was less than comfortable. "Keep up!" he barked at me as he yanked me forward so that I was walking a step ahead of him. I wanted to snap at him and fight back, but I knew that playing along right now was the best thing for me. It was also the hardest thing for me. Holding my tongue was not my forte. My eyes roamed over the space, digesting the world around me. I held back a gasp as I began to recognize my surroundings. This was Alpha Randall's territory—or it had been his territory. They were clearly digging in here for weeks by the way they had the small compound built up.

A small group of rogues watched us closely as we trekked through the center. I felt like I was being led to the gallows, a dead man walking. The talking began to taper off until there was only silence around us. This made me and my wolf anxious. There was animosity in the air, and most of it was aimed at me. Three of the rogues approached us, a female leading the way. The right side of her face was scarred from fire, I reckoned by how it looked. Even with the scars, she was beautiful, in a deadly kind of way.

She and her gang stopped right in front of us. She crossed her arms over her chest to look more imposing. My escort let out an annoyed sound. "What do you want, Moira? Clearly, you can see that I'm busy at the moment," he grumbled impatiently, giving my arm a painful squeeze. I turned my head a bit to glare up at him. He peered down at me from the corner of his eye and lifted a brow like he was innocent.

Moira was focusing her gaze on me as if searching for something before she lifted her nose skyward, sniffing at the air. "This woman smells like him. Want to tell me why that is Kade?" She questioned with a grave voice as her eyes focused back on my escort. I turned my eyes back to Kade who looked more than a little uncomfortable with her line of questioning. She took a menacing step forward when he didn't answer. "Why does she smell like him?" Her dark gaze seemed to spark with killing intent.

I could only figure she was talking about Noah, but I was curious as to why she cared. I mean, I knew his brother hated him, but did they all hate him that much? And why was that so? What exactly did he do to them? This kind of hatred didn't seem like it could really be over something as petty as having a mate—even for a rogue. No, I was willing to bet there was more to the story than that.

Kade released his grip on my arm and took a step back away, which surprised me, considering he was such a large man. I almost wanted to laugh at the thought that he was scared of a single girl.

"I'm going to assume that you're talking about Noah?" I questioned, deciding that maybe I could get some answers from the two-faced wolf.

She snarled at me. "Don't you speak that name again or I'll rip your fucking tongue out!" My wolf snapped her teeth in the direction of the female. She was a threat to both myself and the young I was carrying. She only saw one solution: elimination of the threat.

"How is this even possible? He killed his mate. We made sure…" She stumbled over her thoughts.

"Looks like that whole thing didn't pan out too well for you guys, huh? Cause here I am." I couldn't help the sarcasm or the taunting smirk on my lips.

Moira stared at my face, her lips twitching as if trying to hold back the desire to scream. She rushed forward and closed the small distance between us, wrapping her hand around my throat. "I don't know how this is possible, but I guess that just means I'll get the pleasure of killing that bastard's mate myself this time. How fortunate for me," she whispered to me, arrogance dripping in her words.

I coughed and sputtered as I tried to regain the air to my deprived lungs then narrowed my eyes. "I think… you've…" I coughed some more before I reached up with a clawed hand, swiping at her. This action forced her to release me. I coughed again. "You've severely underestimated me." I rolled my aching shoulders, trying to relax my body as I let my wolf bring me back to the edge again.

"What the hell is going on out here?" David's voice rang out. "I told you to take her to Kellan, not serve her up like a meal to the masses!" He sounded furious.

"Look, Prince Charming, I'm not about to get in-between two she-wolves. I suggest you don't either if you know what's good for you," Kade said with a mocking voice.

"Don't worry. You can take her to Kellan when I'm done and have him dispose of her parts," Moira said as she took a step closer to me. Her presence towered over me. She was going to go for her kill shot. I lifted my gaze slowly from the ground, my eyes connecting with the sight of Kade holding back David. Both males were looking at me with tense expressions, ready to watch my blood spill out across the dirt.

"Say hello to his other bitch for me, won't you?" she whispered into my ear as she dug her nails into my shoulder, holding me steady.

I reached up quickly and gripped her hand with mine. "Why don't you say hello yourself?" I tightened my grip, hunching my body forward as I pulled at her. She stumbled forward, and I used my body to flip her over me. Moira hit the dirt. I stepped away from her, watching as she pulled herself off the ground, her expression looking more feral.

"That was cute," she barked.

"I'll give you a chance to walk away Moira. I really don't want to kill anyone... again" I hope that she would do what I'd suggested because I didn't enjoy the memory of the rogue I had killed, but I knew the likelihood wasn't high. Rogues were beyond reason, and this one seemed more than happy to end my life moments ago. I watched as her bones cracked and popped as she held back, shifting into her beastly form.

She charged at me with her teeth and claws bared. She swiped at me, and I duck down under her arm with ease as I let my wolf take more control of my movements. Moira turned to me again, swiping at me like the desperate beast she had become. I blocked most of her attacks, taking only a couple of cuts here and there. I spotted an opening, and I took it. I swooped down low under her wild movements and popped up in her face. I started punching at her in quick succession. All the energy I had been holding back suddenly had a release.

My hits were coming in too fast for her to block them. I spun away from her when she was wobbling on her feet. A tremble rushed through my body before I rushed forward, kicking her with my leg and hitting her in the stomach. Her body hit the ground and rolled, her body looking like a ragged doll as she went. I stalked toward her as she tried to get up the ground, struggling. I kicked her again when I reached her, causing her to flip back onto her back. I pressed my foot to her throat, anchoring her to the ground.

I stared down at her. A part of me wanted to crush her, but another part of me knew that wouldn't help me or my situation. She stared up at me enraged. "Do it!" she hissed. My shoulders sagged, and I eased back the pressure of my foot.

"You're a coward! That's why you will die in this place! You and your bastard of a mate!" Her body trembled and shook with the rage flooding her system. I gave her a blank look. "If I die... at least I won't die a monster."

"Well, well..." A deep voice spoke out from behind me. "Not what I was expecting to see." I looked over my shoulder to see a familiar face. He looked so much like Noah, except where Noah had blue eyes, this male had deep brown ones.

"You. You're Noah's brother... You're the one who did all of this?" I asked, baffled.

Kellan stood near David and Kade, looking amused. My wolf raged inside me, and I sneered at him.

He let out a soft chuckle. "You'll have to forgive Moira. She has problems controlling her anger where Noah is concerned. He broke her heart when he ditched her for Claire. He also killed her brother, so I'm sure you can understand." Moira let out a growl at the sound of Noah's name, squirming and trying to get out of my hold.

Kellan took a step forward, and I let out a growl. "Stay the hell away from me!"

He scrutinized my form slowly before holding up his hands in surrender. "I am not going to hurt you, Scarlett. You're wounded, and you need medical attention. It would really not benefit any of us if you bled to death." When I didn't respond, he took that as an opportunity to come closer.

I pressed down harder on Moira's throat. "Come any closer, and I'll crush her."

"You think I care?" He questioned with a lifted brow. "Moira knows how things work around here. She challenged you. She lost. The fact that she's still alive is actually a surprise."

"You're a monster!" I spat out.

"Says the woman threatening to crush her opponent to death," he retorted with a smug grin.

I stared at Kellan for a long moment as my mind tried to think of a plan. My eyes drifted away from him to David, who was staring at me with a tense expression, one that I would have possibly labeled as concern if I thought he could feel anything like that anymore. As I stared back at David, I began to formulate a plan in my mind. I turned my attention away from him and back to Kellan, "Fine." I pulled my foot back completely and released Moira, who started coughing and gasping for air.

Kellan held his fake smile. "I'm glad you see things my way." He came forward a couple steps.

"I'm not going anywhere with you," I said through tight lips. Kellan's smile slipped a bit. I could see the anger in his eyes at me challenging him in front of all these people.

"It looks like we're at an impasse then."

"I said, I'm not going anywhere with you, but I will go with him." I pointed toward David. Kellan looked over his shoulder to David who was looking a little surprised and happy at my declaration. Kellan turned his attention back to me, his gaze narrowing into suspicion. "Okay. You heard the woman, David."

David pushed past Kade, knocking him roughly with his shoulder as he made his way to me. When he reached me, his eyes scanned over me. "Do you need me to carry you?" The thought of his hands on me made me want to vomit, but I held back the urge as I nodded my head. I needed to convince David that I was on his side if I wanted to use him to get the hell out of this place.

He scooped me up into his arms with ease. "You surprised me. You fought well, Scarlett. You are strong and clever," he whispered down at me with a look of admiration. "I always regretted rejecting you. Now that we have a second chance, I'm going to claim you like I should have in the beginning. Nothing and no one will sway me this time."

I closed my eyes and forced my body to relax. Everything will be fine, I chanted to myself. Noah will come. He will. Until then, I would protect myself and our pup by whatever means necessary.

47

Scarlett

I was sitting on the cot as the older woman looked at the wounds on my body. Every once in a while, she made a sound in the back of her throat as she poked and prodded me. I closed my eyes, trying to let my mind take me somewhere else, some place where I wasn't surrounded by people who wanted to kill me and the people I had come to care about.

When she placed a hand on my stomach, pressing gently, I grabbed hold of her wrist, and my eyes snapped open. She held my gaze for a moment before lowering it. I knew she knew, and I prayed for her sake she kept her mouth shut or I would take her tongue. My wolf rumbled her agreement, pacing in my mind as she guarded the small glowing light in our belly.

"I'd say it's all psychological at this point," the old woman stated as she removed her hands. I watched as she pulled off the blue gloves, throwing them into a waste bin. She lied for me, but why? What could she want? I narrowed my eyes in suspicion.

"What do you mean?" David asked with a tone of confusion. The woman's knowing glance met mine for a moment before turning her back to us and making her way toward a tall cabinet. "I'd say that she and her wolf are beyond stressed out by the circumstances, and so instead of healing like normal, her wolf is only thinking about survival and by that mark... returning to her mate, I assume." She opened the cabinet.

David let out a low growl. "I'm her mate. Her true mate... that bastard is nothing to her." I had to bite my tongue to keep from snapping at David for talking about Noah like that. He wasn't nothing to me. He was everything to me.

I was surprised by the thought as it rushed through my mind. When had he become so special to me? How had he weaseled his way into my heart?

The woman shuffled some things around before grabbing a bottle and closing the cabinet. "Here." She held the bottle out towards him. He snatched it from her, still riled up about her mate comment. She didn't seem put off by his attitude. I guessed that was usual behavior when you worked with rogues.

"What is this?" He held it up, examining it closer.

"It'll help her to sleep better... which is exactly what her body needs to heal itself. You and the boys need to calm down with the beatings if you want her to be alive much longer," she said, placing her hands on her hips like a disapproving mother. She was trying to protect me and my pup but still, I didn't understand why.

David gripped the bottle in his hand tighter. "No one is going to lay a hand on her... again." He began to shake a bit, and I thought he might lose control, but before that happened he took in a deep breath, calming himself. He turned his attention to me. I gripped the edge of the cot to keep myself from cringing back. He closed the distance between us, lowering himself a bit so that our faces were level. "I'm sorry about what happened out there, Scarlett. I should have stopped that, but there are rules around here."

He reached out his free hand toward my face, and I flinched a bit which made him pause. I noticed the flash of anger in his gaze before he finished his initial movement, lightly brushing some hair behind my ear. "I have to go take care of something. You will stay here and rest until I come back for you." He leaned forward, pressing his lips to my forehead. I dug my fingers deeper into the mattress to force myself to remain close to him.

"Okay."

He pulled back, and I gave him what I hoped was some kind of a convincing smile. It seemed to do the trick because he didn't waste any more time in the room with us. Once he was gone, I let out a sigh of relief.

"You must be Noah's mate," the doctor commented after a couple minutes of silence. I looked at her, meeting her amber gaze before laying myself down on the cot.

"You'll have to excuse me. I'm tired and talking with the enemy isn't high on my priorities," I replied as I stared up at the ceiling that seemed to have some water stains.

The woman let out a soft chuckle. "I'm not your enemy. I'm a prisoner here just like you... Well, sort of."

I chanced a peek in her direction. She was leaning back against the cabinet with her arms crossed over her chest. "How do I know this isn't some kind of trick?" I questioned.

She gave me a smile before looking away toward the small window. "I will never be able to leave here. I was taken prisoner a long time ago and was forced into a mate bond with a man who was not my mate. Even if I hate that man with every fiber of my being... my wolf... well, she can't survive without the bastard."

I watched the woman more closely, realizing that she didn't seem like the other people in this camp. She seemed warm. Her eyes wandered back to mine. "I might never have gotten the chance to be with my mate before he was taken from me, but you..." she gave me an apologetic smile. "I won't sit back and watch that be ripped away from you. You need to get out of here before they find out about the little life growing inside of you."

"Why would you help me? You don't even know me." I pointed out the obvious. I was still feeling suspicious even though a part of me wanted to hope against hope that someone would be on my side.

"You are Scarlett. Your cousin Wyatt was David's beta and is currently being held as a prisoner. You're mated to Noah, who is Alpha Kellan's younger brother, a man known to most of these people as the demon wolf. I know you, Scarlett... well enough." She reassured me.

I narrowed my eyes. "That is a little unsettling. You know all of that about me when I've never met you before."

"I'm one of the pack doctors, and these wolves are chatty once they are high on pain meds," she said with a mischievous glint in her eyes.

"Okay... but that still doesn't explain why you would want to help me. Won't you get in trouble if someone finds out?"

"You let me worry about that. All you need to know is that in that bottle I gave David is a very powerful sleep aid. Find a way to slip it to him by tomorrow night. The guards will be focusing their attention elsewhere, thanks to the impending war, so you shouldn't have much issue getting around." I was stunned by the level of her planning. I didn't know if I could trust her, but at this point, it wasn't like I had many options.

I pulled my gaze away from her. "If you betray me or if this is some kind of trap, you better hope that I die because if I don't..." I paused and turned my head back toward her, our eyes connecting, "you'll be begging for death before I'm done with you."

She didn't back down from my gaze. "I would expect nothing less from the demon wolf's mate." With that understanding between us, I rolled over so my back was to her and closed my eyes. I will get out of here. I will go home to my pack and my mate, I promised to myself.

I didn't know how long I was asleep for, but it didn't feel nearly long enough. A warm hand was touching my shoulder. In my sleep haze, I thought it was Noah... I wanted it to be Noah. I felt a light smile grace my lips. "I was waiting for you," I mumbled sleepily as I rolled over, opening my eyes. I tried not to frown when my eyes found David hovering over me.

His hand traveled up from my shoulder, his fingers brushing over my neck where Noah's claim marred my skin. "Well, I'm sorry I kept you waiting for so long." His words dripped with a double meaning that made my stomach tumble into knots. We stared at each other silently for another minute, each of us lost in our own private thoughts. Mine mostly consisted of how sorry I felt for David, looking at how far he had fallen.

He cleared his throat. "Kellan wants me to bring you to his office." He looked a little guilty.

I pushed myself up onto my elbow, effectively bringing us closer together. "That's fine, David. I understand," I said in a soft voice. His eyes searched mine. I saw the moment his gaze filled with lust. I swallowed hard against my strong desire to push him away and run like the whole lot of hell was chasing me. He needed to believe that I was on his side. I needed to feed his delusion so I could use him. He leaned forward. He meant to kiss me, but luckily for me, the door popped open. "Hurry it up, lover boy!" Kade ordered as he stuck his head in.

David turned his attention toward Kade. "I'm going to kill you if you don't shut the hell up with those comments."

Kade shot him a playful grin. "I'd like to see you try, Prince Charming." He winked before closing the door as David rose up from the bed angrily. I pushed myself the rest of the way up as my muscles screamed from the battle I had been in earlier. I let out a small groan as I got up off the cot which made David turn back to me.

He reached out for me, grabbing my arm in one of his hands as if he was trying to steady me. "Are you okay? Do you need me to carry you again?"

I gave him a forced smile. "No. I think I can manage walking on my own." He gave me a tender smile in return that hurt my heart. I wished for that smile for so many nights, but now, it only pained me. He was lost, and there would be no redemption for him.

He released my arm, only to wrap his large hand around my much smaller one. "Once Kellan is done talking to us. I'll take you back to my space. Well, I guess it'll be our place soon. Anyway, I'll take you there so you can get the rest you need. I promise." He gave my hand a light squeeze. His words didn't give me any reassurance. They only left me feeling more anxious, but I pushed that feeling deep down. I just needed to focus on the plan. I would be getting out of here, and all of this nightmare would be far behind me.

"Then let's get this talk over with. I'm tired," I said with a fake smile and a teasing tone.

David and Kade had me sandwiched so tightly between their large bodies that every time I took a step, I was grazing my arms against them. I would have been extremely annoyed if I didn't realize how this kept anyone else from approaching me. It was not that I doubted my ability to fight off a rogue, but in my current condition, my chances of being successful were definitely questionable. Our speed slowed down as we rounded another corner in the small compound.

A door stood at the end of the small hallway with two men posted on either side. I took in a steady breath, trying to ready myself for whatever was going to happen to me behind that door. I doubted they planned to do any physical damage, but beyond that, I had no idea what to expect. The guards looked at us as we approached them, stopping when we are several feet away. Both guards bowed their heads. "Beta Kade, Beta David..."

Kade snorted in annoyance, moving past the guards, stepping up to the door, and opening it. He turned his gaze back to me. "Ladies first." I rolled my eyes, moving through the open door with David quick on my heels, not wanting to be too far from me. My eyes wandered around the small room. There was a larger desk near a window and a red couch pushed against the wall farthest from me. Kellan stood behind his desk, hunched forward as he looked at something intently.

Delilah sat on the edge of his desk smiling at me viciously. "You look like shit," she said in a peppy tone.

I sneered at her but kept myself from responding to her obvious goading. I was more curious about why she was even here unless their plan was to royally piss me off. Kellan looked up toward the three of us, stretching himself up to his full height. I crossed my arms over my chest. "You wanted to see me..." I said in annoyance.

"Impatient, I see," he replied with a wry grin, not put off with my attitude toward him.

I frowned. "Not really, I just would rather not spend my time with psychotic shifters who are hell bent on destroying the people and society I care about." Kellan threw back his head, letting out a dark laugh before focusing his attention on me again. A big grin was on his lips. He moved away from his desk, taking confident steps around it and bringing himself into full view of everyone.

"You really are a marvel, Scarlett. No wonder my brother wasted no time claiming you." David emitted a low growl at Kellan's statement which got him a quick glance of amusement before Kellan's attention was focused back on me. "Apparently, my brother isn't the only one taken in by your charms," he said teasingly.

"I didn't realize you invited me here to chat about my love life," I remarked snidely. My wolf was pacing around in my head. She had her eyes on everyone, ready for anything.

"What can I say? I'm quite curious about your situation, Scarlett. The fact that my brother had not one but two mates is surprising though I obviously learned my mistake from the first one. I mean, who's to say if I killed you... another mate wouldn't just show up again? The Goddess is a cruel mistress." He crossed his arms over his chest.

"I do have my theories about how this situation between Noah and you developed, but that isn't important. What is important is how we move forward from here. As you can see, I've been collecting things." He motioned with a flip of his wrist to the people in the room. Delilah had a self-important smile plastered on her lips.

I couldn't help but snort. "And what lovely taste you've got." Sarcasm dripped from my words. Delilah leveled me with her death glare but remained rooted to her position.

"David tells me that you've seen your—who was he again—oh, yes, cousin." Kellan waved his hand in a dismissive way, but by the light in his eyes, I could see that he is trying to get a reaction from me. My foot shifted forward slightly as my wolf rushed toward the surface and memories of those men beating my cousin flashed through my mind. A large hand fell on my shoulder, giving it a firm grip. I turned my head quickly, readying myself to snap, but then I realized David was the one holding onto me. I frowned. I forced myself to relax, knowing I couldn't destroy any possible trust I had developed with him.

I swung my gaze back to Kellan as my eyes narrowed into slits. "What do you want from me?" I growled, tired of whatever strange mind game he was trying to play with me.

"Impatient and conceited… not very good qualities to have as an aspiring young luna," Kellan scolded me mockingly. I gritted my teeth together, keeping myself from responding when I recognized the mischievous glint in his eyes as he turned his back to the room. There was a subtle knock on the door before I heard it open. I looked over my shoulder to see Wyatt being dragged into the room by Thorton. The shock of seeing him here now had my mind falling blank and my body freezing up.

Wyatt wasn't putting up a fight. His body was sagging in Thorton's grasp on the collar of his shirt. He was sporting several new bruises. I knew that he was still suffering from the silver that had been injected into him. Concern rushed through me. The only relief I felt came from the subtle rise and fall of his chest, telling me he was still alive.

Thorton dropped Wyatt at my feet like he was trash before stepping over him. "Sir, the scouts told me that Noah is on the move." The sound of Noah's name had me snapping back into reality. I fixed my eyes on Thorton. He was a traitor. He was the one who helped Delilah with her murders and with the kidnapping. All this was clearly planned from the beginning.

My wolf wanted to rip him limb from limb, and I was more than willing to let her. A threatening snarl tore from my throat, and my body coiled, readying itself to spring at its prey. David tightened his hold on me, but that wasn't going to stop me. As if remembering what I was capable of, Kade's hand gripped my other shoulder to help secure me in place.

I struggled in their hold. "You traitor!" I growled. "All those innocent lives..." Thorton looked at me as if I was nothing more than a bug to be squashed.

My body shook violently as I barely held myself from shifting. "I'm going to kill you." My voice sounded more animalistic.

He leaned forward at me with a smirk. "I don't think so, Luna." My nostrils flared up at his mocking. Kellan slapped his palm down on the desk, breaking through the argument. "Enough" He growled, and I could feel the aura of the room change as he began to assert his beast's dominance.

His eyes locked onto me, and I stared back at him. "When you said you were collecting things..." I started as my brain began to process through everything that I'd learned and tried to piece it all together. Kellan gave me a look a curiosity. "This is a game, Scarlett. A chessboard if you will, and I've been setting myself up for the perfect play. If my father taught me anything, it was how to play this game very well."

"So what? We've all been pawns in your ridiculous game?" I questioned.

"Some people have been pawns, but not you, Scarlett. No, you are the most precious piece on the board. You are the queen, the grand piece on the chessboard. But without the queen, the king will fail." He winked at me.

My heart sank at the thought of Noah moving straight into Kellan's trap. He wasn't going to kill me. He was going to make me watch as he killed Noah. That was his plan, and I couldn't let that happen. Wyatt let out a small groan in his unconscious state, and I peered down at him. My stomach twisted into knots as I realized that this was all a display of power, of what Kellan could do to the people I cared about. I clenched my hands into fists at my side, my nails digging into my skin. I couldn't run away. It was too late for that now.

I pulled my attention back to Kellan. "If you think that I am going to sit back and watch you slaughter the people I love, then you've got another thing coming."

"On the contrary, I'm expecting you to put up a fight," Kellan said with a calm certainty.

"I'm not going to fight you," I remarked with a soft voice. I watched Kellan lift a questioning brow. My wolf rose close to the surface, and I could feel her fury on a different level. I saw Kellan's eyes widen for a fraction of a second. The hands holding me loosened their grip. "If I see you again. I'll kill you. All of you. That's a promise." I heard the hatred in my own voice.

His eyes narrowed, and he gave me a confident smirk. "You'll have to get in line. I believe I have cells full of people itching to kill me." He nodded his head in a signal, and David's grip on me tightened. "Now if you don't mind... I have some things to prepare for," Kellan said with a smile. I struggled a bit in David's grip, but I didn't fight too hard as I was formulating my own plan.

"Oh..." Kellan held up a finger as if he has forgotten something. "Just in case you do get a little too riled up..." He looked at Thorton who heaved a sigh as he bent over and grabbed onto Wyatt's shirt, lifting him off the ground. I clenched my teeth together, tightly wanting nothing more than to attack them all.

"I'll keep your cousin with me to ensure your compliance. I mean, we wouldn't want anything to happen to him." I let out a guttural growl as Thorton dragged my cousin away from me. Kellan turned away from me with a confident grin. "Rest up, Scarlett. Tomorrow is sure to be a big day."

48

Scarlett

As David had promised, he took me back to his quarters within the small compound. At first, he looked like he was concerned that I was going to try to run, but when he realized I wasn't putting up a fight, he relaxed. His space was exactly how I imagined it would look: neat and organized. It was funny to think that I had once dreamed about a life where I would share a bed with this man. He had been the only thing I wanted, but now, all I felt toward him was pity. This was a bed of his own making, and now he would have to lie in it... alone.

"Do you want anything to eat or..." David asked, his question falling off as he searched my face.

I shook my head even as my stomach grumbled in protest. "Honestly, I'm tired. I just want to sleep. It's been a long day." I tried to keep the bitterness out of my voice. I thought I saw a flash of emotion in David's eyes, but he gave me a forced smile. "Of course. Let me show you to the bed."

He walked away from me, and I followed after him slowly, not wanting to get too close to him.

My wolf sniffed at the air, taking in everything around us. She didn't like the smell of David. She let out a low rumble of discontent. It wasn't like I could change our current situation, though, so I ignored her.

When I entered his bedroom, I looked around warily as if there might be some kind of danger lying in wait for me. As if he understood my hesitance, he released a loud sigh. "I'm not going to hurt you, Scarlett."

"You hit me earlier." I pointed out as proof of the contrary.

He frowned at my comment. "Yes. Well... you made me angry." He justified his actions. I moved further into the room, wrapping my arms around myself to resurrect some kind of physical barrier between us. "Well, the David I knew would never have hit me," I said in a soft whisper as my eyes drifted over to the bed that I felt anxious about sleeping in. Now that I was looking at it, I would rather stay back on the cot in the medical room.

"That David is dead," he said flatly, and I tried not to cringe at his words. I knew well that he was dead, just like the old Scarlett that died a long time ago. We were simply phantoms of the past haunting each other. I peered up at him, and once again, I felt only pity for him. The anger I had felt for him was disappearing under the overwhelming feeling that our choices had sealed our fate.

His eyes narrowed into tiny slits. "Don't look at me like that." He snapped defensively.

I let out a small, tired breath and looked away from him. "I'd like to be alone now," I said as I moved closer to the bed. I unwound my arms and pulled myself up onto the large bed with a little grunt. I could feel David hovering behind me, but he remained silent. I kept my back to him, not wanting to look at him any longer. He only served as a reminder of the past and of the nightmare I couldn't seem to wake up from. I closed my eyes, exhaustion washing over me.

He moved closer to the bed, and my body tensed up, not sure what he was going to do. I squeezed my eyes tighter together and tried to will him away from me. His fingers hesitantly brushed against my cheek before running lightly through my hair. "I'm sorry, Scarlett," he whispered to me.

"You might have been sorry before, but not anymore. Now, you don't feel anything," I said back to him as I remained frozen and motionless. He didn't respond to my statement in an angry fashion as I half-expected him to.

Instead, he let out a breath and walked away from me. "Rest. I'll make sure nothing happens to you," he said before I heard the soft click of the door closing behind him, plunging me into darkness. I opened my eyes and stared blankly into the darkness. I felt a familiar empty ache in my chest, and I knew it was because I was missing Noah. I wanted him to be here with me, holding me and telling me he would protect what was his. I closed my eyes and let out a deep sigh. "He's coming for you," I whispered into nothingness to reassure myself as I drifted off.

I didn't know how long I was asleep for, but when I came to, I was gasping for air and covered in sweat. My heart was thundering against my chest as my blood rushed through my veins and pulsed in my ears. I must have had a nightmare, but I couldn't recall what happened. I sat up with a small groan and pulled myself out of bed, stretching my stiff limbs. I could tell that the rest had helped me heal my superficial wounds though my shoulder and leg were still pretty achy.

I shuffled my way through the darkness to the door and opened it slowly, peeking out. When I didn't spot David, I eased my way out of the bedroom and into the main area of his little living space. I licked my chapped lips and decided that I was unbelievably thirsty. I moved through the room, hoping to stumble upon something to drink.

"Where do you think you're going?" David's voice rang out behind me, and I immediately stopped in my tracks.

I turned my head, looking back over my shoulder at him. He was leaning against a post of an entry-way into another room. His eyes were narrowed slightly and full of suspicion, and his hair was ruffled and sticking up in several directions, telling me he must have been anxiously running his hands through it. I swallowed the rising lump in my throat. "I'm thirsty."

His face softened into exhaustion, and he let out a small sigh. "Take a seat. I'll get you something." He pushed off the post and disappeared into the room. I turned toward the small seating area and moved toward the couch, taking a seat as he had suggested. I couldn't quite understand why David was treating me the way he was. At times, it was like I saw glimpses of the David I had met all those years ago, then he would disappear again. There was no way he felt anything anymore, right? He was a rogue, after all.

A glass of water was suddenly thrust in front of my face, and I peered up to see David standing over me with a frown on his lips. I reached out and took it from him. "Thank you," I murmured as I placed it to my lips and drank greedily. He sat on the couch next to me, a little too close for my own comfort. I tried to ignore how I could feel the heat of his body seeping into mine. At one time, I would have been elated by his closeness, but now, all it did was make me antsy for more space.

A tense silence hung between the two of us, and I stared down at the cup of water in my hands. David let out a heavy sigh. "Why did you let him mark you, Scarlett?" If I had been drinking at the moment, I probably would have choked and spit it out everywhere. I whipped my head in David's direction to find him staring at me intensely.

I frowned at him. "Does it really matter, David?" His eyes darkened, and I noticed the muscle in his jaw stiffen like he was clenching his teeth together.

"You were... are mine. Mine! If anyone was going to mark you, it should have been me." He growled at me in a dangerously low voice.

I found my hand tightening around the glass. "You rejected me. You had someone else," I snapped at him, meeting his dark gaze with my own. "What did you expect to happen, David? Just thinking about it makes me sick to my stomach. There was only one way things were going to end between us."

David growled at me and reached up quickly, catching me by surprise. His hand snaked around my neck and grabbed the hair at the base of my head. He yanked it hard, and I gasped when my neck was exposed towards him. I squirmed in his hold, but he only tightened his grasp, making my scalp burn and tingle with pain. He glared down at Noah's mark, hatred and envy burning in his eyes. My lips pulled back into a sneer. "You can't change what's already been done. I belong to him, not you. I will always belong to him and never you."

My wolf rushed toward the surface, snapping and snarling. This moment was taking a turn for the worst. My plan to use David was quickly unraveling before me. I shouldn't have opened my mouth. My plan was to build trust with him, but he pushed my buttons. David yanked hard and pushed his face into my neck with a fierce snarl. I slammed my eyes close, and for a moment I thought he might rip my throat out. I was practically panting and sweating from the fear, considering how vulnerable I was in this particular position. He took in a deep breath, dragging his nose against my skin.

"You might bear his mark, but those things can be changed," he whispered harshly against me, making me want to cringe. "You might have his scent on you, but I can put my scent in you." His free hand found its way to my leg and slowly worked its way upward, making my skin crawl.

"David..." My voice came out weakly. "Please..." My heart was beating erratically in my chest at the possibilities racing through his mind. I felt the scraping of his canines against the skin of my throat. "There is nothing to be afraid of, Scarlett. I'm not going to take you while you have some other man's mark on you. When I take you... you will be completely mine. Mine and mine alone."

My body released the tension at his words, and a small breath of relief fell from my lips. I could feel him smiling against my skin. "But I don't see why I can't have a little taste now." The hand on my thigh tightened painfully as his teeth pierced through my sensitive flesh. My eyes opened wide, and a scream tore from my lips as white hot pain scorched through my veins. I began to thrash against him wildly. He pulled back, only to strike out again like a viper. His teeth tore through my flesh again, and I screeched like a banshee. I was sure everyone in the compound heard my screams.

I knew that his bite wouldn't undo Noah's claim on me, but it still burned like acid as his thoughts and feelings crashed into mine. It took a moment for me to realize I was still clenching the glass of now spilled water in my hand. I pulled my arm back, and with all the strength I could muster, slammed the glass against the side of his face. The glass shattered against him, and he broke away from me with a growl of pain. I used his surprise against him and shoved him away from me forcefully. He fell back on the couch, gripping the side of his bleeding face.

I was frantic as I grasped around with trembling hands for anything I could use as a weapon against him. My hand wrapped around the side table lamp, and I jumped up from the couch, probably looking like a wild animal. David was watching me with blazing eyes of fury. I had gotten the better of him. He rose up from the couch and angled his body forward, ready to launch himself at me. I wet my lips nervously but tightened my grip on the lamp. He inched himself forward. "You really need to be taught to be more obedient, Scarlett."

"Rot in hell!" I yelled at him.

"That's no way to talk to your mate," he scolded me with a sinister smile as he shifted forward.

I watched his movements closely. "It's a good thing you're not my mate then."

He growled at my statement and launched himself at me. His body slammed into mine, taking me down to the floor before I could even react. I hit the ground hard, and the air rushed from my lungs as David's body crushed me from above. We scrambled with each other on the ground for a moment, but in my current position, I couldn't really get the upper hand. In a moment of desperation, I bit into his shoulder as hard as I could. A howl of pain erupted from his mouth, and he shook back and forth, trying to knock me off, but I only bit down harder.

My head hit the ground hard, and I saw stars for a moment, making me release my hold on him. He rolled off me quickly with a slew of curses. I shook my head, and my hand fumbled around, grabbing the lamp that is lying a few feet away from me. I moved quickly and launched myself on top of him. Straddling his waist, I pulled the lamp back over my head and slammed it down onto his head as hard as I could. He yelped in surprise at my attack and tried to buck me off, but I tightened my thighs around him to hold myself steady. I pulled back again and slammed the lamp down onto his head with a war cry. His body fell limp under me, but I raised my arm and stared down at him, ready to attack if he moved again.

When I saw the light rise and fall of his chest, I knew he was unconscious. I dropped the lamp, and it crashed to the ground beside us. I pulled myself up off of his body feeling like I had been run over by a train. My hand came to rest against the bloody bite wounds on my neck as I hobbled towards the exit. This wasn't necessarily how I had planned things to go, but I wasn't about to wait around for him to wake up and talk out our little domestic dispute. The doctor did say I should put him to sleep though I think she had something a little more subtle in mind.

My wolf whimpered in my head as she curled herself protectively around our little moon. I knew I needed to be more careful. All the stress could harm my pup, and I didn't want that. I just needed to get to Noah. I just need to get to Noah... I chanted in my head as I staggered out of the room.

•

49

Scarlett

I had almost made my way out of the compound without anyone noticing me. The silver knife burned into the palm of my hand. I fought the reaction to release it, gripping it harder. I had stolen it from a guard after taking him by surprise. It was nice to have some means of dealing out damage since, at the moment, the young in my belly kept me from shifting as I normally would have.

Other than the one guard, I had made it through undetected. I knew that was probably thanks to the fact that everyone was preparing for the impending battle. While I felt comforted knowing that Noah was getting closer to me, I couldn't help the anxiety that was also building. What if something happened to him? What if I lost him? My wolf whimpered at the direction of my thoughts. I quickly pushed them down, knowing that I had to focus on getting out of here, but I wasn't going to leave without the other prisoners. Not without Eva, Wyatt, or the other unknowns.

I moved through the darkness. My nerves were hyper-aware of every sound and movement around me. When I caught the scent of a shifter nearby, I quickly looked for a place to hide. I moved as swiftly as I could to the nearest building, hugging the wall to cloak myself completely in the shadows. The shifter in question came into view. He walked quickly in the direction I had come, and not long after he disappeared from view, three more ran by, following after him.

I gritted my teeth as I kept myself hidden for a few more minutes before I pushed off the wall, quickening my pace toward the holding cells they had taken me from. I could only assume that this sudden commotion meant one of two things. Either David had woken up and told them I had escaped or Noah was much closer than I thought. My heart was thundering in my chest as I searched the darkness, anxious that a rogue would jump out at me.

When the hairs on the back of my neck stood up in awareness, I knew someone was behind me, but before I could react, a hand was slapped over my mouth. I screamed into the hand, readying myself to fight back, but a familiar soft voice calmed me. "Don't make a sound. They are looking for you." The doctor pulled me back into the shadows as another group of rogues raced by us.

Once they were out of sight, she released me. "What happened to the plan? I thought I told you to use the medicine I gave you." She sounded irritated.

"I'm sorry I foiled your perfect plan, but I ran into some trouble. So I improvised. Either way, I'm here, aren't I?"

I snapped back at her, just as annoyed. I could feel her eyes roaming over me in the darkness, probably assessing the damage that had been done.

A small hiss passed her lips, "He bit you." I felt her hand come up, pressing on the still burning wound. I slapped her hand away, frowning at her. "Yeah, but don't worry too much. I bit him back, harder."

The sound of urgent voices in the distance pulled me back into the present. She reached out, grabbing me by the arm. "Come on. We've wasted enough time already." She pulled me quickly behind her as she moved us through the dark. We came to an abrupt stop, and she let out a small curse. I peered around her, curious about what was going on. I spotted two guards standing in front of a small building. There was something or someone important in there.

"What are they guarding?" I asked.

She looked over her shoulder. "Kellan's war prize."

I frowned at her words, my eyes narrowing. The silver blade felt heavy in my hand. "Well, I think it's fair if I take something of his since he has something of mine." Perhaps, I could use her as a bargaining chip to get back my cousin.

She gave me a pinched look. "We don't have time."

"Then I guess we're going to make some. Plus, if we go out there, they will see us either way," I said with a firm tone. She didn't look happy, but she couldn't disagree with my logic.

"Follow my lead," she whispered through tight lips. She stepped out of the darkness, leaving me a little uncertain as she hastily approached the men. They stood up a little straighter when they saw her. "Meredith," one of the men said her name.

She cleared her throat. "I'm here to check up on the female."

The two males looked at each other questioningly before looking back to her. "No one informed us that you were coming."

Meredith put her hands on her hips. "My mate sent me here specifically to check up on her under Kellan's request. If you want to send me away, then I'll let you be the one to explain to hi—"

"No!" the male interrupted her. "No, I am sure it's no problem. We'll open the door for you." I couldn't help but be curious about who exactly her mate was if he can strike fear into people like that. He surely must have been the doctor that David had been referring to originally. The image of the blinded young pup that Kade had dragged into the holding cells came to mind, and I shuddered at the cruelty of the act. The men turned their backs to her, and she looked over her shoulder at me where I was hiding in the shadows. She caught my eyes before nodding her head.

I eased my way out as quietly as possible. Meredith moved quickly at the male unlocking the door. She wrapped her arm around his neck, pressing a hand firmly to his head. I watched her apply pressure as she twisted quickly. The snapping of his bone was the only sound I heard. She released his body, and its dead weight fell at her feet.

The other male lashed out quickly, grabbing her by her throat with a loud snarl. "Traitor!" She tried to break free from his grip. I moved swiftly, pulling the males attention to me at the last second. His eyes opened wide, and I shot him a deadly grin as my wolf pressed her desire for violence into my mind.

"Surprise, asshole!" I whispered as I lifted my hand with the silver blade.

He opened his mouth to release a shout that I silenced as the blade tore into the fleshy softness of his throat. When his blood sprayed out at me, I knew this would haunt me later, but right now it was them or me, and I chose me. I pushed the blade a little deeper, his blood running onto my hand as I held his gaze. "You should have never taken me from Noah," I hissed as his hand relaxed on Meredith and the light fled from his eyes. I could hear her choking as I pulled the blade free, letting the guard's body slump to the ground.

She stumbled back from me when I turned my gaze at her. I could practically taste her fear, and that helped me to reign in my dark urges. I forced myself back into control.

"Demon wolf..." I heard her mumble as her eyes were still trained on me.

"Hardly, I don't think I'm quite deserving of that title, yet," I said back a little breathless. "So, do you want to open that door or do you want to just wait here until more people come?" I questioned when she continued to stare at me, trying to pull her out of the strange trance she seemed to be lost in. Shaking her head, she pushed herself forward and grabbed the keys off the rogue she had killed. I came to stand behind Meredith but kept my eyes scanning the area around us. "Anytime now, Meredith," I said as I glanced over my shoulder to see her shakily fumbling to put the right key into the lock.

My wolf was still scratching under the surface begging for release, but when the sound of the latch undoing hit my ears, I felt her calm down a little. I spun on my heels, moving through the now open door, and Meredith followed cautiously behind me. The room was almost pitch-black except for some moonlight streaming in through a small window. There was a hallway with only one door.

"Give me the keys." I held my hand out in the darkness, and a couple of seconds later, I felt the cold metal press into my other hand. I moved away from Meredith toward the door. "I'm going to let you out," I said to the prisoner behind the door.

There was silence for a moment before a voice spoke back. "You killed that guard." Her voice was raspy as if she had spent many days screaming. I fumbled around with the keys until I finally found the hole. "I did." I knew she must have smelled the blood on me even through the door.

I turned the key, pulling the door open with little effort. I could just make out a female figure standing in the cell near the far corner of the room. She was completely naked, and her hair hung in fierce tangles around her. I could see the silver shackle on her ankle that kept her from going far.

I entered the room with hesitant steps. I held up my free hand. "I'm not going to hurt you. I know what this probably looks like," I whispered to her, knowing the silver blade was still in my hand. I thought I spotted a small smirk pass her lips, but it was gone so quickly that I couldn't be sure. I kneeled down, setting the blade near me as I worked to undo her binding. It was nerve wracking, but when it came undone, my hand reached for the blade as quickly as I could.

The burn on my palm had me relaxing a bit more as I stood up. Now that I stood closer to her I could see more clearly what I was dealing with. That was when I noticed the dominant waves that were rolling off her, something I had missed before. I moved back several steps in surprise, wanting to create a bit more space between the two of us.

She didn't seem concerned by my presence, moving towards the door with powerful steps and taking in a deep breath when she stepped out of the room. "I've been waiting for this day for a long time" Her stormy eyes turned back at me, focusing. They were wild eyes, and they glinted like the silver in my hand.

I'm sure my mouth was hanging open in my shock. "You're an... alph—"

"Alpha" She finished my thought for me as her eyes dipped to the silver blade in my hand, still dripping blood. I noticed the hungry look she got at the sight of it. She took a step towards me as she leveled me with an intense gaze. "But you can call me Grace since I'm indebted to you. Don't worry. You are not the one whose blood I need."

I swallowed hard at her attempt to ease any fear. "Scarlett."

"I know. I heard the one called David talking about you. Lucky for you, he did not notice that you were pregnant," she replied coolly, and my eyes dropped to my stomach.

When I heard the sound of yelling outside, I turned my attention quickly. "Let's hurry up and get the hell out of here," I exclaimed. Grace turned from me with a wicked gleam in her eyes before she rushed away with no care to her nakedness. I felt a little uncertain about what I might have unleashed into the world.

Stepping outside, I came to a halt when I spotted Kade and a couple of other rogues standing there waiting for us. He was wearing a big grin. "Well, Well, Well... looks like the little alpha has finally been set free at last." His eyes were focused entirely on Grace who stood in the forefront with her body shaking slightly. He took a step toward us.

Grace let out a vicious growl that didn't seem to bother him in the slightest. "I've been looking for a good fight. Hopefully, you won't disappoint me like you did in the past."

I took a step back when I felt a blast of energy roll off her. Taking a defensive pose, I glanced at Meredith who was standing in the doorway behind me. I scanned the other rogues. "Go. Get the other prisoners and get them away from here," I whispered as I passed the keys behind me to Meredith, trusting that she would do what I was asking. I felt her fingers brush against mine as she took them before scurrying quickly away from the danger.

Kade's eyes caught mine for a moment before turning them back on Grace. "Maybe I won't kill you right off the bat, after all. Maybe I'll make you watch as I kill your little savior since you didn't get the joy of watching as I killed your mother."

My eyes widened as Grace disappeared. A giant silver wolf now stood in her place. It squared off its shoulders and released a mighty roar into the night as if to signal the drums of war.

50

Noah

"Noah you have to calm down. You need to think smart about this," Ryder said next to me as I paced back and forth, rubbing at the tension in my chest. Only moments before, I felt Scarlett's terror and pain through our bond. I knew something had happened to her. I wanted to rip through the trees and murder anyone who stood in between us. My beast was in a murderous rage over the fact that someone had dared to harm what was ours.

We had made it to the outskirts of Alpha Randall's territory. Now that I knew Thorton had betrayed us, I wanted nothing more than to burn his pack house to the ground.

I let out a growl. "Bring me Christa." I had a bone to pick with the female. I needed to make sure that she didn't know anything about this. When Ryder remained stationary, I turned my heated glare toward him. "Now," I commanded in a low tone. I was sitting on the edge of my control.

He bowed his head submissively and quickly moved to where our horde was stationed in the trees, waiting until I gave the signal to attack. I couldn't help but feel guilt pulse through me as I thought about how I had let Scarlett get dragged into this mess. She deserved so much better than me as a mate... but somehow, the Moon Goddess had cursed her with me.

I should have killed my brother after what happened with Claire, but I had been weak, unable to kill the person who had been with me through everything. I had hoped deep down inside that maybe he was redeemable. I didn't have the strength to kill him. I knew he hated me for what I had done and would always hate me, but I thought as my brother, he would let it be. I obviously made a critical error in my show of mercy.

My eyes narrowed as I stared off into the distance. "This is going to end one way or another, brother," I muttered to myself, clenching my hands into tight fists at my sides.

"Alpha," Ryder spoke behind me, grabbing my attention. I spun on my heels to find Christa standing next to him, her eyes focused on the ground in a sign of submission. I took a step forward. "Look at me." I tried to keep the growl out of my voice. Christa slowly lifted her eyes from the dirt below her feet to meet my dark gaze. I saw the fear in her eyes, but she kept herself from looking away.

I crossed my arms over my chest. "I'm going to ask you some questions, and you are going to answer them honestly because if you lie even once to me..." I paused and growled slightly, "I will not hesitate to kill you."

She nodded her head, and I noticed movement in the trees nearby. I turned my gaze to see Knox move out into the open with his body trembling in a rage. "What the hell do you think you're doing?" He snarled. Dane and Harvey rushed out of the trees after him, grabbing him by arms and holding him captive. He was red-faced as he struggled to free himself. "If you touch a single hair on her head, I will kill you!"

I gave him a genuine smirk at his threat before turning my attention back to Christa. "Did you know about Thorton?" I watched her body stiffen at my question, and her eyes widened in surprise. I focused my hearing on her heartbeat as I waited for her answer.

She swallowed. "He is the one who did this?" she asked me. I could tell from her reaction that she was genuinely surprised. Either that or she was a great actress.

"Are you telling me that you had no idea what he was doing?"

Knox let out a vicious growl at my question, but I ignored the possessiveness of the young pup. Christa shook her head back and forth frantically. "I swear to you I had no idea. I mean, Thorton..." she started, her expression turning to anger, "has always been a man driven by power. He never once saw me as anything other than an object that might buy him more of that. Trust me, I would never have allowed him to breathe another breath if I knew he was plotting anything against you and Scarlett."

Christa dropped to her knees in front of everyone, lowering her head toward the ground in a deep submissive bow. As a child born of alpha blood, I knew that it would be hard to humble to a wolf in such a way. Everyone's attention was completely focused on her, silently waiting.

"I would never dishonor Scarlett or you in such a way." I could hear the sincerity of every word as they left her mouth, and I relaxed my stance knowing that Christa had known nothing about Thorton's betrayal.

I cleared my throat. "Stand up. I believe you." Christa looked up toward me hesitantly before she pulled herself off the ground.

Her eyes were dark as she stared at me. "Alpha." She swallowed hard before continuing. "I would ask that you allow me to be the one to deal with Thorton."

My eyes narrowed in suspicion. "Can I trust you to deal with him without mercy? He sought to undermine me and take what rightfully belonged to me. The only response for such an act is death, and I will have it." I growled as my beast howled with excitement with the image of Thorton's blood coating his fur.

Christa never looked away from me. Instead, she lifted her chin in pride, and I could almost taste the rage pouring out of her. "And his death is something I will gladly you give you, Alpha. I'll make sure that it is slow and painful." We both stood staring at each other for several silent tension-filled moments before a wicked smirk spread over my lips. I knew that Christa would, in fact, be the one to kill Thorton, and she would kill him just as she promised.

I extended my hand to her, and she didn't hesitate to reach out and grasp mine in a firm grip. "So be it. You bring me the head of my brother's beta, and I will take it as a pledge of your complete loyalty to Scarlett and myself," I said to her before we both released each other from the handshake.

A loud roar was heard in the distance, and every person turned their attention quickly toward the sound in surprise. My beast responded to the sound with a loud howl in my mind. My eyes glanced quickly around the small group and met Harvey's. "That was an alpha," he muttered to me with a bit of surprise probably because it had been feminine sounding. The roar had been a cry of war, a cry that I planned to respond to. Clearly, war was what they wanted when they had challenged me and took my mate. And so, war was what I would bring them.

I let my beast take over as he clawed his way out of my skin, taking complete possession of my body. I could feel the shifting and cracking of my bones. Soon, I was looking at the world around me through the red haze of my beast's eyes. I squared off my shoulders and echoed the sound of the female alpha, roaring loudly into the night. All around me, the sounds of bones breaking and resetting were heard, followed by the howls of a hundred bloodthirsty wolves ready for the wild hunt.

51

Scarlett

My body was vibrating from the power that was radiating off Grace. Even the rogues that came for backup stumbled away from Kade with eyes full of fear at the sight of her. She was larger than the alpha males I was used to seeing. There was something in the way that she stood that caused a bubble of fear to build within me. It was almost feral. Kade seemed to relish in the violence that Grace promised and gave her a big grin. "Someone is still a little upset about the whole murder thing," he muttered to himself with excitement.

I looked around for a way to escape, but my attention was drawn elsewhere when I heard a sound that my wolf would know anywhere. I turned my head quickly in the direction of the sound of the howls in the distance. Noah had come for me. The determination to get to him became even stronger, and I knew without a doubt that I would tear this whole compound apart to reach him. I turned my attention back to Kade who had lost a bit of his amusement, having realized exactly the same thing. Grace took advantage of the distraction and snapped her teeth at him. He barely avoided getting a chunk taken out of him, dodging her attack.

"I'll make quick work of this sorry excuse for an alpha." Kade looked past Grace and pointed a clawed finger at me. "And then I'm coming for you, little Luna." My eyes narrowed at him, feeling my wolf stir beneath the surface to meet his challenge.

This only seemed to enrage the beast before me even more, and Grace lunged for Kade, but he laughed as he dodged and landed a hard punch to the side of her muzzle. She let out a whine and shook her head to gain control of herself again. He now stood with his back to me, and I tightened my hand around the blade in my hand. "You're clearly not as angry as I thought you would be. Your attacks lack intention. If you want to kill me, you're going to have to be serious about it 'cause if you don't," he paused as they began to circle each other, "I will kill you."

I could see the bloodlust spark in Grace's dark eyes. I knew that she planned to kill Kade, and it would be gruesome. I had no idea what horrors she had been through, but from what I had seen in the short time that I had been here, I knew that I would feel just as thirsty for vengeance if I was her. Grace and Kade charged at each other, colliding like a clash of thunder. My mind was in awe over the fact that Kade was fighting her without even shifting into his wolf form. I had only seen Noah that way one time, but witnessing this battle, I could see that because rogues submitted themselves completely to their wolf, they were able to tap completely into its power without even needing to shift.

Kade leaped onto Grace's back, wrapping his arms around her neck and clinging onto her tightly. She was struggling to get him off her, snapping her teeth over her shoulder to try to catch his flesh and pull him off. I felt anxiety over the fact that she was starting to stagger in her movements as he continued to crush her throat. In a last attempt to shake him off, Grace reared back onto her hind legs and threw herself into the ground as hard as she could. I cringed at the sound of bones snapping followed by Kade's howl of pain. I knew that he wasn't dead, but at least he no longer had the upper hand.

Grace rolled away from him, struggling as she pulled herself back onto her four legs. She turned back to face Kade, who was now also trying to pull himself off the ground. As she stalked toward him, her lips pulled back into a nasty snarl, revealing her razor sharp teeth. He let out a dark, defeated laugh. "You are perfect just like Kellan promised you would be. Come on, relish in your first kill, Gracie," he taunted her.

I noticed movement behind her and my eyes flashed toward the other rogues that Kade had brought with him. They were moving as a unit toward Grace who was completely absorbed in Kade. He was going to have his men kill her. Coward. My wolf surged forward with the need to protect Grace. I gritted my teeth before I rushed forward. My legs carried me toward my prey. It felt odd with the extra weight around my stomach, but I tried to ignore the discomfort.

This was stupid. I was putting myself and my pup in danger, but I couldn't allow the rogues to win. This was for the future of our entire species.

"What are you waiting for? Attack!" Kade growled.

I had my blade ready, catching one of the rogues by his shoulder before he could shift. I twisted it quickly as he reached for me with his other hand and yanked the silver free. I sneered as I went for him again with a quick jab. Over and over again I pulled the blade free to stab it back into his side. The blood was rushing over my hands and covering my clothes. He sunk to the ground at my feet as my chest heaved rapidly with the surge of adrenaline. I could only imagine how crazed I looked standing over my kill.

I was hit from the side by a strong force that sent me tumbling down to the ground. Sharp teeth ripped into the flesh of my shoulder, and I let out a howl. I twisted and swiped out with my silver weapon, catching the rogue's face quickly. He turned away from me with a howl, and I thrust the blade into his throat before pulling back. He slouched forward, dropping to the ground next to me as he bled out. I pushed myself back up onto my feet, readying myself for another attack. I could feel that I was going into a state of numbness.

This was going to haunt me forever. I would never be able to wash this blood from my hands. Noah had warned me, though. He had told me that I would get bloodier before the nightmare was over.

The other rogue made a go for Grace, so I ignored the pain in my body as I bulleted toward the hideous beast. I rammed into the beast's side with my shoulder, causing its steps to falter. I jumped at it with a cry of a warrior, catching it on the side with my trusty blade driving in deep. It let out a loud whine, thrashing from me as it fell to the ground. I didn't wait for another invitation and lunged for its throat. I sliced and ripped through its tough skin as hot tears of rage poured down my face. I could taste its blood in my mouth. The whimpers the rogue let out only made my desire to silence it forever that much stronger. I didn't want to hear that sound anymore. I couldn't handle it. The cries stopped when I felt the blade scrape against bone.

I tossed a quick, crazed look at where I had left the last rogue, only to see it scurrying away from us as quickly as its legs would carry it. My wolf wanted more blood and death... after everything that these people had put us through. I turned my focus back to Grace who was once again locked into battle with Kade though it seemed more like she was playing with him.

She was avoiding his attacks with ease as if she was finally bored with her game. She rammed her body in his, knocking him back down into the dirt. She stood over him, and I could tell he was waiting for her to go in for the kill. Instead, she shifted back into her human form, surprising me. He stared up at her with hate-filled eyes. "Thought you'd want to tear me limb from limb. Still burdened with your humanity, Grace?"

Grace dropped her body down on top of his, straddling him with a wicked smile on her lips. "Humanity?" She scoffed at his words. "You know killing you isn't about satisfying my wolf. This is about satisfying myself. I want to be the last thing you see before you leave this world." She reached forward and gripped his neck with her hands. He thrashed underneath her, trying to get her to release her hold, but she had successfully tired him out to the point that it had little effect on her. Grace's eyes were pitch-black as she stared down at him. "Make sure you save a spot for your alpha in hell because he'll be joining you shortly."

Kade's face was red, and his eyes bulged as he clawed at her hands in hopes of freeing himself. In one swift jerk of her wrists, she snapped his neck, and his arms fell limp to his sides. I pulled myself off the rogue I had killed, silently watching as Grace stared down at him with a look that was almost filled with inner peace. Slowly, she released her grip on his neck and rising up off of his body.

Grace turned her attention toward me. "You fought well. Thank you for saving me, again," she said with a soft smile on her lips as if we both hadn't been killing machines just a minute ago.

"No problem," was the only response my brain seemed capable of formulating at the moment.

The sounds of howling wolves were more prominent in the distance, and we both turned toward the sound. Grace sniffed the air a bit. "Smells like Alpha's.... two... four of them though I don't know who," she muttered more to herself, probably trying to figure out if they were enemies to her or not.

"That's my mate," I said, "And I need to get to him."

She looked at me with an unreadable expression for a moment before nodding her head. "Then I will help you get to him to repay my debt." I gave her a small smile though I still felt unsure about whether I can trust her, but at the moment, it wasn't like I had many options.

"Keep up, Luna. We've got rogues to kill," Grace said with a bit of excitement before shifting back into her wolf and taking off in the direction of the howls. I stared after her retreating form for a moment before I ran after her. I pressed my blood-stained hand to my stomach.

Soon, we will all be together again.

52

Scarlett

The further we moved toward the howls, the more destruction we saw around us. There were dead rogues scattered about, and the compound was in complete disarray. Grace picked up her speed as she weaved us through the mayhem as if she knew exactly where she was headed and she needed to get there as fast as she possibly could. My legs pushed off the ground as I tried to match her pace, eager to get to Noah and the others.

I picked up the sound of fighting wolves as we rounded the corner near the main building that I had been taken to after the fight with Moira. My eyes shifted around quickly, knowing that we were much closer to the main battle. There could be rogues waiting in the shadows to attack. Grace began to slow down her steps, and her ears twitched as she listened intently to the space around us. Out of the corner of my eye, I saw a flash of black. I turned my head quickly in the direction with a low growl. I stared into the shadows for a moment, waiting for something, but when everything remained still and silent, I turned away.

The moment I did, a beast jumped out of the darkness ready to tear into me. Grace moved like a bolt of lightning, meeting the rogue in the air. She caught it with her teeth by the neck, pulling it back down to the earth with her. It tried to free itself for a moment, biting at her like a rabid dog, but it was useless. Grace's dark eyes met mine before she let out a small snarl and chomped down, breaking the rogue's neck. She threw it away from her with a look of distaste before she moved nipping towards me. I scurried back from her with a low growl, but from the look in her eyes, I could see she wasn't trying to harm me. She only wanted to warn me that I needed to be more careful.

She nudged me with her big head, urging me forward. I did as she suggested and moved away from the now deceased beast. Grace trotted along slightly behind me as we moved closer to the action. I could feel the pull of my mate bond, which was urging me to run to Noah, but I held myself back, knowing that I could run straight into a trap. As if suddenly possessed, Grace bolted toward the front of the compound. I pushed myself to chase after her, wanting to understand what had caused such a drastic shift in her behavior.

I came to a complete halt when my eyes took in the sight before me. Wolves of every shape and color were locked into a bloodthirsty battle. They were ripping and tearing through each other with so much animalistic cruelty that it was hard to imagine that they were humans as well. My eyes scanned the violent scene searching for my mate, searching for

Noah. My heart thudded against my chest with fear that he would be harmed beyond repair. It didn't take long for my eyes to lock on the powerful wolf at the center of the battle, facing off several rogues. His white fur was now stained from what I was sure was both his and his enemy's blood.

I watched as the rogues worked together as a unit as they attacked, trying hard to bring him down. My anger and fear built up as two of the rogue wolves sunk their teeth into his flanks, trying to pull him down to the ground. He let out a fierce howl before he twisted his body, grabbing one and ripping it free from his body, not caring about damaging himself. Once it was off him, he attacked it like a crazed beast. He bit and pulled, shredding the rogues to pieces.

When I saw the movement out of the corner of my eye, I turned to find a rogue coming at me. Its sharp claws tore across my face and caught my eye. I let out a pained howl before lashing out, swiping my blade at it but moved it out of my reach.

Grace appeared at my side with an angry growl though I wasn't sure if it was at me or the rogue. The rogue looked between the two of us for a moment, assessing the threat level that we offered. As if understanding there was no way to beat us, it tucked its tail and ran. I wasn't about to let the beast get away after it got the better of me moments ago. Anger rushed through me as I took off after it. My wolf was excited over the chase our prey was giving us. Grace was by my side with a howl of excitement as she cut in front of me wanting to catch the prey herself. The rogue led us straight into the battle, weaving through the snarling and snapping teeth of bloodthirsty beasts.

A wolf slammed into my side, knocking me off balance. My legs gave out from under me, and I tumbled across the dirt. I growled as I lifted my head toward whoever had knocked me down, ready to tear their throat out. A reddish-colored beast was staring me down with its dark eyes as it was stalking towards me. It took a moment for me to realize who I was staring at, but once I did, I rose up from the ground quickly. My lips pulled back into a snarl. It was Delilah. It had to be.

We slowly circled each other. My wolf was clogging up my mind with images of us ripping our teeth through her flesh and spilling her wet, hot blood onto the dirt below us. This time, my intention was not to walk away until one of us was dead, preferably her.

A blur of silver launched itself between Delilah and me. I growled, ready to attack, until I realized that it was Grace, her hackles raised as she snarled at Delilah. I wanted to snap at her for getting between the two of us, but I knew she was only trying to protect me and my pup. It was probably only instinct for her since she was an alpha and I was a luna.

The sound of Noah howling in pain made my attention roam over the crowd frantically once again. My eyes found him on the ground and on his back as he was trying to fight off a large two-toned wolf who was tearing at him. All I saw was red as I jetted away from Grace and Delilah, barreling through the fighting wolves around me. When I was close enough, I used my momentum to push myself off the ground. I struck with precision, stabbing and twisting my blade into the back of the large wolf and knocking him off and to the ground. I staggered a bit but landed on my feet beside Noah.

The wolf shook its large head as it steadied itself off the ground, looking at me with its dark gaze. I squared off my shoulders and let out a violent snarl that seemed to shake the world around us. I was on the very edge of shifting.

The fighting around us seemed to come to a standstill, and a strange silence engulfed the battle. I had a stare down with the wolf, challenging him to try to attack my mate, because I wanted to rip him apart. However, a sound of clapping broke my concentration, and I turned my head to see the sea of wolves parting and Kellan making his way to us with a smile on his lips. Beside him, David was pulling Wyatt along, his gaze completely fixed on me.

I growled before I pushed back on my wolf, shifting a step back closer to Noah. "Let us leave now, Kellan. Is a grudge against your brother really worth all this death and suffering?" I tried to reason with him, feeling exhausted from all the fighting over the past couple of days. Kellan only chuckled at me in a dismissive way before motioning for David to step forward. He followed Kellan's guidance, pulling Wyatt with him and pushing him down to his knees in front of them.

My heart climbed into my throat at the sight. Wyatt's eyes met mine, and he gave me an apologetic smile. I shook my head in denial as David lifted his free hand and then in a quick motion, sliced it quickly across Wyatt's throat, ripping it open. My legs gave out from under me. I fell to my knees next to Noah who seemed to be barely hanging onto consciousness at the moment. I kneeled there, staring at my cousin who was staring back at me with wide, lifeless eyes. David let go of him, and his body slumped forward into the dirt, his blood pooling around him.

A strange numbness began to wrap itself around me as I stared at the only family I had left lying in the dirt like trash. I had thought... I had believed that in the end, I would save him and we would leave here together. Now, he was gone. A whimper pulled from the back of my throat.

"Now tell me, do you think all the death and suffering is worth it, little luna?" Kellan asked me with a taunting tone. My body stiffened, and my wolf roared to life with me. I pushed myself off the ground, staggering forward as I lifted my gaze toward David. "How could you? He was your beta, your friend... the only family I had left."

"Those bonds mean nothing to me now. He would have died eventually. At least, you were reunited before the end," David said without any remorse. My body began to shake with the force of my rage and bloodlust. I wanted to kill them all. I wanted them all to suffer for what they had taken from me... for what they had put my loved ones through.

"I challenge you, you coward! A fight to the death." I growled at David.

David's eyes narrowed as he peered over his shoulder at Kellan who smiled with amusement before giving him a slight nod. David looked back at me. "I accept your challenge... except when I win, I won't be killing you. Instead, you'll stay here with me without any more trouble." I sneered at his terms but said nothing more. I didn't care about anything but putting an end to the man who I was once fated to be with.

David shifted into his wolf, which was larger in size than I had expected it to be. His fur was black like my own except his face bore a mask of silver. I think at one time I would have dotted upon the beauty of him, but now as I stared at him, all I saw was a monster without a heart.

How could something so pure become so twisted and dark? Mates were supposed to protect and cherish one another, not kill each other. I wished deep down even though I loved Noah and was his mate now that this could have been avoided. Even though David had rejected me, I never imagined this was where we would end up. Yet, I knew in my heart that one of us had to die. He would never let me go, and I would never be happy always having to look over my shoulder.

David and I stared each other down silently. Everything and everyone around us were completely ignored, at least until he shifted his weight forward. All my thoughts of the past were washed away by my wolf's desire to kill. We charged at each other. I rammed him with my shoulder to push him back out of my space before I sliced him with my only weapon. I caught his flank with the tip, digging it in deep. He snarled viciously as he lashed out at me, his teeth sinking into my arm.

I let out a cry of pain but kept my hold on the hilt of the blade. If I lost that, then I would lose everything I had been fighting so hard to secure. He released me as I pulled the knife free, and the two of us separated. I cradled my wounded arm to my chest as we circled one another. I could see that he was limping slightly from where I stabbed him and that sparked in me a renewed fever for his blood. I moved quickly, catching him off guard. I slashed at him over and over again, and he dodged them the best he could. I shook violently as I used the muscles in my body to put more force into my attack. David let out a howl of pain as I stabbed into his side again before he knocked his head into my side in hopes of knocking me loose.

I fought hard to stay attached to him, not wanting to let go of my prey. His teeth sunk into my shoulder in quick, painful bites as if he was gnawing on me. I forced myself to hang on and ignore the harsh pain. Becoming more desperate, David thrashed wildly, which thanks to my now wounded arm caused me to slip free. I was sent flying and landed on the ground with a loud thud. My wolf whimpered as she curled herself around our little moon in my mind. I cringed, knowing I was seriously risking my pup.

David staggered a bit as his chest puffed in and out harshly from all the physical exertion. Even I could feel the exhaustion creeping into my bones, but I couldn't give up until he was dead. That thought helped me start to push myself off the ground.

David seemed to have recovered faster than I had because he charged at me. His big paws pressed down on my bad arm, digging into the fresh wound. I whimpered angrily underneath the pressure, trying to catch him with my blade, but he seemed just out of my reach. His lips pulled back to reveal his sharp teeth. I could tell he wanted me to submit in defeat, but I growled like a rabid beast beneath him. I would rather die than submit, and with that thought, I moved at just the right angle to catch him. My blade went straight through, slicing like butter.

David's leg gave out, and he slumped to his side as he tried to free himself. I twisted my body. I saw weakness in his position and used it to my advantage. His underbelly was exposed. In one swoop I lunged for him. I drove my knife deep into the sensitive flesh there, dragged it down, and sliced him open. David cried out in pain, and I released my hold on the weapon as he fell to the ground completely. His body shook and shivered as it shifted back into his human form, unable to hold his wolf form in his current condition. My eyes scanned over him. I could see that I had inflicted a fatal wound.

Exhaustion seemed to take over, and I slumped forward. I crawled toward David's body, and with my remaining strength turned him so that he was on his back. I was cradling his head in my arms. His eyes were watering, and there was blood on his lips. "I-I'm so s-sorry..." he stuttered weakly as his eyes met mine. I felt pity as I stared down at the broken and dying man on my arm. He had always let others manipulate him into making the decisions he made. In the end, he was the one who was weak—not me. I wiped away a stray tear from his cheek with my thumb.

"I just want you to be happy... I always loved you." He choked on the words, and it took a moment to regain his breath. "F-forgive me."

David didn't deserve my forgiveness, but as I stared down at him, I gave it to him anyways. It was not for him but for me. I didn't want to live with that hatred in my heart for the rest of my life. "I forgive you." He gazed up at me with awe written on his face.

"So beautiful," he muttered as he seemed to stare at something I was sure only he could see. He drew in a shaky breath, and then his body grew completely limp. I knew he was gone, and something in my heart was torn away. I tightened my hold on him and let out a ragged breath. I shook as I lifted my hand, closing his eyes. "May your spirit be at ease on the other side," I whispered, and I truly wished that despite everything that had transpired between us. I removed his head from my lap and gently placed it onto the ground.

I heard movement behind me, but I had no time or strength left to react as a hand grabbed onto my hair and pulled my head back. I didn't cry out or grit my teeth. Perhaps, I was too numb from all the loss and death to react. I stared up to see it was Thorton who was holding me. He clearly had been waiting for the opportunity to attack and waited until I was weakened. I felt a strange laugh bubble out of me. "You're a coward. You knew you couldn't beat me yourself, so you let someone else do the work for you."

He smirked at me. "That may be true, but at least I'll be alive, unlike you."

Kellan moved toward us with steady, calm steps. I watched him closely, and I wondered how he would kill me. Would it be fast or would he drag it on? I couldn't seem to find the energy to care either way. He stopped several feet from me. "This isn't personal, but it's time for me to call checkmate." He pulled his clawed hand back. I didn't dare to look away. I wasn't a coward.

I expected the pain, but it never came. Instead, there is a flash of white, and then Kellan was gone. Before me, Noah stood growling like a mother protecting her pup. Kellan now stood further away, clutching his arm with his hand and glaring at Noah. My own wolf seemed to come to the surface at the sight of my mate alive and well and willing to fight. I was about to try to break free, but Thorton let out a scream of pain.

Suddenly, I was falling forward. I caught myself with my hands and looked over my shoulder quickly to see two wolves ripping Thorton apart. I knew it had to be Christa and Knox.

My attention turned from them quickly when I heard the sound of fighting. Noah was no longer in his wolf form, but he looked very much like he did the day I saw him in the basement. The fight wasn't like anything I had ever seen before, or I would wish to see again. Hands were suddenly on me, pulling me up off the ground. I was prepared to fight, but then I heard a familiar voice. "It's okay, Scarlett. It's just me." I turned to see Christa beside me looking a little worse for wear but alive. Behind her, Knox was standing with his eyes scanning the crowd in a watchful gaze.

I turned my attention to my mate. He had his brother on the ground and was delivering blow after blow. I could see he was lost in a haze of bloodlust at this point.

I pulled away from Christa. My legs were moving me quickly to Noah. "Noah!" I called out to him, but he continued attacking, blood now coating him. He looked like a wild beast. I would have been terrified if I didn't know that inside somewhere, was the man I loved.

"Noah!" I yelled, and that seemed to halt his movements. His fist was pulled back, ready to launch into another round of punches. Kellan coughed and sputtered underneath him but didn't seem able to move. Noah's eyes were trained on me. His chest was heaving up and down as he tried to control himself. I slowly lowered myself to the ground in a submissive manner, knowing this would call to him. "Noah, you don't want to do this," I whispered gently.

He growled low at my words as if to contradict my statement. I ignored it. I pulled my hair away from my neck, exposing the column of flesh to him as I tilted my head to the side. "He's your brother. You will hate yourself if you kill him no matter what he's done to you. Trust me, you don't need his blood on your hands." Noah let out a pained growl.

I closed my eyes. "If you do this, you won't come back. The pack needs their alpha, I need my mate, and our pup needs her father." I sobbed as my hand went to my stomach, waiting for him to make his decision. The silence seemed to envelop everything, and then I heard faint footsteps.

Suddenly, I was being drawn into a pair of strong arms and was pressed firmly against a hard chest. I couldn't stop the sob that wrenched itself free from my throat. I was so happy, and I was so sad. Noah's arms tightened around me, as he nuzzled his face into my neck. I could feel wetness on my skin, and I knew that he was crying. "I thought I would never see you again." I wrapped my arms around his waist and pulled him closer. Both of us needed to comfort each other.

Kellan's dark laughter broke through our moment, and both of us stiffened. "You're still weak, brother, you and that stupid bitch of yours. Your inability to kill me will be your downfall. You know I will never stop hunting you. This will never be over."

I opened my mouth to tell him he could go to hell, but another voice spoke first. "He may not be willing to kill you, but I have no problem with it at all." Both Noah and I pulled away from each other to see Grace stalking out of the crowd covered in blood. In her hand, she was carrying Delilah's head like a gift to be presented to a king. She tossed it down at Kellan's feet with a wicked smile on her lips as he stared up at her with what looked like pure horror.

"Remember me?" she quipped.

Kellan's face was battered and covered in blood, but I could see the fine sheen of sweat against his skin. He looked utterly terrified as he stared up at Grace. "Wait... I—" His words were silenced as Grace shifted into her wolf. She snarled loudly before going for his throat without a second thought. After a couple of seconds, she threw her head back and let out a victorious howl. Around us, the other wolves that Noah had brought with him let out their own howls as the remaining rogues scampered off with their tails between their legs. While a part of me was mourning the loss of the people I loved, I was overcome with peace as Noah pulled me back into his arms. The nightmare was finally over.

53

Scarlett

It felt strange to be back at Noah's pack house after everything that had happened. It was almost surreal. It was hard to believe that it was all truly over, but the silence that surrounded me was enough of a confirmation that this was, in fact, real. I've been held up in my old room since we got back two days ago. My wolf and I both grieved the loss of our old pack, Wyatt, and David. There had been too much death and loss over something so minuscule as a grudge—blood that was forever on my hands now.

I hadn't let anyone into my room, and no one tried to bother me much under Noah's order that I be left alone. I knew I couldn't stay in my room forever. I was acting spoiled as if I was the only person who had lost something. Noah had lost so much more than me through all of this.

There was a gentle knock at the door, and I turned my attention toward it. "It's me, Scarlett," Noah's voice called out from the other side. I could hear the exhaustion and pain in his tone, and it made my heart clench at the thought that I was the one causing him to feel that way because of his constant worrying over me. I uncoiled myself from where I was perched in the window and shuffled my way to the door, my body feeling heavy from my lack of sleep.

I unlocked the door and opened it slowly. It revealed a very haggard-looking Noah. His eyes were quickly scanning over my body as if needing to make sure I wasn't damaged in any way. The sag of his shoulder in a noticeable relief made guilt wash over me.

I pulled the door open further. "Do you want to come in?" I asked in a soft, hesitant tone. He stood still in the doorway for a moment before he walked through the space I had created. I quickly closed the door behind him, not wanting anyone to know he was here in case they wanted to come bother him. I realized now that he was standing in my space that I didn't want to share him with anyone else at the moment. I wanted him completely to myself, feeling like a starved animal at the sight of him.

There was a tension-filled silence between us. We both had so much to say, but neither of us knew where to begin. Noah was the one to break the silence. "Eva and the boy are doing well. Owen and Janie have been keeping an eye on them, getting them the help they need to recover from what they went through. The boy will never get his sight back, but he seems like a resilient young pup. There is already a family willing to take him in, but the other wolf, the Irish one... he said he wouldn't give him over unless he was certain they were a good family."

I gave him a soft reassuring smile. "That makes me really happy." And it did. "But is that what you came here to talk about?"

He returned my smile, shaking his head. "No, not really." He lifted his hand and ran it through his hair, making me realize that he was nervous. All the tension I felt slowly faded away as I let the bond between us ease our nerves.

I took a step toward him. "I missed you. I'm sorry I've been acting like a spoiled brat. You're my mate, I should have leaned on you instead of pushing you away. I should have told you about our pup. I was just afraid." I put my hand to the small swell on my tummy.

His eyes grazed over my stomach for a moment before meeting my gaze, and his lips pursed for a moment. "You're right. You should have."

I waited for him to let me have it. I certainly earned it, but instead, he let out an even breath. "I am not worried about that now. You've been through a lot. I'm just glad to have you both healthy and back here where you belong. All that other stuff... well, we will figure it out as we go."

I tilted my head to the side, my tears pricking at my eyes. "Why are you so understanding? Why can't you be mad at me like I probably deserve?"

Noah closed the distance between us so that we now almost stood chest to chest. His eyes stared into mine deeply as a gentle smile tugged at the corner of his lips. "Because I've been where you've been, Scarlett. There is nothing for me to be mad about. It's only been two days, and you're already reaching out to me." He lifted his hand, placing it against the one resting on my stomach. The touch sent electricity through my veins. I closed my eyes and leaned into his touch, realizing that this was what I've been craving. His touch eased the ache of the loss and made me feel complete again.

"God, I love you." The words were tumbling out of my mouth before I could stop them, but once they're out, I realized I wouldn't have stopped myself, anyway.

"What did you just say?" Noah asked in surprise. I opened my eyes and met his wide eyes. I couldn't help but giggle at the shocked expression on his face as if he thought I would never say something like that to him. Looking back on everything, I could probably see why he might have thought that, but people change. He should know that better than anyone.

"I love you," I said, repeating it slowly for him, "even if you are a big idiot sometimes." I teased with a big grin.

He swallowed hard, then his lips were crashing down into mine. Now it was my turn to be surprised by his sudden attack, but I recovered quickly at the feeling of his lips on mine. My eyes slammed shut, and I threw myself into the kiss, reaching out with my hands and grabbing hold of his shirt. I pulled him closer so that our bodies were pressed tightly together. I didn't want there to be any distance between us, not anymore.

Noah broke away from the kiss. Both of us were panting heavily. He leaned his forehead against mine. "Tell me what you want, Scarlett, because if I don't stop now, I won't be able to hold myself back anymore." His voice was strained and husky.

I smiled to myself. "You. I want you. You're all that I want, Noah, forever." I pulled back a bit, pressing a kiss on his jawline. He let out a growl of approval before he was capturing my lips again. This time, his arms wrapped around my waist, popping me up the ground. I giggled against his lips as I snaked my arms around his neck and my legs around his waist so he could carry me easier.

He pulled back to look at me as he carried me toward the bed. "I love you, Scarlett."

I smiled up at him. "I know. I mean, what's not to love?" I teased.

THE END

Can't get enough of Scarlett and Noah?
Make sure you sign up for the author's blog
to find out more about them!

Get these two bonus chapters and
more freebies when you sign up at
!

Here is a sample from another story you may enjoy:

AN IRREVOCABLE DESTINY
A FATE YET TO BE DETERMINED

UNIQUE
DIFFERENT
FOUND

VIOLET SAMUELS

1

CELINA

Have you ever felt like you can never escape? Have you ever felt like there is no one there for you? Have you ever felt like the whole world is against you and you just want to get away and be free? Have you ever felt that you can never be loved or cherished?

That's my life.

I feel all of these things. You can't change what fate has in store for you. But sometimes, I wish I could just be free and live my own life. I haven't been able to do that for a total of nine years.

My mother and father died when I was seven. I was abandoned and left with my godforsaken pack. I had no regrets when my mother and father died. I spent every second of every day with them, and they never argued. We didn't have any major fights and we all loved each other so much. I didn't think my parents had any regrets either. I think they made the mistake of leaving me alone, though.

You're probably wondering why I'm blaming it on them, aren't you? Well, I don't. I blame my pack for being worthless, unfair, stupid and plain right mean. Childish I know, but true, down to the last detail. Every beating, every bruise, every broken bone and every possible evidence of them abusing me supports that horrid theory.

Ever since my parents died, I've been like a slave to the people I call my pack. I cook, wash, clean, organize and pretty much do everything for them. They throw away money like it's no big deal, and they don't spare a second glance to anyone who's 'lower' than them.

Someone like me.

All the wolves in my pack are gorgeous with either brown or blonde fur and have a mix of either blue, green, brown, or almost black eyes. Having plain blue or green eyes is rare. They have slim or muscular bodies and have the perfect height just to be much taller than humans. Unfortunately, that beauty is tainted by their bitter egos and cold hearts.

My parents were like the pack looks wise, but not personality wise. My parents were kind and thoughtful, always putting others before themselves. They never should've been in this pack in the first place.

The funny thing is, I look nothing like my parents or anyone in the pack for that matter.

Instead of blonde or brown hair, mine is pitch black, pin straight and comes down to just below my shoulders. My eyes are a shining gold that lost its shine many years ago, so now it looks like a light shade of mud. My lips are almost red and, strangely, my skin is pale. I'm not sure why... Most Werewolves have beautifully tanned skin. I'm also a bit shorter than everyone else, but I still have that slim body that anyone would die for. In my parents' opinion, being different is what makes you special. What makes you special, is what makes you unique.

I never believed it, though. All it has ever done was got me teased, and pushed around for being 'different' and 'unique'. It has always been like that. Even with my parents, they always said the pack was just jealous of my obvious beauty, one that I am oblivious to.

Another thing. When I turned sixteen, I made sure I was far away from the pack house, almost on the borders of our territory. The reason? I was shifting. I didn't want to give everyone the satisfaction of seeing my pain, and watching my every bone break after the other. I can honestly say that it is the most painful thing you will ever experience in your life.

When I shifted, I discovered that my wolf was snow white. Not one trace of colour other than white covered me. I was astounded. I had never seen a white wolf. Even my mother's and my father's wolves were brown and blonde, respectively. They told me that when I shifted, never to show to anyone my wolf unless they have my full trust. Nobody has.

I don't know what it means to have a pure white wolf, but I know that I'm different yet again. This time, in a way, I thought I could somehow fit into my pack. I thought wrong. When I came back, I got a beating because I was gone for most of the day, and everyone missed lunch and breakfast. That night, I had to make a three-course meal instead of the usual one, and I had to clean the house until it was spotless. Let's just say I stayed up way past midnight...

I haven't been for a run since. That was three weeks ago. My wolf has been howling in my head, and it feels like she's scratching my insides apart. I badly want to let her out, but I'm too scared. I don't want to get beaten up again.

My wolf has told me multiple times to get away, and I've been considering it for months now. Tonight's the night. I'm leaving. I'm ditching this stupid place and leaving for good. When I told my wolf, she was practically jumping with joy.

I'm making the dinner right now. Although this pack has treated me like nothing, I'm gonna give them something to remember me by, and if that means food, then so be it.

I decide to make one of my favourite courses. For entree, bruschetta with mini prawn cocktails. For main, lasagna with garlic bread. Then for dessert, my personal favourite, chocolate mud cake with whipped cream, ice cream and chocolate covered strawberries on top. If it were me, I would just skip the entree and main and go straight for the dessert.

I set the table for the pack, and as soon as I finish placing the last of the entrees on the table, they walk in through the door. As soon as they get a whiff, they come barging into the dining room, taking a seat and digging in. No 'thank you' or 'this is nice', just like the usual.

I always keep a spare bit of dessert for myself after I finish cooking, so while the rest of the pack eats, I tuck into my mud cake. At least, they let me eat, I guess.

When I hear the bell, I walk back out and collect the empty plates, taking them back to the kitchen. To let them digest a bit, I wash it all up and place it on the drying rack.

I come back out with the last of the mains and am about to walk out when Tina, the pack slut, calls my name.

"Celina!"

I slowly turn around, keeping my hands behind my back, and my head bowed. I'm wearing the correct uniform for serving dinner, and my hair is neatly pulled back into a high ponytail, so I'm not sure what she wants. Whenever someone in the pack calls my name, it's usually because I'm in trouble.

"Why the whole 'fancy-fancy' food? Is it a special occasion? Let me guess... Is it for Damon's birthday? A little present from you?" She snickers at me. I feel all eyes turn to me, but I obediently keep my head down. Damon is the soon to be the alpha of our pack and is turning eighteen in about four days. It's a big thing, and I'm supposed to cook for it...

"I guess you could consider it that. If the alpha is kind enough to accept my gift, of course," I answer in a small voice. I was told from the beginning to address Damon as alpha and nothing else, unlike the rest of the pack.

The room falls silent as every eye turns to Damon, who's sitting at the head of the very large dining table. I look through my long, black lashes to see his face. I'm met with a considering expression.

He nods his head once. "I accept your gift. I will expect a grander and more appropriate gift on my actual birthday, though. Do you understand?" His tone's filled with power and authority.

"Yes, Alpha, I understand," I say, returning to my former position with my head down.

"Good. Now, off you go." He shoos me off, and as soon as I enter the kitchen, I hear their laughs and snickers. I tried not to cry. I've shed too many tears over these heartless people.

They soon finish their meals, and it's time for dessert. I've finished mine by now, so I place theirs on the table with a blank face. They eat up and by the time everyone has finished and has stayed around talking, I've cleared the large table and washed up.

I enter back into the dining room and wait in my usual spot by the door of the kitchen. Every night before I go to bed, I either get hit or nothing for the meals I've cooked. It's the same with breakfast, lunch, and any other meals they eat. As each one walks out of the room, I either get shoved or ignored, which means they liked my cooking. Tina, on the other hand, slaps me across the face. You probably think that's harsh, but that's equivalent to someone else's shove. So just imagine what someone else's slap is to her. It's not a pretty sight.

Damon is the last to leave, and he stops in front of me. I cautiously lift my head and stare into his beautiful blue-green eyes. He has a blank face, as do I. We stare at each other for a moment before he walks out and leaves me alone in the dining room to fix up.

Damon has been my crush since I was about ten, even though he treats me like the worthless thing I am. His brown hair and blue-green eyes are the main aspects that draw me and many other female wolves in. He hasn't found his mate yet either, which means he's available. He wouldn't go for me, though. Not in a million years. I'm too different.

I head to bed in the early hours of the night. The pack no longer requires me after about 7:30 pm, so I am ordered to bed, which I quickly oblige, so as not to get beaten. I still have bruises from the worst ones.

The sad thing is, I believe everything my pack had said since my parents died. That I'm not beautiful, but ugly. That I'm not unique, but different. That I'm not a part of their family, but their slave.

I sigh as I enter my makeshift room. It's bare, except for a large window that lets the moonlight from the full moon flood into my room. My bed is pretty much a sheet on the hard, splintered, wooden floor, and my pillow is a pillow cover stuffed with newspaper.

I won't be sleeping there tonight, though. Not anymore. Not ever again.

I pack what little belongings I have inside a sack – A pair of worn out jeans, an oversized shirt with holes in it, a skirt, one other shirt that appears to be clean, and a pair of socks. I don't own any shoes.

I grab the only piece of jewellery I have, my mother's silver necklace with her and my father's names engraved into the heart-shaped pendant. The pendant has a yin and yang symbol in it, but it's made with little black and white crystals. I slip it into my shirt and proceed to the window.

I open it wide, and without a glance back, or second thought, I jump. I jump to my freedom and my new life.

I shift into my snow white wolf and take off with my sack in my mouth. I don't know where I'm going. I don't know if I can survive. I am only a newly shifted wolf at the age of sixteen.

What do I know? I'll never have to see my 'pack' again. That is enough to make me smile slightly in my wolf form. As I cross the border of the territory, my wolf lets out a howl, filled with happiness and joy.

We're free. I'm free.

Never again will we have to face the Moonlight pack.

If you enjoyed this sample then look for **Unique Different Found**.

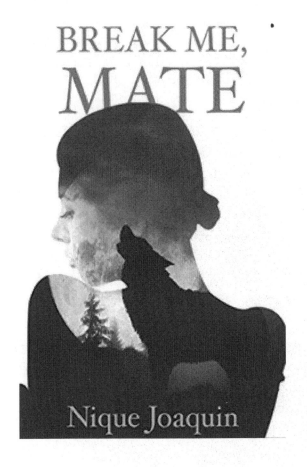

Other books you might enjoy:

Nerd of the Year
Supraja I.R.
Available on Amazon!

Introducing the Characters Magazine App

Download the app to get the free issues of interviews from famous fiction characters and find your next favorite book!

iTunes: bit.ly/CharactersApple
Google Play: bit.ly/CharactersAndroid

Acknowledgements

I would like to take this time to recognize the people that had helped on this book behind the scenes, who held my hand when I felt overwhelmed and who pushed me forward when I wanted to slack off. Without any of you, I am sure none of what I accomplished would be possible.

I would like to acknowledge my publishers being that they were so kind and helpful when I had questions or wanted to make changes even at the last moment (Cause let's be honest, artists of every type are never quite satisfied. There is always something they want to tweak or change).

I would like to acknowledge my Anna Banana, who kept me strong and had my back through all the hard parts of this process. As well as for helping me to grow as a writer. She has challenged me to grow constantly and for that, I am eternally grateful.

I would like to acknowledge my best friend for loving me through all the crazy months of me sitting over my computer with tired eyes and frustrated tears. You make my world such a bright place even at its darkest moments.

And of course, I want to acknowledge all of my potatoes. I do know all that you have done for me. I hope that you guys will continue to be kind and encouraging to other writers following their dreams as you have been for me.

Author's Note

Hey there!

Thank you so much for reading His to Claim! I can't express how grateful I am for reading something that was once just a thought inside my head.

I'd love to hear from you! Please feel free to email me at ashley-michelle.awesomeauthors.org and sign up at ashley_michelle@awesomeauthors.org for freebies!

One last thing: I'd love to hear your thoughts on the book. Please leave a review on Amazon or Goodreads because I just love reading your comments and getting to know YOU!

Whether that review is good or bad, I'd still love to hear it!

Can't wait to hear from you!

Ashley Michelle

About the Author

I'm a twenty-something year old who currently resides on the eastern coastline of the US, but I suffer from a severe case of wanderlust that keeps me from settling down in one place for long.

I've always had an interest in books, from the moment that I learned to read which was a lot older than most kids. Books became my sanctuary during good times and bad. I could become anything or anyone. I got to go on these amazing journeys and meet amazing people all from the comfort of my house. I think it was those younger years that inspired me to create the worlds and characters that I have in the stories that I've written. I simply want to give others the joy of an amazing journey that so many others have given to me.